PR...

"Reminiscent of a ....ara movie, *Jake* kicks c.... ....ee a......... .....pular series from Leigh Gr.....wood.

—Robin Lee Hatcher, author of
PATTERNS OF LOVE

"Leigh Greenwood is synonymous with the best in Americana romance."

—*Romantic Times*

"*Jake* is an exciting, fast-paced Reconstruction Era romance....Readers will definitely want more from this great writer and will want it soon. Leigh Greenwood has another winning series in the works."

—*Affaire de Coeur*

"Exciting and soul searching, *Jake* is bound to win Leigh Greenwood new fans....Only a master craftsman can create so many strong characters and keep them completely individualized. Greenwood's books are bound to become classics."

—*Rendezvous*

"Fun, entertaining and romantic! *Jake* is special—I can't wait for Ward's story!"

The Literary Times

"...unusually perceptive writing with a love story bringing East and West together...."

—*Heartland Critiques*

HER MIND WASN'T ON THE LESSON

Isabelle couldn't concentrate when Jake's body was wrapped around hers. She felt her shoulders against his chest, his thighs against her buttocks, his cheek resting against her hair, his breath against her neck. She couldn't think about anything as silly as a rifle.

"Now you look through this groove to the sight on the end of the rifle barrel," Jake said.

The timbre of his voice had changed. He didn't seem so businesslike and assured, so brisk. He sounded slightly breathless, his voice more of a whisper than a sharp, clear sound.

But he didn't sound as if he was thinking about rifles or targets either. His body was hard with tension. He tried to stand away from her, but he couldn't without releasing his hold on her and the rifle.

Isabelle could feel the heat of his arousal. It burned her skin like a brand. She could feel the tension in his arms as they tightened around her bit by bit.

He seemed to recollect himself. His muscles relaxed.

"You're not looking down the barrel," he said.

She had to at least try to pay attention. If not, she was liable to drop the rifle and throw herself into his arms.

LEIGH GREENWOOD

THE COWBOYS

JAKE

LEISURE BOOKS **NEW YORK CITY**

For Brandon,
My own special orphan

A LEISURE BOOK®

Published by

Dorchester Publishing Co., Inc.
276 Fifth Avenue
New York, NY 10001

Printed in the United States of America.

AUTHOR'S NOTE

Probably no two people will agree on the exact boundaries of the Texas Hill Country, but if you seek out the hills that give rise to the Frio, Sabinal, Guadalupe, Medina, and Pedernales Rivers, you'll find the heart of it no matter where you place the limits.

It's a land of fertile valleys and rocky hillsides, of ancient live oaks, cypress, and maples, of cacti, mesquite, and caliche. In the summer you can wade or step across most of the rivers, but a single heavy rain can send muddy torrents racing across some roads at a dozen places.

The Hill Country is dotted with small towns settled mostly by Europeans of German, Polish, and Czech descent. Historic buildings are constructed of cream-colored, locally quarried tufa limestone. Some neighborhoods still retain their Victorian character. Many towns like Medina, Vanderpool, and Rio Frio are home to only a few hundred people.

Despite the inroads of modern society, the main business of the Hill Country is still ranching. Towns like Fredericksburg and Kerrville may cater to tourists or the business of making money. But if you eat breakfast at the O.S.T. Restaurant on Main Street in Bandera, your companions will be cowboys who still keep their hats on when they come to the table.

There is a real town of Utopia situated on the Sabinal River in Uvalde County. Any likeness to my imaginary farming community of Utopia, which I placed on the upper Pedernales River in Gillespie County, is purely coincidental.

Prologue

Jake Maxwell watched warily as the group of farmers approached the dog trot he called home. With their black clothes, black eyes, and black beards, they sat their mules like so many crows. Jake's hand automatically moved toward his gun, even though he knew he wouldn't use it. They came unarmed. Their defense was their numbers and the united front they presented at all times.

While Jake was off fighting the Yankees, they had homesteaded the best spots on his ranch, plowed up his best hay meadows to plant fields of corn and potatoes. They cut down the trees that shaded his cows in summer and sheltered them from the wind in winter. Far from being thankful Jake had survived the war, they were resentful he had come back to the land his family had occupied for twenty years.

11

Jake owned only a few hundred acres of the thousands his herd needed. Before the war, no one had disputed his right to this corner of Gillespie County. Now a dozen families laid claim to the heart of his ranch.

The farmers didn't waste time on civilities. "We got some bills for damages your cows did to our crops," Noah Landesfarne said.

"They ruined every bit of my corn," another said.

"I warned you to put up fences," Jake said. "You can't expect cows to eat dried grass when they can have tender shoots of corn and wheat instead."

"If anybody should put up fences, it's you," Noah said.

"That's a great expense," the second man said.

Jake was the only rancher in the county. He had been outvoted at the only election. Things hadn't gotten any better when the Reconstruction people came in. They were eying his cattle with the same greedy looks these farmers had.

"This is cattle country," Jake said. "You'll never make a go of farming."

"We each got a bill for damages," Noah said, persisting. "You got to pay them, and you got to put up an indemnity against any future damage."

He handed Jake a piece of paper. The figure written on it made his eyes roll. The other farmers handed him pieces of paper as well. The total was staggering.

"We already talked to the sheriff. You got a month to pay us and come up with the indemnity."

"Who's going to hold this indemnity?"

"The bank."

The farmers owned the only bank.

"What happens if I can't raise the money?"

"We'll take payment in cattle," Noah said. "Three

dollars a head. That's all a longhorn is worth in Texas."

They were worth at least ten times that in St. Louis, maybe more in the gold fields of Colorado.

"You realize your claims would eat up most of my herd."

"Then we won't have any more cows getting in our fields."

Jake knew Rupert Reison. The young farmer made no attempt to disguise his hatred. Jake's temper snapped. "There's no way in hell I'm going to pay you that kind of money," Jake thundered.

He tore the pieces of paper into tiny bits and threw them into the wind. "This has been Maxwell land for twenty years, and it's going to stay Maxwell land!"

"We got legitimate deeds," Noah said. "The sheriff says you owe us damages. You can't let your cows run all over. If it doesn't stop, we'll take to shooting any cow we see in our fields."

"I'll see you in hell first!" Jake exploded. "Now get off my land before I take to shooting you."

But seeing the farmers leave didn't make Jake feel any better. The law and time were on their side. He had to round up his steers and get them to market. But how in hell was he going to do that by himself?

Chapter One

May 1866

Isabelle Davenport studied the eight orphan boys who rode in the wagon with her. They looked so young and innocent, yet collectively they had been thrown out of seventeen orphanages and adoptive or foster homes. Four had been officially adopted but returned because their new parents couldn't do anything with them. Two had gotten into fights with their foster parents. One shot a foster brother. All had run away.

She felt sorry for them, but at times they frightened her. They didn't seem to like anyone, not even themselves.

This was their last chance. If they failed, three of them would go to prison. The two youngest would go back to the orphanage. The others would be turned out to take care of themselves as best they could. Isabelle had only been in Texas one year, but she knew that meant they would have to steal to stay alive. If that happened, most of them would be dead before they reached their twentieth birthdays.

Using her own time and money, Isabelle had located a newly established farming community in the Hill Country willing to take the boys. She hoped that away from towns and the temptation of whiskey, women, and the toughs who always seemed to hang around saloons, the boys would grow into mature, responsible manhood.

"Where are we stopping tonight?" Bret Nolan asked. The sun was sinking into the horizon. The canvas top of the wagon in which they rode had been removed so they could enjoy the spring breeze as well as the view of the surrounding countryside.

Isabelle didn't like what she saw. It didn't look at all like Savannah. As far as she was concerned, it was a desert of hills and canyons with just enough water to keep the sparse vegetation alive. She didn't know how the farmers survived.

"There's a cattle ranch just ahead," Isabelle said. "I'm hoping the owner will give us hospitality for the night."

"I'd rather camp with Indians."

Bret was the twelve-year-old son of a Boston abolitionist who had died attempting to help runaway slaves. Bret hated Texas and everyone in it.

"Maybe his hands will share their bunkhouse," Isabelle said.

"They ain't likely to have a bunkhouse. Ain't nobody from Texas knows how to live indoors."

Bret was always trying to rile the other boys. They mostly ignored him. Bret hated to be ignored.

"Don't know what's worse—Indians, Mexicans, or Texans."

15

"That's enough, Bret," Isabelle said.

"What's wrong, ma'am?" he asked. "Don't you like the truth?"

"Even if it were the truth, it wouldn't be a nice thing to say."

"Oh, I forgot. I'm not supposed to make fun of the lower classes. Even the Irish."

Sean O'Ryan punched him.

Sean's parents had died when he was one. He'd been sent to live with Texas relatives no one ever found. He'd spent most of his thirteen years bouncing from one family to the next, but he wouldn't let anybody insult the Irish.

"Did you see that?" Bret exclaimed.

"Shut up," Mercer Williams said, "or I'll make you walk."

"I wouldn't move a step," Bret countered. "Then you'd have to come back and get me."

Isabelle bit her lip to keep from telling Mercer for the hundredth time that his only job was to see they arrived safely, that this trip was her idea and the orphans her responsibility. Mercer insisted he was in charge. He had wanted to chain the boys to the wagon to keep them from running away. Much against her will, Isabelle had finally agreed to let him take their boots. If Bret were forced to walk, his feet would become cut and bloody from the sharp rocks and cactus.

They rounded a cottonwood- and willow-lined bend in the creek, and the Broken Circle Ranch came into view. It consisted of a dog trot cabin, a low building that appeared to be a bunkhouse, and two corrals. Isabelle's hopes of being able to sleep in a bed vanished.

She told herself she had no right to expect such luxury, but for the first sixteen years of her life she'd

Jake

been part of Savannah's privileged society. No hardship of the past seven years could erase that training or her desire for some of the luxuries rapidly becoming only a distant and taunting memory.

"I'll bet it's got a dirt floor," Bret said.

"It won't make no difference if it's setting in a mudhole," Pete Jernigan said. "The beds will be nailed to the wall."

Pete was nine years old, too young to understand why it was best to ignore Bret.

"You won't get to sleep in one," Bret said. "Ain't nobody giving up their bed for a shrimp like you."

"Let him alone," Sean said, his fair, freckled complexion turning almost as red as his hair. His Irish temper was never far below the surface.

"Sure. I never did like playing with worms."

This time Bret managed to dodge Sean's fist.

"It doesn't look like there's anybody home," Chet Attmore called back from the driver's seat. "Do you want me to see who I can round up?"

At fourteen, Chet was the most dependable and physically mature of the orphans. Isabelle didn't know what she would have done without him and Luke, his thirteen-year-old brother. Chet seemed to find the best trails by instinct. Luke was a genius with horses and equipment.

"Don't nobody set foot out of this wagon until I say so," Mercer Williams said.

"I'll speak to the owner," Isabelle said.

She disliked approaching strangers. With the end of the war and the beginning of Reconstruction, most Texans had uncertain tempers. One look at her well-made clothes and her flower-and-ribbon-bedecked hat, and they immediately classed her as an uppity society woman.

Isabelle climbed down from the wagon. Except for

17

the occasional jingle of the harness as the horses fought off flies with their tails, silence reigned. The ground around the cabin, bunkhouse, and corrals was flat and bare. There was no well or pump, no flowers, no garden, no sign of a milk cow or chickens. There were no curtains at the windows, and the yard hadn't been swept. She didn't see a clothesline, wash pot, or potato hill. There wasn't even a chair in the breezeway that separated the two halves of the cabin.

The place looked deserted.

For a moment she feared Indians might have wiped out the family. Their raids had intensified during the war. So far, the Reconstruction government had done nothing to stop them. Reassured by some clear prints of boots and a shod horse, she marched up to the porch and knocked on the door of the right half of the cabin. She received no answer. She could hear no movement within. It was the same with the other door.

"Try the bunkhouse," Pete called.

"If the boss ain't in, I doubt you'll find his hands in bed," Mercer said.

The bunkhouse was also empty. Isabelle didn't know what to do. She had been told there was no one else between here and the farmers who'd agreed to take the boys. Besides, it was too late to continue their journey.

Isabelle was tired of riding in a wagon. She was sick of the heat, the dust, and the constant jolting. The tension of the journey was eating at her nerves. She'd tried during the first days to foster a positive attitude toward each other among the boys. She had made no progress. They were too cynical, too angry, too distrustful.

"We'll stop anyway," Isabelle decided. "Whoever

lives here has got to come back sometime. Start setting up camp. I expect the owner won't mind as long as we keep away from the cabin."

The boys waited silently for Mercer to unlock the trunk and give them their boots. Isabelle had assigned responsibilities and established a routine the first evening. They'd stuck to it every night of the two-week journey.

Night Hawk, a half-breed Comanche, unharnessed, watered, and picketed the horses out to graze. Bret Nolan brought water and wood. Matt Haskins and his brother, Will, did the cooking. Sean O'Ryan and Pete Jernigan cleaned up. The Attmore boys, Chet and Luke, had no chores because they did all the driving.

Isabelle had tried to encourage conversation during meals, but the boys disliked and distrusted each other. The two sets of brothers paired off. Pete, moody but spunky, hung around Sean for the protection the big, over-grown Irish boy could give him when he shot his mouth off. Bret and Night Hawk balked at having anything to do with anybody.

Isabelle refused to sit through a meal in silence. They would hear the sound of a human voice even if hers was the only one.

"My aunt always said a man should be measured by how well he handled life's difficulties. She believed America was a perfect place for such a test. I imagine she would have thought Texas particularly well suited to separate the genuine from the imitation.

"But she also believed a woman should be pampered and protected. I hesitate to think what she would have done had she been married to a Texan. Right before she died, she told me—"

Isabelle broke off. The boys weren't listening to

her, but they were listening to something.

"What is it?" she asked.

"Somebody comes," Night Hawk said. "White man. Horse wear shoes."

Isabelle could hear the hoofbeats now. He was coming at a fast trot. She got to her feet. She saw Mercer, some distance off from the boys, pick up his rifle. The faces of the boys reflected curiosity, boredom, hostility, even fear.

The rider didn't slow his mount. For a moment, Isabelle feared he would ride his horse right into the middle of their camp. He came so close, and he looked so angry, that several of the boys got to their feet.

"Who the hell are you, and what are you doing on my property?" he thundered. Sitting high in the saddle, he looked huge and intimidating.

"Let me do the talking," Isabelle said.

"If he lets you do any," Chet Attmore muttered, not the least bit alarmed. Isabelle wondered where he and Luke had gotten their cool confidence.

The man's face seemed to relax when he dismounted. Maybe seeing she was a woman allayed some of his fears. A look of confusion appeared on his face as he looked from one boy to another.

He wore threadbare pants that fitted his body nearly as snugly as his skin. The sleeves of his checked shirt were rolled up to reveal big, strong hands and powerful forearms covered with a mat of dark hair. His open shirt exposed a strong neck and still more hair. His wide-brimmed, flat-topped hat shaded his eyes. Every inch proclaimed him to be the most dangerous animal on earth, a mature man confident in his power.

"Good God!" he muttered, "don't tell me these are

all yours, because I won't believe it. You're too young and pretty."

Isabelle moved her lips, but nothing came out. She felt terribly foolish. The sight of this man had nearly struck her dumb. She barely had the strength to stand. Knowing intuitively that he was a threat to all that she was, she fought an urge to flee. That would be absurd. She was only speechless because of surprise. She'd never seen a man quite like him.

By a tremendous effort of will, Isabelle forced her thoughts to what the man had said. While no woman could dislike being called young and pretty, it wasn't proper to say such things in front of the boys. Discipline and respect had to be maintained.

"My name is Isabelle Davenport," she said, trying to sound composed. "These boys are orphans. I'm escorting them to their new homes."

"Then what are you doing here?" the man asked. "This place doesn't look like an orphanage. It doesn't look like a ranch either, but it is."

Isabelle found it hard to concentrate. She'd never met anyone with such rough, uncontrolled energy.

"I was hoping you'd give us permission to stop here for the night," she said. "When we didn't find anyone at home, we—"

"Do you always stop anywhere you please?" the man asked.

Without waiting for an answer, he moved around the group, scrutinizing each boy like an army captain inspecting his troops. Eight-year-old Will Haskins moved closer to his brother, Matt, but the rest stood their ground. The man's hat made it impossible for Isabelle to see anything in his eyes, but what she could see of his expression told her he didn't like what he saw.

"What the hell are you doing with this bunch,

Leigh Greenwood

starting your own gang of outlaws?" he asked. "It's a good thing your man has a rifle. That one looks like he could cut your heart out and eat it."

He was looking at Night Hawk. The boy returned his look in full measure, his black eyes hard and steady, his slim, brown body balanced on bare feet.

"I'm not married," Isabelle said with what she hoped was her most haughty voice. "Mr. Williams is our guard. These boys have all been placed with farmers who live less than a day's travel from here."

His attitude changed immediately. He closed in on her, his expression ugly. "I'll warn you right now," he growled, pointing a finger at her. "I'll shoot the first one who touches my cows."

Isabelle wondered if he would attack her. He seemed angry enough. She couldn't imagine why anyone would want to touch his cows. Longhorns were big, dirty, foul-tempered beasts. She'd as soon touch an alligator.

"We merely want to stop here for the night before going on in the morning." She spoke quietly, hoping to defuse his anger. "We'll make sure we leave the place just as we found it."

"I was hoping you could leave it a little better," he said.

She didn't know what to make of this man. He seemed equally ready to run them off or make fun of them. She didn't find either attitude appealing.

The hair at his collar continued to nag at the edge of some unnamed feeling deep inside her, but she was beginning to feel more like her normal self.

"In exchange for your hospitality, you're welcome to eat with us. Our food isn't fancy, but you're welcome to it."

He lost all signs of belligerence. "Ma'am, anything would be fancy compared to what I can fix."

22

If she had thought to show him how uncouth he was by contrasting her manners with his, she was wasting her time. He picked up an empty plate, served himself from the pot, and sat down. He wasted no time in shoving large quantities of beans and fried bacon into his mouth.

"You got some coffee?" he managed to ask between mouthfuls.

She started to tell him what she thought of men who served themselves from the pot, who sat down while their hostess remained standing, who talked with food in their mouths, but she doubted he would understand what she was talking about.

"I'm not accustomed to serving coffee to a man when I don't know his name," Isabelle said, miffed at his total lack of manners and consideration for her.

"That's a good habit to cultivate, ma'am. It'll save you a heap of trouble in the end."

"Thank you, but your approval isn't necessary. Now if you will be so kind as to tell me your name, I'll introduce you to the boys."

"I don't need an introduction to a passel of scamps I'm not likely to see again. But if it'll settle your feathers, I'll tell you my name. They should have told you that when you got directions to this place."

"They did, but a gentleman always introduces himself."

He stopped chewing long enough to give her a disgusted look. "One of those tea-in-the-parlor and embroidered-lace kinds, are you? Don't know what in tarnation you're doing out here. It must be hell on your sensibilities. For all the good it'll do you, my name's Jake Maxwell. I own the Broken Circle, or what of it your damned poaching farmers have left me. You're welcome to stay the night, but I want you

23

out first thing in the morning. I don't aim to give those thieving bastards reason to set foot on my place again."

His profanity-sprinkled anger startled Isabelle.

He set down his plate and got to his feet. "I guess I'd better pour my own coffee. You seem a mite slow."

Isabelle started, embarrassed. "Sorry, I forgot."

She didn't know why she felt compelled to pour his coffee and hand it to him. As far as she could tell, he was ideally suited to be a rancher. His personality was exactly that of a wild bull.

"Be careful. It's hot," she said as she handed him his coffee.

"I hope so. That's about all it has to recommend it." He stared at it as if he expected to see a tarantula climb out of the cup.

"Isn't it usual to taste coffee before you disparage its flavor?"

"Not when it looks this weak."

She noticed it didn't stop him from drinking it, or handing her the cup for seconds.

"Thirsty," was all the explanation he offered.

She could have sworn she saw mocking laughter in his eyes.

"It wouldn't be too bad if you'd use more coffee," he said when he had finished the second cup. "And don't throw away the old grounds until you've used them three or four times."

"I never use grounds more than once." Her aunt would have gone without coffee rather than do anything so appalling.

"Young grounds don't have any backbone." He set his cup on the ground next to his plate. "Now that I know you're not making off with my priceless antiques, I'll be off."

"You don't sleep here?" she asked.

"I stay at my cow camp. You're welcome to sleep in the cabin. The bed's not much, but it's better than the ground."

"Thank you, but I'll sleep in the wagon."

"You sure? It's a shame to let a bed go to waste."

"I'm sure."

Once again Isabelle was acutely conscious of his muscled forearms, the patch of hair at his throat, the feeling of tightly controlled power. It made her uneasy just to think of sleeping in Jake Maxwell's bed. It was one thing to camp in his ranch yard. It was quite another to allow her body to touch the same sheets that touched his.

"Let one of the boys have it. They can play cards to see who gets it."

"I don't approve of gambling."

"Neither do I, but then, life's a gamble, isn't it? When you look at it like that, cutting the cards for one night in a bed doesn't seem too evil."

Isabelle could think of no reply. Jake mounted up and rode off without another word.

He had hardly disappeared into the darkness when Pete said, "I got some cards." His eyes gleamed with excitement. "Let's cut for the highest card."

The other boys agreed.

"They're probably marked," Bret said.

Ignoring Bret, Pete said to Isabelle, "Shuffle for us."

"I don't know how. My aunt never allowed cards in the house."

Pete stared at her in disbelief.

Night Hawk scorned the white man's bed, but the others were anxious for a chance to get it. Pete won.

"Do you think the runt will know what to do?" Bret

asked. "He's probably more used to sleeping on the floor of a mud hut."

"Tomorrow is an important day," Isabelle said, ignoring Bret and hoping Pete would do the same. "I want you up early so you can bathe, wash your hair, and put on clean clothes. You need to make a good impression on these people. They're going to be your families for the next several years."

"You mean we're going to be their slaves," Bret said.

"You must learn to control your tongue," Isabelle said to him. "Nobody wants to hear their character or good intentions cut up from dawn till dusk."

"Nobody has good intentions toward a Yankee orphan boy."

"Where you were born doesn't determine your character," Isabelle said.

"The hell it doesn't. You're a Southern lady from head to toe. That old cowboy who owns this place is just as bad as the Comanches he's stealing the land from. And any one of these boys will tell you I'm nothing but Yankee scum and won't ever be anything else."

Isabelle didn't argue with Bret. She knew it was pointless.

Later, as she settled into her bed in the wagon, she found herself thinking about Jake Maxwell. She wondered how a man could survive out here by himself. It wasn't possible for him to take care of thousands of cows alone. Of course, he could have a crew, even a wife and family, at his camp.

Yet Isabelle was certain Jake was alone. She could sense it. She had been alone for too long to miss the signs—the wariness, the constant shifting of the gaze, the loneliness that came from knowing there was no one who would care if you suddenly disappeared from the face of the earth.

She could sense it in the boys, too. It was terrible to see in those so young, but she didn't imagine it was any easier for a man.

It certainly hadn't been easy for her.

Something about Jake had made a powerful impression on her. He wasn't the least bit like her fiancé. Charles had been handsome, charming, a perfect gentleman. Yet he had never caused her pulses to race, her body to feel weak, her mind to play tricks.

There was a lingering sense of Jake's presence. She actually wondered what it would be like to touch his powerful arms. She'd seen power, she'd seen roughness, but never a combination like this. It fascinated her. It made her fiancé seem almost boyish.

There was nothing boyish about Jake Maxwell.

Chapter Two

Jake cursed himself as he saddled his horse. He cursed even harder as he rode the short distance through low hills covered in juniper, live oak, mescal bean, mesquite, and yucca. The noise of his horse's hooves clattering over the rocky ground annoyed him. Having to ride through or around canyons that cut deep into the land as they neared the Pedernales River irritated him. Even the abundance of grass failed to cheer him. He barely noticed the profusion of blue, red, and yellow wildflowers.

He was going back to the ranch because of Isabelle Davenport! Just the thought made him furious.

He couldn't sleep for thinking of that woman. His body had been hard with desire all night. It was a forlorn hope. He knew her type—cold, harsh, the kind of woman who could castrate a man with manners and a ladylike disdain for anything physical. She'd lie beneath her husband like a stone. There'd

28

be no kissing, no cuddling, no warmth, no shared excitement. She would endure him because she must and would make him feel guilty for every minute.

She wasn't haughty, but her attitude was superior. If he had been in a better mood, he might have said queenly. It was an unconscious habit, one ingrained from birth. She acted like a princess, an ice princess.

With a string of curses, he whipped his horse into a canter.

Why couldn't he put her out of his mind? He kept picturing her trim waist, the generous swell of her bosom, the whiteness of the skin at the nape of her neck, the softness of her voice, her big blue-green eyes, the utter femininity against which any man was helpless. The only way to kill such a foolish obsession was to go back and let her freeze him to death.

They were up when he arrived. The boys looked like the tag ends of the human race, young outlaws in the making. She was wasting her time trying to make anything out of them. He wouldn't put it past those damned farmers to set them to stealing his cows. They looked just the type to enjoy it.

He had no business getting mixed up with this bunch. He ought to stay away until they'd gone. It wasn't too late to go back.

Then Isabelle stepped around the corner of the cabin. Jake wasn't one to quake and quiver over a woman, but he had to admit that looking at Isabelle was a damned fine way to start the day. He was used to women in shapeless brown dresses, their hair hidden under shapeless bonnets, their faces lined and aged from work, weather, and too many children.

Isabelle looked as if she had just stepped out of a picture book. She wore a yellow skirt of plain design but brilliant color. Her white blouse covered her from wrist to chin. He couldn't imagine how she had

kept it looking so fresh and clean on this trip. Her
hair was brushed until her chestnut curls, clustered
at her forehead and the back of her neck, shone.

But it was her face that transformed the whole.
She looked so young, fresh, and innocent. That was
a dangerous combination. Such a woman could
make a sensible man do foolish things.

"Good morning," she called out. Her mood was
cheerful, but her manner was still formal. "You're
just in time for breakfast."

"I didn't come to eat."

"I didn't suppose you had," she said, approaching
him, "but you may as well join us."

He ought to go, to say he just came by to make
sure they were all right. He dismounted but delib-
erately turned his attention from Isabelle. He had to
get himself under control. "What have you got there,
son?" he said to the boy at the cook fire.

"It's bacon and beans," a younger boy working
with him answered. "Matt ain't got time to fix biscuits."

"Sounds like you're a mighty good cook," Jake said
to Matt. "Where'd you learn?"

"Ma taught him," the younger boy answered.

Though Jake had spoken to him twice, Matt hadn't
raised his head or glanced at Jake. Matt was a tall
boy, blond and blue-eyed, with a well-shaped body.
He was very handsome, but not as good looking as
the younger boy, who was beautiful.

"What's your name?" Jake asked the younger boy.
A thin hand brushed aside the white-blond hair
that nearly obscured his sky-blue eyes. He didn't
come up to Jake's waist, but he looked up at him
without a trace of fear. "Will Haskins," the boy answered promptly. "Matt's my brother."

"Well, Will Haskins, I was talking to Matt. I'd ap-

Jake

preciate if you'd be quiet long enough for him to answer."

"He don't talk," Will said before Jake could turn away.

Jake looked from one boy to the other. Matt still showed no awareness of Jake's existence. Will stared at him, as bright as a penny, his eyes wide, his expression open.

Jake wondered how Isabelle expected to find a home for a boy who wouldn't talk. "Does he talk to you?"

"No."

"Then how do you know what he wants?"

"Matt never wants nothing."

"You'd better eat your breakfast before it gets cold." It was Isabelle speaking. Jake looked up to see that she had poured him a cup of coffee. Matt was holding a plate out to him. The boy seemed to look right through him

Something terrible had happened to that boy. If his brother was anything to go by, he should be bright and willing and full of curiosity.

Jake looked into Matt's eyes. They were empty. He seemed to be little more than a hollow shell, doing what was expected, wanting nothing, thinking nothing, feeling nothing. Jake recognized the signs. He'd seen them often enough in boys shocked out of their innocence by the brutality of the war. It made Jake shiver.

"Come with me," he said to Isabelle. "I want to show you the best trail."

"Let me call Chet and Luke Attmore. They do the driving."

"No, just you. You can show them later."

He ought to stay as far from this woman as possible. She caused him to think all kinds of impossible

31

thoughts, thoughts dangerous to a man alone and missing the comfort of a woman. But the blank look on Matt's face needled his conscience.

"You know anything about these farmers?" Jake asked when they were out of earshot.

Isabelle's surprise was obvious. "Of course. I handled all the correspondence."

"Do they intend to adopt the boys?"

"No, but I didn't expect that," she answered, clearly astonished by his question. "I was fortunate to be able to convince them to take these boys at all."

Jake didn't know if it was fair to jeopardize the boys' chances of finding homes, but he remembered the coldness he'd seen in those men, the cruelty he recognized in Rupert. He couldn't believe they would care for outsiders, especially not orphan boys who'd been sent to them as virtual slaves.

"I don't know much about these men," Jake began, "but I'd ask a few more questions before I handed these boys over. I don't think they're the kind of men to treat these boys the way you want."

"If you know nothing about them, how can you say that?"

"They came in here while I was away and settled on my best land. A month ago, they showed up with bills for damage my cows did to their crops. They know I don't have any money, so they offered to take their payment in cattle."

"So?"

"They're trying to ruin me. They've seen to it I can't get any hands to stay. That ought to tell you something."

Isabelle looked at him with contempt. "It tells me quite a lot," she said. "It tells me you resent men who work with their hands to establish an honest claim to the land, to build homes and cultivate fields to

32

feed their families. It tells me you don't care that your cattle have ruined the fruits of their labors. It tells me you want to avoid debts that are your just responsibility. It tells me you aren't above slandering the reputation of men you admit you know little about."

By the time Isabelle had reached the end of her speech, Jake was ready to hand her over to the farmers. For the sake of the boys he'd tried to warn her, had gone against his better judgment in speaking to her, and she had responded by attacking his character.

Jake threw away his breakfast and poured his coffee into the dust. "I want you and your young hellions out of here the minute they've swallowed their breakfast. Make damned sure whoever used my bed didn't infest it with lice. It's the only mattress I've got. I'd hate to have to burn it."

He took her hand and placed his plate and cup in it. She glared at him, turned rigid by the insult.

"For the sake of your conscience, I suggest you head back to Austin the minute you unload this crew. That way you'll never know if they're worked until they drop or fed slop a pig wouldn't eat."

"Mr. Maxwell," she said from between gritted teeth, "each one of these men has provided excellent character references."

"Have you seen these men for yourself?"

"No, but—"

"Do. Then tell me about their excellent character. Now I've got some cows to brand before my neighbors, who are so full of excellent character, do it for me."

"But if they're going to brand them for you—"

"Don't be a fool. They wouldn't use my brand."

She paled with embarrassment, as well she should

have. She knew nothing about Texas and the hard men who lived here. She should never have left Austin, or wherever she came from. She was no more suited to live outside a city than he was to live inside one.

He stalked away and mounted his horse. Even though anger was chewing at him like a hungry wolf, he looked back at Matt Haskins. The boy had finished his breakfast and was sitting, staring ahead of him out of empty eyes.

That picture haunted Jake as he rode back to his herd.

When Jake left, Isabelle felt as though a giant magnet had released its hold on her. She'd thought of him several times since yesterday, always of something she would change—his clothes, his rough appearance, the feeling of his being a fierce animal on a leash. But she knew that even in Savannah a man such as Jake Maxwell would have ignored the dictates of society.

Isabelle couldn't understand why that thought should excite her. She wasn't a foolish girl indulging in a senseless fascination for a totally unsuitable man. She couldn't imagine a worse fate than to be caught out here, helpless, having to depend on Jake Maxwell.

The man was without character. Didn't he realize how transparent his attack on the farmers was? Did he think she was going to take his word just because he gave it?

She wondered why he was trying to run a ranch by himself. But then, he might not have any cattle. She hadn't seen any. For all she knew, he could be stealing cattle from the farmers.

Isabelle told herself to put Jake Maxwell out of her

mind. What he was or did was no concern of hers.
Her job was to see these boys settled in their new
homes. As for Mr. Maxwell—well, she imagined the
farmers could take care of him.

It was time to get moving, or they would be late.
She looked around until she spied the Attmore boys.
"Chet, tell Hawk to hitch up the mules."

"Yes, ma'am," Chet answered politely.

Chet and Luke Attmore were a puzzle to Isabelle.
She couldn't imagine why no one wanted them. They
were big, nice-looking boys, very mature for fourteen
and thirteen. They were well mannered and did
everything she asked of them.

"Sean, you and Pete hurry with the cleaning up. I
want to be on the road in thirty minutes." Those two
were an odd pair—Sean with his tall, gangly body
and broad face and little Pete with his curly brown
hair and sharp, pointed features. Sean's green eyes
twinkled with cheerfulness. Pete's dark brown eyes
were filled with distrust.

The boys were moving slowly. She knew they were
just as nervous as she was about their new homes,
but time and cruel circumstance had rubbed cal-
louses over their emotions until they could pretend
to feel nothing.

Isabelle knew better. It was in the air around them,
a feeling of desperate hope.

"I'm not finished yet," Bret said when Pete tried to
take his plate. He swung at Pete, but the little boy
jumped out of the way. Sean's big fist knocked Bret
rolling. Pete picked up the dropped plate. He and
Sean moved on as if nothing had happened. None of
the other boys appeared even to notice.

"Hurry up and take off your boots," Mercer ordered.

"Can't we keep them today?" Chet asked. "I don't

want to show up barefooted."

"You'll get 'em when you need 'em," Mercer said.
"Now hurry up and get in that wagon."

Isabelle wanted to brain Mercer for his insensitivity. She made herself a promise that she would never travel with him again. There were many ways to keep boys under control, but treating them like prisoners wasn't one of them.

There was so much pushing and shoving as they climbed into the old army wagon that Isabelle almost missed seeing Pete pull out of his pants the knife Matt used to cut bacon. He raised it over his head and pitched himself at Night Hawk. She was too far away to stop him.

"Hawk!" she screamed.

Night Hawk dropped to the ground and rolled to one side. He was immediately on his feet. He grabbed the younger boy's wrist and threw him to the ground. He fell on top of him, the knife now poised at Pete's throat.

Mercer, aroused from his lethargy, pushed his rifle up against Night Hawk's head. "Drop that knife, half breed, or I'll blow a hole through you."

Isabelle grabbed the rifle by the barrel and pushed it away from Night Hawk. She glared at Mercer. "If you ever again point a rifle at one of these boys, I'll see you're fired the minute we get back to Austin."

"He was going to scalp him."

"Don't be ridiculous. He's just tired of Pete trying to kill him. Let him up, Hawk."

Night Hawk got off Pete immediately, but his gaze was cold and deadly.

"Sean, you're supposed to be watching Pete."

Sean was a good-hearted boy. He always felt guilty when he didn't do what was expected of him. "I can't watch him every second."

Pete had seen his parents butchered by Comanches. He hated all Indians, even half-breeds.

"Pete, sit up front with me. If you attack Hawk again, I'm going to have Mercer tie your hands behind you."

She would be relieved to turn him over to his family. Most of the time he was happy and cheerful, but these black moods settled over him without warning. He had attacked Hawk five times during the two weeks of the trip.

Soon they were all settled and under way. The boys sat crossed-legged on the bed of the wagon, their backs against the sides, their belongings piled in the middle. She sat on a bench where she could watch them, her back to the driver. It was a tight fit, an uncomfortable one by day's end.

"Do you think what that man said is true?" Will asked when the Broken Circle Ranch had disappeared from view.

"What do you mean?" Isabelle asked.

"What he said about the farmers only wanting us so they could work us like slaves."

"Where did you hear that?"

"I followed you." That surprised Isabelle. Though just a year younger, Will's trusting acceptance was a marked contrast to Pete's sharp distrust.

Instantly each boy's gaze was turned on her. Their hopes rode on her answer. It wouldn't do any good to lie. They would know. "I wouldn't put too much trust in what Mr. Maxwell said," Isabelle said.

"I liked him."

Isabelle couldn't understand why. Jake was rude and mannerless. She imagined he would be a brutal taskmaster. That's probably why the bunkhouse was empty.

"The farmers had excellent references," Isabelle

assured Will. "I read them myself. I'm sure they expect you to work very hard. Nobody is making a secret of that. But they and their own sons will be working right alongside you."

"I'll bet we get the hardest work," said Bret, who always assumed the worst.

"I expect you will until you prove yourselves, but once they know you're dependable and they can trust you, I'm sure they'll treat you like one of the family."

"More fool them if they do," Mercer said.

"Don't listen to Mercer, either. Do your work well, and with a willing heart, and I'm certain things will work out for all of you."

They didn't ask any more questions, but she could see doubt had entered their minds. One boy would occasionally glance at another to see what he was thinking. That was a bad sign. Usually they didn't care what the others thought. She would dearly love to say a few words to Jake Maxwell. He was responsible for this.

They had been traveling about an hour when Chet Attmore called out. There was something on the trail ahead. Night Hawk stood up and worked his way forward. Casting Isabelle a nervous glance, Sean grabbed both of Pete's hands.

"It's a man," Night Hawk said. Nobody argued. His eyesight was better than anyone's. "A white man."

Isabelle stood up. She could see the body in the road, but she couldn't tell anything about it.

"He must be dead," Chet said.

"He's alive," Night Hawk said.

"How can you tell?" Bret demanded. "Nobody can see that well."

"I can."

Night Hawk vaulted over the side of the wagon and started toward the body. Isabelle grabbed hold of

Chet to keep from falling as the wagon lurched over a large rock.

"Get back in that wagon!" Mercer shouted.

Night Hawk ignored him.

"Come back here, or I'll shoot."

"He's just going to see if the boy is hurt," Isabelle explained, at the end of her patience with Mercer's stupidity.

Chet Attmore stopped the wagon and all the boys spilled out. By the time Isabelle reached the fallen man, he was completely surrounded. She knelt down next to him.

Though he looked to be two or three years older than Chet, he was just a boy. He appeared to be tall and was thin to the point of emaciation. His hair was dull brown, his brown eyes expressionless, his clothes dirty and threadbare. He looked dreadful.

"Will, run back and get my canteen." Maybe if she bathed his face, he would revive.

The boy's eyes were open, but he was having trouble summoning the energy to talk. He looked weak and undernourished. Isabelle noticed a bruise on his arm. She thought she saw the faint signs of several bruises on his face, but it was hard to tell with the shadows cast by the boys.

"I don't think he's sick so much as exhausted," Isabelle said.

"Whoever beat him did a good job," Sean said.

Will returned with the canteen. Isabelle poured some water into a handkerchief and began to moisten the boy's face and forehead. As the layers of dust came off, she was able to see the bruises more clearly. They weren't new, probably at least a week old, but he had been badly beaten.

"Hawk, help Sean lift him into the wagon. We'll take him with us. One of the farmer's wives is bound to take him in until he gets better."

The boy cried out when Sean put his hand under his back. Isabelle pulled his collar back far enough to see the red welts that crisscrossed his shoulders. They weren't new, probably as old as the bruises. Several of the welts had become infected. She felt her stomach heave with anger and disgust.

"I'm sorry if we hurt you," she told the boy, "but if you can't walk, we'll have to carry you. We're going to Utopia."

The boy struggled to his feet, a look of abject terror twisting his features. "They'll kill me if you take me back there," he gasped.

"Your wounds are infected. You need food and rest. There's nobody else. The nearest town is nearly a week away."

Isabelle was startled when the boy fumbled with the buttons of his shirt. "Look at what they did to me!" he cried as he struggled out of it.

He turned around. Dozens of welts covered his back. Somebody had beaten him unmercifully, left his wounds untreated, his body unfed.

This went beyond anger because he didn't do as much work as expected or didn't do it well. It went beyond punishment for breaking rules. This was cruelty for the sake of being cruel. Isabelle tried to imagine what kind of man would do this to another human being, but she couldn't. Despite two years in the orphanage, she'd had a sheltered upbringing. She'd never seen anything like this.

"Who did this?" she demanded, her voice rough with nausea, her body shaking with rage.

"The gentle, loving man who took me in," the boy said, his voice mocking, "the man who was going to adopt me if I could come to love his family as much as they loved me already. This is what he did when

I didn't work hard enough to please him, when I fell down because I didn't have the strength to work any more, when I ran away because I thought being dead had to be better than living in that hell."

"Did the others know?" Isabelle asked, unable to believe such cruelty would be allowed.

"They were too busy beating their own orphans to care."

Isabelle felt physically sick. She'd never seen or heard of such inhuman treatment. She couldn't have imagined it until now.

"If any man tried to beat me like that, I'd kill him," Sean said.

"Not if your hands were tied."

"Hell!" Bret said. "You mean he tied you up?"

"They tied all of us up, afraid we'd escape."

"Hell!" Bret said again.

Isabelle looked at the faces of the other boys. They were all turned to her, waiting to hear what she would say, waiting to find out what she would do about their futures.

"We're not going to Utopia," she announced.

"What are you going to do with them?" Mercer demanded.

"I don't know," Isabelle replied, "but we most certainly aren't going to Utopia. Hawk, help Sean get him into the wagon."

"We're going ahead," Mercer said. "That's what the agency wanted, and that's what we're going to do."

"It's not your decision," Isabelle said. "Your job is to insure our safety, nothing else."

Mercer pointed his rifle at Night Hawk and Sean, who were about to lift the boy into the wagon. "Put him down. I'll tell the farmers where to find him, but it'll be up to them to come after him."

Isabelle didn't know what came over her. She only

41

knew she was so blazingly angry that she stooped down, picked up a rock, and flung it at Mercer. No one was more surprised than she when it hit him on the forehead. No one was more shocked when he slumped to the ground unconscious. Too horrified by what she had done to think sensibly, she turned to the boy and calmly asked, "What's your name?"

He grinned broadly. "Buck, ma'am. Just call me Buck."

Chapter Three

Chet pulled the wagon to a stop in front of Jake's cabin.

"Help him to Mr. Maxwell's bed," Isabelle told Sean.

"I bet he doesn't want a grubby orphan bleeding all over his bed," Bret said.

"He can have my bedroll," Sean offered, generous as always.

"I'm sure Mr. Maxwell won't mind," Isabelle said. "He offered it freely before." She followed them to the cabin. "I'll see if I can find some medical supplies."

Isabelle was appalled at the condition of Jake's kitchen. It didn't look as though it had been used for weeks, maybe months. She found nothing remotely medicinal except several bottles of whiskey. Apparently Jake Maxwell never got sick or injured. Or if he did, he got drunk until Mother Nature could complete the healing process. She did find some bacon grease. It was old, but it would do. She walked to the door.

"Bret," she called, "bring me some water."

While she was waiting, she found some wood in a box behind the stove. She opened the stove and smothered an exclamation of disgust. The ashes hadn't been carried out. She cleared a space with a poker and put in some dried twigs and bark. She set a match to it. The dry material caught quickly.

"Set the pot on the stove," she told Bret when he arrived with the water. "Bring it to me as soon as it's hot."

She picked up her bacon grease, a bottle of whiskey, and a shallow pan, then hurried to the other side of the cabin. Jake's bedroom was furnished with only a bed and a chest. It didn't look as if it had been used recently. Apparently Jake preferred living out in the open.

"You need to undress," Isabelle said to Buck.

"All the way?" Buck asked, embarrassed.

"Everything but your underwear. I don't think Mr. Maxwell would appreciate having those shoes in his bed."

His shoes were encrusted with something that looked as if it had come from a cow pen. Isabelle brought a chair from the kitchen while Sean helped Buck out of his clothes. For a big, often clumsy boy, he was surprisingly gentle.

Bret brought in some water and poured it into the basin. "It's not hot yet, but I figured you'd want to get started. His back looks a mess."

She was surprised. Bret never showed concern for anybody but himself.

Isabelle had to break the scabs on the worst wounds to clean them. It was all she could do to keep from retching. Buck jerked when she applied the alcohol-soaked cloth to the raw flesh, but he remained still after that. Isabelle would have liked to think he had fainted, but she imagined he simply didn't have the strength to move.

"I bet Mr. Maxwell was planning to drink that," Sean said.

"I don't approve of whiskey," Isabelle said. She fought off the memory of what a man had tried to do to her when his brain was clogged with alcohol. "But it will help keep the infection from coming back."

She finished and rose to her feet. "Now we're going to let him sleep." She stepped outside. Chet was waiting on the steps.

"What are we going to do with him?" he asked, pointing to Mercer Williams, who was lying on the ground next to the wagon, his hands tied behind his back with his own belt.

Isabelle didn't know.

"We could dump him in the river," Bret said. "The wolves and buzzards would clean up anything the fish didn't want."

Isabelle was still horrified that she had hit Mercer.

"I don't know. Maybe Mr. Maxwell will have a suggestion when he gets here."

If he wasn't so angry at her for coming back that he refused to help. She wouldn't put it past him. She had the strong impression he was an impatient, intolerant man.

But Jake and Mercer didn't really concern her. She had to figure out what to do with the boys. She didn't want to take them back to the agency, but she couldn't take care of them herself, and she had no one to help her.

* * *

Jake drove the last of the ornery longhorns into the canyon corral and headed toward his camp. During the year since he'd been home, he'd branded nearly a thousand animals by himself, but the work was slow and dangerous for one man. He had to drive the calf or yearling into a chute and brand it while it was held in place by poles thrust through each end. More than one had broken its leg trying to climb out of the chute.

The Maxwell herd had been virtually unbranded for five years. Nearly half the cattle were mavericks. Jake's mavericks, but he had to brand them to have a claim on them. Even that wasn't always good enough. The Reconstruction government had pushed through a tally law that allowed a man to round up cows regardless of brand and drive them off to sell. The man was supposed to pay the owner when he found him, but he never did. It was legalized robbery.

The farmers of Utopia hadn't tried that yet. They had been too busy driving everybody out of the area except themselves. But who was to say they wouldn't change their minds.

Since winter he'd rounded up more than five hundred steers, but he couldn't drive them to New Mexico alone. He intended to pay the farmers something for their damaged crops—certainly not as much as they were asking—but he had to sell his steers first. If he couldn't, he would lose them and the rest of his stock.

He had just reached the tent he'd set up in a small grove of oaks when he noticed a thin cloud of dust against the horizon. It looked as if it was coming from his ranch. Smoke wouldn't have surprised him. The Comanches would have been happy to burn him out. Maybe the farmers were back. He couldn't imagine what else could cause so much dust.

Whoever it was didn't belong on his ranch. Cursing, Jake threw his saddle on a fresh horse and headed for the ranch at a gallop.

A totally unexpected sight confronted Jake when he rode into the yard. The Davenport woman was back with her orphans, but that wasn't what caused him to stare in surprise. In the big corral, two boys were astride bucking horses. Five more horses—part of the herd his family had owned before the war— trotted nervously about inside the small corral. After his father was killed by a steer, they'd been left to run wild.

One of the riders was the half-breed Comanche. Jake didn't know the name of the other one, but he seemed just as good as the half-breed. The rest of the boys had climbed the fence and were shouting encouragement. Isabelle stood on the steps of the cabin. He came up behind without her hearing him.

"My money's on the half-breed," he said.

Isabelle jumped a foot. When she turned around and saw who it was, she looked relieved. "You scared me half to death."

"Where'd they catch the horses?"

"At the creek when they came to drink. I hope you don't mind."

She was being nice. He ought to turn tail and run, but he itched to get his hands around her waist. It was so small and dainty. Even though she was as neat as a pin and as stiff as starch, she exuded a softness that was nearly impossible to resist.

"Of course I don't mind. I love having strangers commandeer my property any time they like."

Isabelle turned pink. "We had to come back."

Now she looked embarrassed and uncomfortable, which caused all his chivalrous instincts to come stampeding to the fore. If he had any sense at all, he'd cover his eyes, plug his ears, and not stop running until he reached the Pecos.

"I owe you an apology."

"For using this place? Forget it."

"No, for doubting what you said about the men of Utopia."

"Don't tell me they weren't looking their most pious, like they couldn't wait to clasp your little gang of cutthroats to their bosoms."

"They're not cutthroats."

She spoke sharply, her embarrassment fading. Clearly she took any slight to these boys personally.

"Maybe not yet."

"Not ever, if I can do anything about it."

She spoke with such passionate resolve that Jake turned his gaze from the bucking horses to her face. Her expression was one of staunch determination. She really meant it.

"Okay, they're not cutthroats yet. Why didn't you hand them over to the farmers?"

"We found a boy on the road. He'd been beaten and was suffering from overwork and hunger."

"What did you do with him?" Jake asked.

"He's inside, in your bed. I cleaned his wounds as best I could, but he mostly needs food and rest."

Jake turned and headed for his bedroom. Isabelle followed. Buck appeared to be sleeping. Jake approached the bed, his gaze riveted to the welts on the boy's back. He didn't miss the bruises on his face.

Jake felt a cold, killing anger. All the cruelties of the war, the injustices of Reconstruction, seemed to be distilled in this one terrible act. He thought of all the decent, courageous men who'd sacrificed everything they possessed to fight for an ideal while these child-beaters went about stealing his land.

"Which one of those sons-of-bitches did this?" Jake said.

"I didn't ask."

Jake walked over to the chest, opened it, and took out a pistol and holster.

"What are you doing?" Isabelle demanded, fear in her voice.

"I'm going to find out who did this if I have to beat it out of them. Then I'm going to shoot the son-of-a-bitch."

"You can't," Isabelle said as he checked his gun for bullets.

"Why not?" He laid the gun aside and took a handful of bullets out of a box.

"There are too many of them. Besides, they won't tell you. And if you kill one of them, they'll hang you."

"I'll take my chances."

He pushed bullets into empty loops on his gun belt.

"You can't go. If you do, they'll know about us."

He paused. "They know already."

"They know we're coming, but they don't know we're here. If they did, they might come after the boys."

"I'd stop them."

"You couldn't hold them off all by yourself. You couldn't make sure none of the boys got hurt."

"Somebody's bound to get a bit shot up."

"I will not have any of these boys *shot up!*"

Jake wondered what it was that made city-bred women so determined to come out West. They ought to know from the dirt and the heat they wouldn't like it. They certainly didn't approve of the men or anything they did. Everybody would be much happier if they didn't allow females west of the Mississippi, at least not until they built a city to hold them.

"Ma'am, there's Indians and bandits and rustlers out here. Add to that scalawags, carpetbaggers, and that bunch of murdering farmers. None of them cares how they get what they want as long as they get it. You have a choice. You can go back East with your tail between your legs and let them have it—"

"Or you can fight and receive a hero's honors when they bury you." She was sarcastic.

"No, ma'am. Out here, the lucky ones get buried under a few rocks so the animals won't tear their bodies to pieces."

Isabelle swallowed. "And the unlucky ones?"

"Mostly we don't find them. If we do, there's not enough of them left to tell."

He was sorry he'd let his temper get the better of him. She'd made him mad, and he wanted to make her mad right back. But he'd upset her. Now he wanted to grab her and kiss her, tell her she had nothing to worry about because he was going to clean out the whole nest of rattlesnakes.

"I've got to go. I want to catch one of them in his field. That way they can't gang up on me."

"Please don't."

"Don't worry about your boys. You can leave right now and they'll never find you."

"Wouldn't it be better to notify the sheriff? He'd have to go out there if Mercer and I back up your story. Then you wouldn't have to shoot anybody."

"Ma'am, are you worried I'll get shot?" That would be a first.

She looked surprised at his question. "I don't want anybody to get hurt."

"But I have no character. You told me so yourself."

Isabelle flushed with embarrassment. "I hope you will forget I said that. Please wait."

Jake was a sucker when it came to women. When

they were as pretty as Isabelle, he was helpless. Look at him, ready to take on that whole nest of thieving bastards alone. He must be crazy.

"Okay, I'll wait." But he didn't mean to wait long.

The cheering suddenly stopped. Curious, Jake stepped outside. The half-breed's horse had stopped bucking. The other boy's horse was tired, but there was still some life left in him.

"Who are those boys? They're right handy with horses."

"That's Night Hawk and Chet Attmore. They just wanted to have some fun. They've been locked up in the orphanage so long, they've almost forgotten they're boys."

As they watched, Night Hawk pulled the saddle off the horse he'd just finished riding and turned him into the small corral. When he walked toward the other horses twirling a lasso, they scattered and ran.

"What's he doing?" Isabelle asked.

"He's going to catch him another horse," Jake said. "I wonder if he means to break them all."

"Would you mind?"

"There's no point. They'll just be turned out again."

"Maybe your riders could use them."

"Maybe." He had no intention of telling her he had no riders. Besides, he was more interested in watching Night Hawk. He had roped Sawtooth, the meanest horse on the ranch. Sawtooth didn't mind a rope or bridle. He'd follow you anywhere as tame as a cat. But put a saddle on his back and he turned into a monster.

Night Hawk slipped a hackamore bridle over Sawtooth's head and led him into the large corral. There he tied his head close to a corral post. Being unable to move his head, Sawtooth couldn't object when Night Hawk put a saddle on his back.

51

"Smart," Jake said. "That boy knows horses."

"His father is a Comanche chief," Isabelle explained. "He lived with them until he was eleven."

Chet Attmore had finally ridden his horse into submission. While the tired animal stood spraddle-legged, trying to catch its breath, Night Hawk offered his horse to the boys. Matt Haskins stepped forward.

Jake hadn't been able to forget Matt and his empty-eyed silence. The kid he'd seen the night before was in no condition to ride a horse. He stifled an impulse to call a halt to the fun. This was the first sign of life Matt had shown. He watched as the boy prepared to climb into the saddle.

"You may be about to lose your cook," he said to Isabelle. "That's Sawtooth. He'll throw the kid in the dust. Then he'll try to kill him."

Isabelle couldn't have looked any more shocked if he'd said Matt was about to ride a grizzly bear. "You've got to stop him!" she cried.

When Jake made no move, she started forward. He grabbed her by the arm and pulled her back.

"Let's see what the boy can do."

"But—"

"I'll get my rope just in case."

Jake walked over to his horse, never taking his eyes off Sawtooth. He uncoiled his rope, playing with it, letting it lie in his hand, ready to use if necessary.

"Stay on the porch," he said to Isabelle when she started toward the corral. "Sawtooth doesn't know the difference between cowboys and ladies."

Night Hawk kept Sawtooth tied to the post while Matt climbed into the saddle. Night Hawk adjusted the stirrup length and checked the cinch to make sure it was tight. He said something to Matt, then untied Sawtooth.

One second Sawtooth was standing perfectly still.

The next he was a blur of flying feet and heaving muscles. He bucked, spun, reversed, and bucked some more. It was only a matter of seconds before Matt went flying through the air.

The boy got up and was brushing himself off before Sawtooth calmed down enough to realize there was nobody on his back. He stopped and turned, his hate-glazed eyes searching for the man who had dared to ride him. He snorted his fury and charged.

Jake was ready for Sawtooth. He wasn't ready to see Matt standing there, not moving, like he wanted the horse to run him down. His surprise caused him to be a step behind Night Hawk. The boy threw a loop over Sawtooth's neck just in time to keep Matt from being run down.

Sawtooth immediately turned on Night Hawk.

Cursing himself for a hesitation which could have cost Matt his life, Jake threw his rope. The shaggy, dirty gray stallion was caught. He bucked and squealed his fury.

"Get out of the corral!" Jake shouted.

Matt just stood there.

"If you won't get out, then get back on." Jake didn't know what made him say that. He just had a feeling the boy wanted to die, that he had remained motionless because he wanted Sawtooth to kill him.

Jake thought of the hundreds of boys not much older than Matt who'd died during the war, who would have given almost anything to be standing in Matt's boots, and he got mad.

"Come on!" he shouted. "Either you've got the guts to ride him to the finish, or you don't. Which is it?"

It seemed that everything stilled, waiting for Matt's answer. The boys fell silent. Isabelle staggered to the bottom of the steps, her hand over her mouth, her eyes wide with fear. Even Sawtooth turned to look at the boy who stood watching him with empty eyes.

Matt didn't move. Jake wondered if he'd retreated too far inside himself to be reached. He'd seen boys after battle so traumatized by the carnage, by seeing their friends blown to bits, they retreated into some dark place in their minds and refused to come out.

Then Matt took a step. Nothing else about him changed. Just his feet moved. Sawtooth screamed his fury, and the tableau burst into life.

The boys jockeyed for positions on the fence. Isabelle came toward the corral at a run.

"You're not going to let him get back on that horse, are you?" she asked.

"If he wants."

"But he'll get killed."

"He's already half dead. Maybe Sawtooth can save the rest of him."

"How can you talk like that? He's only a boy."

"I wasn't talking about his age. I was talking about his spirit. That boy wants to die."

"How can you know?"

"Didn't you see the way he just stood there, waiting for Sawtooth to run him down?"

"He was too scared to run."

"He's not scared of anything. He just doesn't care."

They both turned to watch Matt as he approached Sawtooth. The horse eyed him with a malevolent gaze. Brave, foolhardy Sean dashed in and grabbed Sawtooth's head, holding him still so Matt could mount. Jake and Night Hawk loosened their ropes.

"Get out of there!" Jake called to Sean. The boy hurriedly climbed through the rails. "You ready?" Jake called to Matt, who showed no sign he'd heard.

"I guess he's as ready as he's ever going to be," Jake muttered to himself.

Jake caught Night Hawk's eye, and they dropped their ropes. Sawtooth went to bucking with renewed fury. In less than a minute Matt hit the ground again. Jake and Night Hawk grabbed the trailing ropes and choked Sawtooth into submission.

"Ready to get back on?" Jake called out.

"No!" Isabelle said. "That's enough."

"Let him decide."

Matt brushed himself off and started toward Sawtooth again. Once more Jake and Night Hawk let go of the ropes and Sawtooth went to bucking, but he didn't leap quite so high, didn't spin quite so fast.

Matt stayed on.

Sawtooth broke into a gallop, then skidded to a halt, trying to send Matt flying over his head.

Matt stayed on.

Sawtooth went back to bucking and jumping and fishtailing and spinning and reversing and spinning again, but Matt stayed on. He stayed on when Sawtooth ran straight at the corral fence. He stayed on when Sawtooth jumped it. He even stayed on when Sawtooth stepped on one of the ropes and nearly went down. He was still on when Sawtooth came to a halt nearly half a mile away, his sides heaving from his exertions.

"Well I'll be damned," Bret said. "I never thought the sullen bastard would do it."

Sean ran up when Matt rode Sawtooth back to the yard. He held Matt steady on his shaky legs when he dismounted, then clapped him on the back enthusiastically. "That was great," he said. "The best riding I ever saw."

"Not as good as Hawk," Jake said, "but every bit as good as Chet."

"I think you're horrible," Isabelle said, "encouraging him to risk his neck on that vicious horse."

Jake didn't answer Isabelle. He was watching Matt, trying to see his eyes. Jake was relieved to see a flicker of life, a tiny spark in the emptiness. Still Matt didn't speak. Will was at his side, talking for him, accepting congratulations.

"Has he ever spoken?" Jake asked Isabelle.

"Not that I know of, but that has no bearing on this."

"It has everything to do with it. There's something still alive in that boy, something that made him step forward, that made him get back on when he fell off."

Now that the excitement of the ride was dying down, the boys gradually became aware of Jake in their midst. They quieted, all looking at him.

"There's four more horses that need reminding what it's like to have a rider on their backs," Jake said.

The tension drained from the group. Night Hawk, Chet, and Sean headed for the corral. Pete, talking a mile a minute, followed Sean. Luke Attmore moved to join his brother. Will looked as though he couldn't make up his mind; then he stayed with Matt.

"It's time to start dinner," Isabelle said to Bret. "I guess you'd better find some firewood and bring some water."

"I want to watch the riding."

"After you do your chores."

"I'm not afraid."

"I never thought you were."

"What's biting him?" Jake asked when Bret left.

Isabelle looked so offended at the way he phrased his question that he thought she might not answer him. But she replied in her most prim style, "He grew up in Boston. He can't ride."

"Well, I'll be damned."

"I certainly hope so if you let any of these boys hurt themselves on those horses."

Jake turned to her. "Can you ride, ma'am?"

"I can drive a carriage."

"That's no good out here."

"I don't live out here, Mr. Maxwell. I don't have to adapt to the brutal way of life you seem to find so ordinary. Maybe I should even say attractive."

"You can say anything you please. If life in these parts is too hard on your sensibilities, I suggest you go inside and tend to your patient. That is, unless you find that too raw for your tender feelings."

Isabelle's expression turned rigid. "I cleaned his wounds when they were dirty and full of infection."

"I know. I can't figure out why you're not stretched out on the bed next to him."

Isabelle eyed him with a fulminating gaze. "I don't know whether you're intent upon insulting me specifically or whether you despise women in general, but I think you're rude, insensitive, and thoughtless. I wouldn't be surprised if you like seeing people endanger their lives. That's just the kind of thing a person of your type would think entertaining."

"And what do *you* find entertaining, ma'am?"

"I wouldn't dream of telling you, of giving you the pleasure of laughing at me."

"And if I promised I wouldn't laugh?"

"I wouldn't believe you."

She looked at him as if he were a cockroach. He was a fool to spend as much as five minutes thinking about her. She could get along by herself. Women like her always did. Their beauty bewitched one poor fool after another.

"I'll do my best to stay out of your way until you leave."

Isabelle looked stricken, all her angry pride gone. "That's just it. We can't leave."

Chapter Four

"What do you mean, you can't leave?" Jake asked as they started back toward the cabin.

"Nothing. It's not your problem."

"It is if you mean to stay on my ranch." He pointed to Mercer. "He's going to be tough to handle when you let him loose."

She groaned inwardly. She didn't want to keep Mercer tied up, but she couldn't allow him to return to Austin before she did.

"What do you suggest?"

"We could give him to the farmers. I imagine he could do a lot of work."

"Mr. Maxwell, I realize you have a very poor opinion of women in general, of me in particular, but—" She stopped. He was grinning. "You're making fun of me."

His smile disappeared. "Would I do a thing like

that?" A more insincere appearance of innocence would be hard to imagine.

"Yes, though I can't imagine why."

"Chalk it up to my perverse nature—you know, like not wanting to sleep in a bed."

He was trying to irritate her. He had succeeded, but she refused to let him know it. "It's the boys I'm worried about. They all have tragic backgrounds. It would wring your heart if you knew."

On second thought, she decided he didn't look like the type to suffer from heart wringing. He was more likely to consider any misfortune their own fault.

"Why can't they get along?" Jake asked. "Some of them look fairly decent."

"They're all decent," Isabelle insisted, "but they don't trust people."

"Sounds like a lot of misfits crying because nobody's mollycoddling them. Of course, if you've been pushing them off on people like your farmers, I can understand."

She might have known he'd manage to make their failures her fault. "I had nothing to with their previous placements."

"Maybe not, but you messed this one up. What happens next?"

She didn't know why she bothered talking to him. He was a man, and they always seemed to think if a woman had anything to do with a plan that went wrong it must be her fault.

"I don't know what to do next," she confessed. "I can't take them back to Austin, but I have nowhere else to go."

"I wouldn't waste my time worrying about them. They can't get along because they don't try."

"I have to worry about them. They're my responsibility."

"Are you related to them?"

"No."

"Then why do you care?"

Isabelle felt like turning her back on him. He was the most callous, insensitive, unfeeling man she'd ever met. Well, no, he wasn't as bad as several she knew, but he was still callous, insensitive, and unfeeling. However, the boys had nowhere to go just now. She'd better bite her tongue before he threw them all out. She sat down on the cabin steps. He dropped down next to her.

"I don't see how you can look at these unloved children and not feel an aching all the way down to the bottom of your soul," she said, avoiding his question. "They only act the way they do because they've been hurt. Their trust has been violated, their innocence destroyed."

"You're avoiding my question."

"And you're exceedingly rude to keep asking it when I obviously prefer not to answer."

"Why?"

"That's none of your business."

"It is if you want me to help you."

"I haven't asked for your help."

"Not in so many words, but when you explained it, you invited me."

"Consider yourself uninvited," she snapped. He was trying to be obnoxious and doing a very good job of it.

"Ever consider letting the boys deal with Mercer?"

"No."

"Don't you trust them?"

She looked at him sharply. "Of course I do."

"Then why not?"

"Because whatever they did would be done out of fear. That wouldn't be fair to them or Mercer."

"A much better answer than I expected."

"I beg your pardon. Did you think I was stupid?"

"Not necessarily."

Isabelle stood up. She had tried to rise in a dignified manner, but she suspected she had jumped up like a six-year-old who'd just been offered a slice of watermelon.

"Sit down."

"And continue to be insulted?"

"I won't."

"You might try, but I don't think you're capable of not insulting me."

"Why?"

"Because your innate prejudice against women is so deep, it colors everything you say. You've probably thought like this for so long, you don't even realize how insulting you are."

He looked as if he were giving the idea some thought. "No, I like women," he said finally. "I just don't trust them."

For a moment Isabelle thought she saw the shadowy figure of a hurt little boy inside Jake, the same as she saw in her orphans, but she dismissed it as too unlikely. Still, even though there was no sign of vulnerability now, some of her defiance left her.

"We haven't decided what to do about your orphans," Jake reminded her.

"It's not your problem."

"It shouldn't be yours. Sit. You're giving me a crick in my neck."

She would have prefered to give him a knot on his head, but she sat. She didn't know why. It just seemed the easiest thing to do. After everything that had happened today, she didn't have much energy left. Still, she knew that wasn't the only reason. When he was around, she felt certain things would work out. Despite his rudeness, his unshakable calm gave her confidence. Anyone who could survive in this wilderness by himself could do anything.

Her gaze was drawn to his strong, muscular forearms. A woman would do almost anything for a man with arms like that. She would. After taking care of herself for so long, the temptation to rely on him was nearly irresistible.

Isabelle was shocked by the direction of her thoughts. She wasn't a silly woman who depended on a man to do everything for her. Neither was she willing to settle for a man who had nothing to recommend him beyond a pair of strong arms.

"The boys are my responsibility," she said. "Why don't we talk about you instead?"

"What the hell for?"

Isabelle was offended by his response. "It's polite to be interested in other people."

"Not out here. If a man wants you to know where he comes from, he'll tell you."

Isabelle stood. "I think it would be best if I left. I seem to be constantly saying something that contravenes your code of ethics."

"Sit down, woman. You jump around more than a prairie chicken chasing grasshoppers. And if you want people to understand what you're saying, stop using those fancy words."

Isabelle felt the remainder of her strength fade away. She wanted to curl up and forget this whole day. She wanted to forget Jake Maxwell, too.

But she couldn't. Despite the insults, his crudeness, his intentional aggravation, there was a raw, uncompromising strength about him that was as attractive as it was alien to her. He stood alone, unafraid, practically defying the world. Isabelle couldn't imagine such a degree of self-reliance or foolhardiness.

There was also an elemental honesty about him. Maybe that was the reason for his lack of manners, his absence of pretense, his refusal to accept any code of behavior but his own. But it was a hard honesty, one that didn't consider feelings or weakness, that required more of a person than most people had to give.

"Is there anything about me you find acceptable, Mr. Maxwell?" She regretted the question the moment it was out of her mouth. She expected him to make fun of her.

"Yeah. You've got a pretty face, nice hair, and a waist so tiny, it doesn't seem big enough to hold you together. But you're an ice princess. You could freeze the warmth out of a summer afternoon. A man could get frostbite if he got too close. I'm sure a lot have tried. I even considered it myself."

No amount of fatigue could make Isabelle spend one more minute in this man's company. "I'm going to see how Buck's doing. I won't take it amiss if you want to return to your camp before I get back."

"Trying to get rid of me?"

"This is your property, Mr. Maxwell."

"It's Jake. Every time you say Mr. Maxwell, I want to look over my shoulder to see who's sneaking up behind me."

"It's not my custom to refer to a man by his first name." Though she had caught herself thinking of him that way.

"Out here that's mostly all we have."

"I still prefer to be addressed as Miss Davenport."

"No problem. Texans are very particular about how we treat women. We don't have enough of them to get careless. When they're as pretty as you—well, you can be called just about anything you want."

Isabelle felt herself blush.

Jake eyed her skeptically. "Don't tell me you haven't been smothered with compliments. I've seen the women they got in Austin. You ought to shine like the sun breaking through after a thunderstorm."

"I have received compliments," Isabelle admitted, "but none quite so extravagant."

"Don't let it go to your head," Jake said. "I don't approve of good-looking women. They're out of place in Texas. If I was to think about getting married—which I'd never do unless I was too old and crippled to take care of myself—I'd look for a homely woman. That way she could keep her mind on her work instead of what do-dad some slicked-up dude might give her."

"If you ever get old and crippled," Isabelle shot back, "shoot yourself. You won't be any good to anybody, certainly not a woman, even a homely one."

Jake was still waiting when Isabelle came out of the cabin. She turned and strode away from him in a manner that clearly said she hoped he wouldn't follow. He had no intention of doing so. He kept on eating his dinner, wondering all the while what twist of fate had sent this woman and her orphans to his ranch.

He didn't feel so amused when it became clear she had no intention of approaching him. It was crazy, but just the sight of her grabbed at his gut. No man could look at Isabelle and not want to possess her, even knowing it meant the risk of frostbite.

When she stopped to talk to the boys gathered around the campfire, Jake decided to take the battle to her.

"Got any more coffee?" he asked Matt when he reached the fire.

Will filled his cup.

"Your brother is quite a hand with horses," Jake said. "Does he ride much?"

"Don't get much chance. We ain't been around anything but nags for more than a year."

"Haven't been," Isabelle corrected.

Will didn't take notice.

"He'll need to talk if he wants to work for anybody."

"Matt won't talk."

"Some men will take it as an insult if they speak to him and he doesn't answer. Might even make it a gun matter."

"Matt won't talk to nobody," Will said.

"Just tell him what I said."

"Okay."

Jake couldn't understand why Will wasn't followed around by a passel of women trying to mother him. His shinning innocence was as rare as Isabelle's beauty.

"Did you mean what you said?" Isabelle asked Jake as he turned away from Will.

Aha! Threaten her precious orphans, and she'd talk to the Devil himself.

"Why shouldn't I?"

"I thought you might have been trying to trick him into talking."

"No need for tricks, ma'am. There's enough troubles already here." He took a swallow of his coffee.

"I don't mean to sound rude, but hadn't you better be getting back to your camp? Of course, I suppose your men can manage by themselves."

"I don't have any men."

Jake could have kicked himself for saying that.

Knowing how impossible it was for a female not to ask questions, he'd set himself up for an explanation he didn't want to give.

"That must make it rather hard on you."

"Yeah." She was going to try to squeeze every bit of information out of him. It wouldn't do her any good, but that wouldn't stop a woman's curiosity.

"There's not many things a man can't do by himself if he puts his mind to it."

"I'm sure you're right."

She looked at him across the fire. He remembered the color of her eyes. That annoyed him. He didn't want to remember that, or the color of her hair.

She sure was a pretty woman. He'd noticed that right off. Her clothes set off her trim figure real well. Not that they exposed any more of her body than absolutely necessary. Miss Davenport didn't believe in unnecessary frills or yards and yards of extra material. Her economic approach led to a dress that covered her body without obscuring it.

Jake decided there was more virtue in economy than he had previously thought.

"Of course, I can't drive them to market by myself. Even a small herd would take several men."

"I suppose it would."

Damn her, looking so calm and sure that he had all the answers when he didn't have a single hand working for him. He wouldn't put it past her to know exactly how desperate he was and be acting like this just for the fun of it.

"I was thinking of making a drive to New Mexico or Colorado. Lots of military forts out there in the market for beef."

"I'm sure the soldiers would enjoy a break in their pork diet."

She didn't sound as if she cared if they ate pork for the rest of their lives.

"The drive's not as far as Kansas or Missouri, but the country's worse."

"Hmmm."

"No irate farmers worried about tic fever chasing you off their land with guns, but there's Indians and Mexican bandits. Comancheros, too."

She sat staring into the fire, not even bothering to respond. She started tapping her foot, probably impatient for him to be gone. Hell, she wasn't even looking at him. He wondered if she remembered he was there. She seemed determined to stay in the shadows cast by the small fire. He couldn't figure out what it was about her that made him care that she wasn't listening. He had never used to let himself get this excited about a female, not even a pretty, soft, feminine one like Isabelle.

Hell, that was obvious! It had been months since he'd been to town. He might not go searching for a woman, but he couldn't ignore one when she was sitting right in front of him. He was human, after all, and Isabelle was fashioned to bring out the humanity in any man.

But there was no point thinking about the color of her eyes, or imagining what it would be like to sit with her in the moonlight on the bank of the river when the willows were in bud. Even though she got to him, made him want to take care of her, be close to her, he needed to remember how dangerous women were. He couldn't trust them.

"I'm sure you'll find the men you need," she said absently.

She wasn't even listening to what she said. She showed about as much interest in him as she did in Mercer.

"How am I going to do that?" he asked, really irritated now.

"Things always turn up when you need them. That's why I'm sure something will happen so I won't have to take these boys back to Austin."

Just what he needed, a Pollyanna. He started to argue with her, but an idea occurred to him that was so stunningly simple, so incredibly obvious, that he felt like a fool for not having thought of it before.

"I'll hire your boys," he said, excitement making his voice louder than he intended.

"For what?"

"Cowhands. They'll help me take my herd to New Mexico."

Isabelle looked at him as if he'd gone stark raving mad.

"Absolutely not. I'd take them back to Austin before I'd let you get your hands on them."

Chapter Five

"I'm not playing nursemaid to a bunch of filthy cows," one of the boys said, the sour one who seemed to dislike everybody.

"I haven't asked you to, Bret," Isabelle said, "but it's easier than farming. All you have to do is ride a horse and sing songs. The cows are too content to graze to cause trouble."

Jake didn't know whether to laugh or be insulted. If she had any idea what it took to convince one of his 1,200-pound "contented cows" to graze quietly instead of trying to gore him and his horse, or stampede, or disappear into some twisting, bolder-filled canyon, she'd change her notions about ranching right fast.

"Why don't you want me to hire them?" Jake asked.

"They're just boys."

"I was herding by the time I was ten."

"Not all of them can ride."

"I can teach them. It's not hard. Even children do it."

"It would take years to turn these boys into cow-hands."

"No, it won't." Jake wasn't giving up. He had found a way to save his neck. "By the time I'm done with them, they'll know how to make their own living. Isn't that what you wanted?"

"Yes, but—"

"Let's cut away the fat, ma'am, and get right to the bone. These boys are only a frog's leap from being jailbirds. You wouldn't have brought them to the edge of civilization if they hadn't already been thrown out of every place that would have them."

If he thought a brutal dose of the truth would shatter her rosy picture of her little gang of rowdies, he was wrong. She didn't hear a word he said.

"They need love and understanding," she said, "not being thrown off horses or gored by your wild cows."

He decided not to point out that only a moment ago his cows were too contented to breathe hard. "You mean you want them to keep going to hell like they are now."

"No, I don't," she said, clenching her hands angrily, "but they're still young boys, children some of them, and they need to be treated that way."

In the way that all children have, the boys sensed something important was happening. They gathered around Jake and Isabelle. He didn't see any longing for respect in their faces. He saw even less desire for affection. They were listening, waiting, watching with hard and distrustful eyes. Taking this bunch under his wing would be like trying to defang a litter of half-grown wolf cubs.

"You can't treat these boys like everybody else,"

Isabelle was saying. "They haven't had ordinary lives. They can't be made to live by ordinary rules."

"In other words, when they get into trouble, I shouldn't punish them for it."

"No, I don't mean it like that. Hawk's mother was captured by Indians. His father is a Comanche chief. He lived with the Comanches for eleven years before his mother was recaptured and he and his sister returned to her family. But nobody would accept them. When his mother and sister died, Hawk ran away to his people. They nearly killed him because they were afraid he was spying for the white man. Now he belongs nowhere, is trusted by no one."

Isabelle's words were passionate, but Night Hawk's eyes were cold, his posture rigid and unbending.

"Pete saw his parents killed by Comanches," Isabelle continued. "He had to watch, knowing he couldn't do anything about it. He hates all Indians, even Hawk. He attacks him every chance he gets."

She looked ready to tell him the story of each boy in the group in order to convince him that they were too frail to survive his rough ways.

"If he's herding cows, he'll be too busy to attack Hawk," Jake said.

"The idea is preposterous," Isabelle said. "They're too young."

"Some of them are fourteen."

"Will is eight, Pete nine. They're practically babies."

"I'm not a baby," Will said.

"He ought to be in a nice home with a motherly woman to take care of him."

Jake let his gaze move slowly from one boy to the next. Their defiant stances showed not the slightest liking for him or any interest in becoming cowhands.

They just stood there, watching him, waiting, as emotionless as carved sentinels.

But they were his chance to get his herd to market, to save something of his inheritance, and he didn't mean to let it slip away because of Isabelle's squeamishness. Now was the time to make her understand that working for him was better than going back to an orphanage in Austin.

"Let's go over to the corral where we can talk in private," he said.

"That's not necessary. I don't intend to say anything the boys can't hear."

"Well, I do, and we wouldn't want to offend their delicate egos, would we?"

She hesitated, then let him lead her away from the boys.

"I agree that some of the boys are too small," Jake said once the boys were out of earshot. "I'll take Hawk, Chet, and Matt. And the big Irish kid if he can stay in the saddle. You can keep the rest."

"That's impossible," she said with a why-can't-you-understand-simple-logic attitude he was beginning to dislike. "You can't separate brothers."

"I don't have time for little kids," Jake argued. "Cowhands have to spend whole days on their own. They have to be strong enough to wrestle a 1,200-pound steer who's determined to do exactly what you don't want him to do, experienced enough to handle a stampede or an Indian attack, mean enough to survive no matter how hard things get."

"Sean won't be parted from Pete."

Jake was desperate. He had a short time to brand his cattle and get them out of the area. If Luke Attmore turned out to be half as good as his brother, he could use him. He could leave Pete and Will in camp. He'd send them back when he started the drive. Isabelle would holler—so would the boys—but it would be worth the fuss if he could get four decent hands.

"Okay, but I won't tolerate crying or sulking."

"What about Bret?"

Jake knew his type—arrogant, bullheaded, useless. "You keep him."

"You can't leave him. He'd feel rejected."

"He ought to be used to that by now."

"Then there's Buck. He's the oldest of all."

"I can't use a kid who's so weak he can't get out of bed."

"He'll get well."

"Good. You can stay here until he's strong enough to travel."

She smiled at him in a particularly superior way. "That won't be necessary. We'll be out of here in the morning, all of us."

"But you said—" He stopped. She had led him on. She had let him bargain and hope, and all the while she had absolutely no intention of letting him have the boys. He was strongly tempted to tie her up with Mercer and let the boys decide her fate for themselves.

"They need jobs and a home. I can give them both."

"You have no home. You live in the woods, or wherever it is you keep your cows. And you don't have a ranch. You're sitting in the middle of nowhere surrounded by nothing, holding on to nothing. Buck told me the farmers plan to strip you bare by fall. You just want to use my boys to save your skin."

"What's wrong with that?"

"Everything! How can I expect you to set suitable standards of behavior when you don't know how to behave yourself? You don't have any sympathy for them, either. You think they're only one step removed from criminals. You're not interested in the boys, only in your cattle. If breaking those horses is any example of the kind of work you expect them to do, they'll all have broken arms and legs inside of a week. That would be almost as bad as leaving them with the farmers."

Jake was furious. It was bad enough she thought he wouldn't look out for the boys' welfare, but comparing him to the farmers was unwarranted.

"I may be rough, ill-mannered, and smell a little sometimes, but I would never harm any boy, even castoffs like your bunch. I saw too many die in the war. Stay as long as you need to get Buck ready to travel. Try to leave the place in one piece."

"If we did that, Mr. Maxwell, we wouldn't be leaving it as we found it."

If he tried hard enough, he could learn to dislike this woman. "Leave it anyway you like. Just make sure you leave."

He stalked away, mounted up, and rode off without a backward glance. He was back in his camp before his temper cooled off enough for him to realize he'd just thrown away his only chance of getting out of Texas with something to show for it.

Buck had turned his suspicions about the farmers into certain knowledge. They did mean to ruin him. They already had a plan. What did he have? Not a damned thing. But he could have if it weren't for one very obstinate, ignorant, extremely attractive female named Isabelle Davenport.

Damn the woman!

Other than an occasional stroll in the garden on a summer's night, Isabelle had rarely been outdoors at night. Aunt Deirdre said no lady had any business outside after dusk. The fifteen nights Isabelle had spent sleeping in the wagon had done nothing to cause her to doubt her aunt's dictum.

But somehow tonight was different.

It didn't seem dark. In contrast to the inky blackness under the trees by the creek, lustrous moonlight flooded the landscape. Uncounted stars dotted the sky. Isabelle could easily see the horses as they stood quietly in the corral. The cold night air was an invigorating contrast to the heat of the day. There was no wind. The night was still.

The little ranch didn't seem so mean and squalid now, nor did she feel so cut off from civilization. Maybe she was getting used to the isolation. She actually felt a sense of freedom. She wondered if the boys felt the same, knowing they would soon be returning to Austin.

She had watched them closely as they got ready for bed. There was never any friendly talk or horsing around among them, but there was more tension than usual this evening. Some of them had been offered a way out, and she had refused. She wasn't sure they would forgive her for that.

"You got yourself in a mess this time," Mercer said. "They hate you."

They didn't hate her—at least she didn't think so—but they certainly weren't happy with her.

"I can't wait for the agency to find out you turned down two possible placements for these young thugs."

"They're not thugs," Isabelle snapped. "If they were, you'd be back there somewhere along the trail, your body left for the wild animals."

"He'd poison anything that took a bite out of him."

It was Bret. He'd been sniping at everybody, doing his best to start a fight. If it hadn't been for Isabelle's intervention, he'd have succeeded. With his dark complexion and thick, black hair, he showed promise of becoming a handsome man someday. It was ruined by his perpetual look of sour discontent.

"Go to bed, Bret."

"Why? We got nothing to do but wait for that kid to get well so we can go back to Austin. Don't be surprised if some of them ain't here in the morning."

"Where would they go? How would they get there?"

"They got horses now. They can go any place they want. I might not be here either."

"That would be a foolish thing to do."

"Why? Nobody wants to go back to Austin."

"You're not going back to Austin," Isabelle said. She nearly cursed herself as the words left her mouth.

"Why not?"

"I have an idea."

"What?"

"I can't tell you now," she said, hoping he would believe her.

"She hasn't got any idea," Mercer growled. "The whole damned bunch of you is going back to the agency. I'm going to see they put you in chains this time."

"Nobody's going to be in chains," Isabelle said, stifling the urge to hit Mercer with another rock. She was appalled at herself. She'd never had violent tendencies until she met Jake Maxwell.

No, that wasn't fair. His values were just different from hers. He didn't do the things she'd been taught a gentleman should, act the way a gentleman should, or believe the right things. On the surface he was everything she'd been warned against, but his effect on her was just the opposite.

She couldn't get him out of her mind for more than

77

a few minutes at a time, and it wasn't merely his physical appearance. There was something compelling about him, something that made her want to believe in him despite evidence to the contrary. He caused her mind and her emotions to conflict, and that had never happened before. It confused and upset her.

She had to get back to Austin before she started to question everything her aunt had taught her.

Isabelle doubted she would ever get used to nights that were nearly as bright as day. It was difficult to move about in secret when any one of the boys could see her merely by opening his eyes. At least the rustling leaves covered up the sound of rocks crunching beneath her feet.

She moved with as much stealth as was possible for a woman who had rarely been required to make a secret of her movements. She eased the poles in the corral back until she'd made an opening big enough for the horses to get out. If they had no horses, the boys couldn't run away.

She circled the corral, waving her arms, hoping to drive the horses toward the opening. They milled about in the center of the large corral, refusing to go near the opening. She was going to have to get inside and drive them out. Gripping her skirts and holding them tightly against her legs, Isabelle crawled between the rails.

She moved a few steps toward the horses. They quickly moved away. She breathed a sigh of relief. This was easier than she had expected. She moved again, and the horses moved as well. Walking with steady steps, she drove the horses before her.

Without warning, she found herself facing Sawtooth, and he didn't look as if he intended to go another step. He also looked as though he was seriously considering grinding her into the dust for interrupting his night's sleep.

Isabelle looked back and was horrified to see that the fence was about thirty yards away. If Sawtooth decided to attack her, it would be impossible for her to reach safety before he ran her down.

Deciding to act as though she wasn't the least bit frightened rather than give in to the terror that was turning her muscles to quivering, useless ligaments, she advanced a step, waving her arms about her head, hoping to look as tall and intimidating as possible. She figured if Jake's size could intimidate her, maybe she could do the same with Sawtooth.

It didn't work quite the same way. Sawtooth backed up a step, but he pawed the ground angrily, snorting his hatred. She was close enough to see his eyes. They seemed to be all white, with only tiny points of color in the center. It made him look like some kind of half-blind demon.

He whinnied, or neighed, or screamed. Isabelle didn't have any idea what to call the terrible sound that shattered the quiet of the night. She knew only that Sawtooth looked madder than ever. He reared on his hind legs until he reached his full height. He was absolutely enormous. She wondered why she had ever thought she could intimidate such a horse.

Sawtooth screamed again, bared his teeth, dropped his forefeet to the ground, and charged.

Even as Isabelle gave herself up for dead, some sense of self-preservation within her refused to quit. Just as Sawtooth reached out with gaping jaws, she threw herself to one side. She could feel the air whip about her as the infuriated animal's shoulder brushed her hard enough to knock her to the ground. She scrambled to her feet just as Sawtooth slid to a halt. He screamed his fury—she was sure what to call it now—and prepared to run her down.

Isabelle turned and fled toward the corral fence. She didn't look back. She didn't want to see that horse ever again. If he was going to kill her, he would have to do it from behind.

Isabelle thought she heard the sound of running feet, of shouts coming from several directions, but she listened only for the sound of Sawtooth's pounding hooves. Then, much to her surprise, she found herself crawling through the rails and practically falling over Will.

"Golly!" he said, his eyes wide with wonder, "were you trying to ride Sawtooth?"

Isabelle wondered why on earth Will should think she wanted to be astride any horse, especially a demented animal like Sawtooth.

Ignoring her even before she had a chance to answer his question, Will climbed the corral fence and screamed, "Atta boy, Hawk! Beat hell outta the son-of-a-bitch!"

For an instant, Isabelle decided the world had gone mad and taken her along with it. Then the sounds of Sawtooth screaming and gravel flying from under his feet caused her to turn. Night Hawk had a rope on Sawtooth, but he was having to beat the infuriated stallion with the end of it to fight off his furious attacks.

The Attmore boys ran up. Luke threw his rope, but Sawtooth ducked his head and it slid off his shoulder. Almost immediately Chet's rope settled over Sawtooth's head. As the animal felt the rope tighten, he screamed and turned his fury on Chet. Just then Luke's second throw settled over his neck.

He was caught. Screaming his rage, he fought the ropes with every bit of power in his body. Isabelle watched as he jerked the boys about the corral like tumbleweed in the wind. Sean took hold of the rope along with Luke. Gradually the four boys wrestled the stallion to the edge of the corral. One by one, they slipped between the poles. Night Hawk and Chet tied their ropes to posts about twenty feet apart. Sawtooth couldn't move without choking himself.

Night Hawk climbed back into the corral and thumped Sawtooth on the head. The stallion bared his teeth and tried to attack him, but the ropes held. His struggle to break loose only seemed to excite Night Hawk even more.

"That my horse," Night Hawk declared to everyone within hearing, excitement making him look more human than Isabelle could ever remember. "I ride him."

Isabelle couldn't understand. She'd as soon have tried to ride a wild buffalo.

"What were you doing in there?" Chet Attmore asked. "He could have killed you."

"Who took the fence down?" Sean asked.

Isabelle decided she might as well confess all her sins at once, but before she could, her attention was distracted by the sound of galloping hooves. To her surprise and dismay, Jake Maxwell practically burst out of the night, riding straight at her. She flattened herself against the corral fence as Jake's mount came to a gravel-spewing halt.

"What's going on?" he shouted as he leapt from the saddle. "Why was Sawtooth screaming?"

Will Haskins very helpfully replied, "He was trying to kill Miss Davenport."

Isabelle couldn't remember a single time in her life when a truthful answer was less welcome.

Chapter Six

Jake stared at Sawtooth and the ropes that held him fast.

"Hawk got a rope on him before he could chew her to ribbons," Will said.

Jake couldn't believe what he was hearing. Isabelle was either crazy, or she didn't have enough sense to know Sawtooth could kill her. "What in hell were you doing in that corral?"

"I was trying to let the horses loose so the boys couldn't run away."

Jake had waked out of an uneasy sleep to hear a horse screaming. He had been afraid Indians had attacked the ranch, killed the boys, kidnapped Isabelle, and were trying to steal the horses. Now she was telling him she had intentionally entered the corral to drive the horses away so the boys couldn't escape.

She was deranged. No doubt about it.

He grabbed her by the shoulders and turned her

so the moonlight was in her eyes. She didn't look insane. Her eyes were a little wide, but that was probably fright. He released her.

"Maybe you got lost in the dark. Society ladies aren't used to running around at midnight."

He hoped that was it. It would be a shame for a woman this pretty to be half-witted. There weren't enough women in Texas.

"I didn't get lost," Isabelle said, rubbing her arms as though trying to remove any trace of his touch.

"You went into that corral by choice?" Surely not even a city-bred female would do something that stupid.

"The boys were disappointed over losing the chance to work for you. Bret said some of them might not be here in the morning. I was afraid they were more likely to run away if they had horses. I'm told there's nothing out there but open plains and Indians intent upon killing as many settlers as possible."

"That's no reason to turn the horses loose."

"It seemed good enough to me."

He didn't try to reason with her. Anyone who would enter a corral with a stallion like Sawtooth wasn't rational.

"Matt doesn't want to go back to the orphanage," Will announced. "They get mad at him when he won't talk. Sometimes they beat him."

"I'll find someone who'll take you both," Isabelle said, "someone who won't beat Matt when he doesn't talk."

"How are you going to do that?" Jake challenged. He couldn't imagine what it must feel like to know you didn't belong anywhere, that you could be given to one person, taken away and given to another at the whim of someone you didn't even know.

"That doesn't concern you," Isabelle said with a dismissing toss of her head. She headed toward the campfire. When he followed, she stalked off to the cabin.

Matt had made up the fire and was making coffee. The boy seemed to have a second sense for what was needed. As Jake watched him wait to drop the beans into the boiling water, he felt certain that all he needed to be normal again was a friendly, stable environment.

"She about got herself killed."

Jake turned to see Mercer Williams, his feet still chained to the wagon wheel.

"She cares more for those boys than she does for her own skin," Jake said. "If you were any kind of man, you'd be helping her."

Mercer shrugged. "My job's to get them to those farmers or take them back to jail. It don't matter to me either way."

"Jail?" Jake knew these weren't innocent children, but he hadn't figured on jail.

"Maybe half of them."

"Matt Haskins?"

"Probably."

"What about his brother, Will?"

Mercer shrugged. "They'll give him to somebody. He's a bright kid, not surly like his brother. Of course, with me chained up like this, at least half of 'em will run off. Best thing, if you ask me. I can go back to Austin, and Miss Davenport can get married like a normal woman."

Jake didn't know which he disliked more, the way Mercer talked about the boys or the look in his eye when he talked about Isabelle. Just knowing what Mercer was thinking made Jake want to smash his fist into his face. Couldn't the bastard see Isabelle was too good for the likes of him?

You, too, Jake said to himself. She might be an ice princess, but he'd actually been thinking about trying to thaw her out. He was a fool to think she would take up with a hayseed like him, even if he took these orphans off her hands. He wasn't in her class.

With an explosive oath, Jake headed for the cabin. When he stepped inside the room, Buck was sitting up in the bed, talking to Isabelle.

"I want those boys," Jake announced.

Both Isabelle and Buck turned to him.

"Seven of them, anyway" Jake continued. "I don't know what I'll do with the little ones, but Luke Attmore's not bad with horses. I figure he'll be pulling his own weight before long."

"I can ride, too," Buck said.

He got to his feet. He was almost as tall as Jake's six feet and as thin as whipcord, but he was still weak and unsteady.

"The first breeze will blow you out of the saddle. Besides, you can't move without breaking open those scabs on your back. You'll have Miss Davenport saying I'm cruel and unfeeling."

Isabelle blushed. She didn't turn red all over, just her cheeks. She'd be appalled if she knew how pretty she looked.

"I don't think you're cruel and unfeeling," Isabelle said. "I said you have no sympathy for the boys."

"They don't need sympathy. They need self-respect."

"I agree," Isabelle said. "On the way back to Austin, I hope to find someone who will give them jobs so they can earn it."

"How do you mean to do that?"

"I'll stop in each community. I'll talk to the mayor or city council. I'll advertise."

"You might as well advertise slaves for sale."

"Do you have a better suggestion?"

"I just gave it to you."

"I can't accept that."

"God, you're a stubborn woman."

"Maybe, but I'm not unreasonable. I spent most of the night thinking about your offer. I still think you're unsuitable."

"What else is wrong with me?"

She hesitated.

"Go ahead, spit it out. After what you've said already, it can't be much worse."

She finally said, "They need decent food, clean clothes, a suitable place to live, regular habits, the kind of things a woman provides. Since I imagine most of them will marry, they don't need your prejudice against women. Neither do they need to learn your scorn for the rules of society. Texas won't always be an untamed wilderness."

Jake had rarely been so angry at a woman. He'd let her take over his ranch, allowed her to fill his bed with dirty boys, let them amuse themselves pestering his horses. He'd even offered to relieve her of most of her worries and she wouldn't because she thought he was a poor example.

"What do you think I'm going to do, take them to a fancy house?"

"Of course not!" she said, blushing furiously. "But these boys need someone to like them, to understand why they hurt so much, someone who might even learn to love them. You can't do that. You see any sign of emotion as weakness."

"Then why don't you come along to make certain I treat them with all the love and kindness their little souls crave?"

Jake couldn't believe he'd let his anger goad him

into saying anything so stupid! Nothing could be worse than having Isabelle on his back all the way to Santa Fe.

"There's no need to be sarcastic, Mr. Maxwell."

"I'm not being sarcastic." No, but he was being a fool. He hoped she turned him down flat.

"Yes, you are. You know you have no intention of taking Bret and Buck. It's cruel to stand in front of him and talk about leaving him behind."

He had to have these boys. It didn't matter what he had to do or had to promise.

"Bring them all, then, every last one of them," Jake nearly shouted. "I don't have any storybooks to read them at night, but there's a Bible around here somewhere. That'll have to do."

Isabelle stood, a look of regal disapproval on her face. "I refuse to stay here and have you make fun of me. If you will please step aside, I wish to leave."

Jake moved over and made a low bow as Isabelle swept by. "Of course, your majesty. Anything you want, your majesty. Let me lie down so you can walk over my back, your majesty."

Isabelle flashed him a look of indignant fury and swept from the room.

Jake stood up, expecting to feel good about getting the better of that uppity female. But all he felt was disappointment. *He had to have those boys.*

"Did you mean what you said?" Buck asked.

"What?"

"About taking all of us, even me."

Jake started to say he'd do anything for some cowhands, but one look at Buck make him realize that taking these boys on would mean more than simply hiring hands. They'd be putting their lives in his hands, just like those boys during the war.

Jake thought of the boys he'd trained, the boys he'd

worked so hard to keep alive, some of them barely older than Chet and Night Hawk. They had come to him brimming with eagerness to fight for the cause. They had homes to protect, families who loved them, a way of life they cherished. They belonged. They had something to fight for, to go back to.

These boys had nothing.

Buck was covered with cuts and bruises, and his clothes were in rags. Jake doubted he weighed more than a hundred and ten pounds. He wouldn't be any use to anybody for at least a month.

But his heart was in his eyes. Hope was there. So was fear. He saw Jake as his savior.

Jake didn't want to be seen that way, but he couldn't turn his back on Buck. He had none of Night Hawk's confidence, none of Chet's maturity, none of Sean's size. He hadn't cut himself off from the world like Matt. He stood before Jake naked, defenseless, unable to hide what he felt, what he feared.

Yet he was willing to fight back, to keep trying. If he were thrown back into the system, he'd fight until somebody killed him one day.

Jake couldn't let that happen to Buck, or Matt and Will, or any of the others. "I'll take all of you if Miss Davenport will go along to do the cooking."

Buck tumbled out the door, almost falling over his feet in his eagerness to find Isabelle. Jake knew there wasn't a chance in a million she'd accept his offer. But if he was to take nine boys on a cattle drive through Indian territory, somebody had to help him.

When Jake went outside, half of the boys were already gathered around Buck, wanting to know what the noise was about. Isabelle stared at Jake as though she couldn't believe what she was seeing. It made him feel like his pants were unbuttoned.

"I won't let you tease the boys like that," she said

when he reached her. "I've already told you why they can't go."

What had possessed him to make such an offer? Did he hope they were so important to her that she'd go for their sakes even though she disliked him? Or was it that he couldn't abandon these boys to worse fates than the one he could offer, even with all the risks it entailed? He thought of Buck's scars, Matt's eyes, Will's innocence.

"All your objections will be cancelled if you went along to make sure I treated them with the tenderness you require."

"You know I can't go. I have to go back to my job."

"Why?"

"Because I'm a teacher. It's the way I make my living."

"You haven't always been a teacher. There's no law that says you have to be one for the rest of your life."

"Maybe not, but it's the only job I have."

"I thought you were so concerned about these boys you'd do anything you could to help them."

"I am."

"I offered to take them on, every one of them. All I asked you to do was to be the trail cook."

"That's impossible."

"Why?"

"I can't cook."

"Every female can cook."

"I can't. I was never taught."

"If these boys can learn to work cattle, you can learn to cook."

"It's not suitable for an unmarried woman to travel alone with so many men," Isabelle said.

"Think of them as your children."

"And you as my husband?"

"God forbid!" Jake exclaimed.

"That won't be necessary. I'll do it for him."

Will and Pete giggled. Some of the older boys grinned.

"Come on, Miss Davenport," Buck pleaded. "We promise not to let anything happen to you."

"That's no good, kid," Jake said. "She's afraid you might want to become part of the problem."

"Me?" Buck squeaked. Then, as realization hit him, he blushed. Isabelle turned white.

"You're abominable!"

"Blame it on the cows. It's hard to behave properly after swearing at wild-eyed steers all day."

"I don't find that an excuse."

"I didn't think you would."

"Nobody'd bother you, ma'am," Chet Attmore said. "My brother and I'd see to that. You could sleep in the wagon every night."

"Thank you, Chet, but it's not just a matter of propriety or cooking or where I'd sleep. I have a job. I can't just disappear without giving anyone an explanation."

"Mercer can explain for you," Jake said.

Isabelle looked around her at the eager faces of the boys and threw Jake an angry look. "It's impossible. After such a trip, I would be a ruined woman."

Jake saw understanding in the boys' faces, resignation, the fading of hope. But he refused to give up. "Why don't you let the boys decide? Maybe they would like working for me, bad example that I am, better than being in a orphanage."

"Who would you take?" Buck asked.

"You sure you won't change you mind?" Jake asked Isabelle.

She shook her head.

"The Attmores, Hawk, Sean, and Matt. Sorry," Jake said when he saw disappointment turn Buck's eyes dull. "I've got to be out of here in a week. I can't take anybody who can't spend eighteen hours in the saddle right now. You're lucky to be alive."

Buck didn't reply.

"Luke and I would work for you," Chet said.

"Me, too," Night Hawk added.

Sean nodded, but he looked unhappy.

"You wouldn't force them to go back against their will, would you?" Jake asked Isabelle.

He could see her struggle with herself. She didn't trust him with her precious orphans. She didn't think he was good enough for them. He didn't know what she thought he could do that was worse than what they'd been through, but she wasn't going to find anybody who would care about those boys the way she did. It was a shame she couldn't adopt them herself. No one would let her do that, but she probably would if she could.

Jake wondered why she was so devoted to the boys, so critical of him. She probably figured they could be saved. He was so old and set in his ways, it would be impossible to train him to live indoors.

"No, I won't force them to go back to Austin," Isabelle said at last. "Any boy who wants can go with you."

Jake breathed a sigh of relief. He had a chance to save his herd and some of the boys, too. But he couldn't enjoy his success because Isabelle looked so defeated and unhappy.

It hurt that she was so upset at letting them go with him. He'd always been respected, occasionally even admired. It irked him she couldn't see past his lack of manners to the qualities others had seen in him. She'd been taught to admire the kind of man Jake could never be. The sooner he accepted that, the sooner he could get Isabelle out of his system.

"You don't have to look like you're signing their death warrants," he said. "I'll do my best to make sure they arrive in Santa Fe without a scratch on them."

"I'm sure you will, but I'll miss them. I hadn't realized until now how fond of them I've grown."

She wouldn't miss him. She'd probably be relieved to see the last of him.

"As soon as it's light, catch yourself a horse from the corral," he said to the boys. "We need about thirty more. You'll find extra saddles in the bunkhouse."

Sean looked at Pete and hesitated.

"Go on," Pete said. "Miss Davenport says she's got another plan. Besides, I'm too little to catch any cows."

"We coming back here tonight?" Sean asked Jake. "Yes."

"I'll help you catch your horses," he said, then turned away abruptly.

"Matt ain't going," Will said. "He ain't going nowhere without me."

"You're too young," Jake said, feeling more like a yellow dog with every word that came out of his mouth. "They'd probably arrest me for kidnapping."

"Matt ain't going without me," Will repeated.

Jake realized Will was frightened at the thought of leaving his brother.

"Miss Davenport will be here with you. She won't let anything happen to you."

Jake thought Matt's gaze focused for a moment, that he actually looked at him. Then the dullness reappeared.

"I won't wait," Jake said, angry with himself for wanting Matt to come along so much. "It's up to you."

Matt didn't move.

Jake

He didn't move when dawn arrived and they brought saddles out of the bunkhouse. He didn't move when they led the horses out of the corral. Jake looked over his shoulder as they rode out to catch horses, but Matt didn't move.

Damn!

Isabelle passed a miserable morning. The boys acted as though they had lost their last chance. They felt it all the more because they had been left behind.

Mercer had escaped during the night. He would reach Austin before her. She tried to be worried about what he'd say to the agency and the school board. But in the face of her worries about the boys, that didn't seem to matter. She sent Buck to bed. He had to build up his strength. Nobody was going to take him while he was so weak.

She had finally admitted to herself that no one was going to take these boys because they wanted to love them and give them a home. They probably looked at them the way Jake and the farmers did. The farmers saw them as slaves. Jake saw them as outlaws in the making.

Yet they were good-looking boys, smart, capable, able if not always very willing. They deserved a chance.

They had a chance, but you threw it away.

Isabelle forced that thought out of her mind. Jake Maxwell didn't really want her to go with them. He would have been horrified if she had accepted him. She had seen it in his eyes when he made the offer.

She couldn't go anyway. She didn't know a thing about cooking over an open fire. She'd have no privacy. She would become sunburned and covered with freckles. She'd probably be raped and killed by Indians.

93

For a moment she wondered whether she should let any of the boys go. But if anybody could get them safely through Indian territory, it was Jake Maxwell. She could still feel his grip on her arms. It was like iron. He had probably left bruises.

He might be attractive if he would take a bath and shave. She didn't like beards. They made her think of lying, cheating men. Not that she could lay those failings at Jake Maxwell's door. His major sin was a complete disregard for the feelings of other people, particularly hers.

Which was another reason she couldn't consider going with him. Her sensibilities would be in ribbons after as much as a week in his company. She couldn't imagine what she would be like after two or three months.

Or years!

She didn't know why that thought should occur to her. She'd rather be tortured by Indians than spend as much as a year with Jake Maxwell.

Will came up to her. "Are we going back to Austin?" he asked, looking worried.

Isabelle hated to admit failure, but there was no point in continuing with a pretense no one believed. "I'm afraid so, for now."

"Do you think anybody will take both of us?"

Will looked at her with his angelically beautiful face, his blue eyes wide, his blond hair almost in his eyes, and Isabelle felt like the worst failure in the world. How could she not have found a home for this adorable boy?

"I tried to make Matt go with that man, but he won't."

"Why not?" Isabelle asked.

"I don't know." A shadow of fear passed over Will's face.

94

Isabelle suspected he knew but wouldn't tell. She felt shamed. Will was barely more than a child. Yet he had already faced the decision of trying to get Matt to leave for his own good. He had more courage at eight than she did at twenty-three. When she took on the task of finding homes for these boys, she had known it wouldn't be easy.

She was a little afraid of losing her job, but she might as well admit she was more afraid of Jake. Petrified, to be exact! She didn't approve of the man, but she was attracted to him. Her thoughts turned to him far more often than necessary.

She had felt a surge of excitement when he asked her to go with him. She'd been telling herself to hold on, that she'd soon be back in Austin. Then she thought of his arms, of his strength, and she'd almost agreed to go with him.

She didn't know what kind of hold he had over her, but she knew he was dangerous. She was afraid that being around him would undermine her common sense. Despite her anger and disapproval, the attraction seemed to be growing stronger.

That annoyed her, perplexed her. She was a strong, sensible, self-reliant woman. She had survived the loss of her only relative, two years in a orphanage, men with more on their minds than support and comfort, the war and its aftermath. Surely she could survive a momentary attraction to Jake Maxwell.

But it wasn't momentary. Something inside her reacted strongly to his presence. The effect in her belly was unsettling, vague, disturbing.

She should be thinking of the boys, not herself. She searched for another solution but couldn't find one. It was Jake or nobody.

She was relieved when the boys returned with

about thirty horses. She was surprised when Jake headed in her direction as soon as they had been driven into the corral. It gave her an opportunity to act on her decision before her resolution failed.

"We had a pretty good day," he said. "We'll keep the best and turn the rest out."

"You'd better keep all of them. I'm accepting your offer. We're all going to Santa Fe."

Chapter Seven

She looked unhappy about it, as if she were sacrificing herself. A martyr, dammit. That's what she thought she was. He wondered if she thought her honor was in jeopardy. Her icy gaze seemed colder than ever.

"What made you change your mind?"

"I couldn't force the boys to go back to Austin. I don't suppose you're any worse than other people who would take them."

She looked him square in the eye, her gaze steady. He had to give her credit. She wasn't a coward. She insulted him to his face.

"You will take all of them, even Buck?"

He had to be crazy. Worse than desperate. Here he was, trying to round up cattle and trail them through Indian territory, and he was taking half a dozen children along with him—children who probably couldn't ride, definitely couldn't shoot, who knew nothing about cows or surviving on the open plains—and all because of an ice princess even the Texas sun couldn't melt.

But there was a different woman inside. He could sense it. He had to find a way to reach the softness she kept hidden in all that ice. He knew it was there. The boys had reached it.

"Yes, even Buck," he said.

Will and Pete grabbed Isabelle's hands and started jumping up and down with excitement. She broke into a reluctant smile.

Jake liked her smile—it transformed her face—but she didn't smile often. He wondered if she'd ever been happy, if she'd ever really enjoyed life. Somehow he got the feeling she'd always been too concerned about good manners and proper behavior to let the juices of life run down her chin.

He wanted to make her smile the way these boys did. Just once he'd like to see her forget the proper way to do things and do what came naturally. He'd like to see her run through the grass with her skirt hiked up to her knees, wade in a creek, walk in the rain, pick flowers when the grass was heavy with dew.

He was certain she would enjoy it if she'd only let herself. A hot-blooded woman was held captive in all that ice. Had to be. Otherwise she couldn't have such a hold on him.

The boys had a hold on him, too, but he could leave them once they were settled. He wasn't sure he could leave Isabelle. He kept finding too many things he liked about her. He especially liked the way her clothes outlined her body while giving her a prim and proper look. She didn't mope around as if she'd already given up on life. She was determined to scrap and tear her way right through to the end.

He liked that. It reminded him a lot of himself.

Isabelle looked up at him, her arm resting on Will's shoulder. "You've got to promise to keep all the boys. You can't toss a couple out after a few days."

"I said I would, didn't I? I may not be worth much, but I don't go back on my word."

"I never meant to impugn your honor, Mr. Maxwell. I was just worried about the uncertainness of your temper."

She actually looked as though she was worried she had hurt his feelings. He'd have to set her right on that score. He didn't have any feelings she could get at. He hadn't had for years.

"You can *impugn* me all you want, whatever the hell that means, but I keep my word. Now you keep yours. The boys and I are going to see about breaking some of these nags. While we're at it, you can see about rustling up supper."

"You seem to have forgotten I can't cook. I'll need Matt to teach me."

"Take one of the little squirts, Will or that Pete fella."

"You can't call them *little squirts*. Their self-esteem has been badly damaged already."

"But they *are* little squirts."

"All the more reason not to call them that."

Good Lord, she was one of those. "Let's get a few things straight right now. I haven't got time to mull over every word I say before it pops out of my mouth. If they don't like what I call them, they'll just have to get used to it."

"Yes, let's do get a few things straight," Isabelle said, squaring up to him and glaring at him as fiercely as a cow protecting her calf. "You'll be considerate of the boys' feelings, or you'll answer to me."

Jake had to laugh. The situation was too absurd for anything else. "Lady, when I'm chasing a thousand stubborn cows over five hundred miles of dusty plains, I won't have time to pay attention to you. When they're stampeding, we'll be trying to keep from losing the whole damned herd. When the Indians come after our horses, we'll be trying to save our skins."

"Then you'd better start now while you have time," Isabelle came right back. "You can begin by moderating your language. I will not abide cursing."

"You will not abide . . ." Jake couldn't finish his sentence. This slip of a female—this weak, defenseless woman—thought she could stand here and tell him what to do. She was nuts. That's all there was to it. Talking to her wouldn't do any good. "Sure, lady, anything you say."

"My name is Miss Davenport."

"I'm calling you Isabelle."

"I won't answer."

"And you're going to call me Jake."

"Absolutely not."

"Well, at least I won't have to listen to your jabbering." He started to leave but turned back. "You need to get your cooking done before dark. It's too easy for Indians to spot a fire at night."

The look of terror that came into her eyes took the starch out of his anger. It beat all how a woman could go from spitting like a wildcat to looking so helpless that a man couldn't help but want to put his arms around her and tell her everything was going to be all right. There ought to be a law against it.

"That's the second time you've mentioned Indians, Mr. Maxwell. Are there truly hostiles about?"

"Yes, ma'am. I figure killing, scalping, and mutilating is just about as hostile as you can get."

"Is it wise to take your cows to New Mexico?

Wouldn't it be better to go to St. Louis or New Orleans?"

"It would if I could get them there, but there are Indians between here and St. Louis. And there are white men even worse between here and New Orleans. I figure my chances are better in New Mexico."

She didn't look relieved.

"It's the way things are, ma'am. And trailing cows is the only way I know to make a living."

She looked a bit frightened. She also looked thoughtful. Jake figured she was regretting her decision. Then she seemed to come to a resolution.

"I guess I'd better get started on dinner. Do you have any supplies?"

"None to speak of."

"You have plenty of beef."

"We can't sell it if we eat it."

He headed toward the corral. He didn't want to have to tell her he was almost out of provisions and didn't have money to buy more.

"Mr. Maxwell."

He stopped and turned. "Call me Jake."

"What are you going to do about the boys when you reach Santa Fe?" she asked, stubbornly refusing to call him by his first name.

"I don't know."

"If you can't find places for them, you've got to keep them on, give them permanent jobs. That's the bargain."

"I'll think about it. But if I do, you'll have to stay as well."

That got her. She hadn't expected anything like that. But then, neither had he.

Jake sat his horse watching Night Hawk, Matt, Chet, and Sean remind the horses what it was like to have a rider on their backs. They had worked their way through half the herd. By noon tomorrow, they would have finished the other half. Some of these horses probably hadn't been ridden since he left for the war. It would take several days, maybe even a week, to fully break them to saddle. Then he'd have seven or eight mounts for each boy who could ride. That was a strong ramuda, plenty for a cattle drive.

Jake wasn't going to admit it, but he couldn't keep down a simmering excitement. He was going to make it. He would get out of Texas with enough cattle to start over somewhere else. Four hands weren't enough to take a big herd to New Mexico, but he didn't have a big herd.

He hoped at least a few of the other boys could stay in the saddle without needing their feet tied under the horse's belly. Luke Attmore was showing himself a good hand with horses. Jake was thinking about putting him in charge of the ramuda.

He didn't know what to make of Bret Nolan. The boy hung around the corral, watching everything, but kept his distance. He never once asked to ride or offered to help. He was a big boy—Isabelle said he was twelve. Jake had plans for him.

Being seventeen, Buck probably knew how to ride. Right now he was too weak to do more than stagger out of bed and lean against the fence, but he had a brightness in his eyes that Jake liked.

Jake's heart leapt into his throat when Will climbed through the fence and came running toward him. The boy seemed oblivious to the half-wild horses that milled about the corral.

"What the hell are you doing here?" Jake demanded. "Don't you see those horses? You could get hurt. Never enter a corral on foot."

"I want you to teach me to ride."

"Why aren't you helping Isabelle?" ·

"Gathering wood and toting water is Bret's job."

"I'll teach you tomorrow. Now turn around and—" Jake was about to tell him to go back to Isabelle when the herd of horses suddenly wheeled and headed in his direction.

"Hold up your hands!" he ordered sharply as he bent low in the saddle.

Will obligingly thrust both hands over his head. Jake hauled the boy into the saddle in front of him. He barely had time to move his horse out of the way of the charging herd.

"See that," Jake said, practically shaking at the thought of what could have happened. "They could have run right over you."

"I just wanted to learn how to ride like Matt," he said.

The combination of his cherubic beauty and a hurt expression slew Jake's anger. "Okay, but on one condition."

"What?"

"You do everything I say. Not just most things. Everything. And you do it immediately, without asking questions."

That clearly was a proposition that didn't meet with Will's liking. He twisted about in the saddle until he could look up at Jake. "Why?"

Jake couldn't imagine why he should be sitting a horse in the middle of his corral explaining to an eight-year-old kid that he was trying to save his life. He glanced to where Isabelle worked over the fire. It was her fault. Nothing like this had never happened until she showed up.

"Horses and cows are wild animals," Jake explained. "They don't like us putting them in pens, riding on their backs, or driving them away from their homes. They fight, and people get hurt. You'll be okay if you learn the rules and stick to them."

"Okay, but you've got to teach me to ride."

"We'll start tomorrow if I have time." He wouldn't. He'd be lucky if he could finish with the horses and round up a few more beeves.

"Why can't I start now? I'm already on a horse."

Jake couldn't help but laugh. "I don't think a corral full of frightened horses is the best place to start."

"You won't let me fall off."

No, he wouldn't. And as the old saying went, it was best to strike while the iron was hot. It was certain Will's interest couldn't be any hotter than it was right now.

"Okay. The first thing you ought to learn is how to saddle your horse, but I guess that can wait."

"I want to drive him," Will said.

Jake chuckled again. "Take hold of the reins right in front of my hands."

"Can't I hold him by myself?"

"Not yet. When you want him to turn to the left, you give a gentle pull on the reins with your left hand."

Will jerked the reins.

"I said gentle. You pull like that, and he'll throw you in an arroyo."

"What's an arroyo?"

"A deep ditch."

Will pulled the reins more gently, and the horse turned slowly to the left.

"Now the right," Jake said.

Again Will pulled gently, and the horse obligingly turned to the right. "How do you make him go?"

"You squeeze your legs and cluck to him."

Will made an odd noise in his throat and wriggled about in the saddle. "He's not going."

The horse moved instantly at Jake's signal.

"Why didn't he do that for me?"

"He will. Getting a horse started is easy," Jake said as he maneuvered his way across the corral. "It's getting him to do what you want that's hard."

"I want that horse," Will said, pointing to a white gelding that pounded past. He was a half-brother to Sawtooth.

"Not yet. We'll start with something a little smaller."

They reached the fence just in time to see Pete come running up. He looked surprised to see Will riding double with Jake. The green-eyed monster of jealousy attacked so swiftly that Jake almost laughed.

"Miss Davenport says it's time to eat," Pete announced. "Why are you giving Will a ride?"

"He's teaching me to ride," Will announced.

"I already know how to ride," Pete said. "But not very good. Will you teach me, too?"

"Sure."

Why not? He had nothing to do but teach pint-sized squirts how to ride horses too big for them and chase cows that had calves bigger than they were. Jake motioned the other boys over to the corral fence. While he waited, Will slid to the ground and took off like a shot.

"I'm going to tell Miss Davenport," he called out.

"Me, too," Pete said, keeping stride with him

Jake shook his head, wondering what he'd gotten himself into.

"Time to eat," he told the boys when they rode up.

"Leave the saddles on. It'll help remind them what it's like to be ridden. When we get finished, we'll ride over and see how the herd is doing."

Tomorrow afternoon he meant to take these four boys chasing cows. He wanted to see how well they rode. After he knew that, he'd attack the problem of what to do with the rest of them.

Three of the boys dismounted quickly. For a moment, Matt's gaze narrowed and bore in on Jake. It was so unexpected, he didn't have time to catch the emotion that flashed there briefly. He would have sworn it was anger, even hatred, but that didn't make sense. There was no reason for Matt to be angry at Jake. Certainly none to hate him.

It was gone so quickly, Jake wasn't sure he'd seen anything at all. Still, it shook him. Matt had been one of the reasons he'd decided to take on these boys. He'd never forget the sight of him standing there, just waiting for Sawtooth to run him down. Jake was certain he could help him.

But not if Matt hated him.

Matt dismounted, climbed through the corral bars, and headed toward the camp without a backward glance. Bemused, Jake watched him go. Then he shook off the odd feeling, dismounted, and headed toward the campfire.

Jake was looking forward to supper. After a day spent in the saddle, he was hungry. He especially wanted some coffee to wash away the thick layer of dust that coated the back of his throat.

He could cook—he had learned during the war—but only enough to keep himself alive. He'd hardly had a decent woman-cooked meal since his mother ran off.

The smell of burnt meat was the first hint that all

was not going to be as he had hoped. The reluctance of the boys to take the plates handed to them was a second. The expression on Isabelle's face when he walked up was the third.

Jake looked at the contents of the plate she handed him and recoiled. The bacon was covered with a coat of charcoal. At least he assumed it was bacon. It was impossible to tell. The beans looked like little brown islands in a muddy stream. He attempted to stab one with his fork. It was as hard as a marble and just as skittish. It jumped out of his plate and hit the ground several feet away.

"Did you cook these?" he asked, furious in his disappointment.

"Of course," Isabelle answered. "They're hot, aren't they?"

He could tell she was nervous. She didn't even look at the boys.

"They're hard as rocks."

"I cooked them for nearly half an hour."

"That's not long enough. How long did you soak them?"

"Why should I soak them? They weren't dirty."

Oh, God, she really didn't know how to cook! "They're dried beans. They need to soak all day!"

"You're shouting." She said it in a normal voice, as though she were correcting a child for something it had done wrong.

"Of course I'm shouting. If I served you charcoal and wet beans, you'd shout too."

"That's bacon."

"It may have been bacon, but it's charcoal now!"

"You're shouting again."

"If you promise to turn this into something that looks even a little bit like bacon, I promise not to shout."

"It's not so bad if you scrape the crust off," Chet said.

"And put some salt on it," his brother added.

"It's probably raw inside."

"It's done," Chet said. "I checked."

Jake stared at the Attmore brothers. He didn't understand why someone hadn't adopted them years ago. They were blond, athletic, looked enough alike to be twins, and could lie with straight faces. This meal wasn't fit for a dog, and they knew it.

"Give me some coffee," Jake said. "Maybe I can wash it down."

He knew immediately the coffee was too weak. A taste confirmed his suspicions.

"You threw out the old grounds."

"Of course."

"I told you to keep them."

"I refuse to drink coffee made with old grounds." She sounded affronted.

"Then you're going to have to make two pots."

"That's ridiculous."

"I agree. You ought to learn to drink decent coffee."

"I made decent coffee."

"If you're going to make the kind we drink here in Texas, first you throw out a third of the old coffee grounds. Never more than that. Then add a handful of new beans to the pot and boil it. When it's black, it's ready to drink."

"That sounds like a recipe for mud."

"Maybe, but it makes good coffee, too. Now what else have you got?" There had to be something else. They'd starve if there wasn't.

"Biscuits and a pie," Isabelle said.

If this was what she did with beans and bacon, he

didn't want to think about her biscuits or pie. He dumped the beans back in the pot. "Leave the pot on the fire. With a little luck, we can have them for breakfast. Did you make gravy?"

"I don't know how."

Muttering curses he made no attempt to hide, Jake scraped as much of the charred crust as he could off his meat. Well, it did look a little bit like bacon. He tasted a piece. Hell, it was hard as leather. "Dammit, woman, this is awful."

"I warned you I couldn't cook."

"Every woman says she can't cook. That way, when she lays out a spread, you'll think she's done something wonderful."

"I do not lie."

Jake looked at his food, and all hopes of a woman-cooked meal vanished. "So it seems. Don't you know how to cook anything?"

"Biscuits," Isabelle answered.

Her answer did nothing to lift his spirits. Biscuits were the most difficult thing of all to cook on the range. During the war, any man who could cook really good biscuits didn't have to do anything else. His friends would be glad to perform all his duties so long as they got to eat his biscuits.

"Give me a couple," Jake said. "Maybe I can manage to choke down this bacon if I wrap a biscuit around it."

"You don't have to eat it if you don't want to."

"Yes, I do. Breaking horses is hard work. It's even worse rounding up cattle. We have to eat this stuff or starve."

"If you'd just leave Matt here until I—"

"I can't spare him. Are those biscuits ready yet?"

"I think so." Isabelle took the top off a dutch oven

and an absolutely heavenly aroma assailed Jake's nostrils. Nestled in the bottom of the oven were a couple of dozen of the most beautiful biscuits he'd ever seen.

Chapter Eight

Isabelle handed Jake two biscuits. He didn't wait for them to cool. He didn't waste them on the charred bacon. He put one straight into his mouth. It was too hot—it burned his tongue—but his teeth bit through the flaky brown crust into a soft white interior. A wonderful aroma filled his nostrils as he chewed and swallowed. He didn't stop until he'd eaten both biscuits. The bacon remained untouched on his plate.

"How?" It was the only word he said.

"My aunt died when I was sixteen," she explained. "I have no relatives, so I was sent to an orphanage. They gave each of us a job. They taught me to make biscuits and bake apple pies."

"But if you could make bread like this—"

"I ought to be able to cook bacon as well," she finished for him.

He nodded.

"They never let me cook anything else. When I left

the orphanage, I worked in places that provided my meals."

Will dropped down beside Jake. He had placed his bacon inside a biscuit. Even with his sharp teeth, he had trouble tearing the over-cooked meat. "Got any jam?" he asked through his mouthful of food.

"There might be some in the house," Jake said.

"I'll see," Pete volunteered. He was up and running toward the cabin before anyone else could move.

It didn't appear anybody else wanted to move. They were all scattered out, keeping their distance. Jake didn't know how he was going to weld these boys into a crew willing to work together, to risk their lives for each other. They were like strangers caught by chance in the same place, all looking for an opportunity to get away.

To what? Where? Nothing and nowhere if he didn't help them.

"I found it!" Pete squealed as he skidded to a halt in front of Jake. "Want some?"

"No."

"I do." Will held up his plate.

Pete offered the jam to Sean, then the other boys.

"Make sure you save some for Will," Isabelle said.

"I went and got it," Pete protested.

"But it was Will's idea. If there's none left, you'll each have to give him some from your plate."

Jake figured he must be dense to have taken this long to realize Pete was intentionally keeping Will until last, hoping there wouldn't be any left.

When everyone who wanted jam had taken some, Pete took a generous portion for himself. Then he set the jar down in front of Will. "Here," he said. He took his plate and plopped down on the other side of Jake. The looks exchanged between him and Will weren't friendly.

Isabelle threw Jake a questioning glance. He could only shrug in answer.

"There are more biscuits," Isabelle said. She opened a second dutch oven. Will was on his feet in seconds.

"Give me some for Jake, too," he said.

"He didn't ask you to get his biscuits," Pete said.

"This is the last pan," Isabelle said before Will could answer. "Two is all you get."

Will plopped down, handed Jake his biscuits, then spooned the last of the jam onto his plate.

"You took it all," Pete protested.

"There wasn't enough," Will said.

"Before you take the last of anything," Isabelle said, "you should ask if anyone else wants more."

"There wouldn't have been any left for me."

"Share your jam with Pete," Isabelle said.

Will didn't like that decision. He looked up at Jake, apparently hopeful that he would rescind Isabelle's command.

"I guess it's fair," Jake said.

Actually, he didn't see why Will couldn't have it all. He'd been shrewd enough to get it while there was still some left. This idea of sharing gave Jake an uneasy feeling. It was too much like people who hadn't done a lick of work getting a share of what their more energetic neighbors had managed to capture for themselves. That sounded too much liked the damned farmers coming in and taking his land and wanting his cows after his family had fought off the Indians for twenty years.

"Hold out your plate," Isabelle told Will.

Pete made the mistake of trying to take at least two thirds of the jam. With a howl of rage, Will threw himself at Pete. Tin plates and forks went flying as

113

the two boys tried to beat the daylights out of each other right in Jake's lap.

Jake yanked them apart. "What the hell do you damned fools think you're doing?" he thundered. The fact that he had jelly and bread crumbs all over him did nothing to improve his temper or his language.

"He tried to take my jelly."

"You took it all."

"I asked for it."

"I got it."

Jake sat the two boys down with jarring force. "The first one who makes a move toward the other goes straight into the creek."

The boys glared at each other, but they didn't feel brave enough to test Jake's threat.

"I'm not sure I agree with this sharing business," Jake said. "It seems to me, since Will got the jelly first, he ought to be allowed to keep it."

He glanced at Isabelle out of the corner of his eye. He could tell she didn't agree, but he'd figured on that. "But I do know it wasn't right for you to take more than half. Don't try to get out of it," he said when Pete started to speak. "You did it right in front of me.

"Now listen up, all of you," he said to the boys, who were watching him closely. "I expect there's going to be fights from time to time. That's natural with this many boys in one place. But there isn't going to be any stealing. I'm not sure what I'm going to do about it, but I can promise you'll never do it again. You keep your hands off what doesn't belong to you. You need something you don't have, you come to me or Isabelle, find it in the hills, or do without. Anybody got any questions?"

Nobody did.

"You two boys clean up your mess and apologize to Isabelle for throwing her food away."

"Will ought to do it," Pete protested. "He knocked my plate away."

"No arguing. And if you ever want to sit astride one of my horses, you won't do anything like this again."

The boys apologized, picked up their plates, and wiped them clean.

"Now, ma'am, you said something about dessert."

"Apple pie," Isabelle said.

"Why don't you offer it around? Pete here doesn't want any. He's feeling unaccountably full about now."

Isabelle picked up a knife and cut the pie into ten narrow slices. He was going to have to tell her to bake two pies next time. It was an insult to offer a man an itty-bitty piece like that.

Jake knew Isabelle was mad when she served the pie without looking at him, but right then he was more concerned about Matt. The boy hadn't stirred when the fight started. Yet he'd been upset this afternoon when Jake pulled Will into the saddle with him. He'd also looked angry when Will sat down next to Jake. It was exactly backward to what Jake would have expected. He didn't understand what was going on in that boy's mind, but he was sure as hell messed up.

Isabelle didn't want any pie. She was too angry at Jake to eat. The man had no feelings. These were little boys—they hardly came up to his waist—yet he treated them as harshly as adults. Didn't he have any notion of how deeply he could hurt these children?

How could he grow up without learning to share? And how dare he liken it to stealing? Pete shouldn't have tried to take too much, but he was just jealous over Jake.

She didn't understand that. Will always stayed with his brother. Pete was usually inseparable from Sean. Yet now both boys were fighting over Jake's attention.

That wouldn't last long, not after the way he treated them tonight. She intended to have a talk with Mr. Maxwell as soon as she could get him by himself.

She waited until he headed toward the corral to saddle his horse and followed. "Mr. Maxwell."

He didn't answer or turn around.

"Mr. Maxwell, I want to speak to you."

Still no response. She followed him to his horse and planted herself directly in front of him. "Didn't you hear me calling you?"

"Oh," he said, feigning innocence, "I thought you were calling someone named Mr. Maxwell. My name's Jake."

"You know I don't approve of informal manners."

"You don't always get to make the rules. This is my ranch."

"I'm well aware of that, but I don't wish to set a bad example for the boys."

"I imagine they know a whole lot more about bad examples than you do."

"That's just the point. They know all about the wrong things and almost nothing about the right ones."

"Well, one of the right things is a man gets to decide what he's called. Call me Jake, or I won't answer. There it is. You can take it or leave it."

Isabelle longed to turn on her heel and stalk away, but she had a feeling such a gesture would be wasted on Jake. "All right, I'll call you Jake when we're alone, but I'll continue to address you as Mr. Maxwell in front of the boys."

"Does that mean we're going to be alone a lot?"

She knew Jake was trying to aggravate her, but she had the oddest feeling that being around him wouldn't be as bad as she had first imagined. Her vanishing common sense again. He was practically the opposite of everything she admired in a man. "I wanted to be alone so I could speak to you about your treatment of Will and Pete."

"And I thought it was for my humble self."

"Mr. Maxwell, you are—"

"What's my name?"

"Jake." She didn't know why the name was so hard to say. "I don't understand how you can go from teasing to being cruel, then right back to teasing again. It's against human nature."

"When was I cruel?"

He looked like he honestly had no idea what she was talking about.

"When you wouldn't let Pete have dessert. When you called the boys damned fools."

"What did you want me to do, praise them for dumping jelly all over me?"

Isabelle saw Jake's desire to tease her disappear. In its place was the familiar harsh expression that said women like her had no business on a ranch. "No, but it was wrong of you to deny Pete pie when all the other boys had some."

"All the other boys didn't try to steal Will's jam."

"He wasn't stealing."

"What do you call taking something that doesn't belong to you?"

"He was only trying to take more than his fair share."

"Which means he was trying to take what didn't belong to him. That's the usual definition of stealing."

Leigh Greenwood

"Mr. Maxwell—Jake—this is jam, not cows or money."

"Oh, so it's all right to take things that don't belong to you as long as they aren't worth much. He could steal my boots, but he shouldn't take my horse."

"Don't be absurd. You need your boots."

"Okay, he could take my underwear as long as he didn't take my hat."

Isabelle felt herself blush. "I should hope you would consider your underwear necessary."

"Not in this hot weather. Just this morning I was of two minds about whether to keep it on."

Isabelle decided this conversation was leaning in directions that made her decidedly uncomfortable. "We're talking about a principle here."

"Exactly. When you take anything that doesn't belong to you, no matter how small, it's stealing."

"I can see there's no reasoning with you."

"Ma'am, it has nothing to do with reason. I've seen men shot for the way they walk or the way they look at you. That makes a spoonful of jam on somebody else's plate seem mighty important."

"You were too severe," Isabelle said, deciding it was useless to try to reason with him. "Pete's only a boy."

"What would you have preferred I do?"

"Talk to him, explain that taking more than his share causes bad feelings."

"Ma'am, where did you grow up?"

Isabelle was baffled by the question. "Savannah."

"Did you have to sleep on the ground, take care of your business in the bushes, and worry some Indian might lift your scalp during the night?"

"Of course not, but—"

"Then a smart woman like you ought to have figured out we play by different rules out here."

118

She knew he didn't think she was smart at all. "The rules of politeness and common decency should be the same everywhere."

"They probably will be when people have time to give it some thought. But right now I'm more concerned about keeping those boys' heads on their shoulders than turning them into fancy gentlemen. You don't touch a man's horse, saddle, bedroll, gun, food, or anything that belongs to him. If you do, he'll think you're trying to steal it, and he'll kill you. There are a lot of other lessons they're going to have to learn to survive. You're not going to like them any better."

"I'm only trying to give them some manners, to fill in some of the gaps they missed by not having homes of their own."

"I guess that's okay, but I don't know anything about raising boys. All I know is cows, horses, and these hills. Those boys are going to need everything I can teach them to get the herd to New Mexico. And you'd better hope they learn fast, because they'll be all that stands between you and some situations that would turn your stomach just to hear me talk about."

Isabelle knew he meant what he said. She'd forced herself and the boys on him. He'd accepted the situation because he needed them, but that was as far as he meant to go.

"If you'll explain to me the reasons for what you do, I'll try to understand," Isabelle said. "I don't promise I'll approve, or that I won't oppose you on occasion, but I will try to understand."

"I guess that's all a man can ask." Jake swung into the saddle. "Now you'd better get to bed. Dawn comes awfully early."

"Are you coming back tonight?" She was appalled

to realize that she sounded as if she wanted him to come back.

"No, but I'll be back for breakfast. And remember, don't put more than a small handful of fresh coffee beans in the pot."

As Isabelle watched him ride away, she wondered about the twist of fate that had put the boys in this man's hands. Would it have been better if they had gone back to Austin? Maybe she could have found someone who understood more about raising boys.

Maybe, but no one who would have taken all the boys. She dreaded to think what would have happened to Buck if he had been sent back. For better or for worse, they had cast their lot with Jake Maxwell.

She wondered about herself. Could she handle the tension between her and Jake? It was useless to pretend she wasn't attracted to him. She would be around him constantly, see him half dressed, his body wet with perspiration, his clothes clinging to him, revealing every contour of his body. She couldn't calm her nerves or quiet her desires by a promise that she'd soon leave.

She felt the muscles in her abdomen tighten. She was in more danger than the boys.

Isabelle thought she heard someone calling her name. But when she opened her eyes, it was still dark. She closed them and started to go back to sleep.

"Isabelle."

It was unmistakable. Someone was calling her. Gathering the blanket around her to keep out the night chill, she sat up. She gasped and clutched the blanket more tightly around her when she saw Jake grinning at her over the side of the wagon.

"It's time to start breakfast," he said.

Isabelle's wits weren't working very well, but she knew it was too dark to cook. "What time is it?"

"Four o'clock."

He had to be crazy. Not even young boys wanted to eat at such a god-awful hour. She pulled the blanket up over her shoulders and lay back down. "Wake me at seven."

"The cook has to get up at four o'clock. The hands have to be fed and in the saddle by daybreak."

He had to be joking, but he wasn't smiling.

"We only get so many daylight hours. I can't afford to waste any of them."

He was serious. He really expected her to wrestle with pots of hot grease when she could barely see her hand in front of her face.

"You'd better hurry up. Once the boys get up, they'll expect to eat."

"No, they won't. They all help."

"That's changed. From now on, they sleep until you call them to eat."

Isabelle threw back the blanket. She was fully dressed, but the morning chill caused her teeth to chatter. "What are you going to do?" she asked.

"Go back to bed." His grin was practically evil.

"You do and you'll be the one frying in hot grease," she said as she got to her feet.

"Where's your sense of humor?" he chided.

"I see nothing humorous about cooking bacon at four o'clock. It would serve you right if I did make your coffee with three-day-old grounds."

"You didn't throw them out, did you?"

She was tempted to tell him she'd thrown them in the fire. "No, I kept the disgusting things."

He breathed a sigh of relief. He offered his hand as she climbed down from the wagon. She didn't take it. Even half awake, she didn't trust herself to touch him.

"It's your coffee," she said turning away and heading toward the site of last night's fire. "You deserve to have it the way you like it—even if it is undrinkable."

He laughed. "You always have to get in the last word, don't you?"

His remark startled her. She had spent her life never being expected or allowed to give an opinion. "Is that a bad habit?"

He grinned. "Only when I want the last word."

Even at four A.M. his smile had the power to ignite a flame within her. She wondered why he didn't smile more often. It made it impossible to stay mad at him. "You get the last word when it's about horses and cows. I get it when it's about food and the boys."

She didn't plan to stand back and let him do anything he wanted. These boys were her responsibility. She intended to keep an eye on everything he did.

"We'll see," he said.

What he meant was *in a pig's eye!*

There was no wood. They'd burned it all before they went to bed.

Jake walked over to the cabin, picked up the ax. "Come on," he said when he returned. "I'll chop, you gather."

"Where?"

"Along the creek."

Isabelle didn't like the idea of entering the dense shadow beneath those trees, but she was determined she wasn't going to let Jake see her anxiety. Her skirt caught on a small bush. By the time she'd freed it, Jake had disappeared into the shadows. She was alone. She felt a moment of real fear. She knew nothing about the wilderness. She had no business being out here!

She heard the sound of an ax. Jake. She felt her body relax.

"Come on. There's plenty of wood here."

"Where are you? I can't see anything."

He emerged from the inky blackness under the trees. "Here."

Isabelle found herself hurrying toward him.

"Take my hand. There's a log in the way."

Isabelle was tempted to try it alone, but she couldn't see in the dark. Resigning herself, she reached out. His hand was big and rough. His skin felt like leather, his fingers strong. He was a natural part of this land, this untamed country that made her so uneasy.

The canopy of trees was not unbroken. Moonlight shone through. As her eyes adjusted, she was surprised how clearly she could see Jake, clearly enough to be dazed at the power of his body as he swung the ax. Wood chips flew through the air. She hurried about collecting them in her skirt. Being busy helped her forget she was alone with him. It seemed no time at all until he had a stack of wood.

"Load me up."

"What?"

"Load the wood in my arms."

Isabelle started into motion. She didn't know what had caused her to freeze. Maybe it was the way he looked at her, with a kind of easy directness she found pleasing. Maybe it was his open shirt and the sight of a sizeable portion of his broad, muscled chest. Maybe it was the unexpected intimacy of the moment. Maybe it was her own recognition of the loneliness of her life.

Whatever it was, everything about Jake seemed

different. Yet he seemed the same. So much so that she couldn't explain why she was acting as skittish as a debutante at her first ball.

She glanced up at him as they walked from under the trees. It shocked her to discover it wasn't his looks she was reacting to. It was his physical presence.

His body.

The realization caused waves of scorching heat to course through her. She was certain her face turned crimson. She had been brought up in the tradition of genteel Savannah. A woman gave careful attention to a man's character, his beliefs, even his family background, but a true lady would never allow herself be influenced by the shape of a man's body.

Isabelle tried to convince herself that she had mistaken her feelings, that it was merely the result of being only half awake. But when Jake's swift stride carried him a few steps beyond her, she found herself staring at his broad shoulders, his firm and rounded backside, his powerful thighs, which strained against the seams of his pants.

No, she wasn't mistaken. The sight of Jake's body had touched a part of her she hadn't known existed. What kind of woman would walk behind a man, staring brazenly at his backside, knowing all the while that it caused strange and uncontrollable feelings to rocket though her body like sightless birds, bouncing off one set of nerves after another until she felt positively frazzled?

She was relieved to reach the camp, to feel the normality of the boys scattered around in their sleep. Matt was up. He had obviously decided to teach her how to cook the bacon. She was embarrassed but relieved.

"Do you know how to start a fire?" Jake asked. Before she could regain enough presence of mind to tell him she'd started more fires than she could count, he said, "I'll show you." He took the wood chips from her. "Come close and watch."

She didn't want to. She needed to be as far away from him as possible, to distract herself from the feelings that were turning her thoughts into nonsense. Maybe if she concentrated very hard on what he was doing, she could forget he was so near.

Jake dug around in the ashes until he found a still-hot ember. He peeled some bark, shredded it, dropped it on the ember. He blew on it until it began to glow red. He blew harder and shredded more bark. Smoke began to rise.

"Now you try," he said.

She was forced to kneel next him to, shoulder to shoulder. She could barely take enough air into her lungs to breathe. She had none left to blow on the smoldering coal.

"You can do better than that."

She had to lean on him to keep from falling forward. She couldn't breathe at all.

"Like this."

He blew long and steady until a tiny flame appeared. Feeding it with chips, Jake soon had a fire going.

"It's easy as long as the wood's dry. Think you can do it next time?"

"Yes." As long as he wasn't so close she couldn't breathe. As long as he didn't look at her with such hunger in his eyes. She had seen that look before, and she knew what it meant. Jake Maxwell wanted her, and he wanted her badly.

Instantly Isabelle was poised for flight.

Chapter Nine

The first time a man looked at her like that, she'd had to fight for her honor. He had stalked her; his eyes had followed her everywhere. She had lived in fear.

She had been governess in a wealthy New Orleans household. Aunt Deirdre's severe training served her well, and for a time Isabelle thought she had discovered the perfect job. Then Henri DuPlange returned from Paris, and everything changed.

He considered servants fair game, and she was a servant. He interpreted all her refusals as coy attempts to wheedle larger and more expensive presents from him. He couldn't believe anyone in her position would find his advances distasteful.

One night he got drunk, came to her room, and attempted to force himself on her. An hour later, Isabelle was in a carriage on her way back to town. She left in her wake a husband with several bleeding scratches on his face, a wife having screaming hysterics, children confused about what had caused such a commotion in the middle of the night, and servants snickering in their quarters.

Henri had had the same look in his eyes as Jake. She would never forget it. She watched Jake warily, but he busied himself helping the boys choose their mounts for the day. While Luke watered the horses at the creek, Jake helped them gather and sort their gear. All the while he answered a steady stream of questions from Will and Pete.

Gradually Isabelle's panic eased. Jake wanted her, but he wouldn't force himself on her.

Breakfast was better. The coffee was still too weak, the bacon and beans were too hard, but the biscuits were perfect. Pete rummaged through Jake's kitchen until he found another jar of jam. Rather than risk a second fight, Isabelle served it herself. She made the mistake of glancing at Jake when she measured Will's portion. His eyes were filled with laughter.

She would probably have made some cutting remark if she wasn't still feeling shaken by her earlier response to him. She felt herself smile back at him. She turned away in confusion.

"The agency shouldn't have tried to farm these boys out," Jake said. "They should have built a house—one shaped like a shoe if I remember correctly—and turned them all over to you."

Isabelle would have liked to believe Jake was complimenting her. She would have liked to believe he thought she could do at least one thing right. But comparing her to a character in a nursery rhyme made that unlikely.

"They wouldn't allow it. They said it wasn't suitable."

She had the pleasure of seeing surprise knock the

127

smile right off his face. He actually looked as though his sense of propriety had been outraged. She hadn't known he had one.

"You're damned right. You couldn't be locked up with boys like"—he glanced involuntarily at Chet Attmore—"of this age."

She wondered if he thought she would succumb to Chet's attractiveness. Standing six feet tall and blessed with the body of a man, the boy was amazingly mature for fourteen. But then, so was thirteen-year-old Matt, blond, blue-eyed and even better looking, though not as sensual. But both were boys. She felt none of the desire that flamed so hot whenever she was near Jake.

"I should have sent you back to Austin," Jake said.

"I wouldn't have gone."

"I never thought you would." Jake got to his feet. "I'm taking the crew to the cow camp to teach them how to round up longhorns that don't want to be rounded up."

"Take me," Will piped up.

"Me, too." Pete didn't mean to be left behind.

"Not today," Jake said. "I'll have my hands full with this bunch. I don't think Isabelle would like it if I brought them back with broken legs and arms."

"I expect you to look after them just as carefully as you would your own son."

"My son wouldn't need looking after."

She had touched his pride. He was a man who didn't like to admit he needed help, especially from a woman and a bunch of boys.

"I can ride," Buck said.

"No," Isabelle protested.

"I'll take it easy."

Jake's gaze raked every part of Buck's body. Isabelle saw the boy attempt to stand up taller in the face of Jake's careful scrutiny. She knew it must wound his pride to be the oldest and still be left behind.

"You need another day to rest and let your back heal," Jake said. "You're still too weak."

Buck wasn't happy with the decision, but he accepted it. The same couldn't be said of Will. He followed Jake to the corral, pestering him to let them go.

"If you're good, I'll let you ride one of the horses tonight."

That didn't satisfy him, but his pleas did grow less loud. Isabelle made a decision. The boys were in the saddle when she reached the corral.

"I want to go with you," she announced.

Jake looked at her as if she were crazy.

"You can't go rounding up cows," Sean said, voicing the opinion the others obviously shared.

"I don't intend to round up cows," Isabelle said. "I want to see the nature of the work you expect these boys to do."

"We don't have time for sightseers," Jake snapped. "This is a working camp, no place for a woman on foot."

"Then teach me to ride."

"I don't have time. Besides, it's impossible in those skirts!"

Isabelle hadn't considered her clothing. "I can drive the wagon."

"There're a couple of arroyos you can't get the wagon through between here and the camp."

"I'll go around."

"You'd get lost."

"You could show me."

"It would take too long."

"One of the boys could show me."

"They don't know the way. Besides, you can't leave the squirts by themselves."

"You don't mean to take me."

"Not today."

"We'll have to talk about this," Isabelle said.

"Sure."

Jake rode off, anxious, she thought, to get away before she could ask him anything else. He thought he'd won. But she hadn't held her own in Savannah society, survived the dehumanizing effects of an orphanage, or escaped Henri DuPlange with her virginity intact to be defeated by a cow farmer more comfortable living in the brush than in his own cabin.

Jake Maxwell had a lot to learn about women from Savannah.

"He's not going to like it," Will said as he trotted alongside Isabelle.

"He's going to be hopping mad," Pete said, apparently looking forward to the fireworks.

"I expect so," Isabelle said, "but Mr. Maxwell is too mature to show such a want of control."

She spoke too soon.

"What the hell are you doing here?" Jake thundered. "And what did you mean by bringing the squirts with you?"

He didn't dismount when he saw her. He rode straight toward them at a gallop. Will and Pete jumped out of the way. Isabelle refused to move even when she felt the hot breath of his mount on her cheek.

"I came to see what you do at this camp," Isabelle said as calmly as she could while being practically nose to nose with his horse. "Since it proved impossible to use a horse or the wagon to get here, I decided to walk."

"Damnation, woman, it's nearly three miles. You're liable to have a heat stroke."

It had been a long walk. Her feet were killing her, and she had long ago given up trying to pretend her dress wasn't stained with perspiration.

"Women aren't nearly so fragile as you seem to believe, Mr. Maxwell, not even in Savannah." She looked around, hoping to find some shade and a place to sit down. She saw nothing to fit either description. Dear Lord, how did Jake survive out here? What did he do when it rained? Or snowed?

"You'll have to go back."

"If you think that after spending an hour getting here, I'm going to turn around and head right back, *you're* the one who's about to have a heat stroke."

"When is he going to explode?" Will asked in a whisper. He had kept close to Isabelle, though Pete had already taken off in the direction of noise coming from somewhere beyond a growth of pines.

"What did he say?" Jake demanded.

"Pete predicted you would blow your top when you saw me. Will's eagerly awaiting the fireworks. I hope you aren't going to disappoint him."

Isabelle was hot, tired, and irritated, but she had to smile at Jake's reaction. He did seem to swell up, probably full of rude and uncomplimentary things he wanted to say to her. She didn't know whether it was pride or a masculine reluctance to be grossly rude to a female, but he managed to bridle his temper. He looked as if he had indigestion. Probably a result of this perpetual Western diet of beans and bacon.

"Since you're here, you might as well see what

we're doing," he said as he started his horse forward. "The camp's not far."

Isabelle hadn't expected him to offer her a ride, but she hadn't expected him to ride while she walked.

"While I *walk*, you can explain the terrain to me," she said, being careful to keep the outrage from of her voice. "Identify some of these plants. I'm unfamiliar with a landscape such as this."

Jake didn't take the hint.

"What's all that noise?" Will asked.

"We're branding. Cows don't generally like it."

Will headed off at a run.

"Stay behind the fence," Jake called after him. He started his horse after Will, then turned in the saddle. "Aren't you coming?"

Isabelle could hardly believe her ears. He was going to ride off and leave her to walk. That was going too far, even for a man who preferred sleeping on the ground. "You'll have to give me a little time. I doubt I can walk as fast as your horse."

There, if that didn't make him mind his manners, nothing would.

"Then you'd better trot."

Isabelle's hands clenched at her sides. She practically bit her tongue to keep from uttering the blistering response that sprang to mind. She would not do anything so undignified as trot, not even if he went off and left her to find her way alone.

She looked up. He was smiling. He had done it just to irritate her. She refused to be baited. She had survived classrooms filled with rude boys. She could certainly endure the taunts of one rude rancher.

"Don't let me keep you from your work," she said.

"I wouldn't think of abandoning you."

Without saying anything more, she headed off in the direction taken by Will and Pete. What she saw

132

when she reached the corral shocked her out of her haughty silence. "My God, they'll be killed."

Matt had a rope around the horns of what seemed to Isabelle to be a huge bull. Chet had a rope around its hind legs. Still the bull wouldn't go down. Sean moved in, took it by the horns, and twisted its neck until it fell with a resounding thud. A small scream escaped Isabelle, and she started forward, certain the bull had fallen on Sean. She started breathing again when she saw him get up, apparently unharmed.

Luke handed him an iron he had taken straight from the fire. Sean pressed it against the bull's side. It bawled in pain. Chet and Matt held the ropes tight. The stench of burning hair and hide reached Isabelle. She gagged.

Sean jumped back on his horse and Chet released the bull's back legs. He lunged to his feet, bawling his fury. He charged Sean's horse, but Matt's rope around his horns jerked him to one side. Before he could get back on his feet, Matt had released the rope. The bull charged, but Matt spurred his horse about the same time Chet and Sean approached the bull from behind. Using their ropes as whips, they drove him back toward the herd.

"What are they doing?" Isabelle asked as soon as she managed to regain the faculty of speech.

"Going after another one."

"Why?"

"All these cattle have to be trail-branded."

"But that bull could have killed one of them."

"Steer."

Isabelle blushed. "How can you sit there and just watch?"

"They have to learn."

Isabelle looked around. "Where is Hawk?"

"Out rounding up more steers."

Leigh Greenwood

"Is it as dangerous as this?"

"Probably."

"Why aren't you helping him?"

"I was until I saw you. You ought to be glad I stayed. You'd be in a hellava fix if I'd brought up some cattle with you standing between them and the mouth of the canyon."

Before Isabelle could reply, yells from Will and Pete turned her attention back to the boys. Chet had cut another steer out of the herd. He attempted to drive the animal toward Matt, but the steer doubled back into the herd.

"Are you going to help or just sit there looking stupid?" Chet yelled.

He cut out a second animal, but he was so angry, he drove it right past Matt toward Sean, who wasn't ready. Sean threw his rope. It landed over the steer's head, but Sean hadn't managed to get it looped securely around the saddle horn. The steer broke away, pulling Sean out of the saddle at the same time.

"Fumble-fingers!" Chet shouted.

"Wake up, you dumb ox!" Sean shouted at Matt. "You're supposed to head him off." He reached up and attempted to pull Matt out of the saddle. Matt pushed him away with his foot, sending him backward into Chet, who had just ridden up. Sean punched Chet, then turned on Matt, pulling him out of the saddle and throwing him to the ground.

Chet jumped down and joined the melee.

Isabelle expected Jake to break up the fight at once. He merely watched. "Stop them!" she cried.

"Why?"

"They could get hurt."

"They're too tired to hurt anybody."

"They shouldn't be fighting."

"They won't once they work things out."

"They ought to do that by talking."

"They will when they finish fighting."

"Why did you stop Pete and Will?"

"Because they were fighting in my lap," Jake said, looking at her as if she were simple-minded.

The boys stopped fighting abruptly.

"Pay attention, or I'll flatten you both," Chet said as he mounted up.

"Go to hell!" Sean said and turned toward his horse.

Matt got off a parting shot at Sean, flung himself into the saddle, and rode off after Chet. Sean threw his hat down, muttered some curses, picked it up again, then mounted up.

This time the boys cut a steer out, roped, and branded it without a hitch.

"See, they worked it out," Jake said.

Isabelle decided she would never fathom the mysteries of the male mind. Maybe it was a good thing Jake had taken over from her—and he had taken over. It was obvious the boys looked to him instead of her. She guessed that was the way it should be, but it was difficult to accept that the boys she cared for so much had practically forgotten her.

She told herself not to expect too much of them. They were without loyalties, distrustful, looking out for themselves first and only. They had to learn to care, to consider others as well as themselves. She hoped that would happen when they felt some security, some sense of belonging. Jake could do that for them. If she really wanted what was best for the boys, she'd support him in every way she could.

She watched as Will and Pete fought to carry the red-hot branding iron. She breathed a sigh of relief when Pete delivered it to Sean without hurting himself, only to worry again until Will had returned it to

Luke. She had never seen Will and Pete so happy.

Maybe she was wrong. Maybe Jake was exactly what they needed. Before she could become comfortable with that conviction, Buck rode up.

"What the hell are you doing here?" Jake demanded.

"I couldn't stay in bed, not with the squirts here."

He gave Isabelle a hurt look for leaving him in bed but taking Pete and Will. Jake cast Isabelle a look that said *now see what your meddling has done.* Almost immediately she heard a sharp whistle. She followed the direction of Jake's gaze. Night Hawk was bringing in a half-dozen steers.

"Can you stay on that horse at anything faster than a canter?" Jake asked Buck.

"Of course," the boy replied, offended. "I may be weak, but I can ride as well as any of the others."

"Then help drive these steers into the corral. Luke, you and the little squirts get the corral gates open. And keep out of the way. You," he said to Isabelle, "climb up on the fence. Don't get down for any reason."

Isabelle started to protest, but she found herself speaking to thin air. Jake and Buck had ridden off to meet Night Hawk. Luke let down one set of poles, Will and Pete another. Matt and Sean rode out to help with the new steers. Chet stayed to discourage any from trying to leave the canyon.

Isabelle hadn't climbed a fence in her life. Aunt Deirdre insisted that climbing was unladylike. She had too many skirts. It was almost impossible to see where to put her feet.

The cedar and juniper rails were covered with rough places where branches had been cut off. The wood gouged her hands. She secured a shaky position and looked to see what Will and Pete were doing. They had scrambled up the rails only a few yards from her. Will didn't like his position. He jumped down and climbed up a little farther away. He changed positions again.

"Don't move," Isabelle said. "The steers will be here soon."

"I can't see," Will complained.

He jumped down and ran across the opening to the other side. Isabelle's heart thumped violently in her chest. Will was by himself. She didn't trust him not to jump down again. Holding her dress so she wouldn't snag it, she climbed down and started to run.

She turned her ankle on a rock and fell.

She tried to get to her feet, but a terrible pain shot through her ankle. Gritting her teeth, she stood up just in time to see a steer headed straight at her.

Jake had started cursing the moment Isabelle walked into camp. He invented new curses when he saw her jump down and start across the opening to the corral, stumble, and fall. He was beyond curses when he saw a steer lower its head and start for her at a dead run.

Before the impulse had become conscious thought, he was spurring and whipping his horse. He saw Isabelle struggle to her feet. He didn't know how badly she was hurt, but he doubted she'd be able to climb the fence before the steer reached her. He took out his rope to throw a loop over the steer's horns.

What if he missed? He wouldn't have a second chance. He had to get between the steer and Isabelle.

Spurring his horse even more furiously, he rode up on the steer's left side. Isabelle hobbled frantically to reach the safety of the fence, but she wouldn't make it. With one last push, Jake drove his horse between Isabelle and the steer. Even as he saw Isabelle scramble to safety, the steer turned on him.

He didn't have time to get out of the way. The steer would undoubtedly gore his pony. When it was down, he would come after Jake.

A rope whizzed through the air to settle over the steer's horns, jerked his head around, and threw his rear feet from under him. The steer went down with a loud thud. Almost immediately, he was on his feet again. Uttering a furious bellow, he turned on his assailant.

But the fall had given Jake the time he needed. His rope settled over the steer's horns, and he was firmly caught. He looked up to see Chet grinning at him.

"He almost got you, sir."

"Jake, dammit!" Jake shouted as they forced the steer through the gate. "My name is Jake!"

"He almost got you, Jake."

"Damned right. Thanks." He and Chet jiggled their ropes free about the same time. The steer spun around. But before he could choose a victim, Chet hit him across the rump and headed him off to join the herd. Jake rode back to where Isabelle was leaning against the fence.

Words of cold fury leapt to his tongue, but the look of pure terror in Isabelle's eyes caused him to bite them back.

"She didn't have to follow me," Will said, clearly feeling guilty. "I can take care of myself."

Jake reached over, jerked him off the fence, threw him over the saddle, and gave him a few whacks on the seat of his pants.

"The first thing you learn out here is to follow orders. The second thing is not to do anything stupid. The third, if you're still alive, is not to endanger anybody else. You did all three." Jake plopped Will back on the corral fence. "You get down before I tell you, and I'll chain you to the ranch house."

Will accepted his punishment without a blink. Jake told himself to keep better watch next time. Will obviously thought nothing could hurt him as long as he was near Jake.

The rest of the steers were approaching the gate. Jake moved his horse to a position in front of Isabelle until they passed. While the boys hurried to put the bars back up, he dismounted. "You all right?" he asked. He didn't like the way she looked. She was too stiff, too white.

Isabelle nodded.

"How's your ankle?"

"Okay. I just twisted it."

"Let me see."

"No. It's all right."

"This is no time for modesty."

"Any time is a time for modesty."

"Suppose you get an arrow in you while we're out on the trail. Are you going to refuse to let me touch you then?"

"I . . . this isn't the same."

"Sure it is. Now sit down and let me see that ankle."

She didn't move.

"If you don't, I'm going to pick you up and set you down myself. Having you injured would be a great nuisance." That hadn't come out the way he meant it.

"I thought I was already such a nuisance that one more thing would hardly be noticed."

"Everything you do is noticed. You're not setting a good example. Now let me look at that ankle."

That got her. She wouldn't do it for him, but she would do it for the boys. He was starting to feel jealous of these kids.

Leigh Greenwood

She didn't move, but she wasn't looking at him. He turned around. All eight boys were watching them.

"Get back to your work," Jake ordered. "Hawk, take Buck with you, but go easy on him. He's still as weak as wet rawhide. The rest of you get back to branding. We can't leave for New Mexico until all of these steers carry proof they belong to me."

He turned back. Isabelle hadn't moved.

"Now that everybody's gone . . ."

She lowered herself to the ground, being careful to gather her skirt under her. She pulled up her skirt until the hem just barely touched the top of her shoe.

"I'm surprised you didn't break your neck wearing shoes like this."

"They're very fine linen walking shoes," Isabelle told him.

"You need leather boots."

"Maybe, but I don't have any. Now are you going to look at that ankle, or are you going to keep complaining about my footwear?"

Jake began to unlace her shoe.

"Is that necessary?"

Chapter Ten

Touching Isabelle had a more pronounced effect than Jake expected. His body hardened quickly. Kneeling was miserably uncomfortable, but he couldn't rearrange himself without being obvious. "I have to take your shoe off if I'm to have any idea what your ankle's like."

Isabelle didn't look convinced, but Jake soon found himself more aware of the shape of her ankle than of her disapproval. He'd never touched a woman's foot before. He'd never considered them attractive. But when they were attached to a woman like Isabelle, well, that was something quite different.

He couldn't see her leg—she was careful to keep it covered—but the foot was small and narrow. Both foot and ankle seemed too fragile to stand up to the rigors of West Texas terrain. He felt the joint. It was definitely not broken. He was acutely aware of the soft warmth of her skin through her serviceable cotton stockings. He had never touched a lady before. He was surprised to find she felt very much like any other female.

He turned Isabelle's ankle slightly. "Does that hurt?"

"No."

He bent it a little more. "How about that?"

"A little."

He thought it must hurt more than a little, but he wasn't going to quibble. "You've strained your ankle. Not so badly you can't walk, but it won't feel good."

"I could tell that."

"You've got to stay off it for a while."

"I can't stay here."

"I've got a camp on the rim of the canyon. I'll carry you."

"I'll walk," Isabelle said. She tried to stand up, but the pain caused her to fall against Jake.

Jake scooped her up before she could object. He liked the feel of Isabelle. Her fragility made her all the more appealing.

"Mr. Maxwell, put me down this instant! I hardly know you. Even if I did, I wouldn't allow you to carry me."

She pushed against him, but Jake was much stronger than she was. "Ma'am, you've got a pocketful of scruples. I suppose that's a good thing in Austin, but they're mighty bothersome out here. When you get hurt, you get taken care of any way you can."

She had lovely eyes. They looked blue today. Finely chiseled nose. Lips moist, soft, parted in surprise. He'd never seen her so close. She looked even lovelier.

He could feel the warmth of her breath as it feathered his cheek. He could also feel the heat of embarrassment warm her body. She turned her head to avoid his gaze, but not before he saw her wet her lips, then take her lower lip between her teeth. She couldn't be any more used to this than he was. But he would have given anything to be able to look into her eyes, to know how she felt about being so close to him.

All he could see was her lashes.

He started to climb the rim of the canyon. After wrestling steers all day, he thought she hardly seemed to weigh more than a child. "Aren't you going to say anything?" he asked when she remained silent.

"Why should I? You'll immediately discount it and proceed to tell me why I'm wrong."

"I'm just trying to help you learn to survive out here."

"Mr. Maxwell—"

"Jake."

"Mr. Maxwell—eeek!"

He pretended to stumble. She startled them both by throwing her arms around his neck and holding on tight. The feeling of her body pressed against his own nearly caused him to drop her for real.

Men out here didn't run across females like Isabelle. She was slim, elegant, poised without being prissy or refined. She was as dangerous as hand-to-hand combat with a Comanche, and he was voluntarily holding her in his arms. Not only had she talked him into saddling himself with half-a-dozen orphans who got in their own way as often as not, she had somehow gotten him to insist she come along. *Insist!* He should have been shouting he'd rather fight the war over again than be saddled with a city-bred female on a trek across West Texas.

Her loveliness must have bewitched him.

"I didn't mean to stumble, ma'am, but your calling me Mr. Maxwell confused me so much, I didn't know which foot to put where." That wasn't what confused him, but she needn't know.

"Are you telling me if I don't call you Jake, you'll drop me?"

"I'd do my best to hang on to you, but a man can't always help himself."

"You're outrageous. You have no scruples."

He grinned. "No, ma'am. They won't fit into my saddlebags."

She glared at him so fiercely, he almost kissed her. It wasn't a conscious thought, just an instinctive reaction, one he barely halted in time.

By the time he reached the canyon rim, he was trembling. He had known he was attracted to this woman, but he had underestimated her appeal and overestimated his self-control. No telling what he'd do given half a chance. She could talk him into anything.

That scared him. He had vowed never to let himself fall into the clutches of a female. He decided it was time to stop teasing and keep his distance.

"Is this your camp?"

"Yes, ma'am." It consisted of a tent and a flat place where he could cook and eat.

"You can put me down now," Isabelle said.

He sat her down on a log worn smooth from his own use. Letting her go was like having the wind knocked out of him. He felt empty, as if something had been pulled out of him.

"If it gets too hot, you can use the tent."

"Thank you. I'll be quite all right."

She looked relieved to regain control of her own person. She was still upset with him.

"Just stay off that foot. It ought to be okay in a few hours."

"Thank you. I will."

Real upset. She spread her skirt until it covered her toes, a clear hands-off message.

"I'll bring you some water."

She looked her most proper and disapproving. "Send Will. I'd hate to keep you from your work."

In other words, get away from me and don't come back. A spurt of anger caused him to say, "Don't worry if you see a couple of rattlesnakes. I keep 'em to hold down the mice."

The fearful look she cast about her routed his irritation. He felt guilty for scaring her.

"Are there really rattlesnakes here?"

"Yes, but they won't bother you if you don't bother them. Yell if you need anything. The boys will hear you."

"Where will you be?"

"With Night Hawk and Buck."

She looked uneasy.

"I'll check on you from time to time."

"That won't be necessary. I'll be all right."

Just like a woman. When she thought he was going to leave her, she was afraid. But as soon as she found out he'd be close by, she insisted she didn't need any help. He never would understand women as long as he lived, or why he felt even the slightest attraction to this one.

But he did. It didn't matter that she was the wrong kind of woman, or that after what his mother had done, he'd be a fool to even consider spending more than one hour with the same woman. There was something about Isabelle that made him forget all his resolutions. He couldn't get rid of the feeling that everything would be different with her.

Isabelle found that if she was very careful to put her foot down flat, her ankle didn't hurt. Well, not much. She should have stayed off it a while longer, but she was bored to the point of screaming. She had watched the boys rope and brand endless cows. They still got into occasional disputes. But as the afternoon wore on, they managed to work out a system that kept their tempers from exploding.

A rock slipped under her foot, and she winced from the pain. She had decided to walk back because she was afraid Jake would insist upon carrying her. She was determined to avoid that. She didn't want her body sending messages she neither understood nor wanted to receive. It hadn't been so difficult when she was certain he was trying to annoy her. She didn't think he disliked her any more. She knew she didn't dislike him.

It was all so confusing. She hadn't felt the least like this with her fiancé. Why did it have to happen now, and with a man like Jake?

Another rock slipped under her foot. She stopped to rest a moment.

She looked about her at the inhospitable land. She couldn't understand why Jake was so fond of it. It was hard, hilly, rocky, and cut with ravines and canyons big enough to hide a herd of cattle. She'd be happy to hand it over to the farmers, Indians, or anyone else who wanted it.

She arrived at the corral shortly after Jake and the boys had brought in another batch of cattle. They were sitting their horses, watching the steers search for a way out. Isabelle wondered just how many cattle the canyon could hold. It seemed to have hundreds in it now.

"I was just about to come get you," Jake said. "It's time we went back."

"There's lots more daylight," Sean said. "I'm not tired."

"Your horse is," Jake said. "I don't mean to take a chance on getting him hurt because he's worn out."

"Can I ride back with you?" Will asked.

Isabelle didn't understand why Jake should glance at Matt. Neither did she understand why the boy's expression seemed angry and threatening. She knew of no reason why he should dislike Jake.

"Ride with your brother."

"How about me?" Pete asked.

"Come on, squirt," Sean said. "I'll give you a hand up."

"How's Miss Davenport getting back?" Chet asked.

"I'll walk," Isabelle said.

"That's impossible," Jake said. "It would take you the better part of an hour on a good foot. You'd never make it without hurting your ankle so badly you wouldn't be able to stand on it for several days."

Isabelle hated to admit Jake was right, especially when it meant admitting she was wrong, but she didn't have any choice. "If you will saddle a horse for me, I'll attempt to keep from falling off before we reach the camp."

"We didn't bring an extra horse."

"If you're willing, ma'am," Chet offered, "you could ride my horse. You can ride bareback if it'll make you feel more comfortable."

"There's not a horse on the place I'd trust Isabelle to ride sideways and bareback," Jake said.

Isabelle wasn't tempted to contradict him. The thought of attempting to stay on a horse without a saddle made her feel faint.

"She can have my horse," Jake said. "I'll walk."

"It'll take forever to get back," Will complained.

"I know," Sean said. "She can ride double with Jake."

"Don't be ridiculous. I—"

147

"That's a perfect solution," Chet said. "There won't be anything for her to hold on to if she rides bareback. Jake can ride behind and keep her from falling off."

"Miss Davenport wouldn't consider it for a minute," Jake said. "It's unladylike, she doesn't ride, and she doesn't like me."

"He's probably woman-shy," Sean said to Chet. "I had an uncle like that. Couldn't come near a female without blushing and stammering and fidgeting like he had bees in his britches."

"You're bound to see her ankles when she mounts up," Jake said.

"I don't see that it makes any difference," Chet said. "You've already seen them, and we won't look."

Jake glared at the boys. Sean grinned expectantly. Chet looked satisfied they had reached a sensible solution.

Isabelle opened her mouth to say she wouldn't be caught riding double with a man in this life or the next but closed it immediately. If she were going to travel to New Mexico, she was going to have to do many things she wouldn't have considered had she stayed in Savannah. Riding double might be one of the least objectionable.

"You'll have to ride astride," Jake said.

Jake had been telling her she was much too hidebound by Eastern restrictions totally unsuitable for the West. She guessed this was one of those times, one of those conventions. It was either ride or walk. Faced with those alternatives, the choice was easy. "I'll ride," she said.

Jake uttered one of his more colorful oaths, then slid to the ground. He stripped the saddle off his horse and handed it up to Chet. "Get started," he said to the boys. "We'll catch up with you later."

"Now," Jake said when the boys were out of sight, "I'm going to lift you onto his back. You've got to throw your right leg over the other side. Otherwise, you'll fall off. Think you can do that?"

Isabelle was certain she couldn't. "Of course I can," she replied.

But she was no more prepared for the feel of Jake's hands around her waist than she had been when he carried her to his camp. Instinctively her hands flew to her waist to cover his, to brace herself, to keep her balance. She could feel his individual fingers as they splayed out against her ribs, the palms of his hands on her sides, his thumbs at her back. She felt captured, held helplessly in his grasp.

It was an odd feeling, completely unlike being in his arms. She felt small and defenseless, as though her strength were nothing. She felt completely encompassed by his overwhelming energy and vitality.

"Bend your knees and jump," Jake said.

She obeyed automatically.

The sensation of his hands around her waist was trivial compared to the exhilaration of being lifted in the air and deposited on the back of a horse who didn't seem entirely sure he wanted her there. She wasn't balanced on his back, and she had nothing to hold onto. She expected to fall off the other side.

But Jake's hands still held her in a vise-like grip.

"Grab hold of his mane and throw your leg over."

She managed to do that just as Jake vaulted onto the horse's back. "Let's go."

Isabelle wasn't startled by the rocking motion when the horse broke into a slow canter. She wasn't much concerned about falling off, though she was certain with every stride that she would be pitched headlong into a cactus. She was much too shatteringly aware of Jake's body pressed against her back, too acutely aware of his arms around her, too intensely aware of his thighs pressed tightly against her own.

She experienced panic, fear, an urgent need to break out of his embrace. Not even when Henri attacked her had her body come into such intimate contact with a powerfully muscled male body.

Yet, as she rode cocooned in his embrace, a new kind of excitement began to grow inside her. It had a delicious edge of anticipation to it. She tried to drive it away, but it was powerful, all consuming. It urged her to lean against Jake; it was heated by contact with his body; it was inflamed by their sensual rubbing together in rhythm with the stride of the horse. It caused heat to flow through her body, arc through her like sparks along the ground after a lightning strike. At the same time it caused the heaviness of desire to pool within her, sapping her limbs of their strength, her mind of its resolution.

This was her first real comprehension of the intensity of her physical reaction to Jake, and it was much too clear to be mistaken for anything else. She wanted Jake, and she wanted him badly.

That shocked Isabelle. None of her previous experience with Jake—liking him, being attracted to him, enjoying being close to him, being touched by him—had prepared her for the shattering effects of desire. It mystified, mortified, and terrified her.

Much to her relief, Jake caught up with the boys before she completely lost control.

"Can I come back tomorrow?" Will called to Jake.

"Me, too," Pete chorused.

"We'll see," Jake said. "It only takes one person to heat the irons and keep the fire going."

"Can I go on roundup?" Will asked.

Isabelle tensed, fearful that Jake, who seemed to

see no danger out here to anyone but her, would let Will go with him.

"Not yet. You need a few riding lessons first."

"I already know how to ride," Will said. "I—"

"Do you recall what I said to you earlier?" Jake snapped.

"Yes," Will answered, subdued.

"Remember it."

Isabelle had never supposed Jake was blessed with an abundance of patience. She was surprised he hadn't lost his temper before now. She expected an uncomfortable silence to follow, but Will chattered on about all the things he could do and what he would soon learn to do. Pete was compelled to match him deed for deed.

"Give them a week," Chet said, "and they'll be ready to take the herd to New Mexico by themselves."

Will wasn't the slightest bit embarrassed. He kept right on bombarding Jake with questions until they reached the ranch.

The ride was over almost as soon as it began. Isabelle was startled to feel the warmth and power of Jake's body leave her as he slid to the ground. She felt a lessening of tension, a dulling of the sharp edge of desire, but there was none of the relief she expected. She felt bereft. Jake gripped her by the waist and lifted her to the ground.

He didn't let go. He kept his hands around her waist and held her close. It was impossible not to feel the heat of his body, not to be aware of his strength, the weakness in her legs. She fought down a compulsion to throw her arms around him and mold her body to his.

"Are you steady on your feet?" he asked.

"Yes."

"Does it hurt when you stand on it?"

"No. If I take it easy while I fix supper, it ought to be fine by breakfast."

"Are you sure?"

She was tempted to say she couldn't stand up that long. It had been a long time since anyone had cared how she felt. But she could tell he thought it was her job, that she ought to cook if she possibly could.

He was right. Once on the trail, no one would have time to take over her chores. She had to do her job, no matter what. She knew Jake would. Besides, she'd been talking to Jake about setting a good example. Now it was her turn.

"Matt's worn out," she said. "He's been in the saddle all day, and he's still got his horse and gear to attend to."

"I'm sure he won't mind if somebody does it for him tonight."

"When you assigned jobs for this trip, did you plan to let the boys skip out when they wanted?"

"No, but—"

"Cooking is my job. I can't expect anybody to do my work for me."

Isabelle took two steps back. It was hard to talk to him when she had to crane her neck to look up at him. "Now I'd better get busy. I don't want to be accused of keeping you from your work."

She walked away, determined not to limp, even if the pain killed her. When she stepped on one of the endless rocks that covered the ground, it nearly did. She recovered her balance and went on, refusing to give in to the pain.

"Bret," she called as she approached the dead campfire, "I need water and wood immediately."

* * *

152

"Does your ankle still hurt?"

Isabelle had finished serving the boys. She'd taken her plate and sat down. Jake got up and came over to her before she'd managed to chew the first mouthful of her food.

"No," she lied, but his asking made her want to cry. Since Aunt Deirdre died, no one had cared how she felt. Most of the time they didn't even pretend. She thought she was accustomed to it. She had tried to be. She didn't understand why it should be different with Jake. She didn't want it to be.

"You stumbled a few times while you were cooking."

She told herself there was no reason for her to be so pleased he had watched her. If her heart beat a little faster, if she felt a little light-headed, it had better be because she had inhaled too much smoke from the fire.

"It's the rocky ground. Everybody stumbles."

"You ought to stay off it for the rest of the evening. Let Will and Pete clean up."

"I intend to."

He sat next to her, chewing mouthful after mouthful of beans and bacon. Apparently he didn't care that the beans where mushy and the bacon hard.

"The boys don't have much muscle yet," Jake said, "but a month in the saddle ought to cure that."

Apparently he was through being concerned about her ankle. She was glad the boys were doing better than expected, but right now she didn't want to talk about them. She was tired, her ankle hurt, she could barely manage to eat the food she had cooked, and she was sick of always thinking about somebody else.

Still, she didn't have a choice. The boys were the reason they were together. Without them, she would never have returned to his ranch. She certainly wouldn't have agreed to go to New Mexico.

"I'd appreciate your teaching them all you can before we reach Santa Fe," she said, forcing herself to ignore her irritation at Jake's loss of interest in her. "It's important they be able to find jobs."

"What are you going to do with the younger ones? They can't hire out as cowhands."

"I don't know."

"You could take them back to Austin. Bret is a little old, but Will and Pete are young enough that—"

"No."

"You can't support them by yourself."

"I'll figure out something."

She wanted him to go away. She didn't want to have to try to figure out how to make someone else happy when she wasn't happy herself. She just wanted time to be alone so she could give herself the sympathy nobody else would. It wouldn't take long. Her ankle would be well in a day or two.

But it wasn't the ankle. She was feeling depressed and unloved. It didn't happen often, but once in a while the loneliness overwhelmed her. Usually she could convince herself it wasn't really important, but today wasn't one of those times. If something were to happen to her tomorrow, there wouldn't be anyone to remember her for more than a few minutes.

That was hard to take.

"Why don't you sleep in the cabin tonight?"

"What?" She'd forgotten the thread of their conversation.

"Sleep in the cabin. You'll be more comfortable than in the wagon."

"I'll be all right."

"You could hurt yourself climbing in and out."

"You worried I won't be able to fix breakfast tomorrow?"

"I'm worried you might really sprain that ankle. I'd have to leave you behind. I can't put up with all these boys by myself."

Well, she supposed he cared, after a fashion.

"Besides, it's not suitable for you to be sleeping out. A woman like you deserves a house with a wood floor and curtains at the window."

She wasn't sure whether he was complimenting her or complaining. "Are you trying to tell me I have no business going on this drive?"

"I'm trying to tell you I don't want you to hurt yourself again."

He actually looked upset. Isabelle felt better. "Thank you. I'd be pleased to accept your offer."

He looked so startled, it was almost comical. Isabelle got to her feet. She felt a lot better. She just might get a good night's sleep after all.

Jake was reluctant to go back to his camp. He knew he shouldn't leave the herd unguarded all night, but he didn't feel comfortable leaving Isabelle with nothing but a bunch of unarmed boys to protect her. He could leave a gun, but he didn't know which boy could shoot the best, which could be trusted to hold his fire until he knew what he was shooting at, which wouldn't consider running away once he had access to a horse and a weapon.

Isabelle and her orphans were giving him a chance to save his ranch, but they were complicating his life. This was worse than the army. At least they gave him food, weapons, and an enemy to fight. Here he was expected to supply everything himself.

Oh well, tomorrow he'd see about sending some of

155

the boys to sleep at the camp. Until then, the herd would just have to take care of itself.

Isabelle was pleased with herself when she woke well before dawn. Jake wouldn't have to wake her today. She dressed quickly and went outside to rouse Bret. The grass was wet with a heavy dew. By the time she had everything on to cook, her shoes were soaked. She did need boots.

The boys were scattered around the camp in their bedrolls, sound asleep. She was relieved to see they had slept with their blankets over their heads. She supposed Jake was responsible for that.

She set about preparing the coffee. She finally had three-day-old grounds. She couldn't imagine why anyone would want such coffee, but Jake was welcome to it as long as he didn't expect her to drink it.

As soon as the coffee was hot, she picked up a big pot and hit it with the biggest metal spoon she had. It made a satisfyingly loud noise. "Breakfast will be ready in five minutes," she called out. "You've just got time to pull on your boots and wash your faces."

"Who needs a clean face to eat?" a sleepy voice demanded.

She was shocked to discover that voice belonged to Jake.

Chapter Eleven

"What are you doing here?" she asked.

As soon as the words were out of her mouth, she was angry at herself for hoping, however briefly, he would say it had something to do with her.

"I was too tired to saddle up and ride back."

"What about your cows?" If she didn't want him to tell her she had nothing to do with his staying, why did she keep asking?

"They've taken care of themselves for years. I figured they could make it through another night. Is that coffee I smell?"

"It'll be ready by the time you wash up."

The boys were waiting to see what Jake would do. Isabelle was certain that if he refused, they would as well.

"Come on," Jake said to them. "A little creek water will get the sleep out of your eyes. You climb on one of those nags half asleep and you'll be picking briars out of your backside for the rest of the day."

Isabelle watched them troop down to the creek, a man leading six boys.

"Will dances around him like a puppy," Bret said spitefully.

Isabelle didn't know why Will clung to Jake so, but she was glad he had a man to look up to.

The boys had hardly returned when Luke came running from the direction of the corral. "Buck's gone," he said, "and he took two horses."

"Something must have happened to him," Isabelle said.

"What could have happened with us sleeping all around him?" Chet asked.

"Nothing happened," Jake said, angry. "He just stole two horses and ran away."

"Buck wouldn't steal," Isabelle said, upset that Jake would think such a thing.

"Why not? Because you took care of his wounds? He's been mistreated by everybody who's had anything to do with him. He probably hates adults as a matter of course. I just hope he didn't head west. I don't want to find his scalped remains along the trail."

Isabelle didn't understand how Jake could talk about Buck's possible death with such cruel indifference.

"You have to go after him," she said. "He isn't strong."

Jake looked at her the way indulgent parents look at a child who's just said something stupid. "He could be as far as fifty miles from here by now. It would take days to catch up with him, if I ever did."

"But you can't just leave him out there."

"I don't have any choice. I don't know where he is. Even if I did, I can't afford the time to go after him."

"You've got to do something," Isabelle insisted, unable to believe Jake wasn't going to search for Buck immediately.

"I am. I'm going to have breakfast. Then I'm going to find out if any of these boys can handle a gun."

"Did you see any tracks?" Isabelle asked Luke, unwilling to give up.

"Yes, but they aren't clear. The ground's too rocky."

"I follow tracks," Night Hawk offered.

"You can trail him a couple of miles," Jake said, relenting, "just to make sure of his direction."

"You're not going with him?" Isabelle asked.

"No." He pointed to the sky, which had already begun to turn pink. "We're late."

Isabelle handed Matt the plate she had in her hand. "Then I'm going."

"You'll do no such thing," Jake said.

"Who'll stop me?"

"I will. Hell, five minutes from here and you wouldn't be able to find your way back to camp."

"I'll go with her," Sean offered.

"Me, too," Chet added.

"None of you are going anywhere. Night Hawk will find out all we need to know. Now, ma'am, if you don't mind, we'll be needing a big breakfast if we're to spend the day in the saddle. I hope you made plenty of biscuits."

Isabelle was tempted to tell him hell would freeze over before she ever cooked anything for him to eat— a phrase she had never thought of using until today— but she decided she wouldn't get anywhere by defying him. The boys had to eat. If she failed to live up to her part of the bargain, he might go back on his.

But she had no intention of letting Buck disappear

159

without trying to find him. She couldn't understand how Jake could, either. Despite living practically like a wild animal, there must be some human decency in him.

She worked in silence, but Will and Pete spent the next ten minutes thinking up explanations for what could have happened to Buck. Their solutions were so hair-raising, Isabelle was relieved when Jake called a halt to their imaginings by announcing it was time to saddle up.

They had barely gotten to their feet when she heard a shout from Sean. "It's Night Hawk and Buck! They've got somebody with them."

The boys forgot about saddling up. They raced to the small hill behind the corral. By the time Isabelle reached the crest, the boys had run to meet Buck.

"I was afraid of something like this."

She turned to find Jake standing next to her. "Afraid of what?"

"Who is that boy?" Jake asked, not answering her question.

"It doesn't matter. Buck is safe."

"I think it's going to matter a hell of a lot."

"What do you mean?"

"You'll see."

Isabelle had never seen the boy before. He was black, tall, and despite a big frame, extremely thin. He looked about the same age as Buck. The horses approached at a walk. Even as Isabelle wondered why they rode so slowly, she knew. The boy was too weak to ride any faster.

"I wonder where Buck found him?" Isabelle asked.

"He stole him," Jake said.

"Don't be ridiculous. Why should he steal another boy?"

"I imagine he was working for your farmers. I

know Buck stole him because I can see a chain around the boy's right ankle."

Isabelle had noticed something dangling but had never imagined it was a chain. "You mean—"

"He was chained at night so he couldn't run away."

Suddenly Isabelle felt herself sway. She reached out. Jake took hold of her hand. He slipped an arm around her waist to steady her.

"Are you all right?"

If she had been before, she certainly wasn't now. She wasn't accustomed to having a man put his arm around her, but she found she liked the feeling. "I'm fine. I'm not used to walking on such rocky ground. My footing is forever giving way under me."

Only this time it was her knees, not her ankle that felt weak. She pulled away from Jake. Just like yesterday, the sensation she felt was loss, not relief.

"You'd better get out your salves and bandages," Jake said. "Let's hope he wasn't treated as badly as Buck."

The boys halted in front of Isabelle and Jake.

"I had to get him," Buck said. "I couldn't leave knowing he was still there."

"Why didn't you tell us what you meant to do?" Isabelle asked.

"I wasn't sure you'd let me. You've got so many boys already, and Mr. Maxwell never did want us. I figured he wouldn't want anybody else."

Isabelle doubted she and Jake would ever agree on much, but she was absolutely certain he wouldn't have left this boy behind. His condition wrung her heart. He was dirty. His clothes were filthy, tattered rags. She was certain he hadn't been allowed a bath. But it was the chain dangling from his leg that caused her to feel greater anger than she had never known. "How did you free him?"

"I sawed the post in two," Buck explained.

"What's your name?" Isabelle asked.

The boy didn't answer. He stared at her out of black eyes that were big with hate.

"It's Zeke," Buck said. "One of those farmers bought him."

"But slaves are free now."

"He wasn't."

"We were just about to sit down to breakfast," Isabelle said. "Later I'll see about those welts on your back."

His expression unchanged, Zeke dismounted and followed Buck to the campfire.

"Next time tell me what you mean to do," Jake said to Buck. "I'd rather have an army of useless critters yapping at my heels than leave even one of you with those devils. Is anybody left?" Jake asked Zeke.

The boy flashed a look full of unquenched anger. "No, but they're expecting some new ones. I heard them talking about it."

"We're the ones they were expecting," Sean said, "but we're taking Jake's cows to New Mexico."

Zeke immediately turned his gaze toward Jake.

"You can come, too," Jake said. "But first get some food in you."

Zeke proceeded to eat like he'd never eaten before. His wounds were easily tended. He had been beaten but not often and not severely. Isabelle wondered who could possibly have placed these boys in such inhuman conditions. Then she remembered she had nearly done the same thing.

Sean entered the cabin holding a shirt and a pair of pants. He handed them to Zeke. Isabelle's heart warmed at Sean's generosity, but Zeke angrily pushed them away.

"You might as well take them," Sean said. "Yours

are about to fall off. You can't walk around in front of Miss Davenport naked."

"I don't want anything from anybody," Zeke said. His entire body vibrated with an anger that seemed to pour out of his soul.

"Then take them until you can earn some money to buy yourself some more," Isabelle said.

"How am I going to do that?" Zeke demanded angrily.

"I don't know," Isabelle answered, unwilling to let him think she had the answers he sought. "Two days ago I was wondering how to keep these boys out of the farmers' hands. Then Mr. Maxwell agreed to take us with him. By the time we reach New Mexico, I'll have figured out how you can pay for the pants."

Zeke glared at Sean. "Okay, but only until I can buy my own."

Isabelle left so he could change. Jake was waiting for her, a worried look on his face.

"He'll be all right. He's mainly worn down and undernourished."

"That's not what's worrying me."

"I'm sure he'll be able to help with the cows."

"It's not that, either. Those farmers have got to be looking for him. They're bound to come here."

Isabelle hadn't thought of that.

"What will they do?"

"Try to force me to give him back."

"You can't!"

"I don't mean to. But if they bring the sheriff, I may not have a choice."

"What are we going to do?" She never doubted he had a plan. He always had an answer.

"I'm going to hide them."

"Where?"

"I don't know yet, but I'll think of something. We'll

keep Bret, Will, and Pete here. I'll move the rest of the boys and most of the horses to the cow camp. They can get on with the branding."

"Shouldn't you go with them?"

"They'll never believe I had nothing to do with it if they don't see me. We can't pretend there's nobody here, so let's give them an explanation they can believe. You can be my cousin, come with her three boys to live with me."

The solution was totally unexpected, but there wasn't time to ask questions. There were too many preparations to make. Jake had to explain to the boys what he wanted done and send the older ones off with most of the horses and all of their belongings.

He set Will, Pete, and Bret to sweeping out the tracks of the extra horses. Then he mounted one of the remaining horses and rode back and forth until he had only four sets of tracks leading into the corral.

"You boys take the food you don't eat," he said to Buck. "You're going to be gone all day."

"Where are we going?" Zeke asked, suspicious.

"I'm going to hide you," Jake said. "The farmers are bound to look for you here."

"I never though of that," Buck said. "I've got to leave. If they find me, they'll kill me."

"Don't talk nonsense," Jake said, brushing aside Buck's fears. "They're not going to hurt you or anybody else. Besides, you had to come here. There's nobody else for nearly ten miles."

Isabelle decided she'd never understand Jake. He seemed so rough and unfeeling, not caring about anybody or anything. Yet he never hesitated to protect these boys.

She wrapped the remaining bacon and biscuits in a clean towel. Buck and Zeke ate all the beans they could hold.

"I don't know how long I'll be gone," Jake said to Isabelle when they were ready to leave. "In case they get here before I get back, you'd better do something to make it look like you're here to stay."

"Like what?"

"I don't know. What do women do? Wash clothes? Clean house?"

"Cook, can, take care of babies."

"You've already cooked, there's nothing to can, and you don't have a baby."

Her sarcasm was lost on him.

"Just come back as quickly as you can."

Considering what the farmers had done to the boys, the thought of being alone when they arrived terrified her. She might not think much of Jake's manners and she might have serious questions about some of his values, but she had no doubt about his ability to defend her. Any man who chose to wrestle longhorns for a living *and liked it* ought to make short work of a few farmers.

"I'll clean the kitchen," Isabelle said. "The boys can start on the bunkhouse."

"There's no point. We'll be gone in a few days."

"As you pointed out, women clean and wash. Nobody would believe I mean to stay in a place like this. Aunt Deirdre would have fainted if you'd asked her to enter that house. The bunkhouse is the obvious place for the boys to sleep."

Like any man faced with a litany of domestic chores, Jake took to his heels. "I'll be back as quickly as I can," he promised.

Isabelle started in Jake's bedroom. As soon as she finished that, she meant to attack the kitchen. It struck her as ironic. She'd never had a home, husband, or children of her own. She'd never cooked, cleaned, washed, or done any of the things women usually did. Yet here she was pretending to keep house for a man she'd met just three days ago, pretending to be the mother of three boys who were no relation to her, pretending she wasn't hoping Jake would stop treating her like a fumbling female he'd be only too happy to be rid of.

After DuPlange's attack, she had been certain she never wanted another man to touch her. But she couldn't stop thinking about Jake's touch. After her years as a governess, she'd sworn she never wanted children. Yet she was risking her future because of an overwhelming need to mother these boys. And now she was about to clean a house.

Jake's room had a spartan emptiness that was so much like him. There was nothing soft about it, nothing useless. She wondered what Aunt Deirdre would have said about him. She probably wouldn't have spoken to him. She was a woman of very rigid standards. Isabelle had often wondered where she learned them. Even in Savannah society, they stood out.

Isabelle's parents had been killed just after she was born. Aunt Deirdre had never voluntarily mentioned any other family. When Isabelle asked, her aunt used to say she had some distant relatives in England.

Isabelle had never wanted to go to England. From Aunt Deirdre's descriptions, it was a strange, cold place that didn't appeal to her. She wanted to meet her American relatives. Aunt Deirdre would only say they'd talk about it later.

Only later never came. One day her aunt suffered a stroke and was unable to move or speak. She lingered for several months before she died. Because Isabelle was engaged to a man from a wealthy family, she was allowed to continue living in her aunt's home. When he was killed in the first engagement of the war, everything changed. Isabelle was only sixteen. She had no known relatives. The house was sold to pay her aunt's debts, and she was sent to an orphanage.

She would never forget that first day. She was lonely, frightened, and still heartbroken over her aunt's death. Nobody cared. Certainly not the other children. All of her things were taken from her and packed away. She was given a uniform and expected to fit in as if she'd never lived anywhere else. She'd been rebuked for crying at night because it kept the other girls awake. The girls poked fun at her "airs and graces." The boys had been just as cruel when she found their rude manners unappealing.

She ran away, but they found her and brought her back.

After that she learned to fight. It never did win her any friends, but she did gain a certain grudging respect. She had counted the days until she was old enough to leave.

When she finally left the orphanage, she was devastated to discover that none of the people she used to know wanted anything to do with her. She was an outcast from the only society she had ever known. She had just enough money to buy a ticket to New Orleans, where she found a job as a governess.

After she left the DuPlange family, jobs in respectable homes had been hard to find. She was a woman with a past. The chance to teach school in Austin, Texas, was like the answer to a prayer.

That was where she had found the boys.

Reconstruction Texas didn't care about them, but she did. She knew what it was like to lose a warm, loving home, to be alone with no one to care. Aunt

Deirdre had been demanding and critical, but her love was unstinting.

The sound of someone riding up ended Isabelle's reminiscing. She was relieved to see Jake, but she was ashamed to let him see how little work she'd done. She'd been daydreaming. She had barely finished his room.

She met him outside. "Where did you hide the boys?" she asked.

"In one of the caves on the river."

"Won't that be one of the first places they look?"

"The current has carved out hundreds of caves. They can't search them all."

"But they'll be cold and wet."

"It's the best place I could think of. What are you doing?"

She pointed to the buckets of water the boys had set on the porch. "I'm about to attack the kitchen."

"Leave it," Jake said. "You can keep cooking in the yard."

She picked up the water and headed inside. "They're farmers. They won't believe I would cook outside when you have a perfectly good kitchen."

Perfectly good was a misstatement.

"If you'll light a fire, I'll put everything that needs washing into hot water. You'll have to empty the ashes first. Do you have any soap?"

"Somewhere."

By the time Jake had a fire going, Isabelle had made an inventory of the kitchen. "There's nothing to eat," she said.

"I know."

"But we're almost out of food."

"I know," Jake said.

She expected more of a response than that. "Then we'll have to buy some. How long will that take?"

"Three or four days."

"We ought to go as soon as possible."

Jake took an unusual interest in a fire that was burning quite well. "We'll have to take some cows with us."

"That'll slow us down."

"I don't have any money," he finally admitted. "And there isn't anybody who'll give me credit. Those damned farmers have seen to that."

Isabelle realized he'd been putting off telling her because he was embarrassed to admit he was broke.

"I have money," she said.

"A few dollars won't do us any good. We'll need supplies for a dozen people for about forty days."

"It's gold."

"That's better, but—"

"Two hundred dollars."

Jake froze. "What in hell are you doing with two hundred dollars in gold? I didn't think there was that much in the whole state."

"The agency gave it to me. It was for the farmers."

"I can't take it."

"It was meant for whoever took the boys. You have, so it goes to you."

Jake looked undecided. She knew it went against his pride to accept anything from someone else, especially a woman. Well, her pride had been cut to ribbons. She didn't see why his shouldn't receive a little rough handling.

She heard running footsteps, and Will burst into the room. "Some men are coming!"

Chapter Twelve

The farmers didn't look the least bit like Isabelle had imagined. She had expected men of ample girth dressed in homespun, riding in a wagon. What she saw was four gaunt, bearded men whose dispositions seemed as sour as those of the mules they rode.

Even if they had never mistreated anybody, Isabelle wouldn't have wanted to turn children over to these men. She couldn't imagine any one of them taking Will up in the saddle or risking their farms for the sake of a bunch of misfit boys.

"Let me do the talking," Jake said.

Isabelle was perfectly happy to let Jake do all the talking. She couldn't think of a thing to say. Bret and Pete had come out of the bunkhouse to see what was going on. She motioned for them to join her. They ran across the yard, looking over their shoulders as if they were afraid one of the men might suddenly try to capture them. Will pushed up against Jake.

Bret and Pete took positions on either side of Isabelle.

"Are those the men who were going to take us?" Will whispered.

"Sure are," Jake said.

"I don't like them."

"Neither do I. Now don't say a word. We don't want them to think we know anything about Zeke or Buck."

As Isabelle watched, a difference came over Jake. It was so gradual that at first she didn't notice, but he seemed to grow a little taller, stand a little more stiffly. There was also a wariness about him. He was wearing his gun, something she'd never seen him do before. He'd moved Will to his left. His gun hand was free.

He was preparing to defend them. That was what had brought about the transformation. She was certain Jake himself didn't even realize it.

The quick flush of gratitude surprised Isabelle, but not nearly as much as the feeling of satisfaction at knowing Jake was willing to defend her and the boys. What had happened in such a short time to transform the crabby bachelor into a man who thought of all these boys as his responsibility, one he took very seriously? She looked down at Will. Jake had let his hand settle on Will's shoulders, unconsciously pulling the boy closer to him.

Isabelle felt sudden moisture blur her vision. How could she have missed this part of Jake? Will and Pete had seen it almost immediately. All she could see was his bad manners, his grubby appearance, his oft-stated objection to having anything to do with her or the boys. Yet at the first sign of danger, he hadn't hesitated to defend them all.

She felt proud to stand beside him. He was a man

a woman could depend on, who would take care of her without thinking he was doing anything special. She watched him slide his hand over the butt of his gun. She almost smiled at the reaction of the farmers. They were afraid of him. That would have horrified her a few days ago. Now it made her want to smile.

The farmers came to a halt in front of the cabin. They didn't get down from their mules. They studied Jake in silence.

"I didn't know you had a woman," Noah Landesfarne said finally.

"This is my cousin, Isabelle," Jake told him. "She and her three boys have come to live with me."

"Didn't know you had any relations around here."

"She's from Georgia," Jake said. "Savannah."

Isabelle didn't know why she decided to speak. The words seemed to come out by themselves. "How do you do," she said, emphasizing the south Georgia accent so much that Pete looked up at her in surprise. She squeezed his shoulder. "It's nice to know we have neighbors," she drawled. "It's been mighty lonely since we got here. I hope your womenfolk will come visit and sit a spell."

The farmers stared.

"You seen anybody by this way?" Noah asked.

"Nothing but a couple of Comanches a week ago. You looking for anybody special?"

"A boy," Rupert Reison exploded. He broke off abruptly at a look from Noah.

"One of our boys didn't come home last night," Noah explained. "We're worried he might have gotten lost. He's not familiar with the country yet."

"You must be nearly crazy with worry," Isabelle said. "I'd go mad if one of my boys got lost in this wilderness. What's your boy's name?"

Noah looked startled, even perplexed. "Zeke."

"That's a nice name. How old is he?"

"Sixteen."

"We haven't seen anybody," Jake said.

"We thought he might have come this way. He'll be without food."

"He'd be hard pressed to find anything to eat here," Isabelle said giving Jake a reproachful frown. "Cousin Jake's cupboards are as bare as a church offering plate. I've been telling him he's got to go to town and get me some supplies. I can't make biscuits out of nothing. I declare, I had more to eat after Sherman took nearly everything we had."

Isabelle was appalled at the sound of her voice. Aunt Deirdre had worked very hard to make certain there wasn't even a trace of Savannah drawl in her speech, and here she was sounding as though she had grown up in the swamps across the river.

"You think he might be hiding in one of the canyons down by the river?" Jake asked.

"He's got to be somewhere," Noah said. "He can't have gone far on foot." Noah's gaze slowly wandered over the whole ranch. It stopped on the corral. "I see you caught up some of your horses."

"They're for the boys," Jake said. "Poor little critters can't ride anything but a wagon."

"They look mighty small to be working cattle."

"Too small," Jake said, "but I thought they might be able to keep them from getting into your fields."

"That ain't going to cancel the money you owe us."

That subject exhausted, silence returned. Clearly the farmers weren't leaving until their doubts were removed.

"Can we look round?"

"Not without me," Jake said. "I don't trust you."

173

The farmers didn't like that, but no one said anything.

"How about the bunkhouse?" one of them asked.

Jake laughed. "Not even a runaway would stay in there. Cousin Isabelle has had the boys cleaning it up so they can use it. See for yourself if you want."

Rupert dismounted and strode over to the bunkhouse. The boys had dragged out all the blankets, mattresses, chairs, a table, the saddles and gear, anything that could be moved. It was obvious no one was hiding in the bunkhouse.

"I hope you don't mind if we go back to work," Isabelle said. "I told the boys they wouldn't get supper until that bunkhouse was clean enough for something besides rattlesnakes to live in it. And I got my work in the house. No man ever knew how to keep a kitchen."

The men stared at Isabelle as if they were unused to hearing a woman talk.

"Hop to it, boys," she said. "Time's a wasting. Go on," she said, when they seemed glued to the spot. "These men aren't going to eat you." She laughed.

The farmers didn't.

The boys slowly moved off toward the bunkhouse. Will cast several entreating glances over his shoulder at Jake.

"Your Uncle Jake has to help these men look for their boy," Isabelle said. "We don't want him to stay lost. Imagine how hungry you'd be if you had missed your supper and breakfast."

One of the men glared at Isabelle.

"Boys eat every meal like they're never going to get anything else," she said. "If your boy was anywhere about, I'm sure he would have come up to the house. Good morning to you."

Isabelle turned and walked back into the cabin.

The minute the kitchen door closed behind her, she felt her legs go weak under her. She didn't know where she had found the courage to chatter away like that. Nor did she know where the words had come from.

She walked over to the window. The boys had resumed their work in the bunkhouse, but they were paying more attention to the farmers than their cleaning. Jake hadn't moved. He watched the men search the ranch. A moment later, he led them toward the creek. They disappeared among the trees.

Isabelle breathed a sigh of relief. She wouldn't be able to really relax until they were gone, but it was good just to have them out of sight.

Will came pounding up to the cabin and burst into the kitchen. "Are they going to find Buck and Zeke?"

"No. Jake won't let that happen. Now you go back to the bunkhouse. We don't want them to think there's anything wrong."

"Will they come back? I'm afraid of them."

"You don't have to be. Jake won't let anybody hurt you."

"Will he shoot them?"

Isabelle was horrified to see Will looking forward to the possibility.

"Maybe we ought to follow them," Will said. "They might do something bad to Jake. He's got a rifle. I saw it. I know how to shoot it."

Isabelle knew Will didn't know the first thing about rifles or stalking people.

"There's no reason for Jake to shoot anybody. When those men don't find Zeke, they'll go home."

"Can I go with Jake to get Buck?"

"Maybe, but if you don't go back and help Pete and Bret, you won't be allowed to go anywhere."

Will returned to the bunkhouse, his dragging steps

indicating what an anticlimax he thought it to be when he could be stalking evil farmers through the woods. Isabelle decided to return to cleaning the kitchen. She didn't need to now, but it would help take her mind off worrying about what was happening to Jake.

Jake had never liked the farmers, but during the last hour he had come to despise them. They weren't careful to keep him from hearing what they said to each other. Threats such as *I'll cut his hide off when I get my hands on him* and *Next time I'll chain the sorry nigger to an iron post* made him want to drag them behind a runaway horse.

He knew that wouldn't help him or the boys, so he led them to the creek, in and out of several canyons, along the river, taking them farther and farther away from where the boys were hidden.

"Suppose he went the other way?" one of the farmers asked.

"Then he wouldn't have come here," Jake said. "He'd head on down the river toward Newcombe's Crossing. Can he swim?"

"I don't know," Noah said.

"Then I expect he'd stay away from the river. Spring storms up country can make it rise pretty fast."

Rupert wanted to search the river. Jake didn't believe he would find the hiding place, but they were bound to find some footprints in the sand or mud. If they did, they'd never believe he hadn't seen the boys.

"You can if you want," Jake said, "but I've got work to do."

He headed up a small canyon and away from the river. The farmers followed him back to the ranch. They barely glanced at the boys or the bunkhouse.

None of them gave any sign they were aware they should take their leave of Isabelle. They mounted up.

"You will let us know if you see him," Noah said.

"Sure, but I expect he's at Newcombe's Crossing by now."

The men offered no comment as they rode from the yard.

Jake breathed a sigh of relief. He'd been worried they knew Zeke had left on horseback. Apparently, since none of their horses were missing, they hadn't thought to look for tracks.

Isabelle came out on the porch. "Are they gone?" she asked.

"Yes."

"When are you going to bring the boys back?"

"Not until after nightfall."

"Are you going out to the cow camp now?"

"No. I don't trust them not to leave somebody to watch us. I don't want them to know about the other boys, and I don't want them to know I'm branding a trail herd. I want to be a hundred miles away before they realize I'm gone."

"When are we leaving?"

"As soon as we buy our supplies."

"When is that?"

"Tomorrow morning. Now, I think I'll spend the afternoon teaching the boys to ride."

Jake was irritated. He'd taken Will and Pete for a ride through the hills. He'd practically had to take Will's horse by the reins to get the boy to return to the ranch.

"I want to help round up cows," he said. "I can do it. I won't fall off."

"Me, neither," Pete echoed.

Actually Pete was the better rider. At his age, being

177

a year older and stronger could make a big difference. Neither boy would be strong enough to handle a rope for several years, but they could certainly ride alongside the herd and keep strays from wandering off.

No, Pete and Will were doing well. Bret was the source of Jake's irritation. Bret didn't want to get on a horse. So far he'd refused to hold a horse or even help saddle one. In fact, he hadn't even entered the corral. Jake couldn't decide what was wrong with him.

Isabelle came out of the house and headed toward them. Jake's brow creased. She was wearing a skirt about eight or nine inches off the ground. He could see considerably more than her ankles. He couldn't imagine what had gotten into her.

"How are the boys doing?" Isabelle asked.

Jake knew she'd been watching from the kitchen window.

"They're doing fine, especially Pete. He's a natural. If he just grows, he'll be a topnotch hand." He waited for her to explain the skirt.

Will rode up. "Watch me," he said proudly then sent his mount cantering across the corral.

"Isn't he going too fast?" Isabelle asked.

"He's doing fine."

"Have you told him?"

"No. Too much praise could ruin him."

Pete had joined Will and was trying to outdo him.

"Boys thrive on praise."

"And end up dead when they get too sure of themselves. Let him worry about how good he is for four or five years. That'll be soon enough."

"You sure you couldn't tell him in three or four?"

Thinking about her skirt almost caused Jake to miss that. "That'll be up to whoever is his boss then."

Isabelle bit her lip. "You're not planning to keep him?"

"I promised to see these boys settled, not take them in. I'm not planning anything past Santa Fe. If I can't sell my herd, I won't have a future."

She looked up, squinting against the sun. "What would you do?"

"My old army captain, George Randolph, has a ranch somewhere south of here. I could always ask him for a riding job."

"But that wouldn't be owning your own ranch."

"That takes money and cows. Right now I've got none of one and a doubtful hold over the other. Now I think it's about time I teach Bret to ride."

"Teach me first," Isabelle said.

Jake gave her a searching look. She was nervous, but she was determined.

"It's impossible until you get boots and suitable clothes."

"I can't do anything about the boots, but I altered my skirt." She showed him a new seam running down the front of her skirt. "I shortened and divided it," she said. "I was sewing when I should have been cleaning."

"You can ride in the wagon."

She shouldn't have done this. If she had any idea what seeing her ankles was doing to him, she'd head straight inside and change into something that dragged on the ground.

"I don't intend to be left here again because I can't ride. Now saddle me a horse. A tame one, if you please," she added in a completely different voice.

Jake saddled an older mare.

The boys came trotting back. "Are you going to ride?" Will asked Isabelle.

"If Jake will teach me."

"I can teach you," Will said. "I know all about riding.

"Me, too," Pete echoed.

"Both of you go to the other side of the corral," Jake said. "I don't want you scaring Isabelle's horse."

"They're going to watch every move I make and report it to the other boys, aren't they?" Isabelle asked.

"You can count on it, but you can foil them by doing everything perfectly." He walked over to her horse. "The first thing you have to learn is how to mount. You need either some kind of step or someone to give you a boost up."

"I'll take a step."

"I don't have one."

"How did Will and Pete get in the saddle?"

"I gave them a boost."

She studied him for a moment. A flush tinged her cheeks. "Then I suppose you'll have to lift me as well."

Jake looked into her eyes. They were almost green today. They seemed to change with her mood. He wondered what green signified. If his body were anything to go by, it was passion. He hadn't been so aware of his need for a woman in weeks.

Isabelle was aware of it, too. Her breathing had become deeper and more rapid. It caused her chest to rise and fall, drawing attention to her breasts, thrusting them forward. Despite a blouse that buttoned up to her neck, he had no trouble imagining the shape and feel of them.

Or the taste.

He started to tremble. His muscles ached with desire. He felt his body harden. His lips felt dry. Instinctively he licked them with his tongue to moisten them. It didn't help. It only made him think of the taste of her lips, the feel of his tongue on her breasts.

Her gaze locked with his. He was certain she knew what he was thinking. There was a trace of uneasiness in her eyes, possibly even fear, but she didn't turn away.

That made it all the more difficult. If he didn't do something, he was going to violate his honor and her trust.

"Turn around," he said, his voice thick with desire. "When I lift you up, toss your leg over."

"I remember," she said.

Jake lifted her into the saddle and forced himself to remove his hands from her waist immediately. It was that or risk taking her into his arms and kissing her. "Now take hold of the reins and do exactly as I tell you."

He led her around the corral, going over the same instructions he'd given the boys. Only this time his mind was more on the effect Isabelle had on him than what he was saying. He was dangerously close to being unable to control himself around her. Had he been looking at cows and sagebrush so long that the sight and feel of a real woman caused him to lose control?

Apparently. He wanted to kiss her, to get his hands all over her. He couldn't help but like women, but after his mother, he would never trust one.

"Let me try it by myself," Isabelle said.

He watched as she guided the mare in figure eights, practiced guiding her with knees, reins, and voice commands. His mother had done the same things. She'd pretended she wanted to learn to be a rancher's wife. She'd fooled them all. They were devastated when she left, when she told them she hated the ranch and everything about it, that she'd always hated it.

A part of Jake had died that day.

Will and Pete rode up on either side of Isabelle. Jake smiled when Isabelle's mare broke into a canter. She looked petrified, but with Pete and Will encouraging her, she had no choice but to keep riding.

She was so beautiful, so delicate. Just like his mother.

His mother had grown up in Mobile, Alabama, the pampered daughter of a well-to-do merchant. She didn't understand Texas. She didn't like it. One day she just left. Jake had never heard from her since.

The smile left Jake's lips. A knot of cold, hard anger formed in his chest.

"How did I do?" Isabelle asked.

"Fine," Jake said, his voice flat. "Now it's time Bret learned to ride."

Isabelle's smile disappeared to be replaced by a disappointed frown. "He doesn't like horses."

"He doesn't have to like them, just ride them."

Before Bret could back away from the corral, Jake picked him up.

"Put me down!" Bret shouted. He struggled, but Jake was far too strong for the boy.

"What are you going to do?" Isabelle demanded.

"He won't get on a horse by himself, so I'm going to put him on."

"No, you're not!" Bret fought even harder.

"I don't think you ought to force him," Isabelle said. "He needs time to overcome his fear of horses. If you just—"

"Will and Pete aren't half his size, and they aren't scared."

"Size has nothing to do with it," Isabelle insisted. "There could be any number of reasons."

"Then I'll get rid of them all at once. Pete, lower these bars for me," Jake shouted.

182

"You touch that bar, and I'll kill you the minute I get away from this bastard," Bret shouted.

Pete didn't even pause. He tumbled off this horse and had the bars down in a minute.

"You're dead, you little snake," Bret shouted.

"The horse won't bite you," Will jeered. "He just wants to trample you into the ground."

"Quiet!" Jake ordered. "Pete, hold my horse."

Bret fought harder than ever.

"When I put you in the saddle, slide your feet into the stirrups and take hold of the reins."

"I'm not riding your damned horse," Bret said.

"I'm putting you on his back. You either ride or fall off."

Jake caught a glimpse of Isabelle out of the corner of his eye. He knew he'd catch hell later, but he didn't know anything else to do.

The moment Jake put Bret in the saddle, he slid off the other side. Jake was on top of him at once.

"Son-of-a-bitch!" Bret yelled as Jake threw him into the saddle again.

"Save your curses for the horse. They're wasted on me."

Bret tried to slide off again, but Jake grabbed hold of his shirt. "Stay in the saddle, or I'll tie your feet underneath the horse's belly."

The boy glared at him with hate-filled eyes. "Let go of me, dammit."

"You going to stay in the saddle?"

"Yes, damn you to hell!"

Bret grabbed two handfuls of mane, but his feet groped blindly for the stirrups. Jake intended to walk the horse, but before he could take hold of the reins, Pete slapped the grey on the rear and shouted, "Giddyap!"

The horse started across the corral at a trot. Bret

bounced up and down like a rock falling downhill. Jake started after him at a run. He reached Bret just as he fell off.

Bret came to his feet cussing mad. "You little bastard!" he shouted as he headed for Pete.

Jake jerked Bret up, tucked him under his arm, and started after the horse, who had stopped about twenty yards away.

"You can beat hell out of Pete later," Jake said. "Right now you're going to ride this horse."

Bret was so furious, the moment he landed in the saddle he jammed his feet into the horse's sides. The reaction was immediate and dramatic. The horse bucked, and Bret went flying through the air.

Pete and Will howled with laughter.

Bret didn't get up immediately.

"Is he hurt?" Isabelle called out.

"He's fine," Jake said. "Just winded."

Bret got to his feet. Before he had time to collect his wits, Jake was at his side. "You're going to mount again. And this time, if you lose your temper and take it out on the horse, you know exactly what's going to happen to you."

Bret didn't offer any resistance.

"It's not hard riding a horse," Will said. "Even Yankees can do it."

Will giggled, but a look from Jake caused him to stop abruptly.

Jake gave Bret a boost into the saddle. Step by step, he taught the boy how to control and guide the horse. Fifteen minutes later, he released the bridle and let Bret ride on his own. As soon as he was certain Bret wasn't going to fall off, he walked over to where Isabelle still sat her horse.

"He ought to be riding as well as the rest of the boys in a couple of days."

"You're a bully," Isabelle said.

Jake had never bullied anybody in his life. During the war he'd had to force boys to do things against their will, but he'd never bullied them.

"This morning, when you were ready to protect us against those farmers, I decided I had misjudged you. I've seen how the boys work for you, how Pete and Will fight over any scrape of attention you'll give them."

"They're decent kids."

"Do you think Bret is going to grow up to be a decent kid after the way you've treated him?"

"I just showed him a horse is nothing to be afraid of."

"You embarrassed him in front of Will and Pete. You violated his right to refuse to ride."

"Violated his right to . . ." Jake didn't know what to say. He had never heard such nonsense.

"You'll be lucky if he doesn't hate you for the rest of his life."

"I'm not interested in whether he hates me," Jake exploded. "A Texan who can't ride can't respect himself."

"You don't know a thing about young boys," Isabelle said scornfully. "They can't be treated like so many wild horses. You can't rope them and ride them until they give in because they're too exhausted to do anything else. You've got to coax the best out of them."

"I don't have the time."

"Take it."

They both stopped. A farmer appeared on the trail going past the ranch. He never once looked at Jake or Isabelle as his mule walked past.

"I knew they'd leave somebody to watch us," Jake said.

"Why?" Isabelle asked, her anger momentarily forgotten.

Jake's gaze never left the farmer. "They don't trust me."

"Do you think they'll come back?"

"Yes."

"When?"

"They'll probably put a watch on the ranch."

"What are you going to do?"

"We're going to Newcombe's Crossing to buy supplies. Then there won't be anything for them to watch."

They were watching the farmer ride across the crest of the ridge when Jake realized Will was speaking to him.

"What is it?" he asked, turning.

"It's Bret."

"What about him?" Jake looked up. Bret was nowhere in sight. "He's run off. He said he hated everybody here, especially you. He said he's going back to Boston."

Chapter Thirteen

"Where did he go?" Isabelle asked.

"Over there." Will pointed toward the trees along the creek that led into a canyon and then to the river a couple of miles away.

"We have to go after him," Isabelle said.

"He'll come back when he's ready," Jake said. "He's embarrassed. The last thing he wants is to have somebody following him, especially a woman."

"What do you mean *especially a woman?*"

"Bret may be a frightened boy, but he's enough of a man to resist the intervention of a woman just now."

"I don't believe you."

"Ask Will."

"Would you want me to go after you?" she asked.

Pete rode up just as Isabelle framed the question. "I wouldn't," he said. "Everybody'd call me a sissy."

"Me neither," Will said, but Jake could tell Will wasn't as positive as Pete.

"I hope a panther gets him," Pete said. "I hate him."

"When he does return," Jake said, ignoring Pete's comment, "I want everybody to act like nothing happened. I don't want him to think he can force people to give him what he wants by doing something like this."

"I can't accept that," Isabelle said.

"Stop trying to undermine my discipline," Jake said. "What those farmers did is mild compared to what can happen before we reach New Mexico. I've got to be certain the boys know what to do and that they'll do it without question."

"I don't believe in treating boys like that."

"It's not a matter of what you or I believe. It's a matter of what has to be done. It's just like getting boys ready for battle. They have to learn to follow orders, or they die."

Jake could see Isabelle struggle with herself, and he felt sorry for her. She was being forced to accept one thing after another that went against her beliefs. He hated doing that to her, but if he was going to take these boys with him, they had to be ready. Otherwise they'd be better off in an orphanage.

Already he'd noticed a change in most of them. They weren't ready to trust him, but they were giving him a chance. Some of them knew he needed them as much as they needed him. Pete and Will were too young to care. They just wanted to feel safe.

"I'll wait until after supper," Isabelle announced. "If he's not back by then, I'm going after him."

Bret didn't show up for supper. Jake had gone off to meet the boys at the cow camp and had come back with beef for dinner. He said a yearling had broken its leg, but Isabelle suspected he'd killed it so the boys would have plenty to eat.

"Good riddance," Sean said at the news that Bret had run away. "He didn't like us and we didn't like him."

"You can't mean that," Isabelle protested. "I know he wasn't always nice, but he thinks you don't like him."

"I don't."

"He doesn't want us to like him," Chet said.

"He also feels out of place," Isabelle continued.

"Who doesn't?" Sean asked.

"But he's a Bostonian in Texas."

"Don't expect me to feel sorry for him," Sean said. "I wouldn't be in Texas if the people in Boston hadn't treated my parents so bad they starved to death."

Isabelle could see she wasn't going to get any sympathy from the boys. That didn't surprise her. It did surprise her that they didn't seem to care what happened to Bret. He was a fellow human being. How could they not care?

She stared out at the darkness under the trees and shivers ran up and down her spine. She was terrified at the thought of going into that canyon after dark. She didn't understand how Bret could remain out there. There was no telling what kind of animals lurked in the shadows. If he didn't return soon, she would have to go after him.

He could be miles away by now. She hoped not. He was only twelve.

They were eating dinner in the kitchen tonight. Jake hadn't wanted to take a chance on one of the boys being seen. They would all sleep in the house or the bunkhouse. Even the extra horses had been picketed out of sight. Isabelle was touched by the effort he was making to be certain no one found the

Leigh Greenwood

runaways. That was all the more reason she couldn't understand why he wasn't worried about Bret.

"Here comes Jake," Will said. The boy had been standing by the newly cleaned window all during supper waiting for Jake to get back with Zeke and Buck. Eyes bright with excitement, Will ran out to meet them.

Something caused Isabelle to glance at Matt. She saw hot anger in his eyes. She didn't understand. Matt had never disliked anybody.

"Did you see Bret?" Isabelle asked Jake when he came in. She started serving plates and setting them down on the table. Fortunately, it was a trestle table. There was only one chair in the whole house.

"It's not likely he'd come up to me."

Buck and Zeke sat down and started eating.

"When you sit down at a table, you wait until everyone is served," Isabelle said. "Since Mr. Maxwell has risked his property and well-being for your safety, I think that's very little to ask."

The boys looked up, stunned, but they stopped eating.

"Jake. I told you to call me Jake, and they might as well start eating now."

"You may make the decisions about cows and riding, but I'll make them about manners. And it's exceedingly rude to start eating before everyone at the table is served."

"I'm not at the table."

"Then get there."

Will giggled.

"You'd better do as she says," Sean warned. "She's on the warpath tonight."

Casting her an exasperated look, Jake sat down, and Isabelle handed him a plate. "Now you may begin."

None of the boys moved. They continued watching Jake.

"You don't have to wait until he starts eating, just until he's served."

Isabelle handed Jake his coffee and retreated to a position by the window. She couldn't stop worrying about Bret. He'd never spent the night outside before. She was certain he was hiding somewhere close to the ranch.

"Why don't you leave him some food?" Jake said.

"What?" She hadn't been listening.

"Put a plate out for him. Then you won't have to worry about him."

"I'm worried about more than his stomach."

"I doubt he is."

"Where shall I put it?"

"On the porch."

"Do you think he'll come up to the cabin?"

"If not, he won't find it."

Isabelle struggled to control her temper. "Wouldn't it be better to take it to the woods?"

"You don't know where he is. Just put it on the porch and call him. If he's around, he'll hear you. If not, it doesn't matter."

"It does matter," Isabelle snapped, "more than your cows, your ranch, or those horrible farmers."

She could feel tears start to fill her eyes. She whipped around, grabbed a plate, and started filling it.

"I don't see how all of you can sit calmly eating your dinner like nothing's wrong."

"He can come in whenever he wants," Chet said. "The door's not locked."

Isabelle gave up. She'd thought it was just Jake, but it was all of them. She took the plate and hurried outside before anger caused her to say something she'd regret. She walked a little way into the yard.

"Bret, I know you're out there," she called. She felt stupid talking to trees but she didn't know what else to do. "I wish you'd come back. Jake wasn't trying to hurt you. He just wanted you to learn to ride. You've got to, you know. You can't always drive the wagon. That would mean you'd always be with me, and you wouldn't like that.

"I've left your supper on the porch. I'd bring it to you, but I don't know where you are. I'll put your bedroll on the porch, too. You'll get cold without it."

She paused. She didn't know what she expected to hear. Maybe she was hoping she could coax him out of the woods. The quiet remained undisturbed.

"Don't be alarmed if you don't see anybody sleeping in the yard. Jake thinks we ought to sleep inside. We'll be leaving soon for Newcombe's Crossing to get supplies. You'll have to come back before then. I can't leave without knowing you're safe."

She walked over to the wagon, dug through the bedrolls until she found Bret's, came back, and set it down on the porch.

"Have you always cared for other people more than yourself?"

Jake's voice coming out of the inky shadows of the breezeway startled her.

"He's upset, cold, and hungry."

"He can do something about it."

"His pride and anger are in the way."

"Pride can be very expensive. Maybe it's better he learn that now when it won't cost him so much."

She looked up. Jake had come out of the dense shadows, but the moonlight turned his face into an eerie pattern of light and darkness. It looked like a mask, cold and lacking emotion.

"I don't understand you. Sometimes I think you're

the kindest, most patient man I've ever met. Moments later you're hard and cruel. How can you be both at the same time?"

He came down the steps toward her. The moonlight flooded his face, turning it into a pale mask. He looked as unreal as the situation in which she found herself, out in the middle of nowhere with ten boys and a strange man, pursued by vicious farmers, preparing to drive she didn't know how many cows across an Indian-infested wilderness to the even more foreign wilderness of New Mexico.

Her life seemed like a phantasmic dream.

She alternated between disliking Jake and an unexplainable yearning to be close to him, between a total lack of understanding of him and a kind of surprise that a man such as he could be interested in her.

"I don't try to be anything," Jake said. "I just do what I have to do. I mean to teach these boys the same thing."

"Why? You didn't want them."

"Let's just say I was shamed by your example."

Isabelle laughed. "If you expect me to believe that, you really do have a poor opinion of my intelligence."

He came closer. Much closer. "You underestimate yourself."

Suddenly the night wasn't the least bit cold. Her pulses pounded in her veins. Her limbs weren't nearly steady enough. "No, I don't. Single women without family can't afford to do that."

"You've got a family, a very large one, if you ask me."

She wondered if he considered himself part of that family. She refused to think about it, even consider it. It conjured up too many impossibilities. "These boys depend on me because they have no other choice. Once they go out on their own, they'll forget me."

"It all depends."

"On what?"

"I'm not sure. I don't understand you."

He actually sounded interested. Isabelle wondered whether he was interested because he found her at least a tiny bit attractive or because he'd never met anyone like her and hoped to avoid repeating the experience.

"It's not hard. I'm no different from anybody else."

He came so close they were almost touching.

"You're unlike any woman I've ever met."

"That shouldn't be . . . surprising. You . . . couldn't have met many . . . out here." He was so close, she had trouble thinking. He was so close, she had to crane her neck to look into his eyes.

"Enough."

Then, to her shock and near terror, he took her by the shoulders and kissed her. It wasn't a passionate kiss, not that she was any judge. It seemed more a questioning kiss, one that didn't quite believe in itself.

That was exactly how she felt. She couldn't be standing here letting herself be kissed by a man she had reviled only minutes earlier. Even a stupid woman knew you didn't stand around kissing a man you didn't like.

Yet she didn't have the power to move. Even worse, she found herself responding to him. She liked being kissed, and she didn't seem to mind one bit that Jake Maxwell was the one doing the kissing.

She must like him. She had to. There could be no other explanation.

"Where am I going to sleep?" Will asked.

Isabelle jumped back.

"You're going to sleep in the house with Miss Davenport," Jake answered, without taking his eyes off Isabelle.

"Where's Matt going to sleep?"

"In the bunkhouse."

Isabelle turned and climbed the steps. "I think you'd better come inside and explain the sleeping arrangements. It'll be easier to do it all at once."

Isabelle didn't know how she could be responding so sensibly. Her entire existence had been turned upside down. She liked Jake Maxwell, heaven preserve her. Even worse, she had liked standing in the yard being kissed by him, abandoned female that she was. On top of that, she had a strong desire to do it all over again.

Aunt Deirdre must be turning over in her grave.

"Do you mind sharing the bedroom with Pete and Will?" Jake asked Isabelle.

"No."

"Buck and Zeke can sleep in the kitchen. I don't want them outside."

"What about the others?"

"They'll sleep in the bunkhouse."

There were six beds in the bunkhouse. Enough for the boys and Jake. She felt a twinge of disappointment, though she wouldn't have shared a room with him, not even with Will and Pete as chaperons.

"I'll sleep in the breezeway," Jake said.

Isabelle felt a coil of tension inside her ease. Jake would be near, but not too near. He showed concern for her, but not too much. There was a twinkle in his eyes, but no grin. She couldn't have endured a grin. That would have meant he'd won something, that she'd lost something.

A twinkle meant they had shared something. Isabelle liked that.

*   *   *

Jake had been awake even before Bret sneaked out of the woods to get the food Isabelle had left for him. He hadn't intended to speak to the boy, but kissing Isabelle had changed his mind.

It changed a lot of things.

Jake wasn't given to a lot of thinking. He mostly accepted things as they were, but not thinking was how he had come to kiss Isabelle. It came over him all of a sudden that it would feel mighty good to kiss her. So he'd just done it.

He'd been right. He did feel good—so damned good, he couldn't sleep—but it set him to worrying. He didn't want to like this woman; he didn't trust females. Yet he had kissed Isabelle, and he wanted to kiss her again. It didn't take a lot of thinking to figure out there was something wrong here. He needed to go back to the beginning, to find out when things started to go wrong.

Everything had been fine until the boys descended on him. First it was Matt and his empty eyes. Then Will and his hero worship. After that came Buck and his scars, Zeke and his chain. One after another, they battered down his defenses until he took them in, all of them, God bless his foolish soul.

Then he had compounded his error by insisting that Isabelle come along on the trail. She told him she couldn't cook, that she didn't approve of him or much of anything he did, and he'd still insisted.

He'd made mistakes before, but he'd never acted like a complete fool.

Maybe he'd let down his guard because she didn't fit any of his preconceived notions. She was pretty and feminine and fragile, yet she had courage and determination. She squared up to him at the slightest provocation. She never seemed to tire, and she never shirked her work. And all the while she managed to look more like a lady than any woman he'd ever seen.

That was why he had kissed her.

No, he'd kissed her because there was something very feminine and provocative about her. She might be a lady, but she was passionate about everything she did. It was impossible to be around her and not have some of her intensity rub off.

And that was why he had kissed her.

No, that wasn't exactly it either. Hell, he didn't know why he'd kissed her. It just happened. He didn't know why he was getting so upset. He'd kissed females before, but never quite like this. Before he'd done it because it was expected of him or because his body wanted it. He'd kissed Isabelle because *he* wanted to.

That might not be so bad, but it didn't stop there. He wanted still more from her, and that was dangerous.

He'd been living by himself too long. He must be getting batty. Isabelle would never love a man she disapproved of as strongly as she disapproved of him. Besides, Jake reminded himself, he didn't want to get tangled up with any feeling remotely close to love. It got in the way of a man's thinking. It made him do crazy things like knock himself out trying to please some woman.

Everybody knew women weren't sensible creatures. They were always wanting what they shouldn't have. They couldn't help it. It was just their nature, the way it was Isabelle's nature to insist upon table manners.

Jake's increasingly frustrated thoughts were interrupted by the sound of someone very inexpertly trying to sneak up to the porch. Bret was bringing the plate back. He set it down and picked up the bedroll.

Jake spoke out of the dark. "If you're going to use that, you might as well come back."

Bret froze, his body poised for flight.

"You can't expect Isabelle to keep setting food out for you. We leave for New Mexico in less then a week. What will you do then?"

There was no answer, but Bret didn't run away.

"You've upset Isabelle. She hasn't been able to think about anybody but you all afternoon. I told her you weren't worth it, but she thinks you're just as important as anybody else."

Bret still didn't say anything. Jake was a little irritated, but he didn't mind talking. He couldn't sleep anyway.

"If you care anything about her, you'll haul your butt over to the bunkhouse. If you're only interested in yourself, I wish you'd hurry up and get yourself killed. Then she can stop worrying about you."

"Nobody cares about me," Bret said, his voice shaking with anger.

Jake sighed with relief. Bret was talking. Half the battle was won.

"I don't know what's in your craw. You've been as angry as a boil about to bust ever since you got here. Maybe you've got a right to be angry. I don't know. I do know you're not going to achieve anything by running away."

"You haven't said anything about me learning to ride so I can help you get your damned cows to New Mexico."

Jake laughed silently. Now they were getting down to it.

"You're a lot like me, Bret, too stubborn for your own good. I won't beg you to help me. I want you to ride because I need you on horseback, but I can do without you. I may not do as well, but I'll get by."

"That's what everybody says. Nobody cares."

"Show me you're worth caring about," Jake challenged. "All I see is a boy who does as little as he can, expects the world to take care of him, and hates them for doing it. You're always pushing the boys away, then thinking they're slighting you. You won't have to think it if you can't ride. They'll make it plain enough."

"It won't make any difference. Nobody gives a damn about me."

Bret was no different from anybody else. He just wanted to be important to somebody.

"Yeah, they do. I give a damn."

Chapter Fourteen

Isabelle was so surprised to see Bret emerge from the bunkhouse the next morning that she gave him a big hug. She hadn't realized he was taller than she was. Neither was he as thin as she had supposed. He was on the verge of turning into a man.

She felt him stiffen, and she quickly released him. Jake was right. He might be young and scared, but he didn't want to be seen to need a woman. Isabelle decided men were strange and contrary creatures to pretend not to want the very things everybody knew they must have.

Everything would have so much simpler if they were like Will. He liked being hugged. The rest of them were prickly with masculine pride. Just like Jake.

"I'm glad you came back. I was worried about you."

Bret shrugged.

"Jake was only trying to help. He says you have to know how to ride. He says—"

"We already talked. Do you need wood?"

"Quite a lot," she said.

She was hurt that Bret seemed determined not to let her care about him. She watched him head off into the trees. He had to be terribly lonely believing no one in the world liked him. She knew. She'd felt the same way.

The rest of morning didn't go as she had expected, either.

"We're going to town for supplies," Jake announced as soon as they were all gathered in the kitchen. The boys stopped eating, their gazes focused on him. They showed their immaturity and fear in the way they were made uneasy by this first change in their routine.

"Will, Pete, and Bret are going with us."

"Why me?" Bret asked.

Isabelle wished he weren't so quick to take offense, but that was past wishing for.

"The farmers think you three boys are fresh from the city. They wouldn't expect me to leave one of you behind. It'll also give them the opportunity to snoop around."

"What are the rest of us going to do?" Sean asked.

"Gather and brand cows. The more we have, the more we can sell. Buck will go with you, but you've got to make absolutely certain he stays out of sight."

"What about Zeke?"

"He's going with us. I've got to find someone to take that chain off his leg."

The countryside didn't look so threatening and unfriendly now. Isabelle noticed the granite hills were nearly covered by live oak, blue-flowering mescal

201

bean, and yellow mesquite. Generous spring rains had prolonged the flowering season. Bluebonnets, Indian paint brush, phlox, and poppies dotted the hillsides and the more fertile canyon floors with their brilliant blues, reds, and yellows. Even the unfriendly-looking yucca and prickly pear cactus failed to detract from her growing sense of the beauty of the land.

She missed Chet and Luke. She had never driven a wagon. She was exhausted. The muscles in her back were so stiff, she could hardly move. Her flimsy gloves offered little protection for her hands. They were red and swollen, filled with stinging needles of pain. Her wide-brimmed hat provided only partial protection from the sun, which seemed to grow stronger and hotter with each passing hour. She could feel the heat of unsightly and painful sunburn on the back of her neck.

She'd been longing to stop ever since noon, but Jake insisted they press on, and she agreed. She didn't want to leave the boys on their own any longer than necessary. They weren't used to taking care of themselves.

Jake was teaching the boys to ride. All day long he'd ridden with them, giving them instructions, correcting first one flaw and then another. He was not an easy taskmaster, but Will bloomed under his attention. Pete found satisfaction in his accomplishments rather than Jake's personal attention. Bret accepted everything with a scowl.

Zeke lay in the bottom of the wagon under a blanket, his chain carefully wrapped so it wouldn't clink and rattle. Isabelle had tried to talk to him, but she gave up when he answered only occasionally and then in monosyllables. It was obvious Zeke didn't like her. Maybe he associated her with someone who had owned him, possibly mistreated him.

"You boys tie your horses to the back of the wagon." Jake's command was sudden and peremptory.

"Why?" Will asked. "I want to ride all the way to—"

"Do as I tell you. Right now!"

Isabelle glanced over at Jake. He was in the habit of handing out orders, but not in quite such a harsh manner.

"You don't have to snap at the boys," Isabelle said. "I'm sure if you explain—"

"Two farmers are behind us. I caught a glimpse of them when they topped a rise. I don't think they saw us, but I can't be sure. These boys have got to be in the wagon with their legs over Zeke before they come into view. If they see them scrambling, they'll be suspicious."

Jake didn't need to say anything else. Even Bret moved with surprising speed.

"I'm going to stay between them and the wagon," Jake said to Isabelle. "No matter what happens, keep moving."

Jake had hardly secured the horses to the wagon and settled the boys into place when the farmers emerged from a low spot in the rolling hills behind them. They were riding horses and moving quickly. Since Isabelle kept the mules at a walk, it didn't take them long to catch up.

"Did you find your boy?" Jake asked when the farmers came abreast.

"No," Rupert Reison replied. "We're looking for him along the river."

"He's probably halfway to the coast by now. If he signs on to a ship in Galveston, you'll never find him."

"Why do you have so many horses?" Rupert asked.

"I've been teaching the boys to ride," Jake said. "No point in spending a whole day doing nothing."

"Why aren't they riding now?"

"Their mother thought it was time they had a rest."

Isabelle couldn't understand why Rupert was still suspicious. She feared there would be trouble if he rode with them for very long.

"We're going to Newcombe's Crossing, too," Isabelle said in the same slow drawl she'd used the day before. "Jake is finally going to get something for me to cook before the boys and I absolutely shrivel up from starvation. You'd think with all those cows there'd be plenty of beef, but no, Jake won't let me touch one. He says—"

"Women can't understand why you can't eat a cow and sell it at the same time," Jake said.

Neither farmer's expression changed.

"I can't see how it's better to sell a cow than starve," Isabelle said. "But men never understand things like that. I'm sure your wives would agree." She rolled her eyes in what she hoped was a passable imitation of a foolish woman. "I can't *wait* to get to talk to a female. I'm so sick of men and boys, I could scream and scream and scream! I tried to get Jake to take me over to your place yesterday afternoon, but he said it was more important to teach the boys how to ride."

"You know what women are like," Jake said.

"I was ready to go on my own," Isabelle continued, "but he said I'd get lost. I told him I found my way from Georgia. I'm so glad you caught up with us. Tell me exactly how to get to your house. I mean to come for a visit the minute I get back."

"We can't tarry," Rupert's friend said.

"I believe women should see as much of each other

as possible," Isabelle called after them as they rode off.

Breathing a sigh of relief, she turned to find Jake staring at her in amazement.

"There's not a man in Texas who wouldn't head in the opposite direction after five minutes of your chatter," he said.

"That's what I was hoping," Isabelle said, of two minds as to whether Jake meant that as a compliment.

"Rupert's convinced something's wrong."

"Do you think he'll come back?"

"No, but I don't think he'll give up either."

"Why?"

"I don't know," Jake said pensively. "I'm convinced there's some other reason he's so determined to find Zeke."

"Can we get back on our horses?" Pete asked.

"Not for a while yet," Jake said. "I want to make certain they're out of sight."

"Follow that track," Jake said.

It was late afternoon. The sun was just slipping beyond the horizon. Isabelle was still hoping they could reach town before dark. The track Jake pointed to was a turnoff.

"Where does that go?" she asked.

"To a man I hope will take Zeke's chain off."

Isabelle didn't hesitate. Zeke was out from under the blanket now. She would have felt a lot better if he'd talk, but his black eyes glared at her with unrelenting animosity. Or maybe he was just feeling miserable from spending the entire day in hiding.

It was dark by the time they pulled up in front of a small log cabin built into a depression in a canyon wall. Twisted post oaks and cedar dotted the rocky slopes. Clumps of red-and-yellow gaillardias and purple prairie verbena brightened the fields around the cabin. Isabelle could see an open shed a short distance away. A big man came from somewhere out of a thicket.

"What do you want?" he asked. He didn't look friendly. Isabelle wondered if Jake had been wise to stop.

"I've got some work for you," Jake said, dismounting.

"I'll need payment first."

"I brought you a horse."

The man walked over to the extra horse. He studied his conformation, ran his hands over his legs, lifted each foot, checked his teeth. "What do you want?"

Jake motioned for Zeke to step down from the wagon. "I want you to cut the chain off this boy."

The blacksmith looked at Zeke, then at the chain. "It's padlocked."

"I don't have the key," Jake explained.

"Lost it?"

"Never had it."

"Not your chain?"

"Nope."

The blacksmith looked back at the horse for a moment, then turned back to Zeke. "It'll take a while."

"You'll have tonight and tomorrow. I'll be back the day after."

"That horse is worth a whole lot more than cutting off some lock."

"You never saw us. We never came here. You don't even know who we are."

"He wanted?"

"Not by the law."

"Where're you spending the night?"

"Here, if you'll let us."

"You better go back to the main trail. I can't pretend I never saw you if I'm caught with you camped in my front yard."

They reached Newcombe's Crossing before sunup the next morning.

"Every cent of that money has to be spent on food," Isabelle was saying. "I can't in good conscience give it to you for guns and ammunition."

"A wagon load of food won't do us a bit of good if we've got a hundred Indians after us and nothing to drive them off. We might as well stay here and save them the trouble of stealing our herd and lifting our scalps."

"I'm sure the army wouldn't let them do such a thing."

"They probably wouldn't if they had enough soldiers, or if they knew where the Indians would strike, or if they could be there in time. We can't depend upon anybody but ourselves."

"The boys don't know how to use guns," Isabelle argued.

"I'll teach them."

As much as she hated the idea, Isabelle gave in. "I need a few things, too."

Jake pulled up in front of a carpenter's shop instead of the mercantile.

"What are we doing here?" Isabelle asked.

"I'm going to see if I can get him to make me a chuck wagon."

"What's that?"

"You'll see when it's done." Even though it was barely dawn, the door of the shop was open. Jake stepped inside. "Are you the man who built Charlie Goodnight's chuck wagon?" he asked.

"Yeah," the man replied.

"Can you build me one by tonight?"

"No."

"Damn. I got to leave tomorrow at daybreak. What can you do?"

"I can build you a chuck box," the man said.

"I guess that's the most important part. Where do you want the wagon?"

"Inside. You can graze your team out back."

The boys helped him unharness the team and roll the wagon inside the shop. He picketed the mules.

"We'll have to walk," he said.

"What's a chuck box?" Isabelle asked.

"You'll see."

"I imagine I will, but I would appreciate your telling me." She was tired of him treating her as if she were even more ignorant and helpless than the boys.

"It's like a cupboard," he said. "It's built into the back of the wagon. Charlie Goodnight came by my place less than a month ago on his way to New Mexico."

"So that's who gave you the idea of going west instead of east."

"If Charlie can, I can, too."

Isabelle opened her mouth to argue, then changed her mind. It was time she started picking her battles.

Very few people were up and about when they reached the main street of town. It wasn't much of a town, just a collection of rough buildings clustered along a single dirt street at the best ford on the Pedernales River. Despite the early hour, the general store was open.

"Can I go in?" Will asked.

"Sure," Jake said. "Everybody can go in, but remember our story. You're family."

Inside, Isabelle headed down an aisle away from

208

Jake. "Aren't you going to help me?" Jake asked. "You're doing the cooking."

"It doesn't matter. I can ruin anything equally well."

Jake had to admit that was true. Isabelle disappeared and returned a moment later with a pair of boots. "You'll need a hat, too," Jake said.

"I already have one."

"A real hat, one that'll stay on your head during a high wind or when you're riding at a gallop."

"I don't expect to ride a horse at that rate of speed."

"You will." Jake looked at several hats until he found one of brown leather with a flat top, a broad brim, and a string to draw up under her chin.

"This'll keep the sun out of your eyes and the hail off your head."

"But my hat—"

"Your hat will blow away in the first high wind. If a horse or a cow steps on it, they'll tear it apart. The only way you'll tear this hat up is with a sharp knife."

Isabelle studied the hat. "I don't promise to wear it, but I'll consider it. Now, unless you need me for anything else, I've got something to do."

"What?"

"That's my concern." And unless it turned out well, he'd never find out what it was.

"Where are you going? Where will I find you?"

"I'll find you."

"When?"

"When are we leaving?"

Jake opened his mouth to answer, but a stream of profanity come out instead. He stomped off toward the front of the store and looked outside. "It's Rupert and his friend."

Isabelle went to the window. "I thought they'd be gone by now."

"So did I. Do you know those men?" he asked the clerk.

The man came to the window. "Sure. They buy supplies here. That's what I thought they were doing here when I saw them yesterday, but they came in asking about two boys. I told them we hadn't seen anybody. I can't see why they want a couple of boys so bad."

"They told us one."

The clerk thought a moment. "No, I remember. He definitely said two."

Jake watched them ride out of sight, a deep frown creasing his forehead. As soon as they were out of sight, Isabelle started to leave. "Meet us at the hotel for dinner," Jake said.

"Okay." She opened her bag and handed him a small, heavy package. "Save something for emergencies."

Jake spent most of the morning ordering supplies. While he did that, the boys looked through every piece of merchandise in the store, trying on hats and boots, digging through piles of clothes, drooling over candies safely resting behind glass covers. They enjoyed looking at the guns, picking out their favorites, pretending they were having a gun battle. Even Bret managed to look less like a sour persimmon than usual.

By the time Jake was done in the mercantile, it was time to eat, so he took them to a restaurant and filled them up with beef and potatoes. No pork. They'd get enough of that on the trail.

He faced a whole afternoon with three boys at his heels. He gave them each fifty cents, warned them not to spend it all in one place, and gave them strict orders to meet him at the hotel by six o'clock.

Then he took himself off to the nearest saloon.

Isabelle wiped her forehead. The heat in the kitchen was terrible. "How can you stand it?" she asked.

"Better than you'll stand cooking outside with the wind blowing dirt in your food and the rain making it nearly impossible to get a decent fire going."

The minute she left Jake, Isabelle had headed straight for the hotel. "I want you to teach me everything you know about cooking," she'd announced when she'd been introduced to the cook. "And you have to do it all today."

The hotel was a two-story wood-frame building with a kitchen and dining room down and bedrooms up. The kitchen was small and furnished with little more than a table and a big iron stove.

The cook looked as though she thought Isabelle might be suffering from too much sun, but an offer of five dollars removed all hesitation. The woman launched into the task with vigor.

"I don't really have to know how to cook anything but beans and bacon," Isabelle said, "but I want to cook them really well."

"We'll see about teaching you a few more things," the cook said. "You won't be on that trail forever."

So Isabelle had learned how to prepare and cook three different kinds of beans, how to cook pork and beef at least half a dozen ways, what to do if one of the boys managed to catch a prairie chicken, how to cook buffalo or antelope, and how to make doughnuts.

"Men go crazy over them," the cook said. "A good batch of doughnuts will make them forget months of bad food."

Isabelle wrote down everything she could. "I don't intend to cook bad food any more."

"Just the same, you learn to make doughnuts. Nobody'll ever call you anything but a right smart cook after that."

Isabelle wasn't so sure. This woman didn't know Jake Maxwell. He wasn't inclined to pass out compliments. She doubted he'd do more than grunt regardless of the meal she served.

Well, it didn't matter. She was learning to cook for herself and the boys. If he didn't like it, he could cook for himself.

Jake was feeling calmer. He'd almost forgotten he was saddled with three boys and one very temperamental female. He'd limited himself to two whiskeys, but he'd spent the afternoon in a saloon inquiring about the trail west. He'd learned that grass was plentiful this year. Spring rains had been heavy and were continuing. The run from the head of the Concho to the Pecos Rivers wouldn't be so bad if the cows were well fed.

He'd also been told the Indians were quiet. The army hadn't done much, but their presence had served to make the Indians more cautious. Jake was feeling at peace with himself when he stepped out of the saloon. That lasted until Pete shouted at him from across the street. Pete himself arrived hard on the heels of the echo.

"The farmers have got Will," he shouted.

Chapter Fifteen

Jake followed Pete at a run. He rounded the corner of a building to see the two farmers standing over Will and Bret. They were under a tree by the bank of the river that ran along the edge of town. Jake slowed to a walk. Will wasn't saying a word. Bret was doing all the talking.

"Everybody says I talk peculiar," Bret was saying. "I growed up in Boston. Pa didn't like it up north, so he went to Georgia. That weren't no good either. Pa weren't too fond of work no matter what state he was in. Chopped himself in the foot with an ax. The dang foot near rotted off, but Pa died afore it could."

"Where's your ma?"

"Probably jawing with some female. Ma said she was sick of us boys. Said she wanted to talk with another woman before she was stuck with us for half a year on that godforsaken ranch. Ma don't like Texas. She wants to go back to Savannah. I don't.

Ma's relations say us boys act like heathens. Uncle Jake don't care how we act."

"Sure I care," Jake said, hoping his voice betrayed none of the anger boiling inside him. "But you're too far gone to save."

As though released from a still photograph, Will ran straight for Jake and grabbed hold of his hand. Jake gave his shoulder a reassuring squeeze. "Why didn't you tell me you were chasing two boys?" he asked the farmers.

An uneasy look passed between the two men. "The other left a while back," Rupert said. "Nobody's seen him around here."

"Then I'd forget about him," Jake said. "If he went toward San Antonio, you'll never catch him. If he went west or north, the Indian's will get him."

"I don't think he went that way, either," Rupert said.

Jake knew Rupert was holding stubbornly to the idea that Jake was somehow responsible for Zeke's disappearance, maybe even Buck's as well. But at this point, even Rupert must have been finding it hard to believe.

"Come on, boys," Jake said. "Let's go find your mother. If I let her stay here too long, she might refuse to go back at all. I hope you fellas don't mind her visiting over your way. She gets powerful lonesome for company."

"Our women don't have time for visiting," Rupert replied.

"Isabelle is the workingest woman you ever met," Jake said. "She'll have their chores finished up in no time."

"They don't much take to strangers," Rupert said.

"Give her five minutes, and she won't be a stranger to anybody."

Jake waited, his arms resting on Pete's and Will's shoulders. Bret continued to watch the farmers with all the apparent curiosity of a twelve-year-old with no guilty secrets on his conscience.

"We have to get back home," Rupert said. "We can't leave our fields untended any longer."

"If I were you, I wouldn't give another thought to losing those boys," Jake said. "I'd just order me up a couple more."

Rupert leveled a particularly malevolent look at Jake before turning and walking away. His companion followed.

"I hate him," Will whispered.

"I don't like him very much, either," Jake answered. "What did he ask you?"

"He asked me about my daddy."

"What did you tell him?"

"I told him I didn't remember much, and I don't."

"Did he ask you anything else?"

"Yeah, but Bret wouldn't let me answer."

Will wasn't pleased about Bret butting in, but Jake was. Will was too young and innocent to understand what was going on. Bret understood very well. Jake smiled at Bret. "You sounded just like Isabelle, talking a mile a minute and not telling them a thing."

Bret shrugged off the compliment. "I was thinking of what they'd have done to me if we hadn't found Buck," Bret said.

"But I don't want a bath," Will objected. "I had one before we left Austin."

"That was three weeks ago."

"I wash my face in the creek every morning."

"That's not the same as a bath."

"It feels like it."

They were back at the hotel. The bathroom was

small and narrow. A large tub filled with steaming water took up most of the space. It aggravated Isabelle that she should have to appeal to Jake for support. She wondered if he would take a bath as well. He had surprised her by cutting his hair. It made him look twice as handsome. She wasn't sure she could stand much more.

"We'll all get a bath," Jake said to the boys.

"Then we'll have a nice dinner and sleep in a real bed," Isabelle said. "It'll be a long time before you have either again."

Isabelle and the boys were already seated in the hotel dining room when Jake walked in. She had been right to be apprehensive. Washed, shaved, and wearing clean clothes, Jake was breathtakingly handsome. Even the boys noticed it.

"You don't look so hairy," Will said once Jake joined them at a large rectangular table. The room contained twelve rough-hewn tables, some trestle, some provided with chairs. Isabelle had chosen the only one covered with a table cloth.

"He shaved," Pete informed him. "I'm never going to shave when I grow up."

"Girls like men to shave," Bret said. "They don't like woolly bears."

"I don't care what girls like," Pete said. "I don't even like 'em."

"Me, neither," Will agreed.

"Isabelle is a girl," Jake pointed out.

"No, she's not," Will said. "She's a lady."

"Thank you," Isabelle said, feeling herself blush, "but I think we should postpone this discussion for about six or seven years."

"All girls want to do is get married," Bret said, ignoring Isabelle. "I'm never going to get married."

Jake

Isabelle listened in amusement while the four males discussed women and the virtues of marriage as if she weren't there. Maybe, like Will, they didn't figure either subject applied to her. She certainly wasn't interested in marriage. After her experiences with men, she preferred to depend on herself.

But even as that thought crossed her mind, a whole barrage of contradictory thoughts shoved it aside. It was impossible to sit this close to Jake and not feel the magnetic pull of his presence. He was like a physical force. She could feel the tension between them. She wondered if he felt it, and if so, what he thought about it.

She smiled as she watched him. The boys were saying one absurd thing after another. No matter how sharp-tongued Bret was, Jake managed to keep the conversation light. They acted like puppies crawling all over the lead dog.

Jake was allowing it, maybe even liking it. He was an entirely different Jake from the man she had come to know on the ranch. He smiled. Oh, did he smile. Her stomach did a wild somersault every time. He had a tiny cleft in his chin, and his Adam's apple moved up and down as he talked. She hadn't noticed it until he shaved. She could see the faint mask of his beard. Her fiancé's face had been perfectly smooth. She preferred Jake's slightly rough appearance. It didn't promise anything he wasn't.

She'd never known he could be charming, but he so entranced the waitress that Isabelle thought she was going to offer to cut his steak for him. His mood was so contagious, people smiled when they glanced over at their table. Isabelle imagined all the others thought they were a family enjoying their outing on the town.

A cold, empty feeling turned her smile stiff. She

had no family. She was alone. She was just here long enough to help these boys. She would go back to Austin when it was over. That's exactly what she'd expected when she started on this trip, but everything had changed.

She had come to like the boys. She wanted to be as important to them as they were to her. She couldn't imagine not seeing them again, not knowing how they would grow up, not seeing their wives, their children. They were part of her life. They were her family.

And Jake was the glue that held them together.

His blue eyes twinkled at her. Will had said something, but she'd missed it. Smile lines appeared around Jake's eyes. His lips parted to reveal even, white teeth and a tiny dimple in his cheek. The smile was so warm, so inviting, so genuine, she felt as if they really were a family.

She wished Jake would kiss her again.

The thought shocked her, but she didn't back away from it. She didn't care what it said about her. She remembered his kiss, the softness of his lips, the strength of his arms around her. She had felt safe, wanted, desired, attractive. There was none of the predatory feeling she got from Henri DuPlange. Jake drew her to him despite her disapproval.

She had never felt so wonderful as when she was in his arms. She remembered every second of the walk to his tent after she twisted her ankle, every minute of the ride back to the ranch with his body practically enfolding her own.

Somebody's knee touched hers under the table. Common sense told her it could have been any one of the boys, but her body told her it was Jake. So did his eyes. Some of the brightness faded to leave them looking smoky, clouded with desire.

Heat surged through Isabelle's body from head to toe. She felt as if the temperature had gone up thirty degrees. She hoped she wasn't blushing. She was certain she was. She knew how to behave in the drawing rooms of Savannah, but when it came to Jake, she was just as innocent and naive as Will.

"I think it's about time we put these rascals to bed," Jake said. "I want to leave before dawn tomorrow." Dinner was over. They had sat talking while Jake drank three cups of coffee Isabelle knew were not made with three-day-old grounds.

"We don't want to go to bed," Pete said.

"Can I see a saloon?" Will asked.

"No, you may not," Isabelle said. "You're going straight to bed. You may not think it now, but you're tired. I don't want you whining all the way back to the ranch."

"I don't whine," Will protested.

Isabelle had to admit Will was the most cheerful of the boys, but she was feeling unaccountably aware of Jake's presence, and that was making it difficult for her to concentrate on what she was saying.

Jake stood up. One look and Isabelle wondered if she had the strength to move. Why did he have to wear such tight pants? They were indecent. Anyone who questioned whether Jake was a man only had to look.

Isabelle looked away, mortified. Jake held out his hand to help her up. She wanted to refuse. She wasn't sure what contact with him would do to her right now. But she didn't think she could get up without help.

"You're tired, too," Jake said. "What did you do all day?"

"You'll find out soon enough," Isabelle said. She

had to get control of herself. People probably assumed she was his wife, but they would frown upon a display of naked desire. As much as Isabelle didn't want to admit it, that's exactly what she was experiencing. She wanted Jake Maxwell, and she wanted him so badly, her limbs trembled.

"You go up," Jake said to Isabelle. "The boys and I are going to take a short walk to settle our suppers. I'll look in on you when I get back."

Isabelle watched them go with a sense of loss. She might have been ready to fall down with fatigue, but she would have given anything to be invited to go along with them. Aunt Deirdre would have said ladies must preserve their dignity. Isabelle was finding she would rather have the roughness of Jake and the uninhibited chatter of Will Haskins, even the bitter complaints of Bret Nolan. Being seen as a lady was flattering, but it wasn't much fun.

"Can't we just look inside one saloon?" Will asked.

"Yeah," Pete agreed. "Just one peep."

Bret, too, watched Jake anxiously, even though he refused to betray his eagerness.

"Okay, but you're not to tell Isabelle. She'd have all our heads."

There wasn't much to see in Newcombe's Crossing, just a couple dozen buildings, a third of them saloons. The boys rushed forward to peer into a saloon that was more tent than building.

"They're not doing anything," Will complained.

"Yes, they are, you little idiot," Bret said. "They're drinking whiskey."

"They're not fighting or shooting anybody," Pete pointed out.

"They aren't even arguing," Will said. "They're just sitting still, talking and drinking."

"That's what people do in saloons" Jake said.

"Where are the women?" Bret asked. "I thought there was supposed to be half-naked women."

"Only in fancy saloons," Jake said.

"Are there any fancy saloons here?" Will asked.

"Nope," Jake said.

"It's a big gyp," Bret said.

"Are the saloons in Santa Fe like this?" Pete asked as they walked along, peering in windows as they went.

"Pretty much," Jake replied.

"Hell, I'd just as soon stay with the cows."

Jake nearly laughed. Wouldn't Isabelle love to hear that?

But that started him thinking about Isabelle all over again. Just the thought of six weeks on the trail with her caused his body to stiffen. He could understand his physical need, the desire to lose himself in her body. After all, he was a man, and he'd been without a woman for a long time. What he couldn't understand was the way she made him feel.

He'd never had much time for the niceties of living. Life was tough. You got tough, or you died. That's just how it was. He never questioned it.

But Isabelle did. And what was more, he had started to feel he ought to do something about it. Now wasn't that a hell of a development!

"Can we go to a cockfight?" Pete asked.

"No," Jake answered without hesitation, "not even if they had one, which they don't."

"What's a cockfight?" Will wanted to know.

"Two chickens fighting," Bret explained.

"Ugh! Who wants to see that?"

"Nobody but a Texan," Bret said as he turned away from a window that featured boots and saddles.

"How about a dogfight?" Pete asked, not ready to give up.

"No fights," Jake said. "It's time you squirts went to bed. You're too bloodthirsty for me."

Will laughed. "You're just fooling." He skipped forward, then turned around so he could watch Jake as they walked along. "You're not afraid of anything."

The look of hero worship rocked Jake down to his boots. Nobody had never looked up to him, not even the boys he trained during the war.

He wasn't the kind of man a boy like Will ought to look up to. He knew because his old army commander, George Randolph, had been that kind of man. He never lost his temper or shouted, not even in the hottest moments of battle. He never lost control. No matter what happened, you could always depend on George to have the answer.

Jake wasn't like that. He cussed, drank, used women when he needed them, and generally did as he damned well pleased. He didn't have any manners, he didn't bathe all that often—the cows didn't care how he smelled—and he would just as soon live in a tent as in a cabin.

He had no idea what to do with these boys!

He wasn't the kind of man they ought to emulate, and he was a fool if he thought for one moment he could be.

They crossed the street at the end of town and started back. "Isabelle will have my hide if I keep you brats up too late," Jake said. "That woman can be mighty fierce when it comes to you boys."

"I don't mean Isabelle," Will said. "I mean Indians and robbers and things."

"Sure, I'm afraid of Indians."

"No, you're not."

Hell, now he wasn't allowed to be scared of a

bunch of crazy men who wanted to kill him and take his scalp. "Sure I am."

Will's faith was shaken, but he persevered. "But you wouldn't run from them."

"If I had a faster horse, I sure as hell would."

"Wouldn't you even fight 'em?" He was badly shaken now.

"Sure I would."

Will beamed. "You're just trying to fool me. I knew you weren't scared of Indians."

Jake started to explain.

"He's afraid of them because it's stupid not to be afraid of somebody who's trying to kill you," Bret said. "But he wouldn't run away because he ain't no coward."

"Oh," Will said, taking a moment to digest that.

"There's a difference," Bret said impatiently. "Damn, are all Texans as dumb as rocks?"

"I'm not dumb," Will shouted, squaring up for a fight.

"Are you trying to make people hate you," Jake asked Bret, "or can't you help it?"

Bret turned sulky. "He's always asking stupid questions."

"No question is stupid if the answer teaches you something." Jake pulled Pete from a window full of candy and ladies' apparel.

Bret didn't answer, but his wrathful expression didn't encourage Jake to think he'd changed his mind. He knew Bret wanted to be liked, but he couldn't understand why he seemed to do everything in his power to make people dislike him.

"I hate it when he looks at you like you're a god or something," Bret said. "You're nobody. You can't do anything but chase cows. My grandfather wouldn't even talk to you. Hell, you smell so bad, he wouldn't let you come close."

Will launched himself at Bret. Before Bret could push Will away, Pete attacked him. Next thing Jake knew, the three of them were rolling around on the boardwalk, fists flying. People passing by looked, smiled, and kept walking.

If Jake had had any doubts about his being an unfit guardian, here was all the proof he needed. He couldn't even stop them from fighting. How in hell had he gotten himself into such a position? More to the point, what was he going to do about it?

"Break it up," he ordered. When his words had no effect, he took Will and Pete by their collars and lifted them off Bret. "When I tell you to do something, I expect you to do it," he said, giving each boy a shake.

"But he said you smelled," Will protested.

"We'll all smell pretty ripe before we reach Santa Fe, including Bret, but you'll learn there's worse things than smelling bad. Now brush yourselves off. We don't want Isabelle asking questions. Women never understand it when men fight."

Pete and Will brushed vigorously, but both looked ready to jump Bret again if he said so much as one word. Bret looked ready to take on the whole world.

"Turn around so I can get the dirt off you," Jake said to Bret. When he didn't move—he looked ready to fight Jake if necessary—Jake took him by the shoulders, spun him around, and brushed his shirt and pants vigorously. He gave all three of them the once-over, then shook his head. "You'll never pass muster. Look, I'll get Isabelle to talking, and you slip past when she isn't looking."

"Is that all you're going to do?" Pete asked.

"What do you want me to do?"

"Beat him or something."

"Will that make him like me?"

"No."

"Will he stop thinking I smell?"

"No."

"Then I guess I'd better think of something else."

"What?"

"That's between me and Bret."

"You mean you're not going to tell us?"

"If it were you, would you want me telling everybody?"

"I wouldn't care," Pete said. "My last people beat me all the time."

"I never liked it when they beat Matt," Will said. "I wanted to kill all of them."

Jake got the feeling he'd survived another crisis, but he wasn't sure how. He ought to be learning something, instead of sliding through by the seat of his pants. Oh well, he only had to last until they reached Santa Fe. He stopped at the water trough to wash their faces.

"Okay, brats, back to the hotel, and mum's the word."

It didn't work. They met Isabelle in the hallway upstairs. She noticed the dirt immediately. Her gaze swept from one boy to another until it settled on Jake.

"They're exhausted," he said as nonchalantly as he could. He hustled the three boys past Isabelle and into the room. "We're all going straight to bed. We're leaving at dawn."

"Good. I'm worried about the boys."

Jake had forgotten the boys—all of them. Isabelle was still fully dressed, but she had let her hair down. It fell over her shoulders like a reddish-brown mantle. It was hard to believe how much difference it made. She looked like a princess without the ice, somehow accessible, reachable, human. She looked feminine and desirable.

Jake felt something inside him clutch and clamp down. Lust, hard and urgent. He'd felt it before, but it had never felt as if he were being assaulted by hot branding irons. He could feel it churning in his gut. He wanted to reach out to steady himself, but there was nothing to grab.

He put his hand out. Contact with the wall steadied him. "You look very nice tonight," he managed to say with an appearance of calm. "I like your hair down."

She touched her hair in the self-conscious way all women had. "I washed it."

He longed to run his fingers through it, bury his face in it. "It makes you look younger." That wasn't the right thing to say.

"I'm not that old."

"And nicer," he added. "Younger and nicer and not so schoolteacherish."

He was getting in deeper and deeper. She turned pink. Probably with anger. If he'd been one of those men with a silver tongue, she'd be turning pink with pleasure. Judging by some of the things he said, his tongue must be made of corroded iron. Being around her made it worse. He never felt like such a rough, stupid, clumsy fella as when he was trying to say something nice to Isabelle.

Will stuck his head out the door. "Which is your bed, Jake? I want to sleep with you."

"I'm not sleeping with Bret," Pete said, pushing his way into the hall.

Both boys were in their underwear.

Isabelle grinned. "You'd better go settle the sleep-

ing arrangements before you have another fight on
your hands. Good night."

She closed her door, and it was as if some physical
support had been taken away. Jake felt as if he were
about to slide right down into the floor. With a strong
effort, he pulled himself together. If the boys ever
discovered he was mooning over Isabelle like a love-
sick calf, they'd never let him forget it.

"In that case," he said, giving each boy a shove toward the door, "I guess I'll sleep with Bret."

Chapter Sixteen

Jake sat up in bed with a start. He thought he had heard someone cry out. But he could hear no sound inside the hotel. He got up, walked over to the window, and looked out.

The street below was quiet. The last drinkers had probably gone home hours ago. This wasn't Austin or San Antonio. The only people who lived near Newcombe's Crossing were farmers and a few ranchers.

Behind him Pete and Will slept the sleep of the innocent. Their covers off, their arms and legs flung about at all kinds of angles, they were in as much of a tangle as when they had jumped Bret. Bret looked more at peace than he ever did awake.

As Jake turned away from the window, he heard it again. The sound was too muffled to tell if it was a man or a woman. It was too faint to tell if the person was dreaming or in real trouble. He decided to wait until he heard it again. He couldn't go back to sleep until he made up his mind one way or the other.

He didn't have to wait long. This time he could tell it was coming through the wall from Isabelle's room. He jumped into his pants, opened the door quietly, and stepped out into the hall.

Virtually no light came in through the window at the end of the hall. He trailed his hand along the wall until he came to the door. He knocked softly, but got no answer. He knocked again and waited. Still no answer. Could he have been mistaken? He couldn't be sure as long as the door was locked.

A window! There must be one in Isabelle's room. Jake went back into his room and looked out the open window. A narrow porch roof ran across the front of the building. He felt a wood splinter drive itself into his foot as he climbed through the window, but he kept going. He reached the window and looked in.

Isabelle was in bed, but she was moaning and flinging her arms into the air. Jake was afraid she was sick. He climbed in and hurried over to the bed. Her movements had thrown the light covers onto the floor.

Another moan broke from Isabelle, and she twisted about in the bed. She tried to say something, but Jake couldn't make out any words. He put his hand on her arm. Mumbling something unintelligible, she immediately threw it off.

"Isabelle, are you all right?"

She didn't answer.

"It's Jake. Tell me what's wrong."

Still no answer. He didn't know what to do. He'd never dealt with a sick woman. He would have summoned someone if he'd known whom to call.

She lay quietly now. He should climb back through that window and scramble into his own bed, but he sank down next to her. Despite his vow never to marry, never to trust a woman, especially a pretty, city-bred woman, he could not deny the attraction that had flared between them from the first moment he saw her.

Now he could sit close to her, watch her, maybe even touch her, without fear that she would glare at him or move away with a look of fear and disgust. Maybe he could figure out what it was about her that made him feel so mixed up inside.

His father had once told him he'd know when he met the right woman. He said it would be as though they were meeting for the first time but had known each other all their lives.

That didn't fit him and Isabelle. They looked at everything from nearly opposite points of view. They distrusted each other—mostly because they were so different.

He told himself to stay away, but he wanted to spend hours looking at her, talking to her, touching her. He had kissed her, held her in his arms, and he hadn't been able to think of anything else since. She had bewitched him, and he couldn't do anything about it.

He reached out to touch her. He knew he shouldn't, but he couldn't stop himself. He'd never known a woman could be as soft and sweet-smelling as Isabelle. It wasn't the smell of perfume. It was a simple, clean smell, like a morning breeze when it was laden with the scent of spring flowers.

But it was her softness that mesmerized him. All his life he'd had to be strong to survive in this harsh land, tough to survive the brutal war, numb to the pain of losing people who were important to him. Little by little, life had squeezed the softness out of him. Then Isabelle appeared; her softness matched his toughness every step of the way.

He touched her cheek, and the effect on his body was immediate. Everything he felt for her was distilled into a single, nearly overpowering feeling. Need. He wanted her so badly, he was about to explode. He jerked his hand back, fearful that if he didn't, he wouldn't be able to stop himself.

She brushed her cheek with her hand as if she were swatting at a fly. He smiled to himself. Even in her sleep she insisted he keep his distance. That was something else he admired about her. She had her standards, and she wasn't about to lower them for him or anybody else. If she had any idea what he was thinking now, she'd throw him out the window.

He hadn't been this close to a female in nearly a year. His body was hard with pent-up hunger and the tension of not doing what nature so desperately wanted him to do. He gripped the edge of the bed. It was that or find himself caressing breasts separated from him by nothing more than a thin gown. Or exploring the curve of her hip. He could just imagine the warmth and softness of her skin.

He could also imagine her shock if she woke up to find him caressing her body. She'd probably take the boys and head straight back to Austin. He didn't want that. He had to keep her with him. He had the terrible feeling that if he didn't, he would never see her again.

Isabelle suddenly cried out and started to toss about in the bed. Jake was afraid she would roll onto the floor. He tried to scoot her back on the bed, but that only made her fight harder. She hit, kicked, and pushed, as if her life depended on it. He had no choice but to put his arms around her and hold her still.

The response was stunning. She stopped fighting

and threw her arms around him. She held on more tightly than he thought any woman could. She put her head against his shoulder and snuggled close. He hardly knew what to do.

Almost as abruptly as she had stopped fighting, she started kissing his neck and cheek, then his ear. He felt as if he were holding red-hot coals in his hands. It was more than he could stand.

Jake kissed Isabelle hard on the mouth, and her eyes popped open.

Immediately she was wide awake. "What are you doing here?" she demanded, her eyes round with shock.

Isabelle was stunned. She had awakened from a dream to find her dream mirrored by life.

Henri DuPlange had been stalking her again. Tonight he had caught her and dragged her off to a small house somewhere on the plantation. No one was close enough to hear her screams; nobody was around to stop him from raping her.

Jake had appeared and knocked Henri down with one blow. He had picked Isabelle up and carried her to his waiting carriage. She had thrown her arms around his neck, relieved to be free of Henri, delighted to be in the arms of the man she loved.

Now she found herself truly in Jake's arms, and he was kissing her with even more fierceness than in her dreams. Immediately her body was ablaze with the yearning she had struggled so hard to deny. Her breasts, pushed hard against his chest, became achingly sensitive, her nipples firm. She tried to pull away, but Jake wouldn't let her.

"What are you doing here?" she asked again.

"You cried out in your sleep. I heard you through the wall."

She glanced at the door. She was certain she had locked it.

"I came through the window." He paused. "I couldn't just lie in bed and do nothing."

Still he didn't release her. She couldn't release him either. The fire raging inside her wouldn't allow it. It had gotten a firm hold on her senses and wouldn't let go.

"Are you sick?" Jake asked.

She shook her head. "It was a bad dream."

"Did he hurt you?"

"No."

She held him tightly. She didn't intend to. It just happened. His arms tightened around her.

"Did anybody ever hurt you?"

"No."

"But they tried?"

"Yes."

He held her tighter. No one had held or comforted her since her aunt fell ill. She hadn't realized how much she missed it. She was glad she was strong and self-reliant, but it felt awfully good to know that for the moment someone else would provide all the strength.

"What did you do?"

"I left."

The fires inside her had turned to liquid heat. Her body felt taut, her nerves strung so tightly, she thought they would snap. Yet her limbs trembled uncontrollably. She felt hot and cold. She knew she ought to send Jake back to his room, but she didn't want anything so much as she wanted to stay in his arms and have him kiss her again and again.

Such conduct went against everything her aunt had taught her. Aunt Deirdre had always stressed that a woman's reputation was her most precious possession. She believed all men were beasts. She would have hated Jake.

But Isabelle couldn't imagine even one of the men Aunt Deirdre approved of simply holding her as Jake was doing, kissing her only because she was frightened and needed comfort. Behind their polished manners and clever conversations, they were concerned with little more than their own pleasures.

Isabelle could tell from the tension in Jake's body that he was subject to those same desires. But his behavior proved he wasn't ruled by them.

"Didn't you have anywhere you could go?"

"No."

"No one?"

"No."

That didn't feel like the devastating admission it used to be. But then, Jake had never held her in his arms like this. Her fiancé had been content to kiss her hand and brush her cheek with his lips. Aunt Deirdre had approved. Isabelle had thought she was supposed to be satisfied with that. Now she knew she never would be.

Jake was kissing her eyebrows, the end of her nose. She wondered if her mother would have given her the same advice as Aunt Deirdre. Surely if her father had held her mother like this, kissed her like this, felt like this, she would have winked and whispered something wonderfully tantalizing in her daughter's ear when they were alone.

"You shouldn't be alone," Jake was saying. "You should have been married."

"I was engaged."

Jake froze. He held her away from him. She could see him beginning to withdraw.

"I didn't love him. I didn't know it then, but I do now."

His arms tightened around her again.

"What happened?"

"He was killed in the war."

His lips touched her forehead. She was struck by their softness. Everything else about him was so rough, harsh, abrupt. But his lips were soft and warm and moist. She tilted her head back, and he kissed her on the lips.

This time there was nothing proper or well-behaved about his kiss. It was hard, greedy, and hot. She felt scorched by the intensity. She was unprepared when his tongue pushed between her lips and up against her teeth. Aunt Deirdre had never said anything about this. Neither had the girls at the orphanage.

Almost by instinct, she opened her mouth. His tongue touched her own shocked and flaccid tongue. It poked and prodded until her tongue roused itself from its lethargy. With a series of sinuous moves, Jake's tongue encircled hers in a dance that was at once erotic and maddeningly tender.

Isabelle hesitated at first. She didn't know what to do. She teetered on an edge; she knew somehow this would plunge her into an abyss of physical pleasure. But the lure of Jake's tongue was too enticing. Abandoning all restraint, Isabelle allowed herself to follow where her body led.

Never had she been so aware of her physical self. It seemed that her tongue was connected to a nerve that ran through every part of her. Her entire body, right down to her toes, felt so sensitized that she was unable to keep still. She pressed herself against Jake, hoping to squeeze every ounce of pleasure from his kiss. She didn't want to leave any part of the experience unexplored.

"So you're all alone," Jake said when he finally

lifted his mouth from hers.

"Yes."

That seemed to upset him.

"I shouldn't be here. You need somebody to protect you. You need—"

"I have you."

She hadn't meant to say that, at least not the way it sounded. It presumed too much.

"Are you sure?"

"Yes."

What had she said yes to? She wasn't sure. But it felt right. It felt even more right when Jake began to leave cluster after cluster of kisses on every part of her face. When he started kissing the side of her neck, she felt her bones turn to water. She threw back her head, hoping he would kiss her throat.

He did.

But he didn't stop there. He kissed her shoulders, the hollow of her throat, her ears. She felt his hands in her hair, on her back, her sides. With the tip of his tongue he traced an outline of her lips. She shivered with pleasure. He took her ear lobe between his teeth and tugged gently. She nearly melted.

The feel of his warm breath in her ears was the most erotic sensation she'd ever experienced. She was certain a lady shouldn't enjoy it, but she couldn't help herself. She hoped he would go on and on until she dissolved from an excess of pleasure.

But she soon found she had underestimated her body's capacity for pleasure. Jake's hand moved from her back and covered her breast. An "oh" of astonishment was superseded by a gasping intake of breath when his fingertip found her firm nipple and began to gently rub it through the soft material of her gown. If her body had been on fire before, it now turned to liquid flame.

Jake kissed her again, and his tongue invaded her mouth to engage in another sinuous dance. Driven by the ever-widening ripples of pleasure his fingertips were sending through her body, Isabelle took Jake's lip between her teeth. He groaned with pleasure.

Isabelle wasn't aware that Jake had unbuttoned her gown until he slipped it over her shoulder. Immediately her attention was divided between her breast and the trail of kisses he scattered across her shoulder, along her collar bone, and down her chest until he reached the mound of her breast.

Isabelle grew rigid with anticipation. But her expectations were nothing compared to the reality of his taking her nipple into his warm, moist mouth. Isabelle was certain she would explode. Her breast seemed on fire with a kind of heat that deprived her of strength. Simultaneously it filled her body to overflowing with an energy so fierce she could hardly contain it.

She wanted to throw herself at Jake with a fury that would break the grip of the tension that was turning her body into a writhing, aching thing that no longer responded to her commands.

She made no objection when Jake slipped her gown over her shoulder to expose her other breast to his lips. She didn't try to stop him when he took her nipple between his teeth and she heard herself utter a shuddering moan of ecstasy. Nor did she object when he slipped her gown under her hips and off her body. The roughness of the coarse cotton sheet against her skin felt glorious.

She didn't feel the cool night air. She was too warm. The multitude of sensations Jake aroused in her body overwhelmed her so that she wasn't aware of his hand until it moved between her legs. In a moment of jolting realization, all her aunt's warnings came rushing back. Aunt Deirdre had said this day would come, that men wanted only one thing from a woman. She said a woman must wait until marriage to allow a man such liberties.

Isabelle had had no trouble denying other men who had looked at her with lust in their eyes, but she wanted to make love to Jake. She hadn't realized it until this moment. It wasn't something she'd thought about. Nor did she try to rationalize it. She simply wanted it.

She didn't think she could stop herself.

It took a moment before she could open herself to Jake. It wasn't that she was afraid of him. It wasn't that she didn't want to. Her muscles wouldn't relax. It was new. It was frightening. Everything he had done so far was so overwhelming, she wasn't sure she could stand any more.

For a moment she was certain she couldn't. But even as fear threatened to take hold of her, it melted away, leaving her relaxed and eager.

Jake's invasion caused her to gasp. He touched the very core of her being. She became enmeshed in a coil of yearning. She might die from pleasure, but she would not escape the need.

Jake continued to touch her, to gently rub, until Isabelle felt every muscle in her body tense to the snapping point. She was helpless before the waves of pleasure that poured over her in ever increasing strength and speed. She writhed in the bed, moan after moan escaping from her until she thought she would cry out from the delicious agony.

Just as she was certain she could contain herself no longer, a gigantic wave lifted her to a shuddering peak and she thundered down the other side. She felt flooded. Then the tension flowed from her, and she came down the other side of that wave in a kind of mindless state. She had never been so utterly exhausted.

Yet she'd never felt so completely wonderful.

She didn't understand the magic Jake had wrought, but she knew her aunt could never have experienced any of what had just happened to her. If she had, even once, she couldn't have warned Isabelle so frequently against men.

But her aunt had never met a man like Jake. He didn't possess the social skills she thought necessary. He would never dress or live in a style her aunt could have found acceptable. He was a man who didn't need colorful trappings to detract from his shortcomings.

Because he didn't have any.

He was exactly what every woman wanted and feared she'd never find. The packaging was a little unexpected, but Isabelle had had time to inspect the contents, and she knew Jake was the kind of man she'd hoped her fiancé would be. The kind she knew now he never could have been.

Isabelle felt the waves of pleasure start to rise again. She didn't know it could happen twice. But before her surprise could be overtaken by the surging desire, Jake withdrew his hand. She was about to ask him what he was doing when he invaded her again. This time he stretched her to the limit.

She knew instinctively that this was what her aunt had cautioned against. Remembering the warning that she would suffer great pain, Isabelle tensed.

But there was no pain. Only a thin, knife-blade of discomfort, and then mind-numbing pleasure sweeping over her in waves as Jake moved within her. Isabelle forgot her aunt's warning. She gave herself up to sensations that battered at her senses until she was helpless to resist. She let herself be carried deeper and deeper into the vortex until she felt herself losing consciousness. Then, as before, she felt the tension break and something flood through her.

She was only dimly aware of Jake as he tensed, shuddered, then collapsed beside her.

"Are you all right?" Jake asked.

Isabelle didn't know how much time had passed. It seemed like several lifetimes.

"You haven't said anything," he said when she didn't answer.

"I don't know what to say."

"You don't have to say anything as long as I gave you pleasure."

"Mmmm." He'd given her far more than she'd ever thought possible.

"I'd better go."

A cold draft invaded the cocoon of warmth that encased her. She snuggled closer to him, but she could already feel him withdrawing.

"I don't want the boys to wake up and find me gone. Are you sure you're all right?"

"Yes, I'm fine."

But she wasn't fine. He was running away. His withdrawal was like a rejection.

He paused after he put on his clothes. "Are you sure nothing's wrong?"

"Absolutely. Go on. I'm half asleep already."

She lied. The warmth of his presence had been replaced by the chill of his absence. How could she sleep when she'd just traded her honor to a cowboy for a few minutes of feeling wanted, no matter how wondrous and intense?

Now that her few minutes were up, he had climbed out the window and disappeared. She was just as alone and unwanted as ever.

Chapter Seventeen

An hour later Isabelle was still awake, her body rigid from shock. She shivered from cold fear. She couldn't believe what she had just allowed to happen, what she had encouraged Jake to make happen.

She had ruined herself for a few minutes of pleasure, for a fleeting sense of security, a longing to feel she was important to someone else.

She didn't blame Jake. He'd given her plenty of opportunity to refuse. She had given in to her physical need of him. She had asked nothing of him, yet she had given him everything. What could have possessed her to do anything so crazy?

The physical attraction was enormous. She admired him. She was thankful to him for what he was doing for the boys. She loved his strength, the feeling of security she had when she was around him. But none of these things was reason enough to give herself to a man.

The only acceptable reason would be that she loved him.

But she didn't love him. She couldn't. How could she when she argued with him constantly, disagreed with half of what he did, thought most of his decisions were wrong? No, she didn't love him, but she'd let him make love to her. How was she going to face him in the morning, ride back with him to the ranch, travel across Texas with no company other than that of a few boys?

Just thinking about "making love" caused her to groan. It had been lust, pure and simple. After the way she'd acted, he'd probably expect her to hop behind the bushes every night the minute dinner was over.

But no sooner had the thought occurred to her than she knew Jake wouldn't force himself on her. He wouldn't need to. She was more likely to drag him into the bushes than the other way around. Her body had betrayed her once. There was no reason to suppose it wouldn't do so again.

Isabelle got up from the bed and lighted the lamp. She started to dress. She couldn't go with Jake. It was absurd to even consider it. She couldn't face him again. She would go back to Austin. He could take the boys. He'd probably do a better job of taking care of them if she wasn't around.

But even as she made her decision, Isabelle regretted it. She had never met a man like Jake. She could love him. She'd come very close already. Much closer than she had realized. But he didn't love her, and it was time to go before she was helplessly in love with a man who neither liked nor respected the kind of woman she was.

*　　*　　*

Jake had harnessed the mules and loaded the wagon. The boys had eaten and were anxious to see if the blacksmith had gotten the chain off Zeke. Jake was anxious to see what Isabelle thought of the chuck box the carpenter had built to store her food and cooking equipment.

But he couldn't find her. She wasn't in her room. He had checked. She hadn't left a message. That wasn't like Isabelle.

"She musta been the lady who left before dawn," the clerk said when Jake asked. "Didn't see her myself, but old Joshua said she was a looker."

"Where did she go?"

"Asked about getting a ride to Austin. Old Joshua told her to see Sam Stone. He's driving a wagon that way this very day."

"She's not taking us back to Austin, is she?" Pete asked.

"She can't," Will said. "She promised."

"Promises to orphans don't count," Bret said.

"Isabelle's promises always count," Jake said. "You boys stay with the wagon, and make sure nobody helps themselves to our food. I'll be back in a jiffy."

He found her sitting outside a ramshackle cabin, her back straight, her eyes staring straight ahead.

"What are you doing here?" Jake asked. "We should have started back to the ranch an hour ago."

"I'm not going," Isabelle said. She didn't look at him. "I'm returning to Austin."

Jake had known something was wrong, but he hadn't expected this. "Is this about last night?"

She seemed to grow even more rigid.

"Because if it is, I—"

"I'd appreciate it if you would erase last night from your memory. I don't hold you responsible. You came to me only because you thought I was ill."

"Nobody has to take responsibility for what I did," Jake snapped.

"Nevertheless, I do. It has made me aware that I have a weak physical nature."

"Pig's feet!" Jake stepped in front of her so she had to look at him. "I don't know who told you such nonsense, but you're just about the strongest female I ever met. You're certainly the most stubborn and hardheaded."

"That has no bearing on—"

"You're no different from any other woman who's been taught to be frightened of men and to hate making love."

"But a lady—"

"I bet you were told a lady had to suffer for the sake of children, that you had to endure the disgusting attentions of your husband because it was your duty."

He could see the confirmation in her eyes.

"My ma was told the same thing. She hated it when my pa touched her. She also hated the ranch. She wouldn't do a lick of work outside the house. She said Texas wasn't a fit place for a woman. Pa, David, and I did half her work, but it didn't make any difference. She hated Texas, and she hated us for making her stay here."

He didn't know why he was telling her all this. He'd never told anybody. Even after nearly twenty years, the hurt was still too raw. But now that he'd started, he couldn't stop himself. It was like a poison he needed to get rid of.

"Pa told her if she'd just forget all that high society rigmarole her mama had taught her, she'd learn to be happy. Well, Ma forgot all right. You know what my fine, high-born Ma forgot?"

Isabelle shook her head.

"She forgot her husband and two sons. She put us right out of her mind and ran off to Austin. But that wasn't exciting enough for her, so she went to St. Louis. Got herself a job in one of those high-toned gambling clubs. You know the kind, where you have to have a personal recommendation to get in."

Isabelle shook her head.

"Ma took up with a trader. I guess she decided a man's touch wasn't as bad as she thought, especially when it was softened by a lot of money."

"What happened?" Isabelle asked.

"I don't know, and I don't care."

But that wasn't true. His mother had married her trader and moved to Santa Fe. As far as he knew, she was still there.

"I didn't mean to get sidetracked," Jake said, embarrassed and angry with himself for exposing a secret that still had such power to wound him. "I just get so mad when women tell each other they aren't supposed to enjoy a man's attentions. It's just as natural for a woman as it is for a man."

"But we're not married," Isabelle said.

"That has nothing to do with it."

"It ought to."

"That's what the rules say. Real life doesn't follow rules."

"Well, I have to live by the rules," Isabelle said. "And the rules say a woman must not give herself to a man before marriage. If she does, she will be banished from society."

"There's no society in Texas."

"I don't mean to live in Texas. The society I was raised in, the society I was taught to care about, does care very much."

"If you cared so much for this society of yours, why didn't it take care of you when your aunt died?"

Isabelle didn't answer.

He moved closer until he could look her in the eye. "Why?"

"I don't have any relatives. There was no one to take me in."

"There's always someone when people care. You said you were engaged."

"My fiancé died."

"Then why didn't his family take you in?"

"Why should they?"

"A Texas family would take you in. They'd keep you, too, if you couldn't find a husband."

"I had been in a orphanage."

"What else?" He moved still closer, putting pressure on her.

"I didn't have any money," she shouted at him. "I was poor."

That's what he'd thought. He stepped back. "And you're still letting those people make rules for you."

"They're not just for me. They're for everybody."

"Nobody makes rules for me."

"It's different for men. I have to abide by the rules, or I'll lose my job."

"As far as anybody knows, you haven't broken any rules."

"*I* know."

"Nonsense. You've just discovered you're a warm, loving, giving woman who will make some man a warm, loving, giving wife. You ought to have a dozen children."

She half smiled. "I'd never survive."

"You're a lot tougher than you think. A month ago you'd never have believed you could cook a meal over an open fire."

"I still can't."

"We eat it. That's what counts."

Jake could hardly believe what he was doing. Isabelle had no business on a cattle drive to New Mexico. He didn't want to become emotionally entangled with any woman, especially a woman like Isabelle. So why did he always seem to be practically begging her to go with him?

Isabelle looked at her hands folded so firmly in her lap. Then she looked up at Jake. "Thanks for trying to make me feel better. It was very nice of you."

Jake threw up his hands in frustration. "Nice be damned!"

"I promise I'll think about what you said, but I still can't go with you."

"What about the boys? Are you going to abandon them?"

"They don't need me. They don't even listen to me any more."

"I thought you were worried I'd be too hard on them."

"Buck survived the farmers. They'll survive you."

"What's going to happen to them when they reach Santa Fe?"

"You'll find jobs for them." She looked up, her gaze pleading as well as worried. "But you've got to keep Will and Pete. They're small, and they adore you."

"These boys need a mama, a stable home, a father who'll be around to give them a hand when they need it, to wallop them when they need that. I don't even know if I'll have a ranch."

"What would you do with them? I've got to know."

"Give them away, send them to an orphanage. Hell, I don't know." He half turned away.

"You can't do that."

He spun back to face her. "I can dump them anywhere I please, and there's not a damned thing you can do to stop me if you're sitting in Austin."

"But you wouldn't. I know you better than that."

"Who's going to watch them when I ride ahead to look for water or a bedding ground? What's going to happen to them if we get attacked by Indians? I've got to think of the other boys, of the herd. I can't be hauling Will and Pete behind me everywhere I go."

"You can't send them back."

"I won't have to if you come along."

She hung her head. "I can't."

He knelt in front of her and looked up into her downcast eyes. "You want to come along, don't you? Don't you?" he asked when she didn't answer.

She nodded

"Then why don't you?"

No answer.

"Do you think I'll try to seduce you?"

A pause. "I'm not sure."

"Do you think I'd succeed if I did?"

A longer pause. "I'm not sure of that, either."

Jake sighed then took her hands in his. "I'm not going to try to convince you that you did nothing wrong, but I promise I won't touch you for the entire trip. I won't kiss you. I won't even tell you you're pretty. I won't talk to you unless I must, and I'll keep as much distance between us as possible. I can't handle this trip by myself. I need your help."

Isabelle pulled her hands away but didn't look up. He could see she was struggling with herself.

Jake stood. "Before you give me your answer, know that if you get on that cart to Austin, I'm putting Will and Pete on with you."

Isabelle looked up at him. "You can't do that."

"I can, and I will. You can't waltz in here, shove ten boys on me, have an attack of conscience, and run off and hide."

"I'm not hiding."

"Yes, you are. You're afraid of me and yourself, of what might happen between us in the future. You're running away."

"Is that wrong?"

"It's unnecessary. You made a mistake. Everybody does. You learn from it and keep going. It's what you'd say to the boys. You wouldn't tell Buck to go hide because some bastard nearly beat him to death, or Zeke because another bastard chained him up like a dog."

"You think I'm a coward, don't you?"

Jake reached out and pulled her to her feet. "I think you're a strong, courageous woman, but you're frightened and confused. You don't understand what's happening, but you won't find the answers back in Austin."

Isabelle pulled away. "So what am I supposed to do?"

"Come with us to Santa Fe. You'll never forgive yourself if you leave those boys. They mean more to you than anything that happened between us."

Isabelle started to pace. Jake knew she was strongly attracted to him—she would never have let him make love to her if she weren't—but her deepest attachment was to the boys. She just needed him.

Jake didn't like that. He wasn't in the market for a wife or a family, but he'd found himself surrounded by boys who seemed to gravitate to him as if they were bound together by the ties of nature.

On one level, the pull between him and Isabelle was just as strong. But it was an attraction that had its foundation, its entire being, in their physical nature. When it came to everything else, they could hardly have been more different.

So why was he irritated that Isabelle loved the boys and not him? He couldn't explain that one. It wasn't as if he wanted to get married, or settle down, or even have a mistress. Women like Isabelle didn't marry ranchers. He'd seen ranchers' wives. He knew.

Isabelle stopped and turned to Jake. "I'll go, but there are conditions."

There always were with a woman. For them a simple yes or no was impossible.

She kept her distance. "I must tell you I find you extremely attractive. I don't understand it, but it's so. I'm not certain I can uphold my end of the bargain. If I can't, I won't go."

That was certainly hanging her laundry out to dry. She had more guts than he thought. "The boys will always be around," he said. "That ought to help."

"I shouldn't need help."

"If it makes you feel any better, I could use a little help myself. It's not going to be easy thinking about the sweet taste of your lips and having to talk about beans and coffee."

"Mr. Maxwell, you promised—"

"It's still Jake. I'll keep my promise, but there's no point in your thinking all the temptation is on one side. Now what are your other conditions?"

Isabelle blushed. He was tempted to tell her how attractive she looked, but he was afraid it would scare her off.

"You must pay the boys a decent wage. I don't know what that is, but they should receive something for their work."

"Assuming we get there with a herd to sell, I'll pay them forty dollars."

"You must agree to keep the boys until I can decide what to do with them."

"Do you mean, bring them back to the ranch?"

"If necessary."

"Are you going to stay as long as they do?"

Isabelle turned pale. "I'll do my best."

"If I have to give guarantees, so do you."

She seemed to lose the control she'd had all morning. "How can I do that when I might shamelessly throw myself at you at any time?"

He couldn't help but smile. No woman had ever threatened to assault him. "I promise to scream so loud the boys will come running."

"Don't make fun of me," she said, her fists clenched, her voice tight with humiliation. "I don't want to want you, to like your kisses, to like the feel of your arms around me, to like being near you, but I can't help it. Hell, I even find you attractive in the morning with your hair standing on end. See, now you've started me cussing."

Jake was speechless. Isabelle's words had caught him like a powerful fist in the small of the back. Instantly his body was stiff with desire. Last night hadn't satisfied his hunger for her. It had only made it more intense. He could deny it when he thought she didn't want him, but he couldn't when he knew she wanted him as much as he wanted her.

"I want you, too, but I promise you we won't make love until both of us agree it's what we want."

Isabelle backed away. "That's not the kind of guarantee I need."

"It's the best I can do."

"Why did you call it *making love?* We don't love each other." The strained look in her eyes told him this question wasn't the result of idle curiosity.

"We have a strong feeling for each other. Maybe we aren't sure exactly what it is, but it's there. You would never have let me stay otherwise. I wouldn't have stayed."

"I thought men wanted women . . . any woman."

"Maybe some men do. I don't."

She was silent for a long moment. Then she seemed to sigh, square her shoulders, and come to a decision. "We'd better get going. I imagine Zeke's beginning to wonder if we're coming back."

Zeke was inside the blacksmith's cabin when they arrived. The chain was gone and the abrasions on his leg had been treated.

"That's one hungry boy," the blacksmith's wife said. "You make sure you feed him proper."

Zeke looked less angry, less tense, but he didn't speak. He climbed up into the wagon and pulled the blanket over him.

"You don't need to do that," Jake said. "The farmers went home yesterday."

The blacksmith led out the horse Jake had given him and tied it to the back of the wagon. Then he brought out an ornate black leather saddle and bridle and dropped them into the wagon.

"The horse is yours," Jake said.

"I don't need your horse or this saddle," the blacksmith answered. "Zeke may. You never know when he might have to run for his life."

"He won't have to run again," Jake said.

Jake watched the smoke curl lazily upward from the still smoldering timbers. He knew the farmers hated him, but he could hardly believe they had burned him out. It was obviously not the work of Indians or bandits. There was nothing haphazard or hurried about it. Someone had pulled up all the posts from the corrals and piled them and the rails inside the bunkhouse and the cabin. Jake wouldn't have been surprised to learn they had poured coal oil on the dry wood to make it burn hotter. They must have tended the fires to make sure they burned evenly. The boys poked around the edge of the rubble, but nothing was left.

"Who could have done this?" Isabelle asked, stunned.

"Rupert," Zeke said. "He's the one who owned me."

"He thinks I had something to do with your disappearance," Jake said.

"You can get him back," Zeke said. "I know a way."

"It would be a waste of time," Jake said. "They'll all swear they were home all day. They won't admit Rupert bought a slave and beat and starved him either. They're in this together. Whatever one man does, he does for all of them."

"But to burn down your home!"

"There wasn't much to burn."

It hadn't been much of a house as houses go, but it was his home, the only one he'd ever had, the one he'd fought a war for, the one he'd returned to when everything else was lost. Now it, too, was gone. He was strongly tempted to accept Zeke's suggestion and head straight for the farmers' settlement. Half of them would be dead before dawn.

But he wouldn't do that. That would only create more hate and more orphans.

The safety of Isabelle and the boys was the main reason he wasn't going to take his revenge. He and his herd were all that stood between them and having to go back to Austin. Getting to New Mexico was the best possible revenge.

"Back in the saddle," he said to the boys. "We're heading for the cow camp."

"It'll be dark before we can get there," Isabelle said.

"I know, but I want to be on the trail before dawn. After this, I don't dare wait another day."

* * *

The camp was ominously quiet. All trace of activity had been removed. Jake rode up to the fence across the canyon mouth. It had been covered with so much brush and vines, it was almost impossible to see.

"Where is everybody?" Pete asked.

"Where's Matt?" Will asked, obviously worried that his brother might have left him.

"Do you think anything happened to them?" Isabelle asked.

"No. I figure they know the farmers burned the cabin. They've tried to wipe out all signs of the roundup."

Jake was feeling guilty he had left them unarmed.

"But where are they?"

"Let's check the tent."

The extra saddles and other equipment were piled inside the tent. The extra horses were picketed nearby, but there was no sign of the boys.

"I don't understand it," Isabelle said. "Where could they have gone?"

But Jake wasn't listening to Isabelle. He heard the faint sound of singing—not good singing, but there was something very familiar about it.

"Stay here," he said. "I'll go look for them."

"I'm coming with you," Isabelle said.

"No need. They'll need to eat soon. I want them all to have full stomachs when we hit the trail."

"Bret and the boys can start the fire," Isabelle said. "I'm coming with you."

Jake gave in. She had to know sooner or later. It might as well be now.

They didn't have far to go. After they crossed a small ridge, the sound grew louder. Jake guessed they were in a cave he remembered on the far side of the canyon. He used to hide there when he was a boy.

"You sure you don't want to go back?" he asked Isabelle.

She subjected him to a searching glance. "You're hiding something, and I mean to know what it is." She paused and listened. "Why are they singing in that peculiar manner? I never knew any of them was interested in music."

"I doubt they are. It's their condition that brings it on."

"What condition?"

"You'll see."

It took them a little while to pick their way across the canyon and up the far wall.

The boys were gathered around the remains of a small fire. Night Hawk, Luke, and Buck were asleep. Chet leaned against the stone wall, his eyes barely open, his formal demeanor still in place. Matt lay close by, leaning on his elbow, staring into space. Sean was singing in a thin, adolescent tenor. He was standing, swaying unsteadily from one side to the other. Two empty whiskey bottles lay on the ground.

"They're drunk!" Isabelle said in stunned disbelief. "They're dead drunk."

Chapter Eighteen

Isabelle couldn't believe the boys were drunk. They were so young, so innocent. She was thankful that she and Jake had taken Will and Pete with them.

"It's not that bad," Jake said. "Matt and Chet are awake, and Sean is still on his feet."

"Don't try to defend them," she said in disgust. "They know they're forbidden to touch alcohol. That's one of the first things they're taught."

Sean stopped singing abruptly at the sound of voices. He peered anxiously into the dark. "Is that you, Jake?" he called.

"Yes," Jake said.

Sean looked relieved. Chet struggled to his feet at the sight of Isabelle. Matt continued to stare into space.

"I sure am glad you're back," Chet said as he pulled himself erect. "We didn't know what to do."

"They burned the ranch," Sean said. "Luke and I

wanted to stop them, but Chet said it was more important to keep them from finding Buck."

"Is that why you piled everything into the tent and hid up here?" Jake asked.

"Yeah. Hawk wanted to lay for them, but Chet wouldn't let him do that either."

"Chet was right," Jake said, turning to Chet, who was having great difficulty remaining on his feet. "I always did think you had a good head on your shoulders. I'm making you foreman of this crew."

Isabelle walked into the center of the group. She looked furiously about her, then turned her blazing gaze on Jake. "You find all of them drunk, and all you can do is compliment them and make Chet foreman?"

"I had to do it by morning. Now seemed as good a time as any."

"But they stole your whiskey and got drunk."

"They shouldn't have done that."

"Is that all you're going to say?"

She couldn't believe he was just standing there. It must be a man thing. Boys had the right to get drunk, but just let a female try it!

"They did a good job disguising the fence," Jake added. "Whose idea was that?"

"Mine," Chet said. "Since we didn't have any guns, it was the only thing we could do. Did you have a good trip?"

"Pretty good. We got the chain off Zeke, and we got plenty of supplies. We met the farmers a couple of times, but—"

"How can you stand here chatting?" Isabelle demanded. "Do something this instant."

"We're moving out before dawn tomorrow," Jake said. "Get all the sleep you can. You're going to need it."

257

Chet's legs couldn't hold him up any longer. He gradually sank back to the ground. Sean watched, a confused expression on his face.

"I want you back in camp," Jake said. "Chet, now that you're foreman, it's your job. See to it."

"Yes, sir," Chet said, still in a heap.

"He can't even move himself," Isabelle snapped. "How's he going to move the others?"

"He'll work it out," Jake said as he took Isabelle by the arm and led her away.

"Let me go," she said, trying to break away. "I haven't had my say."

"We've both said all we're going to say," Jake said, firmly forcing her to walk in front of him.

Isabelle was furious. Every time she decided Jake was perfect for the boys, he did something like this. It was obvious that he was totally unconcerned about their moral character. He had found them stone drunk and hadn't said one word against it. What was more, he didn't intend to punish them. That was intolerable. She couldn't accept it.

"Do you mean to say anything more?" she demanded when the ground leveled out enough for her to stop having to watch her feet.

"What do you want me to say?"

"That's obvious."

"Not to me."

"You can begin by telling them it's wrong."

"Haven't you told them already?"

"Of course I have."

"Then they know it."

"But they got drunk."

"That doesn't mean they don't know it's wrong. It just means they did it anyway."

"That's even worse."

"Probably."

She stopped and turned to face him. "Is that all you mean to say, *probably*?"

"Most likely."

Isabelle spun around and started back to the cow camp. "I never thought you'd let these boys do something as stupid and dangerous as this and not say a word about it."

"Haven't you ever done something you knew was stupid and dangerous?"

"No."

"You brought those boys out here."

"That might have been dangerous, but it wasn't stupid."

"You were meaning to give them to the farmers."

"I didn't *know* what they were like. If I had, it would have been heartless and inhuman, not stupid."

"Okay. But what I'm getting at is, those boys know all that already. They probably found that whiskey the first day we were gone."

"They knew about it before that," Isabelle said. "I used it to clean Buck's wounds."

"That's even better."

"What do you mean?"

"They've known about it for a week, but they never touched it until there was a crisis. They were scared. They didn't know what to do, so they got drunk."

"That was useless."

"Of course it was, but when they're drunk, they aren't afraid. We weren't here to help them, so they did the best they could."

That was a peculiar point of view, one she never would have thought of. "That sounds like the kind of thinking a man would do. But the fact remains, it was wrong and they need to be punished so they won't do it again."

"Don't worry. They'll be punished plenty. I don't think you'll be seeing any of them wanting whiskey for a long time."

"What are you going to do?"

"You'll see."

It was hard to argue with Jake when he was behind her and she had to watch her feet or fall down the side of the canyon. It was just like him to get her where she couldn't concentrate, then try to make her back down, but she wasn't giving up that easily. "I can't accept that."

"Okay, say what you want, but remember two things."

"What?"

"This is the first freedom these boys have known in a long time. They're bound to do things they'll regret. There's no point in trying to teach them a lesson they've already learned."

"What's the other thing?"

"Experience is the best teacher."

"Do you plan to stand around and let *experience* do all the work?"

"These boys aren't children. They're practically grown. They're not going to listen to you or me. They'll put up with a little guidance, but that's about all. If I let them do their own learning in the little things, maybe they'll listen to me in the big things. If I start pushing on them now, they'll never listen to anything I have to say."

"That's all you're going to do?"

"Yeah."

She looked at him, standing there so tall and strong and sure of himself. Maybe he was right. What did she know of boys or men? She'd been wrong about Jake at every turn. And now, even though she thought he was making a terrible mistake with the boys, the thought uppermost in her mind was that she wanted to be in his arms again.

He would hold her. She knew that. He might say he would keep his distance, but he was tempted. She could see it in his eyes. All she had to do was reach out, touch him, and his resistance would crumble.

What was she thinking! The first sign of trouble, and she wanted to fling herself into Jake's arms. That was as bad as getting drunk.

"I'd better see about fixing supper."

"They won't need much. I want them to have their biggest meal in the morning. I don't mean to stop until they drop from exhaustion. I want to put as much space between us and those farmers as possible."

"You ready?" Jake asked.

"Give me two minutes," Isabelle replied. "The biscuits aren't quite done yet."

Isabelle was certain she had barely closed her eyes when Jake woke her to fix breakfast.

"Can I wake them up?" Bret asked, already looking forward to the boys' suffering from hangovers.

"Let Jake do it," Isabelle advised. "They're not going to like anybody today."

The boys had come stumbling in last night just before Isabelle went to bed. They had carried Night Hawk. They had barely been able to crawl into their bedrolls before dropping off again.

Isabelle lifted the lid of a Dutch oven. The biscuits were perfect. "Okay," she said to Jake. "It's time."

Jake stepped between Night Hawk and Buck, held up the lid of a Dutch oven, and began hitting it with an old horseshoe. The din was terrible. The boys jerked up out of their bedrolls. Some held their pounding heads, pain visible in their agonized expressions.

Night Hawk launched himself at Jake, but he was hardly able to stand on his feet. Jake moved aside, grinned broadly, and continued to hit the lid as loudly as he could. Just when Isabelle thought she couldn't stand it any longer, he stopped.

"You've got thirty minutes to eat and saddle up," Jake announced. "When we bed down tonight, we're going to be twenty miles from here. Anybody who doesn't want to go, make up his mind now. I'll give him a horse, and he can head back to Austin."

Buck pulled the blanket over his head, but Zeke wasn't having any of that. He jerked the blanket off. "Get up, you damned fool. You want to end up with more stripes on your back?"

Without waiting for Buck to move, Zeke hauled him out of bed and shoved his head into a bucket of cold creek water. Buck fought like a downed steer. When Zeke finally let him pull his head out of the water, he was wide awake.

"Anybody else need help waking up?" Zeke asked. They were all moving except Night Hawk. Zeke emptied the bucket over him. He came off the ground with murder in his eyes.

"Come on," Zeke said, taunting him. "It was Indians sold me to those farmers."

Sean grabbed hold of Night Hawk and headed him toward the coffee.

"You were a little rough on them, weren't you?" Jake asked Zeke.

"The farmers were rougher," Zeke replied.

Isabelle had never seen such a miserable, subdued crowd. She was a little irritated when no one noticed breakfast was better than usual, but she told herself to wait. The boys were too hungover to notice anything that didn't jump up and move off their plates. Even Pete and Will kept quiet.

She wondered how the boys were going to be able to ride when they couldn't walk. She was certain they couldn't when Luke failed to cinch his saddle tightly enough. It slid off the horse, taking Luke with it.

Jake was on him in a flash, telling him he was holding everybody up, and if the farmers caught them he would be partly to blame. Luke worked doubly hard to get the saddle back on the horse and catch up with the other boys. Even Bret saddled up and helped move the herd out.

"Jake was mad as hell, wasn't he?" Will asked when only he, Isabelle, and Pete were left in camp.

"Keep working and don't cuss," Isabelle said. "We have to have this wagon loaded and be on the trail before they get out of sight."

"That won't be a problem," Pete assured her. "They're so hungover, half of 'em will be trying to chase bushes back into the herd."

Isabelle doubted any of them were that badly off, but Jake had eight boys in his crew, six of them hungover. She wondered if they would get five miles.

By noon Isabelle knew she had greatly misjudged Jake's determination to make twenty miles the first day. She also knew the boys were undergoing a more severe punishment than anything she or Jake could have devised.

Sean had tied a bandanna around his head. He soaked it with cold water every half hour. Luke groaned each time his horse changed gait. Night Hawk, riding in sullen silence, took his anger out on any cow that tried to turn back. Chet was white-faced from the strain of trying to concentrate. Buck threw up. Isabelle didn't fool herself into thinking they wouldn't drink again, but she was certain they'd give more thought to when and how much.

The sun beat down on them with an unrelenting intensity. She could feel trickles of perspiration run down her back and between her breasts. She was certain she was filthy. The moisture made the dust stick to her skin.

They were passing out of the hill country with its deep canyons. The grass had become more sparse, shorter, more coarse. This was clearly a less hospitable land. No wonder the settlers had left it to the Indians.

She'd had plenty of time to watch Jake in the saddle. She'd never realized how attractive that man could look astride a horse. He sat tall in the saddle. No matter how hot or tired he was, he never slumped or slowed down. He was everywhere, offering encouragement, guidance, assistance. He seemed to sense where trouble was going to crop up before it happened. He seemed to know when a boy needed a little gentle support or a rough jostling.

For the last hour, he'd had Will and Pete riding flank. She would have preferred to keep them with her in the wagon for a few more days, but they were busting their britches with pride knowing they were finally *real* cowboys.

Isabelle decided she would never understand men, even little ones. Nothing appealed to them like danger. She thought of her fiancé's eagerness to go off to the war. Now here were Pete and Will, still children, anxious to pit themselves against big, ornery longhorns.

Matt had somehow managed to work his way into the position behind Will. His dislike of Jake had continued to grow until it blazed in his eyes. She assumed it was jealousy. It grew stronger the more attached Will became to Jake.

Jake rode up, and Isabelle couldn't suppress the tendrils of excitement that raced all through her. She didn't know why she had ever thought her fiancé handsome. He paled in comparison to Jake. She felt her body start to tense. She tried to calm herself, but she couldn't stop her heart from beating faster or force herself to breathe normally.

"Everything okay with you?" Jake asked when he came abreast of the wagon.

"Yes."

Actually, she was miserable. She didn't know why she'd ever thought it was hot in Savannah. There she could sit in the shade or catch the breeze off the river. She always had something cool to drink. She was tempted to follow Sean's example and pour water over her head.

"I'm going to ride ahead and look for a place to stop for tonight," Jake said. "I ought to be back in two or three hours."

Isabelle opened her mouth to object but closed it again. She had to carry her weight on this trip. If that meant being left with the boys for several hours, then she would have to get used to it.

"Chet is responsible for the herd," Jake said. "If anything goes wrong, he's to get the boys out of the way and let the cows take care of themselves. That goes for you, too."

Jake rode for a moment without speaking.

"I've given him a gun," he said finally. "I want you to have one, too."

He held out a Colt revolver. She recoiled.

"I don't know how to use that."

"Just point it and squeeze the trigger. You'll miss, but the noise will probably scare anyone off."

When she didn't take it, he leaned out of the saddle

and placed it on the seat beside her.

"I'll be back as quickly as I can."

Isabelle had never considered herself a coward, but she was ready to admit she felt a lot better when Jake was around. The reality of being alone on this vast landscape was far beyond anything she had ever imagined. Only a few hills broke the expanse of flat, grassy prairie that stretched to the horizon.

It didn't seem to bother the boys. To them it meant freedom. They were too young to realize that everything came with a price, especially freedom. The desolate nature of the land warned her the price could be their lives.

They all depended on Jake.

So she was greatly relieved when she spotted him on the horizon. She smiled when Pete and Will deserted their place with the herd and struck out to meet Jake, each trying to outride the other. She couldn't tell who won, but she could tell Jake wasn't pleased. He had a lot to say. When he finished, the boys rode back to their positions with the herd.

"Why did they go back?" she asked when he rode up to her wagon.

"Because I sent them."

"They've been waiting for you all afternoon." Nobody had told her that. The boys had stayed with the herd, but she noticed they watched the horizon where Jake had disappeared more than they did the cows.

"They've got to learn they can't go off and leave their work. Everybody's depending on them to do their share."

"But they're little boys. They're too young to understand."

"They're not too young to understand responsibility," Jake said.

"But—"

"I don't intend to be too hard on them, but they've got to learn. Now, I'm going to tell you how to get to the bedding ground. Are you any good at following landmarks?"

"What kind of landmarks?" she asked.

"Hills, creeks, any sort of large tree or rock, the sun."

"I don't know. I never tried," Isabelle replied, stunned. All trees, hills, creeks, and rocks looked pretty much the same to her. As for following the sun, she didn't know it was possible.

"It's easy. Just listen carefully."

He rattled off a lot of directions she was certain no one on earth could follow.

"Got all that?"

"I don't know."

"Say it all back."

By some miracle she managed to repeat it all and mix up only one rock with a small hill.

"If you can't do better than that, you might end up in Mexico or the Indian Territories," Jake said.

"Why don't you show me?"

"I've got to stay with the boys."

"If I can find my way, surely they can."

"I think it would be better," Jake said. "Safer."

Instantly the tension was between them, alive and pulling them toward each other like roped steers. She could see it in his eyes, in the way his body tensed. His jaw line was hard, his teeth clenched.

"Surely you don't think—"

"I made you a promise I intend to keep. I can't do that if we're alone together."

"Is it that hard?"

How could she ask such a question when her own body was suffering agonies? She was practically squirming at the memory of what he'd done to her only two nights ago. How much more difficult must it be for Jake? Men were supposed to be slaves to their desires.

"Do you think I made love to you on a whim?" Jake asked.

"I—"

"You're a very beautiful woman. You would stand out in a town much larger than Austin. Out here, you're a vision that makes a man begin to wonder if he's not delirious. I can't go with you. I don't dare. I'll send Hawk. You should reach the bedding ground in about two hours."

"I can find my way."

She was certain she would get lost, but she needed time to calm down, to get control over herself. She couldn't keep reacting this way every time she was close to him. This trip would come to an end. Jake would disappear. She had to be ready when the time came.

This trip was turning out better than Jake had hoped, but it wasn't turning out the way he wanted. He'd wanted to do something to help Matt start speaking again, but the boy disliked him more and more each day. Jake considered himself a pretty decent guy, but he didn't want Will idolizing him. The thought gave him the willies.

He wasn't having much success with the others either. Maybe Buck liked him, but he was just another boss to the rest of them. They wouldn't notice if he left as long as somebody else took his place. He hadn't cared at first, but he'd started to like these boys, to care about them. He naturally wanted them to like him in return. He guessed he'd made a wrong move.

Isabelle was definitely a plan gone wrong. She wasn't supposed to come along, but she had. He wasn't supposed to be attracted to her, but he was. He wasn't supposed to like her, but he found himself liking her more and more each day. He wasn't supposed to lose control, but he'd already made love to her and his body was aching to do it again.

Worst of all, he found himself wanting her to like him. It had all come crashing down on him when he realized he'd begun to alter his plans for the future so Isabelle would fit into them. He kept thinking of how she was different from his mother, forgetting how they were similar, forgetting he didn't want to get married, thinking only that he didn't want to let her go.

He had to be crazy to think she wanted anything to do with a man like him. She felt a strong physical attraction for him, but that horrified her so much, she had been ready to abandon the boys and flee to Austin.

Everything went around and around in his head, like a dog chasing its tail, yet nothing changed. The more he wanted Isabelle, the more unattainable she seemed to become.

He didn't know how to handle women. There was a whole vocabulary, an entire way of responding that was foreign to him. His ma and pa had fought like two wildcats. He didn't know any couples who got along any better.

He wanted Isabelle, but he didn't want marriage, family, trusting, loving, hurting. He wanted them to enjoy themselves as long as their passion for each other lasted.

He didn't know how to go about achieving that,

but he could start by complimenting her cooking. She might not believe him, but it wouldn't hurt to try. He just had to make sure she didn't catch him tossing his food into the bushes.

Chapter Nineteen

"This is good!" Jake exclaimed. "Who cooked it?"

He knew he'd said the wrong thing before the last word was out of his mouth.

"I mean, who *taught* you to cook like this," he said, hurriedly trying to retrieve the situation.

"I'm a woman, remember," Isabelle snapped. "We like to say we can't cook so when we do we'll get lots of compliments."

So much for clever maneuvering, Jake thought. Nothing for it now but the truth, rough as it was. "Last week you couldn't cook hot water. Now you turn out a stew that's as good as anything I've ever eaten."

"I have supplies."

"It's more than that. I'm sorry for what I said. I really didn't mean it."

Isabelle didn't look mollified. "The cook at the hotel taught me."

"So that's where you went. It is good, isn't it, boys?" he asked Will and Pete. They were in their usual places on either side of him.

"It's better than anything Matt ever cooked," Pete said.

"Twice as good," Will said. "Why don't you marry her? Then you could adopt us and we could stay with you forever."

Jake couldn't help but glance in Isabelle's direction. She looked almost as stunned as he felt. He was shocked by the idea. But what shocked him most was that it didn't seem so farfetched.

"Don't you think she's pretty?" Will asked.

"Sure," Jake said, trying to sound as casual as possible. "I think she's beautiful."

"Me, too," Pete said. "If you adopted me, would that mean I could stay here and not go to any more strange houses?"

Jake didn't know how to answer that question without raising hopes that were impossible to fulfill. Will was waiting just as anxiously for the answer. He looked around. Buck, Sean, and Luke were watching him. Bret and Zeke weren't, but they'd stopped eating. Chet and Hawk were watching the herd. Only Matt seemed uninterested.

"A man doesn't marry a woman just because she can cook," Jake said.

"Why not?" Will asked. "I would."

"There's a lot more to a woman then cooking," Jake replied.

"But you already said you thought she was beautiful."

"There's more than that, too."

"What?"

Jake felt as if he were sitting on a griddle.

"I'm not a good person to ask," Jake said. "My ma

ran off when I was younger than you. Didn't much like women after that."

"You like Isabelle, don't you?"

"Yeah, but I don't know much about women. I haven't been around very many."

He knew he wasn't going to get away without giving these boys an answer. The question might never be this important to them again. If he missed this chance to teach them something now, he really wasn't fit to be responsible for them.

"Marriage is a whole lot more than food or looking pretty. After all, everybody gets old."

That wasn't the right tack. How was he going to explain what he barely understood himself?

"People shouldn't get married unless they feel something very special for each other. There's times they'll disagree about something that's really important. They've got to love each other enough to let the other person have their way."

"I wouldn't do that," Pete said.

"And after they're through fighting, they've got to be able to forget all about it and just remember how much they love each other."

"Matt wouldn't forget," Will said. "He never forgets anything."

"You can't hold grudges," Jake said as he poked Will in the stomach with his index finger. "And when the person you love makes a mistake, you can't say *I told you so.* You can't even want to."

"What if you are right?" Bret asked.

"It wouldn't matter. You'd want them to be happy more than you'd want to be right."

"Do you know anybody like that?" Bret asked. He was clearly skeptical.

"No."

"I don't, either."

Leigh Greenwood

"But that doesn't mean it's not possible." He was getting off the track. "Being with somebody all the time can be pretty awful unless you like each other a lot."

"You could always go to a saloon."

"You ought to like your wife better than going to a saloon, better than gambling, better than anybody else."

"Doesn't sound like much fun to me," Pete said.

"It can be."

"I want my wife to be pretty," Will said.

"I'm not getting married," Bret said. "I don't like women."

"I might," Pete conceded, "but she'd have to cook."

"Why can't you cook?" Jake asked, relieved the conversation had drifted away from the Will's question. "Maybe she can run the ranch."

"Men don't cook!" Pete protested. "Besides, no girl can ride and rope like a man."

That statement seemed to clinch the argument for the boys, and a silence fell.

"You never answered Will's question," Buck said. "If you adopted us, would that mean we wouldn't be given to anybody else?"

Trapped! "You'd better ask Miss Davenport," Jake said.

All eyes turned toward Isabelle.

"I'm not sure the agency would let any man adopt so many children," she said. "But if they did, no one could take you away. You would be Jake's sons."

Buck turned back to Jake, his mouth open to speak.

"Before you get your hopes up," Isabelle said, "you ought to know he can't adopt any of you as long as he's unmarried."

"Then I think you ought to marry Miss Davenport

and adopt all of us," Will said. "I don't want to belong to anybody else ever again."

Jake put his arms around Will's and Pete's shoulders. "Why should anybody want to adopt you two scamps? That would be worse than living with a badger and a bobcat."

Both boys laughed, and Will threw his arms around Jake. Jake would have been touched by the show of affection if the anger blazing in Matt's eyes hadn't turned to hate at that moment.

Isabelle didn't know how she managed to finish her dinner. Will's question had shaken her right down to bedrock. It was the key to the riddle. As absurd and preposterous and impossible and frightening as it was, she loved Jake and wanted to marry him.

So much for common sense. So much for Aunt Deirdre's teaching and plans. She had fallen in love with a cowboy who preferred sleeping on the ground and cooking his meals over an open fire to living in a house. He had only a nodding acquaintance with basic hygiene and absolutely none with the way she'd been taught men were supposed to behave.

She didn't care. As long as he held her in his arms, he could eat with his fingers and pepper his sentences with cuss words. As long as he loved her as he had two nights ago, she'd sleep on the ground and count herself fortunate.

But that was the problem. He didn't love her.

She wondered if he meant what he told the boys, that he wanted more from love than a pleasant face and a willing body. It had surprised her, but it had pleased her as well. She hadn't know he understood so much about love, or cared.

But she had misjudged Jake from the first. Because she'd been raised in Savannah, she had kept thinking she knew more than he did. He was constantly showing her how wrong she was. It was about time she consigned most of Aunt Deirdre's warnings to the rubbish pile and started all over again. If she wanted to be the wife of a cowboy, she was going to have to start thinking like a cowgirl. Looking down her nose at most of what Jake said and did was no way to begin.

Besides, she didn't know what she had to be so proud of. She was dependent on Jake, not the other way around.

Jake watched the boys as they came in for breakfast. Matt got up from where he and Will had been sitting. He gave his plate to Isabelle and headed for his horse. It was his turn to be on guard duty. He threw Jake an angry look. Jake was certain it contained fear as well. Jake had given up hoping he could help Matt. The boy hated him, and this was beginning to have an effect on Jake's relationship with Will.

The child felt caught between Jake and his brother. When Matt was with the herd, Will was himself. But when Matt was around, he was uncomfortable, jumpy. Jake kept his distance. No point in making things worse for Will. He wondered what the kid thought about his idea of adoption now.

Jake had thought about it a lot. The last four days had gone better than he had hoped. They had traveled about seventy miles. The Hill Country with its canyons and trees was far behind them. Ahead stretched a flat, treeless plain. Isolated clumps of cottonwoods and willows could be found along the banks of the few spring-fed streams that provided water to the dry wilderness.

The boys had settled in to their jobs. He no longer had to watch them every minute. Chet was turning into a remarkable foreman for a boy his age. Jake understood less and less why he hadn't been successfully placed.

The more miles Jake put between himself and the farmers, the better he felt. He had never quite gotten it out of his head that Rupert hadn't given up on finding Zeke. The second boy had to be Buck, but why did he want him so badly? After they burned his ranch, Jake didn't put anything past Rupert.

Will was headed in his direction. The kid was walking funny. Jake hoped he hadn't developed a saddle sore. In the middle of a cattle drive, that was almost as bad as having a boil on your bottom.

"Why aren't you helping with the dishes?" Jake asked. Pete and Will had short hours in the saddle, but they made up for it by helping Isabelle.

"I sat on a cactus," Will said. "I got a thorn in my bottom."

Jake tried not to laugh. If Matt hadn't been so determined to sit as far away from Jake as possible, his brother wouldn't have gotten into a cactus.

"Well, you'd better ask Matt to get it out."

"He's gone."

"Ask Isabelle."

"I'm not letting some girl touch my bottom," Will said, shocked at the very thought. "I ain't no sissy. I want you to take it out."

"Women are a whole lot better at this sort of thing than men."

"I want you," Will insisted.

"Okay," Jake said, "but we'd better go down in those willows by the creek. A fella needs privacy for this sort of thing."

Will grinned and reached for Jake's hand as they headed off.

Jake had the oddest feeling that this was what it would feel like to walk with his own son some day. After his experiences in the war, he'd decided he didn't want children. Then he'd had this small mob foisted on him by Isabelle, and everything in his life had changed. More importantly, he'd changed. He wasn't sure just how, but liking to have Will hold his hand was one way.

"You sure nobody can see us?" Will asked as they went deep into the willows. "I don't want Bret to know. He'll tell everybody."

"Nobody can see us," Jake said. "I guess you'd better pull down those pants. The sooner we get rid of that thorn, the sooner we can get out of here."

Will's backside was white and thin. The thorn was easy to find, but it wasn't easy to extract. Sitting down had pushed it below the skin. Jake had to use his knife to get it out. Will tried very hard not to cry. Except for a couple of grunts and one moan, he took it like a man. Jake was just about to compliment him on his courage when he heard something crashing through the willows.

Afraid a steer had somehow gotten away from the herd, Jake turned in time to see Matt launching himself though the air at him. He held a very large knife in his right hand. The look of rage and hate in his eyes caused Jake to fear the boy had finally gone insane.

Jake had opened his mouth to ask Matt what the hell he was doing when he realized the knife was aimed straight at his own throat. Matt was trying to kill him. Jake dropped his knife in order to get a good grip on Matt's knife hand.

"Stop! Stop!" Will screamed. "He wasn't going to do it."

Matt didn't heed his brother. He didn't even seem to hear him. He fought like a demon to break Jake's hold on his wrist.

Jake was amazed at the boy's strength. Jake outweighed him by at least fifty pounds and was twice as strong, but it took Jake nearly a minute to wrestle the boy to the ground. Jake pinned his arms. He held his body in place by sitting on him. Matt continued to struggle frantically, but he couldn't overcome Jake's superior strength or weight.

"He wasn't going to do it," Will shouted at his brother, tears in his eyes. "He wouldn't do it. I know he wouldn't."

"I don't know what Will's talking about," Jake said from between gritted teeth. "I wouldn't hurt him. But if you don't drop that knife, I'm going to break your hand."

Matt still fought, but Jake found a pressure point in Matt's wrist. His grip slackened, and the knife fell to the ground. Jake picked it up. It was one of the knives Isabelle used to slice bacon. It was extremely sharp and had a blade ten inches long. It could have gone clean through his body.

"Now tell me why you were trying to use this knife on me," Jake demanded.

Matt responded by fighting to get loose.

"Tell me before I batter your head against the ground."

"It was because of me," Will said, still crying. "He thought you were going to . . . going to . . . do that thing."

"What thing?" Jake demanded.

"Matt told me I was never to let anybody touch my

bottom." Will said. "He said if they did, I was to kick and scream."

Jake heard the sound of several people crashing through the willows. "Pull up your pants," he told Will. He moved off Matt. "Sit up, but don't move. We have to talk."

Seconds later Isabelle broke through, followed by Pete.

"What's wrong?" she asked. "I heard shouting. Did you get the thorn out?"

"Yes. Take Pete and Will back to the wagon. Matt and I will be there in a minute."

Isabelle's gaze fell on the knife. She opened her mouth to speak, but Jake shook his head. He looked around until he found Will's thorn. "Here. You can show it to everybody."

"Damn, that was a big one," Pete said. "Did it hurt?"

"Naw," Will said.

"Go on," Jake said. "You still have to help Isabelle clean up."

"I doubt I'll get any help out of him tonight," Isabelle said, but her attention was on Matt. The boy sat with his head between his legs.

"We'll be along in a little bit," Jake said. "Why don't you make some more coffee?"

Isabelle was clearly reluctant to go. "Are you sure he's all right?"

"That's what I'm going to find out."

"You sure I can't help?"

"Not this time."

She didn't look convinced, but she left. Jake waited until the sound of her footsteps had died away.

"Now tell me what this is all about," he said to Matt.

The boy didn't move. He continued to sit with his

head between his legs, his body shivering as he swayed back and forth.

"What happened to Will? Who did it?"

Still Matt didn't move, but it seemed he shivered worse. Jake figured the pressure was building up inside him. If he just waited long enough, the boy would say something.

Jake couldn't decide what anyone could have done to Will. He hadn't seen any signs of abuse—no scars or bruises. Will didn't act as if he had been abused. He was too open, too loving. Matt was the one who acted frightened and withdrawn.

Matt! Of course. Jake felt like a fool for not seeing it sooner.

"He did it to *you*, didn't he?" Jake said. "What was it, Matt? What happened?"

Matt started to shake violently. He tried to scramble to his feet, to get away, but Jake grabbed hold of him and forced him to sit back down.

"You can't keep it inside you forever," Jake said.

Still Matt refused to speak. His shakes got worse. His teeth chattered. Jake could feel his muscles quivering uncontrollably.

Whatever had happened, Matt had thought Jake was about to do the same thing to Will, so he'd attacked him. But what could be so terrible that he would attack him with a knife?

"Who was it?" Jake asked. "If it was one of the foster parents, we can tell the agency. They'll make sure it never happens again."

Matt didn't speak, but he shook his head.

"Who then?" Jake asked.

"Uncle."

Jake almost missed the word. It was spoken so softly, his voice was so rough from disuse, it was barely understandable.

"What did he do?"

"Liked boys," Matt said. "Young boys."

A hazy picture started to form in Jake's mind. It was too indistinct to see clearly—he knew little about such things—but he was disgusted by what he sensed might have happened.

"Did he touch you between your legs?"

Matt nodded.

Jake felt his skin crawl. One of the boys he'd trained during the war told him about being touched that way by an older man. The boy still had nightmares years later.

Suddenly Jake understood. Matt had attacked him when he was with Will, when the boy was bending over with his pants down.

Jake thought he was going to be sick. He couldn't imagine any man doing such a thing. But that an uncle would do it to his own orphaned nephew was unbelievable.

"Did he force you to take your pants down?" Jake asked.

Matt nodded his head.

"How many times?"

Matt shrugged his shoulders.

"For how long?"

"Three years."

Jake felt hot rage bolt headlong through his veins. Three years was an eternity to a boy Matt's age. He must have felt he was living in hell. Jake wanted to find the bastard and kill him.

"Why did it stop?"

Matt jumped to his feet so quickly that Jake almost lost him. But he caught him by the shoulders before the boy could get away.

"You've got to tell me, Matt. You've bottled this up too long. If you don't get it out, it'll drive you crazy."

Matt was shaking so badly, Jake caught him under the arms to hold him up. Jake wasn't sure the boy could speak.

"Come on, Matt. You've told me the worst part. Now let's have the rest. Let's get rid of everything."

"I saw him looking at Will," Matt finally said in a hoarse whisper. "I knew what he was thinking. I told him he could do it to me and I wouldn't say a word to anybody, but he wasn't ever to do it to Will."

He wiped some slobber off his lips with his sleeve and looked up at Jake.

"One day he took Will into some trees back of the smokehouse. I wouldn't have known, but I heard Will whimpering. He had Will bent over a limb when I found them. They were both naked. He was going to . . ."

He stopped. The shaking had started again. He looked away. Jake thought he might try to run away again, but he just stood there.

"What happened?" Jake asked.

"I couldn't let him do that to Will," Matt said.

He had started to cry. Huge tears rolled from his eyes. He looked up at Jake, pleading.

"I couldn't."

"What happened?" Jake asked again.

"I found a butcher knife in the smokehouse. I buried him in the middle of the hog pen."

He was crying hard now. Just standing there in front of Jake, defenseless, crying out the torment he'd kept locked inside for so long.

"Are they going to hang me?"

Jake was gripped by a terrible anger. It wasn't enough that this boy had had to live with abuse. He had lived in fear of being hanged as well.

"Nobody will touch you. Not ever. I swear it."

Jake put his arm around Matt's shoulder and drew

him close. Matt threw his arms around Jake and sobbed.

Jake wondered why all the cruelties of the world seemed to be visited on helpless children. Maybe it only seemed that way because he'd seen so many. He thought of all the childless couples in the world who would have given half of what they possessed for a son like Matt. Yet he had ended up with an uncle who sodomized him, an uncle he had killed to protect his younger brother.

How did you go about saving a soul that had been ripped apart like that? Jake didn't know. He wasn't even sure it was possible. The child had been living in fear of his life. Jake didn't know how he had stood the strain. No wonder he didn't speak.

Matt's sobs finally stopped. He let go of Jake, embarrassed at his weakness. "I'm sorry."

"Don't be."

Matt wiped his eyes.

"Are you going to tell?"

"I ought to tell Isabelle. She needs to understand."

"I don't want her to know."

"Why?"

Matt looked down and shuffled his feet.

"Out with it."

"She'll think I'm dirty." He looked up at Jake. "You probably don't want me to stay on the drive with you."

Hellfire and damnation! The boy's burden was even more terrible than Jake had imagined. Matt thought he had been turned into something so reprehensible, no one would want anything to do with him.

"There's nothing dirty about you," Jake said. "I always thought you were a fine young man. Knowing what you've gone through, what you were willing to do to protect your brother, makes me think even more of you."

Matt looked relieved, but he didn't look as if he really believed Jake.

"I know Isabelle will feel the same way. She'll probably want to smother you with attention. But I won't tell her if you don't want me to."

Jake knew the boy longed to say no.

"Okay, but don't tell her today."

"Matt, nothing that happened made you dirty. You're still the same good-hearted boy you were before it happened. Don't let it ruin you."

Jake could tell Matt didn't believe him, but he was young. He would never forget, but he had time to get over the worst of it.

"Now let's get back. You're supposed to be on watch. If those steers stampede while you're gone, the boys will never forgive you."

Chapter Twenty

Isabelle decided God had made a serious mistake when he didn't make man in the image of woman. After Jake told her what had happened to Matt, she had been determined to do everything she could to let Matt know he was still a cherished member of the group. Jake told her she was not to say a word or even act like she knew—on pain of having her neck wrung.

Isabelle had been furious, but she decided she'd wait and let Jake realize he was taking the wrong tact. When he'd been a miserable failure, she would step in and show him how to treat a sensitive boy like Matt.

Things hadn't gone exactly as she expected.

Jake had treated Matt with the same callous disregard for his feelings he always had. Not only had Matt not seemed to mind, he had virtually blossomed under treatment that would have had any ordinary woman crying herself to sleep night after night. He still didn't say much, but he did talk. He was never obvious about it, but he liked to be near Jake. He never tried to sit by him the way Will did, but he was always close enough to hear everything he said.

Isabelle was waging her own battle to stay close to Jake without seeming to do so. A cattle drive was not a good place to be near anybody, especially when she drove the chuck wagon. She was up early and washing dishes after everybody had left with the herd. She caught up with the herd about the time Jake told her where he meant to camp for the night.

She left the herd, arrived to cook the evening meal, and spent most of the evening cleaning up and getting ready for breakfast the next morning. She wanted to drop from exhaustion, but she couldn't when Jake never slowed down. He was always in the saddle or teaching the boys to shoot. She hated to think how much ammunition was used up shooting at imaginary Indians.

Then he decided to teach her to shoot.

"I don't want to learn to use a gun," she told him. "I don't believe in killing."

"Neither do I," Jake said, "but I believe in dying even less."

Isabelle resented that the few moments Jake was willing to spend with her had to be spent talking about guns. He had kept his word. He had stayed away from her. She had gotten exactly what she wanted, and she hated it.

"We've been very lucky so far, but we can't expect to make it all the way to Santa Fe without trouble. You're the most vulnerable of all. You've got to know how to defend yourself."

There had been one change. He had been sending

one of the boys with her each day. The last two days he had gone himself. The first time it happened, her heart had hammered with excitement. But she hadn't counted on his iron control. He had insisted she let him drive while she took a nap.

She had tried to argue, but it did no good. It never did. He was the most stubborn man God had never created. It annoyed her even more that he was usually right.

They should be leaving the bedding ground right now—the herd had already left—but he had decided this very minute was time to teach her to shoot. She considered refusing but decided it wouldn't be worth the trouble. Besides, as much as she disliked guns and the idea of killing anyone, she had a terrible feeling she would someday need to defend herself. Or Jake.

"It's not hard," Jake told her as he handed her an unloaded rifle. "Here, hold it. Get to know the feel of it."

She'd rather have him hold her. She knew the feel of that already, and she liked it. A lot better than this rifle. It was cold, awkward, and heavy.

"Don't hold it like it's a snake," Jake said. "It won't hurt you."

It might as well have been one. She liked it just about as much.

Jake took the rifle from her. "Hold it to your shoulder like this."

He handed it back. She tried to copy what he'd done, but it was awkward. She shifted to the left side, and it felt better.

"You're left-handed?"

"Yes. Is it important?"

"It keeps me from trying to teach you to shoot with the wrong hand."

She still didn't hold the rifle to Jake's satisfaction.

"Here, let me show you," he said.

He stood behind her and put his arms around her. Isabelle liked that a whole lot better.

"You've got to rest it against your left shoulder like this."

He pulled it tight against her shoulder.

"Support it with your left hand like this." He took her left hand and placed it under the barrel of the rifle. "Put your right hand on the trigger like this."

He took her hand, placed her index finger on the trigger, and wrapped her fingers and thumb around the stock.

Isabelle offered no resistance, but neither did she pay close attention to what he was saying. She couldn't concentrate when his body was wrapped around hers. She felt her shoulders against his chest, his thighs against her buttocks, his cheek resting against her hair, his breath against her neck. She couldn't think about anything as silly as a rifle. She could have been holding a cannon or a peashooter and wouldn't have known the difference.

"Now you look through this groove to the sight on the end of the rifle barrel," Jake said.

The timbre of his voice had changed. He didn't seem so businesslike and assured, so brisk. He sounded slightly breathless, his voice more of a whisper than a sharp, clear sound.

"You're not doing what I asked," Jake said. "There's no point in firing a rifle if you're not going to aim it first."

But he didn't sound as if he was thinking about rifles or targets either. His body was hard with tension. He tried to stand away from her, but he couldn't without releasing his hold on her and the rifle.

She could feel the heat of his arousal. It burned

her skin like a brand. She could feel the tension in his arms as they tightened around her bit by bit until he actually hurt her.

He seemed to recollect himself. His muscles relaxed.

"You're not looking down the barrel," he said again.

They both knew it was impossible. The rifle was shaking too much for either of them to sight anything smaller than a medium-sized hill.

"What do I do when I look down the sight?" she asked.

She had to at least try to pay attention. If not, she was liable to drop the rifle and throw herself into his arms.

"Make sure your target is in the middle of your sights. Then you squeeze the trigger like this. Don't jerk it. It'll throw your aim off."

She had her sights aimed on Jake. Only it wasn't as simple as shooting him. Her mind told her she was being incredibly foolish. Her emotions whispered that despite outward appearances, this was the one man who could give her everything she wanted. Her body screamed that she was wasting time. It wanted to consume Jake here and now.

Suddenly the tension was too much. Her muscles sagged, and she leaned back against him. That set off an immediate reaction in Jake. His breath ended in a sharp gasp, and his body became rigid. He stepped back abruptly. The rifle fell from her loosened grasp.

Isabelle turned around. Their gazes locked. The rifle was forgotten. They stood looking at each other, unable to move, unable to speak. Then one of the mules stamped its foot, and the spell was broken. Jake lifted his arms from his sides, and Isabelle walked straight into his embrace.

Their kiss was hot and fierce. All the restraint, the frustration, the banked desire of so many days burned away the remaining traces of hesitation. Isabelle forgot her reservations about the future. She forgot she was turning herself into a fallen woman. She forgot she would probably never see Jake after the end of this drive.

She cared only that she was in his arms and that he was kissing her with all the passion she so fervently desired. Jake was the most real thing that had ever happened to her, and she meant to hang on to him for as long as she could.

She pressed her body hard against him. She wanted to feel her breasts ache from the pressure of being pushed against Jake's hard chest. She ground her body against his hardness. She wanted her loins to burn with the need to have him inside her.

When Jake's impatient fingers fumbled with the buttons to her dress, she undid them for him. She was eager to feel his hands on her body, to feel his warm, moist lips scorch her firming breasts with his desire.

A moan escaped Isabelle when Jake's teeth raked a sensitive nipple. The feel of the morning air did nothing to cool her heated flesh. Nothing but union with Jake's body could put out the fire that was burning in her loins.

Isabelle leaned against the side of the wagon. As Jake's teeth and tongue ravaged her breasts, he pushed his knee between her legs. Isabelle could barely stand. She clamped his leg between her thighs and squeezed. The pressure felt delicious. It tickled and teased the tension that centered there.

The moment she released the pressure, Jake's hand found its way between her legs. He didn't tempt or tease her. He didn't need to. Her body was already slick with moist heat. He parted her flesh and entered her. His fingers went straight to the sensitive nub. Isabelle's entire body shuddered when he began to rub ever so gently.

It took only a moment before the magic being worked by Jake's hand all but made her forget the wonders his lips wrought on her breasts. He drove deeper and deeper into her, gradually increasing the pressure, increasing the tempo little by little until she felt waves of pleasure rush through her body.

Isabelle clung to Jake, her body twisted and tormented by the swell of passion that surged through her. Without warning the waves broke, and she felt the tension drain from her in a physical release.

It was several moments before her breathing returned to normal. Only then did her shattered senses focus sufficiently for her to see that Jake was no longer a partner in her sensual journey. Not even a guide. He had backed away and stood staring at her, his face a mask of shock and shame.

"I didn't mean to do that," he said.

Isabelle struggled to regain control of her mind and body. Jake was rapidly moving away from her. She had to stop him before he ran away altogether.

"I wanted it as much as you," she said.

"But I promised. I gave my word."

"I know, but—"

"You told me you couldn't control the need inside you. I promised I'd do it for you. *I promised.*"

"I wanted you, Jake. I wanted you to want me."

"I do. I want you so much, it's hard to think about anything else. Why do you think I make the boys ride with you so much of the time?"

She was relieved to know he'd stayed away because he didn't trust himself. She'd never been able to entirely banish the fear that having made love to her once, he had no further interest in her. Her need for Jake went far beyond her physical desire.

She rebuttoned her blouse.

"You're a lady," Jake was saying. "You're too good for anybody like me."

"Don't be absurd. I'm just a woman."

"You'll never be *just a woman*. You'll always be what you were raised to be. You couldn't be anything else if you tried. Any more than I could be anything but what I am. You belong with soft music, warm lights, compliments whispered in your ear. I belong out here with the thorns and the dust."

"I don't want to be put in a glass cabinet and taken out only to be admired," Isabelle said, horrified at the kind of life he seemed to think she wanted. "I may not be as good at surviving thorns and dust as you are, but I prefer it to the life you described. I want to be alive, Jake, to feel alive. You've taught me the difference."

"It was the boys."

"No. It was you and your determination to rub my nose in it until all the snobbery was worn away."

But she couldn't convince him of that now. He was too shocked at what he had done to listen to her, or believe her if he did. She must make him understand that she wasn't the same woman she had been a few weeks ago, but he wasn't ready to hear that now. He was too angry with himself.

"We'd better be going," he said. "I don't want one of the boys coming back to see if something happened to us."

"Jake—"

"My pa brought me up to honor my word. He wouldn't accept my hunger for you as an excuse for breaking it."

Isabelle couldn't help but smile. "I do, Jake. I think it's the very best reason."

"It won't happen again. I pro—"

"Don't promise, Jake. I don't want you to."

"You don't think I can keep my word this time?"

"I don't want you to."

He took a moment to think that over. She wished she knew what he was thinking, but whatever it was, it had unsettled his mind.

Isabelle didn't have to think anymore. She knew what she wanted. She loved Jake and wanted to marry him. That didn't make any sense. She had no idea how she could possibly make such a marriage work, but she refused to worry about practicality. She loved him, and he loved her. She was sure of that even if he wasn't. They'd find a way. She knew they would. Jake could do anything.

And she had discovered she wasn't the person she'd thought she was. She might even learn to use a rifle.

Jake resisted the impulse to ride so far ahead of Isabelle that he couldn't see her. He knew he was trying escape his conscience, not Isabelle. He shouldn't have made love to her. He had promised to keep his distance. Now, at the first real temptation, he'd given in and taken her in a rutting heat.

She said she wanted him as much as he wanted her. A knife-edge of desire raced though him, making him hard and hot. Even now he trembled with the effort to keep from turning back and making love to her until this driving need released its vise-like grip. Her wanting him made it that much harder not to give in.

He reminded himself of his mother. She couldn't have endured the only kind of existence he could offer Isabelle. Isabelle might try, but she would ultimately run back to the only society she understood.

He could never settle for an affair that lasted until their passion was spent. He doubted he could ever exhaust his need for her. He'd never expected to feel this way—never wanted to—and it frightened him. It made him just that much more afraid of loving her. Once he loved her, he would follow her anywhere.

And that would be the end for both of them.

But she didn't love him. She couldn't. She wanted him to make love to her, but a woman of her type looked for something quite different in a husband.

He'd best keep his distance until they reached New Mexico. After he sold his herd, he'd make certain she had enough money to get back to Austin. He'd find something for the boys as well. He couldn't leave without knowing they were safe and happy.

And he would leave. He couldn't stay around Isabelle knowing he couldn't have her. Maybe he'd go to Colorado and start a new ranch. Maybe he'd go back to Texas and get another herd. The boys could help him. Maybe he would abandon his ranch and take a job as an ordinary hand. He was certain George Randolph would give him a job if he asked.

Wherever he went, it had to be so far away from Isabelle that he would never see her again.

Isabelle knew something was wrong even before they reached the herd. The cows were spread out, grazing, not bunched and walking forward in that long, meandering column. There wasn't a boy in sight.

"Somebody's been hurt," Isabelle said, certain nothing else could have caused the boys to go off and leave the herd.

Leigh Greenwood

"They'd better be hurt real bad to have let the herd wander," Jake said. "I'll ride ahead and see what's wrong."

And leave her to bring up the rear just as if she wasn't burning with curiosity as well.

A totally unexpected sight met Isabelle when she drove up. The boys were standing around a dead steer. Sean and Hawk were holding a boy who struggled hard to break loose. Chet was explaining to Jake what happened.

"I don't know how he got so close without one of us seeing him," Chet was saying, "but next thing I know, he's driving a steer into this wash. By the time I got here, the thieving varmint had killed it."

"Who are you?" Jake demanded. "What are you doing out here by yourself?"

The boy was only a child. He looked to be eight or nine at most. The sun and wind had burned and blistered his face. Someone had cut his dark brown hair in uneven batches. A battered, wide-brimmed hat nearly covered his face. Shapeless brown pants and an over-sized checked shirt dwarfed his thin body. Isabelle doubted he weighed more than seventy-five pounds. His heavy boots were several sizes too large, but his hands were slim and delicate. Isabelle decided he would be a handsome little boy when he was cleaned up.

The child refused to answer Jake. When Isabelle climbed down from the wagon, he started struggling. When he found Sean was too strong, he bit him. He bit Hawk, too. Before either could recover, the child threw himself at Isabelle. He grabbed her around the waist and hid behind her.

"Don't let 'em kill me!" he cried in a high voice.

"Nobody's going to kill you," Jake said, trying without success to pull the child from behind Isabelle.

"But I can't have people stealing my steers."

"I didn't steal it," the child said, still dodging Jake. "I took it."

"It's all the same to me," Jake said, unable to see any difference between the two.

"Are you hurt?" Isabelle asked Sean and Hawk.

Sean shook his hand. "He didn't break the skin, but it hurts like hell. What's wrong with you, you little son of a bitch? Only a girl bites."

"You put your big hands on me again, and I'll bite you again," the boy answered defiantly.

"You boys go back to the herd," Jake said. "Isabelle and I will take care of this. And next time you leave those steers on their own, one of you had better be dead or damned near it."

The boys didn't want to miss anything, but they mounted up and rode off. "Now," Jake said turning back to the urchin, "you can start by telling me your name."

"No."

"Okay. Until you give me something better, your name is Brat."

"It's not," he replied indignantly.

Jake ignored him. "Now, Brat, what are you doing out here all by yourself? There can't be another white man within two hundred miles."

"My name's Drew."

"Glad to make your acquaintance, Drew. Now tell me, where's your family?"

Tears suddenly filled the boy's honey-brown eyes. "Dead," he said. "Injuns killed 'em. I'm glad I bit that big one."

"You shouldn't have. Hawk is only half Comanche. How did you get away?"

Drew didn't look repentant. "Ward helped me."

"Who's Ward?" Isabelle asked.

"The man who helped me. His horse broke a leg. He was gonna ask if he could hitch a ride with us when the Injuns attacked. He killed 'em, but they shot him. I killed that beef so we could have something to eat. We already ate everything we took from the wagon."

"Where is this Ward?" Jake asked.

"Down the wash a ways. We been watching you."

"Take us to him," Jake said.

"You gonna hurt him?"

"Of course not," Isabelle assured him. "We're going to help you both."

Drew looked to Jake for confirmation. "Yeah, that's right. Now hurry up. We've got to catch up with the herd."

Drew didn't seem entirely convinced Jake meant no harm, but he started down the wash. Isabelle guessed the boy was unused to making decisions that could determine whether he lived or died. But she had a hunch he was the kind of child who would get used to it very quickly.

"How long have you been out here?" Jake asked.

"Dunno. Seems like forever."

"Was there anybody else with you besides your parents?"

"No."

"What possessed your pa to travel alone? He was asking for trouble."

"That's what people told him, but Pa never listened to nobody."

Without warning, Drew darted into a thicket of juniper and vines that clung to the side of the wash.

"Don't come any farther," a voice called out.

It came from a different part of the wash.

"We've come to help," Jake said. "Drew shot your

dinner, but he can't bring it to you. We thought we'd lend a hand."

"What have you got in mind?"

"It depends on whether you can walk."

A man crawled from behind a bush using his arms and one leg. His pant leg was split down the seam, exposing a bandaged thigh. He was a tall, thin man with a slightly Spanish cast to his features. Or maybe it was the Spanish style of his clothes. He had straight black hair, fair skin, and deep blue eyes. Next to him was a saddle, bridle, and saddlebags of black Spanish leather worked with silver. Whoever he was, he was not a poor man. He spied Isabelle and his attitude changed.

"My apologies, ma'am, but I'm afraid I can't greet you as I would like." He sounded positively courtly. "I'm Ward Dillon. When I'm able, I will most assuredly kiss your hand."

"That's not necessary," Isabelle said. "I'm more interested in seeing your wound."

"It's not a sight for a lady."

"I've seen quite a few unladylike sights in the past few weeks, and I haven't fainted yet," Isabelle replied, irritated that he was treating her just the way Jake had done. Was it necessary to dress like a slattern before men thought she could do anything beyond carry a parasol and fan herself because of the heat?

Ward turned over and lay on his back. "Sorry to be so rude, but my strength is gone."

Jake examined him warily. "I guess he's worth saving," he said.

Isabelle was shocked, but Ward chuckled.

"I'd appreciate it if you'd give it a try. From the look of things, you could use at least one vaquero old enough to shave."

Isabelle was shocked to see a broken arrow shaft protruding from his leg.

"You'll have to wait until we get back to the wagon to remove that," Jake said.

"Then let's go," Ward said.

They mounted him on Jake's horse. She knew the pain must be excruciating, but Ward never said a word.

"Come on out, Drew," Ward called once his strength returned. "We may as well go along with this lady and gentleman. I doubt we'll get another offer."

Drew came out, but he didn't look as though he trusted Jake.

"He's not quick to accept strangers," Ward explained.

"She is," Jake said, indicating Isabelle, "especially if it's a kid."

"My name is Isabelle Davenport," Isabelle said. "And this ungracious man is Jake Maxwell. I was responsible for some orphan boys who needed jobs. Jake had a herd that needed taking to New Mexico. We decided to combine our resources."

Ward grinned.

"She started out with eight," Jake said. "But before I knew it, she shook a tree and two more fell out."

"Now it looks like we have an even dozen," Isabelle said.

"You ain't got me," Drew declared.

"They have us both," Ward said. "I'd appreciate it if you didn't give them any trouble. They're going to have more than enough with me."

Chapter Twenty-one

Removing the arrow shaft proved to be more difficult than Isabelle expected. Jake could only get it out by pushing it through the other side. Isabelle thought she would faint. Ward did.

"Use plenty of whiskey to clean it," Jake said. "We don't want him to get gangrene." He examined the ugly wound closely. "Frankly, I don't know why he doesn't have it already."

"Is he gonna to be okay?" Drew asked. The boy was as white as a sheet.

"We'll have to wait and see," Jake said. "It's a nasty wound. Now get up in the wagon. We've got a long way to go before we make camp this evening."

Ward regained consciousness about a half an hour later.

"I see I survived," he said to Isabelle.

"The wound is infected," Isabelle said.

"I know. I used all my carbolic acid trying to prevent gangrene. I hope I was successful." He looked around. "Where are we going?" He didn't seemed overly concerned about the prospect of dying.

"Bed ground for the night. Maybe we can stop early."

"No," Ward said. "I know a place about twenty miles from here."

"That's too far after our delays," Jake said.

"You're very close to the major north-south Indian route," Ward said.

"The boys can't drive the herd that hard—they've only been at this for a week—and I can't leave Isabelle on her own."

"You take care of the boys. I'll make sure the wagon gets there."

"You know these plains?"

"Like the back of my hand."

Jake looked undecided. "Tell me about this bed ground," he finally said.

Ward did, and he told Jake how to get there.

"Okay, but you make sure you keep your eyes open."

Isabelle was relieved that Jake didn't want to leave her.

"Go on," she said. "The boys need you more than I do."

That wasn't true. She'd never needed anybody as much as she needed Jake. The boys would outgrow their need. She never would.

"Tell me about yourself," Isabelle said to Ward as they started off. "And don't leave out what you were doing in the middle of this godforsaken country by yourself."

Isabelle watched Jake disappear in the distance. It didn't take long. One minute he was there, and the next he was gone. It gave her an odd feeling. She wanted to reach out and ask him to come back. She shouldn't have felt so alone, not with Ward and Drew in the wagon.

She felt abandoned. She and Jake had forged a new link in their relationship this morning, one that was elemental. They were joined in a way that was integral to her existence as a human being. She had become a small part of him; he had become a large part of her. She didn't think Jake knew that, but she did.

Jake didn't like it. The hoofprints were old, but there was no question that more than a hundred Indian ponies had traveled north along a route the herd had to cross. The Indians would come back. The only question was when. Unless there was a heavy rain, it would be impossible for them to miss the trail left by the herd.

They would follow—of that Jake was certain. But right now, he was more worried about the next eighty miles. Ward's ideal bed ground was the headwaters of the Concho River. That was the last water until they reached the Pecos River. Four days of scorching, dry plain. He had planned to spend a day resting the cattle, giving them a chance to graze as much as they wanted. Now he wasn't sure.

Then there was the question of what to do with Ward and Drew. He didn't suppose they wanted to go all the way to Santa Fe, but he couldn't turn around and take them back east. Neither did he want to add another orphan to his responsibilities, not that it would make much difference at this point.

He was getting ahead of himself. For a man who'd spent most of his life avoiding commitment, he sure acted anxious to grab hold of it now. Ward could take care of himself, and Drew probably had family anxious to take him in. They could send for him at Santa Fe as well as anywhere else. Jake would have enough to do trying to figure out what to do about Isabelle and the boys.

They didn't arrive in camp until after dark. By the time they had watered the herd and let them spread out to graze, the boys were exhausted. Jake was dog tired. The herd had fought every step of the extra five miles.

The boys' inexperience had kept Jake moving at a gallop most of the day. He'd worn out four horses. He had to go easier tomorrow. He didn't have enough horses for that.

His exhaustion probably explained why he was feeling so uncharitable toward Ward. He could have used an extra hand rather than having two extra people to worry about. Still, it wasn't like him to feel irritated about a man who might still lose his leg.

"That was mighty fine eating, ma'am," Ward was saying. "It's been a long time since I've tasted better."

"That's only because you've been lost with nothing decent to eat," Isabelle said, pink with pleasure at the compliments Ward had been handing out so generously. "A good beef stew is a treat for us. I was getting tired of pork."

Ward eyed Jake. "I don't know if Mr. Maxwell is equally fond of his stew. I imagine he's thinking of how many dollars it cost him."

"My name's Jake," Jake said. "I like the stew. It's right tasty. Isabelle is turning into a real good cook."

The compliment didn't sound nearly as nice as he'd hoped. He'd been planning to tell Isabelle how much he liked the stew. He was still waiting for her to forgive him for assuming somebody else had cooked that first meal after they got back from New-combe's Crossing.

"Drew, get up and serve those boys," Ward said. "Miss Davenport will never get a chance to eat her dinner."

Drew didn't look entirely pleased, but he got up.

"There's no need," Isabelle said. "The boys know how to serve themselves."

Jake figured Isabelle grew up with somebody waiting on her. His ma said that's how all society ladies were raised. The whole family would sit down to this big table with the head of the household at one end. That would be Jake. Only he'd never sat at the head of a table in his life. He bet Ward had.

"You just leave those plates, ma'am. Drew and I will see to them."

"You'll do no such thing," Isabelle said as she submerged the plates in water that had been heating on the coals. "You've got to keep still so your wound doesn't break open. And Drew needs to finish his dinner."

The boy cast Isabelle a grateful look and dug into his food before Ward had time to think of something else for him to do.

"A lady like you shouldn't have to do all this work," Ward said. "I feel like a shiftless lout just lying here and expecting you to look after me."

Jake thought he ought to thank his lucky stars somebody was looking after him. If Drew hadn't shot that steer, he'd be back in that dry wash trying to figure out how to keep himself alive and not finding many options.

"Jake will tell you everybody has a job to do," Isabelle was saying. "The boys all help with the herd, but Pete and Will help me when I need it."

"It still doesn't seem right. My mother never did such rough work."

"I don't suppose mine would have either if she had lived, but Jake will tell you this a different world out here. Everybody has to do their share."

Jake wondered how it had become his fault that West Texas was full of Indians and rattlesnakes and that fine ladies had to soil their hands washing dishes. For a dried-up piece of rawhide dripping blood and guzzling coffee, Ward Dillon was acting damned high in the instep. You'd think he was the one born a lady instead of Isabelle.

Jake's coffee cup was empty. He started to ask Isabelle to fill it for him, but he stopped himself. He got up and poured his own coffee.

"No need to get up," Ward said. "Drew could have done that far you."

"Probably, but I wouldn't want to be responsible for the kid starving to death," Jake snapped.

He didn't know whether Ward was just trying to show his appreciation that he wasn't dying under a clump of sage or whether he had a genius for getting other people to do his work for him, but Jake was getting damned tired of his unctuous ways. He could look bad in Isabelle's eyes all by himself. He didn't need any help from this piece of driftwood.

Jake swallowed his coffee, cursed when it burned his throat, and put his cup and plate into Isabelle's hot water. "We're leaving first thing in the morning."

Ward looked surprised. "You should lay up a day to allow the herd to drink all they can before you start. It's eighty miles without a drop of water."

"I know," Jake said, wondering if Ward thought he was the only man who'd ever set foot in West Texas. "I also know about a hundred Indians went up the trail a couple of weeks ago. They don't usually stay

long. I don't want to be anywhere near here when
they come back."

"Indians!" Isabelle exclaimed. "I hope it's not the
same ones that killed Drew's parents."

Damn! Now he'd frightened Isabelle. "There's Indians from here to Santa Fe," Jake said. "This bunch
is probably no different from the rest. I just don't
want to meet up with them."

"When do you want breakfast?" Isabelle asked.

"An hour before dawn. From now on we'll travel
at night and rest during the heat of the day. It'll be
easier on the cattle."

It wasn't easier on Isabelle. The first day passed
without incident, but things got more difficult by the
second. Cooking a meal in the middle of the day with
the sun bearing down on the back of her neck and
the wind blowing trash into the pots did nothing to
improve her temper or the taste of the food.

Drew, Pete, and Will had spent most of the night
scouring the area for wood. There was virtually nothing between the Concho and the Pecos but buffalo
chips. Isabelle had accustomed herself to a great deal
during the past weeks, but Jake figured she'd turn
the wagon around and head back to Austin before
she'd cook with buffalo chips.

Ward fashioned a walking stick out of a limb. He
hopped around worse than a one-legged soldier. Jake
would have been happier if he'd kept on being a useless invalid. He got in the way more than he helped.
Of course, Isabelle thought Ward was wonderful.
Jake didn't know why women always fell for that sort
of thing.

"You really must stay off your feet," Isabelle said
when Ward insisted upon grinding the coffee. "You'll
be more help to Jake when you can ride again."

"I couldn't consider leaving you to cook for all these men without anybody to help you."

"Drew can give me all the help I need," Isabelle said.

"I want to ride," Drew said. "I'm just as good as any of them." He pointed to the younger boys. "I don't mean I don't want to help you, ma'am, but I'd rather earn my keep."

God, Jake thought to himself, they must go to school to learn that much blather. It rolled out of their mouths as though it were the most natural thing in the world.

It made him feel more like a dirt clod than ever. He couldn't think of pretty things to say. When he did, they came out wrong. He hadn't been brought up like Ward and Isabelle. Hell, he didn't know about half the things they took for granted. Isabelle liked talking to Ward. Jake could tell from the way she smiled at him.

He couldn't blame her. The only person he could blame was himself for keeping on dreaming about the impossible.

Not a single hill broke the monotony of the flat plain. The grass hadn't yet dried and turned brown, but the sun blazed down with blinding intensity. The herd had been without water for a day and a half, and they were beginning to feel it. They milled about, bawling their discomfort. As the steers' thirst became greater, they started thinking about the last place they'd found water. All morning one steer after another tried to head back to the Concho River. The boys had spent most of their time driving bunch quitters back into the herd. Their horses were exhausted.

"Take it easy on your horses," Jake told them over and over again. "We don't have many to spare." For a drive like this, he needed eight or nine horses per rider. They had four.

Ward was standing over the Dutch ovens when Jake came in to eat. "I cooked the beans," he announced. "They won't be half as good as Miss Isabelle's, but the poor woman's nearly exhausted."

Far from looking exhausted, Isabelle looked magnificent. Jake continued to marvel at how she could look so crisp and neat when everybody else looked as if they'd been dragged through a mud puddle and left out to dry. It was all too easy to picture himself coming home to her at the end of each day.

But even as his need for Isabelle grew stronger, even as he began to question his vow never to marry, his old prejudices reared their heads with renewed vigor. Every day brought him closer to Santa Fe and the memory of what his mother had done to his family.

He'd thought the anger had died years ago, but he was wrong. It was still there—waiting, simmering. He felt the internal tension increase a little each day. He tried to tell himself it would be different with Isabelle, but the way she acted with Ward demolished that piece of self-deception. Regardless of how well she was surviving this trip, she hadn't forgotten how she was brought up. After the boys left, she would have no reason to stay in this wilderness.

His mother used to throw up her hands and declare she couldn't live in this wasteland another minute. Then after shouting and cursing her husband for taking her away from Mobile, she would start crying and pulling her hair. Next she'd take to her bed, staying there for as much as two weeks at a time, moaning as if she were about to die.

He kept telling himself Isabelle wouldn't do that. She had responded to challenges by learning how to do her work better. Then they found Ward, and Isabelle took to him like a long lost friend. He found himself wishing that Indian had shot Ward through the tongue instead of the leg. At least then he wouldn't have been able to talk so much.

"Isn't she a wonder?" Ward was saying as he hobbled alongside Jake. "She can drive that wagon for hours, then cook a meal better than you can find in a restaurant, all in the wind and the dirt, and she looks as pretty as a picture, as though she just stepped out of her *boudoir*."

Jake didn't know what a *boudoir* was, but he was dead certain it was something that belonged in a house a good deal fancier than any he'd ever be able to afford. If Ward didn't stop taking the words out of Jake's mouth before he had a chance to say them— the ones he knew at any rate—he was going to dump him in the next wash so the Indians could finish the job.

"Isabelle has always looked fresh as a daisy," Jake said, disgusted with and envious of Ward's easy command of the flowery compliment. "We've gotten so used to it, we hardly notice it any more."

"I'd notice her if she looked that way every morning for a hundred years."

Jake abandoned the battlefield. He could tell when he was outgunned. "We all think Isabelle's pretty special," Jake said. "Just ask any of the boys."

He accepted his plate and looked for a place to sit. The boys were seated in a circle around the fire in the middle of the endless plain. It felt as if they were they only people in the world.

"She's twice as pretty as any lady I know," Chet said. "And twice as nice."

"If it weren't for her, I'd be in jail," Sean said.

"And I'd be dead," Buck added.

As the boys tried to top each other praising Isabelle, Jake couldn't help but glance at her. She really did look especially pretty today. Damn Ward. He never gave him a chance to say anything first. Still, maybe it was just as well. Sweet words got a man into trouble. They also started a woman thinking more than he intended. Women never could understand there was a difference between *I like you very much* and *I want to get married.*

For Jake, the difference was crucial. The moment he finished eating, he got to his feet.

"We got to get going, boys. The next day and a half are going to be brutal."

"You ought to rest more," Ward said. "I never heard of anybody driving a herd like you're doing."

Isabelle sent Jake a questioning look. It made him nervous to go against conventional wisdom, but knowing those Indians could cut their trail any minute helped. The Indians could travel as far in one day as the herd could in five.

"Those steers are so miserable they can't settle down," Jake said to Ward. "Look at them. They're doing nothing but walking as it is. Might as well be walking toward the Pecos. They'll get to water a lot quicker."

"If they don't die first," Ward said.

"They won't die from walking," Jake said, "just thirst." He was talking more to Isabelle than Ward. "Every extra hour it takes us to reach the Pecos, the more steers we'll lose. How are the mules holding out?" he asked Isabelle.

"Fine. But we don't have any more water for them."

"How about for us?"

"It's getting low. It won't last more than two days."

"It won't have to. With luck, we'll reach the Pecos

311

before midnight tomorrow."

Isabelle walked with him as he headed for his horse. "Are you sure?"

"No," he said, deciding to be honest, "but it seems best to me to keep going as long as they can. Once they stop walking, they won't be getting closer to water no matter where it is. How are you holding up?"

"I'm fine." She smiled. "With Ward and Drew helping, I've got it easier than anybody else."

"How's his leg?"

"Much better. I was worried about gangrene, but it seems to be healing."

"The man is tough as leather."

"With a silver tongue," she added, smiling. "He sounds like some of the men I grew up with in Savannah."

"If he starts bowing and kissing your hand, he'll have to find his own way to Santa Fe."

Isabelle smiled again. He wished she wouldn't do that. It made it a lot harder for him to remember his vow. It made it doubly hard to remember why it was okay for him to like Isabelle but not love her.

"I don't think I'd like that any more than you would."

"That's how fancy gentlemen act."

"I'm not a fancy lady any more. I'd feel rather strange if anybody tried to kiss my hand."

But she didn't feel strange when Jake kissed her lips or her breasts. He almost smiled. She really wasn't the same woman who had driven up to his ranch weeks ago. That woman had been afraid even to sleep in his bed. He ought to get in the saddle and get going, but he lingered, unwilling to end the moment.

"Things are going to be rough for the next while. I expect the boys will have to eat on the run. It's going to be all we can do to keep this herd from turning back."

"I can help," Drew said.

Jake hadn't seen the boy come up.

"You'd better stay with Isabelle."

"I can ride better'n any of them," Drew said, pointing scornfully at Hawk and Chet, Jake's two best riders. "Gimme a horse, and I'll show you."

"You can ride with me," Isabelle said.

"Jake is gonna need all the help he can muster to git this mess of steers to that river," Drew said, stubbornly holding to the issue. "No point in my riding in the wagon. My pa put me on a horse when I was three."

"Okay," Jake said. "Ask Luke for a horse. If you can stay on, you can ride flank between Zeke and Buck."

Drew was off like a streak.

"I don't think—"

"It's his pride," Jake said. "He's just like Pete and Will."

"But he's so fragile," Isabelle said.

"So are you, and you survived. You look prettier than a bluebonnet today."

Isabelle looked a little flustered. "I'm really as tough as old hickory. I found that out at the orphanage."

"You look a lot better than any piece of wood," Ward said as he hobbled up.

Jake, a similar compliment on his lips, had to stifle the desire to throttle Ward on the spot.

"Drew tells me you're going to let him ride with the herd," Ward said, seemingly unaware of Jake's annoyance.

"I'm going to give him a chance."

"I wish you'd keep an eye on him. He's not as robust as he ought to be."

Jake decided he was going to leave Ward at the first settlement he came to. Putting up with him all the way to Santa Fe was more then he could endure. Not even Jake's father tried to second guess him so often.

"I'll do that," Jake said. "Now I'd better get going before Drew drives the herd all the way to the Pecos by himself."

Chapter Twenty-two

Isabelle kept the wagon north of the herd, away from the dust stirred up by over four thousand hooves. Her body was covered with fine grit, but water was too precious to waste washing. She was certain her face had become permanently lined from squinting into the afternoon sun. And from anxiety.

She was worried about the boys. And Jake. They were exhausted. They had been in the saddle for nearly three days with virtually no sleep. She had insisted that Will and Pete get some rest, but the other boys refused to sleep as long as Jake didn't. They nodded over their food. Isabelle suspected they fell asleep in the saddle. She was certain only Jake's vigilance had prevented an accident so far, but he had to be near the end of his resources.

"How long before he falls out of the saddle?" Ward asked.

"Who?" Isabelle asked, jerked out of her reverie.

"Jake. Who else are you thinking about?"

Isabelle felt herself blush.

"He's driving the boys too hard," Ward said.

"He's not driving them at all. They're driving themselves."

"It doesn't matter. They're exhausted. Somebody is going to get hurt."

Isabelle had been trying to convince herself not to worry. Ward had just put an end to that.

"Have you ever wanted something so badly you'd take any risk?"

Ward thought for a moment. "No, but I came close once."

"This herd is all Jake has. It stands for everything he hopes to have."

"But the boys."

"It's much the same with them. They never had a chance until now. Jake's success will be their success. I don't mean the money, though that's important. When they get those steers to Santa Fe, and they *will* get to Santa Fe, they will have accomplished something nobody can take away from them. They won't be useless orphans any more, and they'll owe it all to Jake."

The wagon bumped and lurched over rocks and uneven ground until Isabelle thought every joint in her body would be jarred loose. The contents of the cupboard rattled and bumped, the plates and cups producing dull ringing sounds, the ovens and pots dull thumps.

"How about you?"

"I was going to take them back to Austin to look for some more farmers."

"I'm sure they're happier on a horse than they would be behind a plow, even though they're about to fall out of their saddles."

"I've got to be at the river when they get there. I mean to cook the biggest dinner they've had since they left the ranch."

"Who're you trying to impress, the boys or Jake?"

"All of them."

"Why?"

"Because my future is in front of us."

"Does he know that?"

"I don't know. He's fighting mighty hard, but I have a chance now that you've come along to make him jealous."

"Me!"

"Yes, you." Isabelle laughed softly. "Jake's not very good with words. You've been saying all the things he wishes he could say." She smiled, quite pleased. "I thought he was going to hit you yesterday."

"Is there something going on I ought to know about?"

"I'm trying to get Jake to marry me."

"He ought to be straining at the bit."

"Jake's convinced himself he's never going to get married, and I'm exactly the kind of woman he's never going to marry."

"But if—"

"I don't know why. He hasn't told me yet. He also thinks he's not cut out to be responsible for these boys."

"But you just said they knock themselves out for him. I know the little ones idolize him. If I see Will trying to imitate his walk one more time, I'm going to bust out laughing."

"Jake doesn't see it that way. He had to work with boys during the war. A lot of them got killed. He's afraid to feel anything for these boys."

"Have you told him—"

"You don't tell Jake anything. I've tried. You have

to let him find out for himself."

"He might never do that."

"I see no harm in giving him a little bit of help."

"Are you asking me to become a partner in your nefarious plot?"

"Of course."

Jake could tell the minute the first steer scented water. The steer's head went up, he uttered a sound somewhere between a grunt and a bellow, and he started to run. Jake spurred his horse to the front of the line.

"They're going to run all the way to the river," he shouted to Chet. "There's nothing you can do to stop them, so don't try. Get Hawk, Sean, and Matt up front with you. You've got to make sure the herd stays on the trail to the crossing. Otherwise, there's a thirty-foot drop to the river with quicksand at the bottom."

"What are you going to do?" Chet asked.

"I'm going ahead to make sure Isabelle and the wagon get across before the herd arrives. Watch out for the squirts."

Jake reached the river just as Isabelle and Ward started to unload the ovens. "Set up on the other side," Jake said.

"But it's better over here," Ward said. "More wood, better shade, better grass."

"I saw lightning to the north. The river could be up several feet by morning."

Ward looked ready to argue, but Isabelle promptly reloaded the ovens.

"I'd feel safer if you drove," she said to Ward.

"It's no different from any other river," Jake said.

"I'd still feel safer with Ward driving."

Jake had to bite his tongue to keep from saying

something he knew he would regret. Besides, he didn't have time. The herd would arrive soon. Isabelle would be trampled if she was in their way.

Jake didn't understand her reliance on Ward. He had to remind himself that Ward had been helping her and filling her ears with compliments for the last five days. That's what she was used to, what she'd grown up expecting. She didn't look so tired. She had revived like a thirsty desert flower. Her response to Ward was proof she didn't belong in Texas.

He'd have to find some way to keep them apart. He wanted to lay up here at least one day to give the boys a chance to rest and the herd opportunity to drink its fill and graze a bit. He wanted them as fat as possible when they reached Santa Fe.

When they moved out, Ward would be in the saddle. He wasn't going to be sitting next to Isabelle all day, filling her ears with pretty compliments, arguing with Jake over every decision. Maybe he'd make Ward ride drag. By the time he'd breathed dust all day, maybe his throat would be too dry for compliments. Just because Jake didn't intend to marry Isabelle didn't mean he was going to let her fall for a fancy piece of cowhide like Ward Dillon.

The rumble or four thousand hooves reached his ears, and the herd appeared in the distance. Jake could count about forty steers. The rest were enveloped in a cloud of dust stirred up by thousands of pounding feet. Sean and Hawk rode on either side, keeping the racing herd on the trail. Jake was suddenly apprehensive about the rest of the boys. He wished he had stayed with the herd rather than let his jealousy make him follow Isabelle.

The lead steers hit the water at a dead run. Their momentum carried them right through the river. Jake found himself busy turning them back so they wouldn't overrun Isabelle and the campsite. For a moment he was completely enveloped by the cloud of dust. Gradually it cleared, and he could see the leaders fanning out along the west bank of the river. Some of the herd stopped in the middle of the river. Those lagging behind pushed to get to the water, turning the river into a dangerous, milling mass of horses and cows desperate for their first drink in nearly four days.

Sean, Buck, Zeke, and Bret entered the river to keep the herd together. Hawk, Luke, and Matt did the same on the river bank. Jake saw Drew and Will with Chet. Before he had time to breath a sigh of relief, Pete appeared out of the dust cloud and rode his horse into the water to join Sean.

But he didn't make it. A half-dozen impatient steers raced around Luke and plunged into the river from the embankment. One of them came up under Pete's horse, throwing the horse on its side and Pete into the swirling water. Pete bobbed to the surface and immediately began splashing about in a frantic manner that told Jake the one thing he didn't want to know.

Pete couldn't swim.

Jake spurred his horse toward the river, but his path was blocked by hundreds of tightly packed steers. It was impossible to get through. He moved down river until he could reach the bank. Pete was being washed toward him, away from the ford toward the quicksand. Jake uncoiled his rope and threw it, but it wasn't long enough to reach Pete.

Before Jake could jump into the river, Bret dived off his horse and started swimming toward Pete with swift, powerful strokes. On the east bank, Chet shouted at Pete and threw his rope, but the boy was too frightened to swim for it. He continued to struggle frantically, which only exhausted his strength and caused him to go under a second time.

The current continued to carry Pete farther downstream, where the banks quickly rose to thirty feet above the surface of the river. If Jake dived into the river now, the force of the dive would bury him in quicksand.

Pete surfaced again, but he was too disoriented to grab hold of Chet's rope which landed nearly over his head. He fought grimly, silently, but he went under for the third time just as Bret reached out for him. Without pause, Bret dived under the surface of a river made muddy by hundreds of steers upstream.

Jake held his breath. Each second lessened Pete's chances of survival.

After what seemed like an eternity, Bret broke the surface. He had his arm around Pete.

"Swim over here!" Jake shouted. "Avoid the sandbar. It's quicksand."

Hawk came up behind Jake. A moment later Isabelle and Ward arrived in the wagon. They watched in tense silence as Bret made his way through the swirling water toward the west bank. Jake tossed his rope. "Put this under Pete's arms," he shouted. "Put Hawk's rope around yourself."

Pete was a dead weight, but Bret managed to get the rope under his arms. Using his horse, Jake hauled Pete's limp body out of the river and over the bank.

"Is he dead?" Isabelle asked, when the white-faced boy was laid on the ground.

"I don't know," Jake said. "He was under a long time."

Jake turned Pete over with his arms by his side. He knelt over the boy and began to lift his arms rhythmically.

"What are you doing?" Isabelle cried.

"He's trying to get the water out of his lungs," Ward said. "If he wasn't under too long, he may still revive."

Jake told himself not to panic, not to go too fast, to keep a steady rhythm. He'd seen a boy revived this way during the war. He knew it could work.

If Pete hadn't been under too long.

Suddenly Pete made a gagging noise. A moment later, water gushed out of his mouth and nose. Then he coughed, deep racking coughs that brought up more water. When he stopped, his face was pink from the exertion. Jake turned him over, and Pete opened his eyes.

"I think," Jake said, "you need to learn to swim."

"Where did you learn to swim like that?" Jake asked Bret. They were sitting well away from the campsite, watching the river, which had risen several feet in the last few hours. Everybody had finished dinner. Will and Drew were cleaning up. Isabelle and Ward had spent the last several hours at Pete's side, fussing over him like two mother hens. Sean hovered nervously in the background, trying to do something to relieve his feeling of guilt. The other boys were taking turns watching the herd as it grazed in the soft twilight.

"We used to spend the summer at my grandfather's place on Cape Cod when I was little. I could swim by the time I was three."

Bret's tone was bitter, his expression angry. Jake doubted the wound of being disowned by his family would ever heal.

"It was very brave of you to dive in after Pete."

Bret shrugged. His expression was set and mulish.

"It wasn't much. I couldn't let him drown, even if he is a dumb Texan."

Bret was clearly uncomfortable with compliments. He had fled when Isabelle tried to smother him with praise. He was almost rude when Pete tried to thank him. Jake couldn't understand why the boy should feel more comfortable being an outcast.

Jake got to his feet. "There are a lot of people here who would like to be your friend if you would just let them."

"I don't want any friends, especially from Texas."

"I think you do. I think you want friends very badly."

Jake had intended to go check on Pete, but he changed his mind. He could see Ward and Isabelle still hovering over him. He wanted to talk to Isabelle, but he didn't think he could stand one more minute of Ward without saying something he would regret. He might have to accept that Ward was more to Isabelle's liking than he was, but he didn't have to like it.

And he damned well didn't. He had to get to sleep. He had the last watch. Besides, as long as he was sleeping, he wouldn't be thinking about Ward and Isabelle.

Isabelle wouldn't listen to him. She wouldn't even speak to him. When he tried, she pushed him away with a mocking laugh.

"Go away," she said in her slow drawl, exaggerated for the benefit of the men who loved to think of her as some exotic Southern flower brought to perfection under the sultry nights of the Mississippi delta.

"You've got to come back," he pleaded. "I miss you. The boys miss you, too."

She looked at him with the kind of scorn a woman

can achieve only when it was mixed with hate. "You don't miss me. You miss having someone to cook your meals and wash your clothes. You don't need a wife. You need a slave. Any female would do."

How could he make her realize it was her they missed? Hell, he'd lived for years on beans and bacon, only washing when he fell into a river. He didn't care if he spent the rest of his life sleeping under the stars. He wanted Isabelle because she was the only woman in the world he loved or could ever love.

But she'd never believed that. Or never thought it was important enough.

"You won't have to cook or wash clothes ever again. The boys and I will do it."

He got too close. She pushed him away, then turned her attention to the mirror. She was using too much makeup. She didn't even look like herself. Her chestnut hair had been dyed flame red. Her lips were a slash of vermillion in a sea of white powder, her eyes so heavily penciled they looked as if she were wearing a mask. Her dress exposed more of her than he'd seen in five years as her husband.

But it was her expression that had changed most. It was hard and cruel. So was her laugh. And she was laughing at him now, the sound emerging from a face that looked like a caricature of the woman he loved.

"I wouldn't go back to that hellhole if you gave me ten servants. I loathe the heat and the dirt; I despise the smell of cows. But most of all, I despise the smell of *you.*"

The door opened, and Ward Dillon entered. He wore a black suit, gold vest, crimson tie, and a ruffled white shirt. When he saw Jake, a mocking smile curved his lips and danced in his eyes.

"Aha! I thought I detected the smell of cattle. I

thought the city ordinances prohibited bringing cows into New Orleans."

"He didn't bring his cows," Isabelle said, "just himself."

They both laughed.

"Are you ready, *chère?*" Ward asked Isabelle. "The customers are getting restless. Everybody's starved for the sight of you."

Isabelle smiled at Ward the way she used to smile at Jake. "I'm done. How do I look?"

"Perfect as always."

"How can you say she looks perfect?" Jake shouted. "She's smeared her face with paint. Half her body is exposed to the sight of every drunk who wants to gawk and paw at her. She doesn't look perfect. She looks like a whore!" Jake grabbed Isabelle by the arm. "You're coming home with me."

Isabelle tried to jerk her arm loose. "I'm never going back to that place again. I hate it, and I hate you. I'd sleep with every man in New Orleans before I let you take me back."

Jake was through listening. He was taking Isabelle home. She'd be unhappy at first, but she'd soon see that living a clean, decent life on a ranch was much better than putting her innocence and beauty on display. She'd soon understand that no amount of money, jewels, furs, mansions, or servants was worth the loss of self-respect.

"Let her go," Ward ordered. "She doesn't want to go with you."

"I'm taking her home."

"This is my home," Isabelle cried.

"Then you're living in hell."

"I was living in hell when I was married to you."

"You're still married to me. You're still my wife."

Ward hit him. Before he could get up, Ward hit

him again. Jake pulled his gun and shot him.

Isabelle screamed as the scene around him dissolved into a series of revolving images. He saw Ward fall, blood rapidly staining his white shirt.

Out of nowhere, police appeared to drag him away—not to jail, not to his trial, but straight to the gallows. As the noose was fitted about his neck, he saw Ward get up from the floor. The bloodstain faded. He wasn't dead. He wasn't even wounded.

Jake tried to tell the policemen, but they tightened the noose and put a hood over his head. Jake could hear Ward and Isabelle laughing. The sound grew louder and louder until it hurt his eardrums. It stopped only when they pulled the lever and the floor dropped away from under his feet.

Jake woke up, his body damp with perspiration. He could hear Sean singing to the cows. He sat up. The boys lay scattered about, all sunk in exhausted sleep after the strenuous drive. He looked over his shoulder. The chuck wagon stood where it had when he went to sleep. Drew, Ward, and Pete slept on the ground nearby, Isabelle inside.

It had been a dream. It wasn't real, but it gave him chills.

It hadn't been a dream before. His mother had left her husband and two sons. She had gone to St. Louis. He'd tried to find her when he came home from the war to tell her his father and brother were dead, but she wasn't there. They said she'd gone to Santa Fe.

It didn't do any good to think about it. He'd been over it dozens of times, and it always came up the same. Delicately nurtured women couldn't stand the only kind of life he knew, the only kind he wanted. Will would have to look for another solution. He couldn't have Jake and Isabelle for parents.

Jake couldn't go back to sleep. He dressed quickly, but instead of saddling up as he intended, he turned toward the wagon, drawn by a force he could neither name nor deny. He looked inside.

Isabelle slept on her side, a blanket folded under her head for a pillow. She looked so young and innocent, her skin milky white, her hair and brows inky black. She looked almost as unreal as in his dream, but there was nothing artificial about her.

Jake was sensible enough to know the real Isabelle existed somewhere between those two extremes. The question was where.

"She's unbelievably lovely, isn't she?"

Jake nearly jumped a foot at the sound of Ward's voice. He was only glad it was Ward rather than an Indian, who wouldn't have given him any warning at all.

"Yes," he said, more calmly than he felt. "Much too lovely for Texas."

"Once she gets these boys settled, I expect she'll be heading back to Savannah."

"I reckon so," Jake said, turning to face Ward. "What will you do when we reach Santa Fe?"

"Don't know. Probably drift."

"Where?"

Ward glanced at the wagon. "Wherever looks most interesting." He paused. "What are you going to do?"

"Go back to Texas and get another herd. There are a lot of cows in Texas that need taking to market."

"It'll make it hard to get married if you're away from home more than half the year."

"I didn't say anything about getting married. Women don't take to men like me." If he didn't have a home, he wouldn't be tempted to do something foolish, like ask Isabelle to stay with him.

"Some do."

"Most don't."

Ward let his gaze wander to the wagon. "You asked?"

"Don't need to. She made it plain she hates everything about me and Texas. I didn't have a fancy education, but I can understand plain English."

"I'm not so sure about that."

Jake was tired of talking to Ward, and he was too jumpy to keep standing around doing nothing. "I'm going to relieve Sean. He needs the sleep."

"Want me to come with you?"

"You'd better take care of that leg. If it breaks open, Isabelle would never forgive me."

Jake rode out and sent Sean to bed. He was trying to make up his mind if he could send Buck to bed and handle the herd alone when the other rider on duty came toward him. It was Ward.

"I couldn't stand you hogging all the nobility," he said with a grin. "You can tell Isabelle you did your best to keep me in bed."

Ward rode on by. In a few moments, Jake heard the sound of a pleasant baritone floating on the night air. Ward was singing a Spanish song, but it wasn't a rough folk song. It sounded like something a woman would learn from her singing master. What on earth would Ward be doing with a singing master?

Then he remembered that Ward had the same background as Isabelle. They got along so well because they were two of a kind.

Jake shook his head to get rid of that indigestible thought. It didn't matter where Ward came from. He'd made it plain he was interested in Isabelle. She'd already shown she was interested in him. Jake had better start thinking of his cows and forget the foolish idea that had been growing in the back of his mind for the last several days.

He turned to watch the lightning against the sky. He was glad the storm hadn't come this far south. The horses would have been up to their fetlocks in mud by now.

When Isabelle woke, the Pecos was out of its banks and still rising.

"Gather all the wood you can find and move to higher ground," Jake told her after they'd finished the first breakfast they'd eaten in daylight since they started the drive. "I mean to spend the rest of the day here. We'll head out tomorrow morning."

They were halfway to the new camp when Will gave a shout. "Look!" he shouted, pointing behind them across the river.

Isabelle looked around, and her breath stilled in her throat. As many as a hundred Indians had come to a halt across the swollen waters of the Pecos. Comanches!

"They meant to ambush us and take the herd," Jake said. They probably would have taken Isabelle. Only the Pecos stood between them and death.

"What do you think they'll do?" Isabelle asked.

"There's nothing they can do until the river subsides."

"How long will that take?"

"I don't know. Maybe as much as a week."

"Then we're safe."

"They can travel as far in one day as we can in five."

"Will they follow?"

"I don't think so. We'll be in Apache territory before they can reach us."

"But they're just as bad."

"Better the Apache who doesn't know we're here

than the Comanche who does."

Before Isabelle could respond, Pete jerked a rifle out of the wagon and headed toward the Indians at a dead run. His speed showed he had recovered from yesterday's near-tragedy.

"Son of a bitch!" Jake took after him as fast as he could run.

"What's he doing?" Ward asked.

"I think he's going to try to kill some of those Indians," Isabelle said.

"Son of a bitch!" Ward muttered. "If he shoots even one of them, they won't stop until they hunt us down."

Pete scampered along like an antelope. Jake had never tried to run in high-heeled boots. He was certain he already had blood blisters on both feet. But if he didn't stop Pete before he killed somebody, bloody feet would be the least of his worries.

"You can't shoot those Indians!" Jake shouted at Pete.

"I'm gonna kill at least one of the bastards," Pete shouted. He didn't turn around. The wind ripped the words out of his mouth and carried them back to Jake.

Jake had been watching for something like this ever since Pete attacked Night Hawk, but the Indians had come up on him by surprise. Before he'd had time to think about Pete, the boy had stolen the rifle and gone. Thank goodness he hadn't had time to teach Pete how to shoot. He just hoped his father hadn't either.

That hope died when he saw Pete drop to his knee, raise the rifle, and fire.

Jake didn't have to wonder whether the bullet hit

its target. An Indian let out a yelp, and his horse went to bucking fit to be tied. Nobody went down, so he'd probably only grazed the horse, but Jake didn't think they'd be so lucky the second time. Making a desperate spring, Jake reached out and grabbed Pete by the shoulder.

Pete whirled and hit him in the head with the stock of the rifle. Jake nearly passed out as both he and Pete tumbled to the ground.

Jake wanted to lie there and concentrate on his aching head, but he rolled up on his hands and knees in time to see Pete kneel and take aim.

Jake threw himself at the boy. The rife went off, and they tumbled over and over.

Jake hit his head on something hard. He almost lost consciousness. He fought off the darkness as he looked around for Pete. The boy was getting to his feet with his gaze on the fallen rifle. Using the last of his energy, Jake threw himself at Pete. He landed on top of the child, the rifle bare inches from the boy's fingertips.

Fortunately, since Jake was afraid he was going to pass out any minute, Sean ran up. He looked across the river.

"I don't think he hit anybody."

Pete was sobbing, hitting and kicking Jake with all his strength. There was nothing here of the boy who followed Jake around, copied his walk, worked to earn his praise. This boy was so consumed by a deep anger that he didn't care about anybody, not even himself.

"Why did you stop me, you son of a bitch? I hate you! I hate you!"

Jake pinned Pete's arms to his side. Pete tried to butt Jake with his head. When he couldn't, he screamed out his fury.

Isabelle and the other boys arrived.

"I think we'd better get the herd moving," Jake said to Chet. He looked to Isabelle. "Take Will and Drew with you."

She hesitated only a moment. "Sure."

Drew and Will didn't want to be shepherded away from all the fun, but Isabelle soon had them headed toward the wagon. Pete continued to fight as hard as he could, but his strength and stamina were soon exhausted.

"Are you ready to listen?" Jake asked.

Pete's answer was to struggle some more, but it was only a token resistance. His previous fits of anger hadn't lasted so long or been so severe. Jake had been sure he would get over it with time. Now he wasn't sure.

"I'm going to tell you one more time," Jake said. "You can't go around attacking every Indian you see."

"I will!" Pete shouted. "I will, and you can't stop me."

"Then you can't stay with us," Jake said. "I'll leave you at the first fort we come to. Isabelle will write to the agency. They'll send somebody to get you."

Pete looked at him with a mixture of fear and defiance in his eyes. The hold of his anger was lessening. "Miss Davenport won't leave me. She said she'd never leave any of us."

"She'll have to leave you because you're endangering all our lives."

"I was just trying to kill those damned bastards. They killed my ma and pa. I wish I could kill all of them."

He was upset now, not so angry.

"If you had killed just one of them, they would have waited until the river went down and followed us. They would have killed all of us and stolen the herd. But the worst would be what they'd have done to Isabelle."

"What would they do?"

"Worse things than you can imagine."

"Worse than being killed?"

"Much worse."

"I don't believe you."

"You've got to promise me right now you won't attack another Indian."

"No."

"You positive?"

"Yes."

"Okay, here's how things are going to be until I find somewhere to leave you. You'll ride in the wagon with your hands and feet tied. I'll untie your hands when you eat, but they'll remain tied the rest of the time, even when you sleep."

"Isabelle won't let you do that. Sean won't neither."

"They won't have any choice. I'm in charge of this drive. I make the decisions."

Jake waited.

"What if I promise not to bother Night Hawk?"

"Hawk isn't going to murder and scalp us. They will."

Pete stared at the Indians across the swollen river. "I wish I could kill every one of them."

"I can understand that, but you've got to realize you're never going to find the Indians who killed your parents. And shooting other Indians won't bring them back."

Pete didn't respond.

"Come on. We've got to catch up with the others," Jake said as he took Pete by the shoulder.

"I can walk by myself."

"Can I trust you?" Jake said keeping his hold on Pete's shoulder.

"How long do I have to promise?" Pete asked.

"For as long as you're with Isabelle or me."

"What if you marry Isabelle and adopt me?"

Jake knew that would never happen, but he didn't figure this was a good time to tell Pete.

"Then it will be forever."

Pete thought for a while longer. "Okay, but if you don't marry Isabelle, it's all off."

"That seems fair enough," Jake replied.

"Then get your hand off my shoulder. I ain't no sissy. I don't go back on my word."

Jake chuckled. Pete was back to normal.

Chapter Twenty-three

Jake didn't have a good reason why his instincts failed him.

Maybe he was too concerned with the boys. He'd been thinking about them more and more. He couldn't forget Will's idea that he and Isabelle should adopt them. Marriage was out of the question, but he didn't see why the boys couldn't stay with him. They weren't old enough to hire out as regular hands. They needed a few more years of someone looking out for them. He didn't mind doing it.

Maybe he was too concerned with getting the herd to Santa Fe. They were so close he could taste it, but anything could still happen. Indians and Comancheros had been known to steal herds within sight of army forts.

Maybe it was Isabelle. No matter where his thoughts turned, they always came back to her. He fought a constant battle with himself. How could he think he loved Isabelle when the very thought of marriage brought on nightmares? He hadn't slept well in weeks. It was impossible to consider not sleeping for the rest of his life

But it was getting equally impossible to think of the rest of his life without Isabelle. The battle was tearing him apart. He'd had that dream about Isabelle every night since it first happened. It was always the same. He was so tired he found himself dozing in the saddle.

That's what was on his mind when he should have been paying attention to his back trail. That's what he was doing when the first gunshot shattered the quiet.

He looked in the direction of the gunfire. Firing into the air, four men rode out of the stand of pine and cedar that covered the low hills on either side of the valley through which the herd was passing. Jake guessed they meant to stampede the herd, drive off the riders, then steal the herd at their leisure.

He had to stop them. His whole future depended on this herd. A dozen scenarios for how to do that flashed into his head at once. Then he saw a fifth man with a rifle sitting his horse up on the mountainside. The man fired, Buck's horse reared, and the boy came off.

He was shooting to kill!

None of the boys wore a gun except Chet. Jake hadn't thought they had enough experience to know when or how to use a gun. Only he and Ward carried rifles, and Ward had stayed behind with Isabelle. They wouldn't catch up with the herd until midday.

Jake had to safeguard these boys by himself. There was only one way. He had to get the herd between them and the rustlers, but first he had to get that rifleman off the mountainside.

Jake took precious seconds to jerk his rifle out of the scabbard and fire several hurried shots at the rifleman. He didn't hit him, but he did drive him back into the trees. The bushwacker would try again—Jake hoped not before he had time to get the boys out of rifle range. He jammed his rifle back in the scabbard and spurred his horse into a gallop.

When he reached Chet, the boy was trying to keep the cows from stampeding.

"Let 'em run!" Jake shouted. "Head them right at those bastards. Then get the others and drop back!"

"But they'll steal the herd."

"Let 'em have it! Once the herd starts running, get the boys back to the wagon with Ward and Isabelle. Make sure Luke holds the horses. We can't get the herd back without mounts."

"What are you going to do?" Chet called out.

"Buck's down."

"You can't get to him before the steers do."

"I've got to try. Now get out of here before they start shooting at you, too. Go on!" he yelled when Chet hesitated. "You can't help me get the herd back if you're dead."

Jake turned his horse and started working his way though the herd. They weren't running yet, but they would soon. He had to reach Buck first. The first rustler was closing in on the front of the herd. Jake pulled his gun and fired at the rustler over the head of the steers. The rustler's horse stumbled and went down.

Jake drove his horse as fast as the animal could go. The steers were running now. He could see Buck ahead on foot. The first few steers would go around him. Then one would hook him and the rest would run over him.

He had to get there first.

He glanced up on the mountainside. The rifleman was back and preparing to fire.

Jake pointed at the rifleman on the hill. "Duck!" he shouted to Buck, hoping the boy could hear over the noise of the running herd.

Buck dropped to the ground just before the sound of a rifle shot split the air. A steer next to where Buck had been standing bellowed in pain as a bullet knocked off one of its horns.

Jake slowed his horse as he neared Buck. He leaned over and extended his hand. "Climb on," he shouted. For precious seconds he brought his horse to a standstill. Buck virtually leapt up behind Jake. "Hold on!" Jake shouted. "We've got to get out of range. That guy is hell with a rifle."

The herd was running hard, the rustlers were following, but the rifleman was still on the mountainside. He was taking aim again.

"Stay as low as you can," Jake shouted as he spurred his horse up a small hill toward a sheltering belt of pines. "We'll be out of range in just a minute."

Jake's horse took to the hill with a vengeance. For the first time in his life, Jake was thankful for the blood of Sawtooth in his herd. He had almost reached the trees when he felt the pain. He never heard a shot. He almost thought he imagined it. But when a terrible weakness came over him, he knew he'd been hit.

He tried to speak, to warn Buck. But even though he moved his lips, no words came out. He was losing his grip on the reins. He couldn't sit up. He was going to fall.

Hell, he was going to die right here in the middle of a godforsaken plain in New Mexico Territory. Rustlers were going to get his herd and Ward was going to get his woman. Why in hell had he survived four years of war to die in a place that wasn't even on the map? At least the army would have given him a decent burial, marked his grave, and sent his weapons home.

Damn, damn, damn! He'd really messed things up this time.

Ward was talking to Isabelle when they heard the shot.

"Why should Jake be shooting?" she asked. "Do you think something's wrong?" Things had gone so well, she'd almost forgotten the possibility of danger.

"That was a rifle shot," Ward said. "He probably shot an antelope or a deer. Fresh meat would be a welcome change from all this salty pork."

A rapid burst of rifle fire eliminated any notion that Jake was hunting. Something was wrong. Isabelle whipped up her mules, but Ward immediately grabbed the reins and pulled them to a halt.

"What are you doing!" she demanded, shocked. "We've got to find Jake. He may need help."

"There's nothing you can do," Ward said. "Turn the wagon into those trees."

Isabelle fought to regain control of the reins. "If you think I'm going to hide when Jake and the boys are in trouble, you have a very peculiar notion of the kind of woman I am."

"I have a very good notion," Ward replied, keeping a firm grip on the reins, "but you have no idea what a danger you are to everybody. If you're captured, we'll all be at their mercy."

Isabelle opened her mouth to protest.

"Do exactly as I say, and we might come out of this with a whole skin. Drive the wagon into those trees and stay there. No matter what you hear, don't come out. Take a rifle, and if you see anybody, shoot to kill. You won't get a second chance."

"What are you going to do?"

"I'm going to find Jake and the boys. I'll send them back here. You'd better get bandages and hot water ready. Somebody's liable to be hurt."

It went against Isabelle's instincts to hide in the trees, but she kept telling herself that if she were captured, Jake and the boys would do something foolish and dangerous. She just wished she'd paid more attention when Jake tried to teach her how to ride and use a rifle. Then she wouldn't have to hide in the trees like a skulking coward.

A woman like her was useless to a man like Jake. If she married him, she'd be a stone around his neck.

Isabelle saw them long before they entered the meadow nestled between two hogback ridges. She didn't have to count to know several were missing. She could soon make out Sean and Matt bringing the young ones back. She didn't see Chet and Luke. Nor Zeke and Hawk. Buck was also missing.

She didn't see Ward or Jake.

She heard a lot of crashing through the trees. A few moments later she saw Luke and Zeke bringing the horses under cover of the timber.

"What happened?" she asked Drew, who was the first one to reach her.

"Some men came at us down a mountain. Chet made us stampede the herd into them, then come back here as fast as we could."

"Where's Chet?" Isabelle asked Sean.

"He's making sure everybody gets back," Matt explained. "He said it's what Jake told him to do."

"Where's Jake?"

"Buck was down. Jake went to get him."

"What about Ward and Hawk?"

"Ward went by us like the Devil was on his tail," Sean said. "He kept yelling for us to find the wagon and protect you."

Isabelle had been so distracted, she hadn't been paying attention. Now she realized Zeke had climbed into the wagon. He had found the guns and started handing them out.

"Put those back," Isabelle said. "Jake said you weren't to have them unless he was here."

"He's not here," Zeke said, "and we don't know if he's coming back. I don't know what those white devils want, but I don't mean to let them shoot me down when I've got a perfectly good gun right here."

"Me either," Will said, stepping to up get his gun.

"Don't you give Will a gun," Isabelle ordered. "Pete or Drew either. If the rest of you must have guns, take one pistol each. Then form a circle around us. Let me know the minute you see or hear anything. And nobody, *nobody*, I repeat, is to shoot until I give permission."

The boys didn't say anything, but they did seem to be following her instructions. "I need wood and water," she said to the others. "Ward said there may be injuries. We'll have to eat in any event."

"Make sure the wood's dry," Zeke said. "We don't want any smoke. That's how the farmers caught me when I ran away."

Only a few minutes passed before one of the boys yelled that he saw Chet coming. Isabelle was at the edge of the trees to meet him.

"Where's Jake?" she asked.

"He went after Buck," Chet said, sliding from his exhausted horse. "He said the rest of us were to come here."

Isabelle tried to calm the panic building inside her. She was alone in this trackless wilderness with these

Leigh Greenwood

boys depending on her, and she hadn't the slightest idea what to do. She looked at the protective perimeter they'd formed and began to wonder if she was in charge at all.

"What happened?"

"Rustlers attacked the herd."

"I know about that. Why was Buck down? He's a good rider."

"That's the part I don't understand," Chet said. "There was a man up on the mountain with a rifle shooting at him."

"Why Buck?"

"Maybe because he was riding point. Maybe he thought if he got Buck, there'd be nobody to stop them taking the herd."

"Wasn't Hawk riding with him?"

"Yes, ma'am, but he disappeared."

Nobody had seen Jake. No one knew what had happened to Buck or Hawk or Ward. She asked everybody.

"Let me have your gun," Isabelle said to Chet.

"What for?"

"I'm going to look for Jake."

"Sorry, ma'am, but I can't let you do that."

"You can't stop me," Isabelle said.

"I don't want to, but I will."

"And I'll help him," Zeke said.

Isabelle couldn't believe the boys were actually threatening to keep her there against her will. That was absurd. When they found out she meant to go, they wouldn't stop her.

"We don't have much of a chance," Zeke said, "but I don't aim to let you ruin it by running all over the countryside yelling for a man who's perfectly able to take care of himself."

"You don't know that."

"You don't know he isn't."

"He's not here."

"Neither are several others."

"They could all be hurt."

"We won't help them by getting shot as well."

"I'm not stupid, Zeke. I know—"

"You don't know nothing!" the boy snapped in a strangled whisper. "He might be working his way back here right now. You go out there, and he's going to have to get himself killed just to save your dumb ass."

"That's enough," Chet said. "There's no call to talk to Miss Davenport like that."

"She's fixing to get us all killed."

"No, she's not. Now apologize and get back to your position."

"I ain't apologizing to nobody stupid enough to go out there looking for somebody when they don't have a notion in this world where that somebody is. Hell, she can't even ride a horse. She'd probably shoot herself if you let her have a gun."

"Apologize, Zeke."

"You going to make me?"

"If I have to."

Zeke jumped Chet, and the boys went down in a heap. In less than five seconds, every boy was gathered around the circle screaming their support for their favorite.

"Quiet!" Isabelle hissed. "Do you want every rustler within ten miles to know where we are?"

The boys stopped shouting, but only Sean made any effort to keep a lookout. Everybody else was intent on the struggle between Chet and Zeke. It wasn't long before Chet got Zeke down with his forearm across his throat.

"Apologize," he gasped between clenched teeth.

Zeke used every bit of his strength to throw Chet off, but he was pinned securely.

"Apologize, you son of a bitch, or I'm going to choke the life out of you."

Zeke shook his head and Chet pressed his forearm across his windpipe.

"I'll kill you if I have to. It'll be one less fool to worry about."

Isabelle suddenly realized this was no trial of strength to see who was going to be in control. Chet meant what he said. He really didn't care. "Stop," Isabelle said, trying to pull Chet off Zeke.

Matt and Luke pulled her back. "Leave him alone," Luke said. "Zeke's been asking for it."

"But Chet's choking him."

"Zeke's got a choice," Luke said. "If he doesn't want to die, he can apologize."

Isabelle realized she didn't know anything at all about these boys. Chet and Luke had beautiful manners, yet they talked about choking Zeke like it was no more important than killing a prairie chicken for dinner.

Zeke must have given in. Isabelle couldn't understand what he said, but Chet let him up.

"I apologize," Zeke told Isabelle when he got to his feet. Then he turned on Chet. "I'm going to kill you, you son of a bitch."

"You'd better look behind you before you try it," Luke said.

Isabelle got chills down her spine. Luke was only thirteen. How could he talk like that?

"Stop this, all of you. Chet's in charge until Jake gets back. No one is to question that. I'm not going anywhere, at least not now. Get back to your positions. Anybody could have sneaked up on us while you were all urging Chet and Zeke to kill each other.

I'm ashamed of you. We've got to work together if we're going to get to Santa Fe safely."

The boys didn't look apologetic.

"You think he's dead?" Pete asked.

"No," Isabelle replied as firmly as she could. "Jake has survived a war, Indians, those farmers, and I don't know what all. He can survive a few rustlers."

"I think he's dead," Pete said as he walked away. "I think he's lying somewhere with a bullet through his head and blood all over him."

Isabelle refused to think Pete could be right. Jake wasn't dead. Jake couldn't be dead. She would feel it, wouldn't she? You couldn't lose part of yourself and not know.

"Chet said Buck's horse went down," she said. "He might be hurt, have broken an arm or something. Jake could be setting it before he tries to bring him back."

"He's dead," Pete said as he drifted off to his lookout.

Ward rode in an hour later. Even before he dismounted, Isabelle knew he hadn't seen Jake or the boys.

"I can't find a trace of anybody," Ward said as he dismounted. "Let's hope that wherever they are, they're together."

"What about the rustlers?" Chet asked.

"They took off after the herd. All except one."

"Is he hurt?" Isabelle asked.

"He's dead."

"Serves the son of a bitch right," Chet said. "Did you see anybody with a rifle, a man on a horse up the mountain?"

"No."

"You've got to find Jake," Isabelle said.

"I've already looked everywhere I can think to look," Ward said.

"Then look again. I'll look if you won't. I can't just stand here doing nothing, knowing he may be lying wounded somewhere out there needing my help."

"Jake's a resourceful man. He's survived much worse than this many times before."

"Then why doesn't he come back?"

"I don't know. You'll just have to wait until he gets here and ask him."

"What about Hawk?"

"I didn't see him either."

Isabelle started toward the horses, but Chet blocked her path.

"You've got to let me go," she pleaded. "I've got to look for Jake."

"No."

One word. Short and unchangeable.

"Sit down, Isabelle," Ward said. "There's nothing you can do."

She looked from one grim face to another, faces she'd always seen as childlike or youthful, innocent and hopeful. Now they surrounded her like a ring of dark sentinels. They were no longer friendly.

"How can you leave him out there by himself?" she demanded. "He wouldn't leave you. He'd be here right now if he hadn't gone after Buck."

"Jake said I was to get everybody back here and wait for him," Chet said.

"But what if he can't come back by himself? What if he's wounded?"

"One of us will go after him," Ward said, "but it won't be you."

Sean volunteered. Isabelle watched him saddle up and ride out. She looked around for something to do.

If she had to stand here waiting, wondering, fearing, she would start to scream.

"I'll fix something to eat. It's been a long time since the boys have had time to do anything but gobble their food."

"Sounds like a good idea," Ward said. "They'll be rested with full stomachs when Jake's ready to go retrieve the herd."

Isabelle tried to block everything out of her mind. She realized now that she'd never loved her fiancé. She'd been upset when he was killed, but she hadn't felt anything like she felt now—empty, hollow, yet the big space inside of her filled with a worse pain than any she had ever imagined.

She had thought she couldn't marry Jake, that she couldn't be the kind of wife he needed. It had hurt, but that was nothing compared to the pain of knowing he might be dead. As long as he was alive, there was always hope that somehow they could work things out. If he was dead . . .

She couldn't finished the thought. She had to pay attention to the biscuits. She'd almost added a cup of salt instead of flour.

Four boys had gone out and returned without finding Jake and Buck when Night Hawk rode in just after dusk. Isabelle ran to meet him. "Have you seen Jake?"

"He not here?"

"I thought you went after him."

"I follow the herd. I see where they take them." He held up a gun belt and holster. "I see that one not go with them."

Isabelle reeled under the impact of yet another shock. Night Hawk had killed a man with even less show of emotion than Chet.

"Have you eaten?"

It seemed a useless thing to ask, but she couldn't think of anything else.

Hawk shook his head.

"There's plenty left. Help yourself."

She couldn't serve him. She hadn't the energy.

"Do you think he's dead?"

Isabelle was sitting alone, staring into the darkness. She looked up to see Will. He looked like a little boy now, scared and alone. She held out her hand. He took it, and she drew him down on the rock next to her. She put her arm around his shoulders. He resisted only a moment before he threw his arms around her and held on tight.

"They all think he's dead. Everybody. I asked them."

"He's not dead," Isabelle said. She had to keep saying it to herself. It was all that enabled her to hold on.

"How do you know?"

"I just do. I can feel it."

"Can anybody tell when a person dies if they love them?"

"Who said I loved Jake?"

"Everybody knows that."

"Yes," Isabelle said, willing to admit out loud what she'd known for so long. "That's how I know."

"I told Matt he wasn't dead. I said you'd know." Will loosened his grip enough to look up into her eyes. "When is he coming back?"

"I don't know."

"I don't like it when he's gone."

"Neither do I."

"Are you going to marry him if he comes back?"

"Why do you ask that?"

348

"Because I want you to adopt me and Matt. Will you?"

"I don't know. There are nine other boys. I don't know that Jake would want to adopt that many."

"But I want to be adopted the most. Pete says he doesn't care. Bret says he hates everybody. I don't think Zeke likes anybody either."

"We can't pick some and leave others. I have to find a home for—"

Isabelle broke off. Zeke had shushed everybody, then held up his hand for silence. Nobody moved. Isabelle strained her ears, but she couldn't hear anything.

"What is it?" Will asked in a whisper.

"Shush!" Zeke's command was imperative. "Somebody's coming."

"How many?" Ward and Chet asked at the same time.

"I can't tell, but it sounds like just one."

"I go." Night Hawk melted into the darkness before either Chet or Ward could stop him.

Isabelle had jumped to her feet, her body so taut, her muscles hurt. Though she tried as hard as she could, she couldn't hear anything that couldn't be the breeze whispering among the trees or a mouse rustling among the leaves for its dinner.

Abruptly she heard voices, then the sound of running. Every person with a gun or rifle was pointing it in the direction of the sound that was quickly growing nearer. Even before she could make out the shapes in the dark, Night Hawk called out, "It's Jake and Buck."

Jake's horse seemed to burst out of the darkness. Isabelle took one look and felt the life go out of her. Jake's body slumped forward in the saddle, held up by Buck's straining arms. The boy turned his tear-stained face to Isabelle.

"He came back for me," Buck said, his face aged by grief. "He was trying to shoot me. When Jake came after me, he shot Jake."

"Who was trying to shoot you?" Ward asked.

"Rupert Reison," Buck said. "That's who killed Jake."

Chapter Twenty-four

It was like a bad dream. Everything moved in slow motion. Isabelle hadn't let herself believe Jake could be dead. She had kept her hopes alive because to do anything else would be to give up. Jake would never give up. He wouldn't want her to, but now he was dead, leaving her with the boys and a love that remained an unopened bud.

The boys laid Jake on the ground and stepped back. They seemed to accord him more true affection now than when he tried to help them learn to respect themselves.

Will started to cry.

Jake looked so still. He'd always been so alive, so full of energy. The boys had placed his body at an awkward angle. It wasn't right. She couldn't leave him like that.

She knelt down beside him.

"Isabelle, don't . . ."

"I'm just going to move him. He looks so uncomfortable."

It seemed impossible that everything she had loved so much was gone. Vanished, as if it had never been. How could something so powerful disappear? It ought to last longer than the stone that formed the mountains.

The pain would last as long as she lived.

She moved Jake's head. His skin was still warm and pliant. "Somebody get his bedroll from the wagon," she said as she crossed his hands on his chest. "We can't leave him like this."

She didn't know who got the bedroll or who helped her spread it over his body. All but his face. She wanted one last look.

One last kiss.

She knew she shouldn't, but she didn't care. She leaned over and touched his lips with her own. They were dry, as though parched with fever, his breath warm on her cheek.

Isabelle froze.

She was afraid she was imagining things. When she felt that faint caress a second time, she knew it was no illusion.

She scrambled to her feet. "He's still alive! Bring the wagon. We've got to get him to a doctor."

"Isabelle, you're upset. Why don't you sit down over here. I'll—"

"I'm not crazy, Ward. He's alive! I felt his breath on my cheek. Twice."

After a startled moment, Ward bent over Jake. He looked up. "He is alive, but just barely."

"Hurry, we've got to—"

"He'll never make it to Santa Fe. Where was he shot?" he asked Buck.

"In the back."

Ward turned Jake over. There was a small hole in his shirt. Ward took out his pocket knife and cut the shirt open. "I need some light," he said. "Do you have a lantern?"

"In the wagon," Isabelle said.

"Get it."

"He needs a doctor," Isabelle said.

"He's going to have to depend on what we can do for him," Ward said. Bret lit the lantern with a stick from the fire and brought it to Ward. "Hold it where I can see," he ordered. "Higher. More to the left."

No one spoke while Ward studied the wound.

"The bullet will have to come out. I don't know if that'll save him, but he'll die if it doesn't."

"He needs a doctor."

"He's got one," Ward said.

"Where did you learn to do that?" Isabelle asked.

Ward had removed the bullet. They made Jake as comfortable as possible on a bed of blankets over pine needles. Isabelle was preparing to sit up with him through the night. Chet had organized the watch. None of the boys were asleep. They remained close to Jake, watching, waiting.

"I was a surgeon in the war, the one some of the young soldiers used to refer to as the War of Northern Aggression."

"You must have been very good."

"We all were, or came to be. We got lots of practice."

"But why—"

"I grew up the idealistic son of a wealthy rancher. I wanted to do more with my life than tend cows. Medicine seemed the ideal vocation. Then the war came, and I realized I had no idea what it meant to be a doctor. I hated it."

"But why were you wandering about in Texas?"

Ward chuckled, but Isabelle doubted he was amused.

"You want the sordid story of the death of my idealism? Maybe someday. I haven't yet learned to live with it myself. To share it would be impossible. Let's just say I fell in love with the wrong woman."

"I didn't mean to pry. I just wondered—"

"Anybody would."

He stood and stretched. "I'm tired. I think I'll go to bed. My leg still isn't up to the kind of riding I did today."

Isabelle looked up at him. He looked more troubled than exhausted. "Thank you for saving Jake."

"I merely removed the bullet. We have to wait and see if Jake can save himself."

"He will. I know it."

"Do you plan to tell him you love him?"

"I don't know. I'm not sure I'm the right woman for him."

"Balderdash!"

"He doesn't want to be married."

"Maybe he's changed his mind."

She didn't answer. It was impossible to explain her confused feelings. Chet had told her how Jake sacrificed the herd to protect the boys. She no longer had any doubts about his not caring enough for the boys, of wanting to use them, of putting his profit before their safety.

She felt ashamed for having doubted him. She should have figured out long ago that Jake didn't think he was anything special. He probably didn't think he'd done anything out of the ordinary today.

She thought he was magnificent.

He would make a perfect father for all these boys.

Well, maybe not a father—some of them were too old for that—but she couldn't think of anyone better suited to shepherd them into manhood.

She desperately wanted to be at his side. She had come to love these boys. She knew several of them would never return her regard—she wasn't sure Zeke could even learn to like her—but they needed a mother as much as they needed a father. Isabelle couldn't imagine letting anyone else do that.

Which brought her full circle. Jake didn't want to get married, and she was the wrong kind of wife for him if he did.

"None of that makes any difference," Isabelle said. "Everything depended on Jake being able to sell the herd. Now he has nothing. He won't marry anyone."

"Would you still marry him?"

"Yes."

"Tell him."

"You don't understand."

"No, I don't. But then, I made a mess of my own life. I'm in no position to give advice."

"I haven't done any better."

Chet came to sit next to Isabelle. "How's he doing?"

"The same."

Silence.

"What's going to happen to us?"

"I don't know."

"Jake's broke, isn't he?"

"Yes."

"He doesn't have any money at all?"

"No. All he had was the herd."

Silence.

"Was he planning to use the money to buy a ranch?"

"He hadn't made up his mind. I think he was trying

to decide what would be best for you boys."

"Will was always talking about him adopting us."

Silence.

"Do you think he would?"

"I don't know. I do know he meant to take care of you."

"He can't without money, can he?"

"The agency won't let him."

Silence.

Chet got to his feet. "You going to stay up all night?"

"Yes."

"Good."

He turned and walked away.

Jake felt himself floating on a sea of pain. It radiated out from his chest to every part of his body. No matter how hard he tried, he couldn't move. His limbs were weighed down with stones. He felt as if he were suffocating. Every breath was an effort, yet he struggled on. He had someplace to go. He didn't know where, and he didn't know what he was supposed to do, but he had to get there. It was more important than the pain.

He wondered where he was now, if he was alone, why he couldn't move. Occasionally he thought he saw a face floating above him. He tried to speak but couldn't. He didn't know if anyone tried to speak to him. It must have rained. Once he felt drops of water on his skin. The sound of his breath leaving and entering his lungs roared in his ears, but he didn't mind. As long as he could hear that sound, he knew he was still alive.

All through that night and the next day, Isabelle never left Jake's side, not even to cook. He was burning up with fever. Ward tried to reassure her, to tell her that was normal. She knew it was. She also knew that of the fever didn't break, he would die.

She kept Will and Drew busy going back and forth to the stream for cool water. She constantly bathed him from the waist up. Ward checked periodically, but Jake's condition stayed the same.

She was anxious about the boys. When they weren't on guard, they gathered in a tight group on the far side of the wagon. It worried her that every time Ward walked over to them, they fell silent. She knew they were planning something, but she couldn't concern herself with that now. She could think only about Jake.

His temperature broke in late afternoon. He opened his eyes twenty minutes later.

"Don't move," she warned him when he tried to turn over. "You've been shot in the back."

He took a minute to absorb that. "What about the boys?"

"They're fine."

"Buck?"

"You brought him away without a scratch."

He seemed pleased with that.

"And the herd."

"It's gone."

She could see the vitality drain from him. A moment later his eyes closed and he was unconscious again.

"He's okay," Ward assured her. "It's his body's way of making sure he rests."

Isabelle prayed Ward was right.

Isabelle knew something was up. The boys all gathered before her. They looked very solemn. For a moment she feared they were going to tell her they were leaving, but she pushed that thought aside. They didn't have any place to go.

"Ward says Jake's going to be all right," Chet said. "It'll be a while before he can ride again, but he's going to be fine."

"We're going to get the herd back."

"You can't do that. It's too dangerous. Wait until Jake gets better."

"We talked it over," Chet said. "If we wait any longer, they'll have time to take the herd into Mexico and sell it."

"That bastard followed us because of me," Zeke said. "I'm not letting Jake be robbed by a bunch of no-good skunks."

"But you're just boys," Ward said. "You don't know what to do."

"We've worked out a plan," Chet said.

"I'm sure you have, but I can't let you go."

"You can't stop us."

"I—"

Ward's protest died. Every boy had a gun, and they were all pointed at him.

"You're to stay here with Jake," Chet said.

"You can't do this," Isabelle protested. "Will and Drew are only children."

"We've talked it over, and we're all going," Chet said.

Isabelle realized there was no use protesting. She remembered the look on Chet's face when he wrestled Zeke to the ground. There would be no changing his mind.

"Be careful," Isabelle said. "I couldn't stand it if anything happened to one of you."

"We've got a plan," Chet said again.

"I'll come with you," Ward offered.

"No. Someone has to stay here. We took a vote and decided on you."

"Don't I have a say?"

"No. It's your job to make sure nothing happens to Jake and Miss Davenport."

Ward seemed almost amused at the seriousness with which Chet assumed the mantle of leadership.

"I'll do my best."

It was a very solemn group of boys who saddled up and rode out of the trees. Isabelle prayed they would all return safely. She was glad they appreciated what Jake had tried to do for them. She just wished they could have found another way to show it.

"Are they really going after the herd?" Ward asked, nearly as dazed as Isabelle.

"I never knew those boys," Isabelle said, staring into the darkness that had swallowed the boys she had come to think of as her family. "Not any of them. I thought they were children. Now they're going to face men who are thieves if not killers as well."

"I can still try to stop them."

"I'd want to hold them close. Jake would say I had to let them go. He'd say this is something they have to do for their own self-respect."

"Even when they're as young as Drew and Will?"

"Odd, isn't it? In Savannah, Will would be in bed by now, tucked in by his nurse, the toys put away, the picture books on the shelf. Even Matt would have been home long ago. Now I'm letting them go off into the night to face men with guns, and I'm supposed to accept it as normal."

"This isn't Savannah."

"Sometimes I think I would give anything to be back there, to be somewhere where I understand life."

"And Jake, could he live there?"

She looked down at the face that had become so dear to her. "He might try, but it would take the heart out of him."

"I think you underestimate the man."

She had seen more of Jake than Ward had. Jake would try, but he wouldn't be the man she had fallen in love with despite the laws of common sense and the rules of the society that had nurtured her. He had to be free, even if it meant Indians and rustlers and nights spent sitting on the ground praying he wouldn't die.

"No. I just understand what kind of soil it takes to nurture a man like Jake."

Jake woke up again about midnight.

"Looks like I'm going to live," he said in a gravely voice.

"It looks that way," Isabelle said. She hoped he didn't hear the catch in her voice.

"That bullet should have killed me."

"It would have if Ward hadn't taken it out. Did you know he's a doctor?"

"Oh."

She guessed that didn't seem important to Jake now, only that he was alive. It was important to her. It was the reason Jake was alive.

"How did the boys take the loss of the herd?"

"Not very well."

"Tell them we're not done yet. There are more cows back at the ranch." He had to rest. His strength was gone.

"I'll tell them. Now go back to sleep. You've got a lot of getting well to do."

"Will you stay with me?"

"Yes."

He smiled and closed his eyes.

Chet watched the two men arguing at the camp-fire. A third lay on the ground some distance away. It was impossible to tell if he was sick or injured. He groaned in pain, but the two men didn't pay him any attention.

It was the sound of a gunshot that helped them find the campfire so quickly.

"I'm going in alone," he told Hawk and Luke, who crouched beside him. "I'm going to give them a chance to give up."

"You can shoot that good?" Hawk asked.

"Yeah, he can," Luke assured him.

"Why didn't they leave somebody with the herd?" Zeke asked.

"They probably figured if we hadn't come after them by now, we weren't going to," Chet said. "You sure Sean can take care of the little squirts and the herd?"

"He's got Buck and Matt to help him."

"I should go," Hawk argued. "I move with no sound."

"I want them to hear me," Chet said. "I want to give them their chance."

But he hoped they wouldn't take it. They were the same kind of scum who'd shot his father in the back. They'd tried to kill Buck and they'd nearly killed Jake. They deserved to die.

Like the men who'd shot his father.

Chet made a lot of noise as he moved through the underbrush. The men were still seated when he walked out into the open, but their hands were close to their guns. They visibly relaxed when they saw Chet.

"What are you doing out so late, kid?" one of them said. He grinned and winked at his companion. "You get lost in the dark?"

"I've come for our steers," Chet said.

The men were instantly alert. "*Your* steers?"

"Yeah, me and the other kids. You shot Jake. They're ours now."

"Get outta here before we shoot you," a rustler with a mustache said.

"There's two kids up in the woods right now, their rifles aimed at your hearts. Either you drop your guns and ride out, or you draw and die where you sit."

The man with the mustache laughed. "You going to make us?"

"Yeah."

"How?"

"Ever heard of Lacy Attmore? He taught me to shoot the center out of a playing card before I was six."

"Lacy Attmore's dead," the man said, scornfully.

"So is the man who shot him in the back."

"Now look here, kid, we don't want—"

"Drop your guns or draw. You got ten seconds."

"Let's talk this over."

"I don't make deals with cheats, thieves, and yellow-bellies. You're all three."

"Why you snotty-nosed son of a bitch, I'll—"

"Draw!"

"You're damned right I'll draw!"

The clearing exploded with a cannonade of gunfire. The man with the mustache stared at Chet as his gun fell from his hand. "Who are you, kid?"

"I'm Lacy Attmore's son. He'll be waiting for you in hell!"

The others came down the slope. Night Hawk

checked the bodies. "All dead," he announced.

"How about the other one?" Chet asked.

"It's Rupert Reison," Zeke announced. "He's been gut shot, but he ain't dead. Let's kill him now."

"No. I want to know why he tried to kill Buck."

"Because he beat Perry Halstead to death," Buck announced as he stepped out of the pines. "He saw me when I found the body. That's why I had to run away."

The boys returned shortly after mid-morning. They brought the herd and Rupert Reison.

"How did you do it?" Ward asked in amazement.

"There were only three of them left," Chet said. "They'd gut-shot this one."

"I wanted to kill him," Zeke said, "but Chet wouldn't let me."

Ward knelt beside the unconscious man.

"You can look at him, but you can't help him," Zeke said.

"You can't let him die," Isabelle said.

"You could if he had done to you what he did to me."

Isabelle didn't know what to say, but she had to do something to make these boys understand that killing wasn't the answer. But how could she do that when this man had tried to kill them? Jake would understand. He would know what to say.

"But what was he doing with rustlers?"

"He hired them to steal the herd as a cover for killing me," Buck said. "But when they got the herd, they didn't need him any more. They shot him and left him to die."

"He tried to kill Jake," Chet said. "He has to die."

"He will," Ward said. "There's nothing I can do for him."

"But why did he want to kill Buck?" Isabelle asked.

"He had two of us working for him," Zeke said, "me and Perry Halstead. Perry wasn't very strong. He couldn't work very hard. Mr. Reison beat him worse than me. One night he jerked Perry out of bed and hauled him off. Perry never came back. Mr. Reison said he ran off."

"But he didn't," Buck said. "Next day I found a dog digging in fresh earth. When I pulled him away, I saw a hand. It was Perry. Rupert saw me. That's when I ran away."

"You should have told me," Isabelle said.

"I was afraid you wouldn't believe me."

Isabelle wasn't certain she would have. Even knowing what the farmers had done to Buck, it was hard to believe anyone could beat a boy to death and then try to kill another to cover up his guilty secret.

It was even harder for Isabelle to understand the unbending nature of these boys. They felt no urge to forgive. One man had committed murder, two others had attempted it, all had tried to steal horses and cows. Therefore, they had to die. They had passed sentence and rendered judgment.

"You should have told Jake," Isabelle said. "He would have believed you." Jake wasn't blinded by a belief in the basic goodness of all men.

But Isabelle believed in the basic goodness of these boys. She knew Jake did, too. He'd nearly died trying to protect them. She was certain there was decency inside them—forgiveness, too. She could never be a mother to most of them—they were beyond that—but she made a promise to herself right then and there that she would teach them to love and to forgive.

For until they could forgive, they would never really love or be worthy of it.

*   *   *

Will ran up so fast, he nearly plowed into Jake.

"Whoa!" Ward said. "You're about to do serious damage to my patient. It would ruin my reputation if he died now."

"She's a girl!" Will cried, ignoring Ward. He yanked at Jake's sleeve to be sure he had his attention. "You gotta get rid of her. We don't want no girls here."

Jake opened his eyes. He'd been dozing in the cool shadows of a huge oak. A panoramic view of the valley stretched before him. Somewhere in the distance, a stream murmured softly as it tumbled over its rocky bed.

"I thought you liked Isabelle," Jake said.

"It's not Miss Davenport. It's Drew."

"What's he done?"

"He's not a he. He's a she."

Will had waked Jake out of a light sleep. He didn't have all his wits about him. He was clearly going to need them to follow this conversation. He sat up. "Okay, start from the beginning, and don't yell." His head was still ringing.

Will dropped to the ground like an empty potato sack. "Drew is a girl. Chet said he saw her."

Jake turned his gaze to Ward, who was carefully inspecting the activities of a colony of ants as they busily conveyed some bread crumbs to their tunnel.

"What do you know about this?"

"More than I told you."

"So it seems."

"She didn't want anybody to know," Ward confessed with a guiltless sigh. "It seemed like the best idea. There couldn't be any question about her traveling with me or with you and the boys."

"What's your bright idea now that the secret's out?"

Leigh Greenwood

"I have none. I'm relying on Isabelle."

Isabelle and Drew were approaching, accompanied by Chet and Pete.

"I don't suppose you could swear them to secrecy," Ward said none too hopefully.

"Only if you cut Pete's tongue out."

Drew didn't wait to present her case. "I'm not leaving," she stated, planting herself squarely in front of Jake. "I can ride just as good as any of them."

"But you're a girl," Will said as though it were an incurable disease.

"I don't want to be a girl," Drew said, "and I'm not going to be one."

"What's your real name?" Jake asked.

"I told you. It's Drew."

"Your Christian name," Isabelle prompted.

Drew hung her head. "Drucilla." Her head popped up and she glared at Will and Pete. "I'll flatten the first one who calls me that."

"Drew is just fine," Isabelle said. "But we've got to decide what to do about your being here."

Drew drove her fist into Chet's stomach. He attempted to look as though she hadn't hurt him, but it was an effort.

"You wouldn't have to do a thing if Mr. Long Nose had minded his own business," Drew complained.

"I thought you were hurt," Chet said. "She had blood all over her," he said to Jake. "I thought she was dying."

Jake looked confused.

Ward grinned. "Her first time?" he asked Isabelle. She nodded. "Drew was as frightened as Chet."

"Will someone tell me what in blazes—"

"Later," Isabelle said. "First we have to decide what to do about Drew."

"Is she going to keep on bleeding?" Jake asked.

"Not for about a month," Ward said, smothering another grin.

Jake was relieved. "Then act like nothing happened. We'll be in Santa Fe long before then. Her people can worry about it."

"I don't have any people," Drew said. "I want you to adopt me like you're going to adopt Will."

Jake hadn't anticipated this. "You're not an orphan. You're bound to have family back East. Besides, we can't keep a girl with all these boys."

"Why not? You're keeping Miss Davenport."

Jake decided this was too much trouble to handle in his wounded condition. But when he got well, he was going to give Ward a black eye for the rude noise he made.

"Jake is not *keeping* me," Isabelle said.

"Will said you were getting married."

"That's not for Will to decide."

"Well, are you?"

Isabelle looked at Jake. He took the coward's way out and shrugged his shoulders.

"We haven't discussed it."

"Could you keep me until you make up your mind?"

Isabelle looked at Jake again. "I don't see why not. Once Jake sells the herd, we'll go to Santa Fe. Everything will be decided by then."

Chapter Twenty-five

Jake looked out over the little valley. It was a peaceful place. A tiny stream flowed lazily along the valley floor. Waist-high grass rippled in the warm breeze. Hillsides covered with pines and cedars offered shade and cool breezes during the hottest part of the day. The herd was spread out along the valley's length, grazing on the rich grass. Three boys at a time took turns at three-hour shifts. The others dozed in the shade, fished in the stream, or hunted for game.

It had been a halcyon eight days, but Jake had recovered from his wound. It was time to move on.

"It is lovely, isn't it? It almost makes you want to stay here forever."

Jake turned to find that Isabelle had followed him. He wished she hadn't. Just knowing she was near made him want to take her in his arms and make love to her until he forgot the rest of the world and all the reasons why he couldn't ask her to marry him.

"Chet's been wonderful," she said. "He's organized everything by himself. I haven't had to do anything."

"I'd love to know how he talked Ward into taking a shift like everybody else."

"He offered. He said it would make the numbers work out evenly."

"He's been trying to pretend otherwise, but that man is an experienced rider."

"He said his father was a rancher."

They were talking around what they both knew they had to discuss. It wasn't going to get any easier. Better to do it now and get it over with.

"What you said to the boys last night was real nice."

"It was no more than they deserved. I wouldn't have anything if it weren't for them."

"But to offer them shares in the herd . . ."

"It seemed only fair."

"They told me to tell you they won't take it."

Jake looked at Isabelle. "Why not?"

"They figured they didn't do anything you weren't paying them to do."

"I wish you'd talk to them."

"I agree with them."

They had him backed into a corner.

"What are you going to do now?" she asked.

"First thing tomorrow we're going to hit the trail. The army fort is only a two-day drive from here."

"I mean, after you sell the herd."

Now they were getting down to it. "I'll pay everybody what I owe them, and you and Ward can take them into Santa Fe."

"Aren't you coming?"

"No."

"Why not?"

He might as well tell her. Maybe she would understand. "My mother's in Santa Fe."

"Wonderful. You'll get a chance to see her after all these years."

"I don't want to see her."

"Do you remember what you told Matt? You said keeping the hate inside was destroying him."

"You don't know what it's like to have your mother walk out on you."

"Jake, I lost my whole family. They put me in an orphanage. It's not easy, but you get over it."

"But they died. They didn't walk out."

"You can't change what happened, but you can break its hold on you. Go see your mother. Get rid of the hate and fear that is destroying you, destroying what we could have together. You've got to meet her some day."

"No, I don't. I don't intend ever to see her, speak to her, or even think about her."

"What are you going to do?"

"Go back to Texas for another herd. I'm thinking about becoming a professional drover."

"What's that?"

"A man who takes herds to market. I'll be able to give some of the boys jobs."

"What about Will and the others?"

"You and Ward can take care of them."

"Ward and me? What makes you think—"

"I've seen you together. You're always saying they need a home, a stable environment, a father and a mother. I can't give them that. I don't have a home, and I don't have a wife. You and Ward would make a perfect couple. Besides, the boys like him."

"You could have a wife if you wanted."

"There's only one woman I want."

"Who do you want, Jake?"

"You, dammit. You know that. Why did you make me say it?"

"Because you never said it before. Sometimes I wasn't sure."

"How could you doubt it? I've wanted you so much I couldn't sleep."

"You can have me, Jake. All you have to do is ask."

"It's not that easy, and you know it. You can't stand my way of life, and I can't stand yours. We wouldn't last a week before we started arguing over everything from getting up at four in the morning to my coming to the table smelly."

"I wouldn't—"

"You told me that first day I was lower than dirt. I haven't moved any higher since."

"Don't hold that against me. I don't think the same way now."

"That's what you think today, but you'd change your mind fast enough. My ma sure did."

"Jake, your mother is not the only woman in the world. Do you believe I'd do something like that to you?"

"Don't you understand? Ma didn't want to do what she did. She couldn't help it. Being out here drove her crazy. Being stuck with three men only made it worse. You'd be stuck with a dozen."

"Things are different now."

"No, they aren't. I've watched you and Ward. You perked up like a bluebonnet in a spring shower when he showed up. You talk about the same things, laugh at the same things. You're two of a kind. You're not like me, and you never will be."

"Jake, listen to me—"

"No! I've thought about it until it's nearly driven me crazy. I've tried to figure out what I could do to make things different for you, but there's no way. I told myself to marry you anyway, that a few months was better than nothing. But I'd always know you would leave, and I couldn't stand it. I couldn't look into your eyes and see them grow colder each day. I couldn't stand feeling your body grow stiff when I came near, seeing you turn your head when I entered a room. Every day when I got up, I'd be afraid it would be the last day I'd see you. I couldn't stand that."

"Jake Maxwell, how dare you stand there telling me what I'm going to do, that I'm going to fail just because your mother did! I don't care if a thousand other women failed. What makes you think I'm going to be like them?"

"It's not you, Isabelle. It's the way you were raised. There's nothing out here you like."

"There's you. There'd be the boys."

Jake didn't think he could stand it if she said she could do it for the boys.

"My mother had two sons. She wanted to stay, but it wasn't enough for her."

"I'm not your mother."

"No. You're a lot more beautiful. I couldn't stand to see you wither and fade."

"Don't be ridiculous. People don't wither from the sun and wind."

"Women do. I've seen it. I couldn't do that to you."

"You're not doing anything to me. I want to be your wife. I want to be at your side. I don't care if I get a little sunburned in the process."

"It's not just that. It's—"

Isabelle looked at him with disbelief. "You're not going to change your mind, are you? Here I am telling you I love you, that I want to share your life, give those boys a home, maybe even have children of our own, and all you can do is tell me I'm going to turn tail and run just because your mother did."

"Isabelle, you can find a dozen men who'd be only too happy to marry you and be a father to those boys. If you only give Ward half a chance, I bet he'll—"

"Oh, shut up, Jake. I've listened to your nonsense until I can't stand it anymore. I like Ward, but I don't love him. He doesn't love me. We were only trying to make you jealous. A wasted effort, apparently. I've already found the husband I want and the ideal father for these boys. It's you. The boys like you, and I love you—fool that I am. I know you were terribly hurt when your mother left, but that was twenty years ago. You can't let it ruin the rest of your life."

"I'm not. I'm just facing up to things that can't be changed."

Isabelle grabbed hold of him as if he were a goose she was about to put into the cook pot. She wrapped her arms around his neck, pulled his head down, plastered her body firmly against his, and kissed him hard on the mouth. Jake's knees nearly went out from under him. How was he supposed to do the right thing when Isabelle was determined to give him what he wanted most in the world?

It was impossible not to kiss her back, impossible not to press his body against hers. Impossible not to want her so much that his body trembled with desire. It would be so easy to give in.

With tremendous effort of will, Jake gripped Isabelle by the shoulder and held her away from him. "No." His voice was a hoarse whisper, barely understandable. "I won't let you ruin your life."

"It's my life," Isabelle replied, her own voice thick with passion. "I ought to get to decide what to do with it."

"Not with me," Jake said. "You don't agree now,

but as soon as you get back to Austin, you'll see I'm right."

Isabelle's mouth compressed into a thin, angry line. Her hands balled into fists. "I hoped I could change your mind, but you're more stubborn than I thought. Well, I'm stubborn, too. I'm going to wait. You can hang around here sulking and feeling sorry for yourself, but when you're done, I'm going to be waiting. But you'd better not take too long, because if you do, I'm coming after you.

"You can't have the boys—any of them. Any man afraid to face his own mother isn't fit to rear a houseful of teenagers. Now before I lose my temper entirely, I'm taking the boys to Santa Fe. They're going to have a bath and buy some decent clothes. I'm going to have a meal I don't have to cook. And so help me, if you say one word about that making me a city woman, I'll drive that chuck wagon right over you."

She turned and stalked off. Twelve yards away, she stopped and turned around. "You're wearing my brand, Jake Maxwell," she said. "You just remember that if you change your mind and decide to go into Santa Fe."

Jake knew he wouldn't change his mind. If he couldn't face Isabelle, who loved him, he was too much of a coward to face the woman who'd deserted him and left a scar that still wouldn't heal.

As Jake watched Isabelle and the boys ride off toward Santa Fe, he felt as though his heart were being torn out of his chest. He never imagined saying goodbye would be so hard. She wouldn't let him have any of the boys. She said if he wanted them, he would have to come to Santa Fe to get them.

So that was that.

There was nothing to keep him in New Mexico any

longer. He'd sold his herd. He'd even found a buyer for the chuck wagon and the extra horses. He had made more money than he'd expected. He could go back to Texas and hire a new crew to round up the rest of his cows, buy another herd, buy a ranch, do just about anything he wanted. With Rupert dead and his treatment of Perry Halstead exposed, he doubted the farmers would cause him any more trouble.

But none of those options appealed to him. He couldn't set foot on the ranch without being reminded of Isabelle and the boys. The money, his success, didn't mean as much as he'd expected. He thought he had done it for himself. He had, but it meant much more when he shared it with Isabelle and the boys. It was their success, too. Not just his.

He kept telling himself he'd made the right decision. But if that were true, why did he feel so terrible?

Because you're a coward. Cowards feel rotten because they can't stand their own cowardice.

He'd been decorated for bravery during the war. Why did he feel like such a coward now?

Because you're afraid to let yourself love, to let yourself trust. You're so afraid of failure, you're willing to forego your chance at happiness.

There wasn't any chance. He knew what would happen. He was only postponing the inevitable.

You've changed. Why can't Isabelle?

Had he changed? What was different about him now? He wanted Isabelle. He was even willing to marry her. No, he *wanted* to marry her, and for much more than his physical need of her. He couldn't imagine his world without Isabelle. Her crisp blouses, her trim figure, her boundless energy, her hunger for the comfort his body could give her combined to make him feel like a different person.

She might argue with him at every juncture. She might be as stubborn as his longhorns. She might make him change a lot of his habits, but she was as essential to his happiness as the rolling Texas hills which had been his home since his birth. It didn't make a bit of sense for him to go back to Texas if she didn't go with him.

He wanted the boys, too. Not just as cowhands. They helped fill up the hole inside of him that came from the loss of his family. Will's adoration still made him uneasy, but he liked having the kid around.

Matt was talking more, Pete didn't look as if he wanted to kill Hawk, Chet was maturing into a remarkable leader, and Bret might learn to trust if he wasn't betrayed again. He didn't know about Buck and Zeke. They had their own still-buried angers, but Sean, Luke, and Drew were doing just fine.

How would they feel when Isabelle told them he wasn't coming back?

Jake had to laugh when he remembered how Isabelle had laid down the law. She didn't ask him, she told him. She'd made up her mind. He could agree with her or not. Man, that woman had a temper.

Why had he never seen it before?

Because you were too busy making decisions for other people. You had all the answers.

But he didn't. He'd vowed never to get married. He had sworn never to trust a woman with his love. He was positive no delicately nurtured female could survive being a rancher's wife. But he hadn't made any of these decisions. He'd let his anger at his mother, his sense of betrayal, make them for him. The same thing would happen all over again if he didn't do something about it.

He knew one thing for certain. He couldn't do

without Isabelle. Every passing minute proved that. He felt more and more desperate. Any risk was worth taking as long as it meant there was a chance he could have Isabelle.

He picked up his saddle and headed for his horse. He was going to Santa Fe. He was going after Isabelle. But before he did, there was a woman he had to see.

He went to the last address he had for his mother, and they told him at the house that she was in town with her son. She was driving a green wagon. He couldn't miss her. She was the only woman in Santa Fe who drove a wagon wearing white gloves.

Jake saw the boy first. He looked so much like his older brother, David, that Jake nearly stopped breathing. He knew it was rude, but the closer he got, the harder he stared. David had been twenty-four when he was killed, but Jake remembered what he had looked like at sixteen. This boy was the spitting image of David.

This boy was Jake's half brother.

Jake pulled up when he reached the wagon. "Howdy," he said to the boy. "I'm looking for your ma."

"She's inside the store," the boy said.

"I'll wait. My name's Jake. What's yours?"

"Kurt."

He could tell he was making the boy uncomfortable, but he couldn't stop staring. Learning he had a half brother had been a shock. Discovering he looked exactly like David had staggered him. He kept expecting the boy's image to dissolve into something totally different.

But it stayed the same.

"How old are you?" Jake asked.

"Sixteen."

He'd been born just three years after his mother left. Jake imagined this boy getting all the love and comfort denied him and David, and he started to shake with an anger that had been boiling inside him for nearly twenty years.

Jake looked around when Kurt's expression changed to a relieved smile. A woman was coming down the boardwalk.

"That's my ma." Kurt jumped down from the wagon.

Jake dismounted and looped his rein around the hitching post.

"This man's been looking for you," Kurt said as his mother approached the wagon. She handed her son her packages and turned to Jake.

"Hello. I'm Mrs. Stuart. What can I do for you?"

Jake stared at the woman standing in front of him. She didn't look like the mother he remembered. She looked much too old. Her hair was completely white. Her face was deeply wrinkled. Yet the wrinkles didn't detract from fine eyes that looked huge in her face. She was dressed with quietly expensive taste. Silver and turquoise circled her neck and dangled from her ears.

More striking to Jake, she seemed to be at peace with herself, to be calm and in control of her feelings. There was none of the frenetic energy, the desperation Jake remembered.

Jake had expected to feel rage, bitterness, disgust, scorn, but it was like trying to be angry at a stranger. This woman wasn't the mother he remembered.

He stopped shaking. He had a peculiar feeling he'd stepped out of his world. Nothing felt real.

"Are you all right, Mr.—Sorry, I don't know your name."

"I'm fine," Jake heard himself saying. His voice sounded as if it was coming from far away. "I'm just a little unsure of what to say. I'm Jake, your son."

His mother's eyes grew wide with surprise. Her color faded. Then a sad smile brightened her face. "God be thanked!" she said softly. "I've prayed you would come."

Jake found Isabelle and the boys in a restaurant. They had put three tables together and were sitting so close, they rubbed shoulders. White-washed adobe walls reflected the light from several lanterns suspended from large black beams that stretched across the ceiling. The lanterns on each table illuminated their faces much like the campfires of their fifty-two nights on the trail.

Jake stood just outside the door, watching. They hardly looked like the group of ragamuffins he'd dragged across seven hundred miles of some of the worst country in the Southwest. They'd all taken a bath, had their hair cut, and put on new clothes. Matt and Will's hair gleamed straw-blond; Hawk's glowed inky black. Finally wearing clothes that fit her—though still dressed as a boy—Drew looked feminine.

The room virtually crackled with their energy. Jake heard Pete and Will's voices raised in argument—how many had he settled already?—and knew he wanted to be part of their exuberant excess. Just being around them made him feel more alive. There would be plenty of years for peace and quiet later.

Isabelle looked lovely. He didn't know how it was possible—maybe it was those starched, white blouses—but she didn't look like a woman who'd just crossed a wilderness, cooked a hundred meals over open fires, driven a wagon through rivers and over mountains. She looked so feminine, so quietly elegant, so absolutely beautiful, it made his body tighten just to think of touching her cheek or kissing her lips.

He'd been a fool to think she couldn't endure living wild. She'd been through the worst, and she still looked magnificent. Even if he had to follow her all the way to Savannah, he couldn't let her go.

"Jake!" Will shrieked the minute Jake passed through the doorway. The boy plowed his way across the room, grabbed hold of Jake's hand, and pulled him toward the table. "You've got to come quick. Isabelle's gonna make a ranch, and she's not gonna let you have it."

Jake looked across the room at Isabelle. She was looking at him, her face drained of color. He laughed. He couldn't do anything else. He was back where he belonged, with Will, the rest of the boys, and Isabelle. Everything was going to be all right. He could just feel it.

He grinned down at Will. "Do you think if I hired all her hands away, she'd join her ranch with mine?"

"Drew won't come. She swears she's sticking with Isabelle no matter what."

"She's not very big. Maybe we could kidnap her."

"I don't know. Drew's a girl. Matt says you can't have fun with a girl."

Jake walked over to the table. His gaze never left Isabelle. "What about it? Do you think you could join your operation with mine?"

"I sincerely hope so," Ward said, with a decided look of relief. "I'll have to help her if you don't."

Isabelle's gaze never wavered. "It depends on the kind of deal you're offering."

"It's a little complicated. Do you mind if I sit down while I explain?"

"Take my chair," Chet said.

"Why don't all of you gather around," Jake said. "It concerns everybody."

They made so much noise, they drew the attention of the other diners. They smiled at Jake, probably thinking it was some kind of family reunion.

It was.

"First," Jake said, when all the boys had come close enough to hear, "I want to go back to Texas and gather another herd. If I'm going to buy a good ranch, I need more money than I have."

"Where are the cows coming from?" Ward asked.

"I've got plenty more at the ranch," Jake said. "I don't think the farmers will bother us this time."

"Where will you buy your ranch?" Isabelle asked.

"I haven't decided, but we can make up our minds on that later."

"We?" she asked.

"Yes, we."

Her eyes searched his face. He smiled at her, hoping she would find the answer she sought. She smiled back at him—tentatively, but a smile nonetheless.

"What else?" she asked.

Jake let his gaze travel over the intent young faces that surrounded him. "I want to adopt all the boys."

Will let out a squeal and pitched himself at Jake, climbing over Chet to get there. "I told Matt you'd adopt us," he said. "I told him ages ago."

It took a minute for Jake to get Will quiet and settled on his lap. "I realize all of you may not want to be adopted, but before you decide, there's one thing I want you to consider. You're still underage. You could be taken away from me at any time. If you're my legal sons, you can stay as long as you want."

"They won't let you adopt me," Zeke said. "White people can't adopt black kids."

"I'll find a way," Jake said. "And you can stop trying to look like you're not here, Hawk. I mean to adopt you as well. Don't think you can sneak off. I'm still better at tracking than you are."

The boy actually smiled. Jake hadn't thought it was possible.

"You going to offer to adopt me?" Ward asked.

"Considering the way I've been acting, I'm surprised you'd ask, even as a joke."

"Well, I—"

"But I would like you to come with us until you make up your mind where you want to be. You've been trying to hide it, but you've a damned fine horseman. The boys need somebody to fix their cuts and broken bones, and Isabelle needs somebody to talk to who knows what civilized people act like. Maybe you can teach me and the boys."

"You realize your little scheme depends on—"

"I know exactly what it depends on," Jake said, turning to Isabelle. "It depends on Isabelle agreeing to be my wife."

"She will," Will piped up. "She's been in love with you for ages."

"If you don't mind, Will, this is one question I'd like to answer for myself," Isabelle said.

"But you told me you loved him."

"I know what I said, but there's more to it than that."

"Oh, you mean sex. Pete told me all about that."

"No, I don't," Isabelle said, blushing from hairline to fingertip. "And if you want me to adopt you, we're going to have to have a serious talk about what little boys should and should not mention in public."

"Like sex?"

"Definitely."

"Oh."

"Come on, brat," Matt said, hauling his little brother out of Jake's lap. "I'm going to put a sock in your mouth before you ruin the whole setup."

"I'm not ruining anything. She said—"

Matt put his hand over Will's mouth.

"Escape while you can," Ward said. "I'll undertake to keep track of the brood."

"Feed them. I'll pay the bill."

Jake escorted Isabelle out of the room. "Where shall we go?" he asked.

"I think my room would be best," Isabelle said.

Chapter Twenty-six

Isabelle wondered if she'd be able to reach the top of the stairs. Her legs felt very wobbly. Doubts and speculation dashed through her mind at a fever pitch. Her limbs felt weak from desire. Jake wanted her. He wanted to marry her. Everything she wanted was within her grasp.

Or was it?

Jake never changed his mind. Jake never listened to what anyone else had to say. Yet, here he was saying he wanted to adopt all the boys and marry her. What had caused him to change his mind?

Isabelle was tempted to say she didn't care, that she would take him on any terms, but his refusal to come with them to Santa Fe had given her time to think. She loved Jake, but she wasn't going to marry him if he still thought she was going to flee back to Austin and abandon him and their children. He was going to believe she was just as dedicated to their marriage as he was, or he would find himself living with nothing but cows.

He had to say he loved her. If she had to put up with cows and sweaty bodies at her table, liking an awful lot, strong regard, and irresistible physical attraction were not enough. That kind of sacrifice required an unstinting commitment of love.

Isabelle waited until Jake entered the room. She closed the door and leaned against it. "Do you want to explain why you've changed your mind, or do I have to guess?"

"I took your advice."

"That must be a first."

He ignored her snipe. "I went to see my mother."

That caught her off guard. She didn't know what she'd expected, but that wasn't it.

"I don't understand why you're in such a good mood. Before all you had to do was think about your mother, and you looked like you were ready to shoe horses with your teeth."

"I can't explain it myself," Jake said. He moved about the small room, a bundle of nervous energy. "I think I expected to see the woman who left our ranch twenty years ago. I hated that woman. I was ready to blame her for everything that's happened since then. I tried to blame her anyway."

"What happened?"

"Mrs. Isaac Stuart didn't look like Ma. She didn't even act like her. She has a son who looks exactly like David. By the time I met her husband, I was so numb, I didn't feel anything."

"Did you ask her why she left?"

"She said I had every right to hate her, that she'd probably feel the same way. She wanted to take David and me with her, but Pa wouldn't let her. When he proposed, he promised they'd live in San Antonio.

Then he changed his mind. He wouldn't even let her visit her family. Then after she left, she wrote to us for nearly fifteen years, but Pa always returned the letters unopened. She showed them to me. There must have been a hundred. She said if she had known Pa had died, she would have written to me. The last she heard, David and I had gone to war and the ranch was deserted."

"That still doesn't explain why you've suddenly decided you want to marry me."

He grinned at her, that quirky kind of grin that caused her stomach to do somersaults. "You won't believe I've suddenly seen the error of my ways?"

Isabelle nearly laughed. "I've been pointing them out since I met you, and it hasn't changed a thing."

"I told her about you. She said I was a fool to think you couldn't learn to live at the ranch. She said she would have stayed if she had loved Pa. She might have stayed if he had loved her. She couldn't endure the thought of living the rest of her life without love."

Jake walked toward Isabelle. He held out both hands. She put her hands in his, and he pulled her close to him.

"Neither could I, but I had decided that before I came to Santa Fe. I even decided I would move to Austin if necessary."

"You'd never survive."

"If you can make it on a ranch, I can make it in Austin."

"Actually, now that I know what to do, I'm almost looking forward to living on a ranch. I think I must have been trying to get to Texas all along. Why else would I have found my way from Savannah to New Orleans to Austin to your ranch? There must be a strain of peasant blood in me. Aunt Deirdre would be horrified. She always maintained that I had the blood of English nobles in my veins."

"Then you will marry me?"

He tried to pull her close, but Isabelle put her hands against his chest.

"I think you've forgotten something."

"What?"

"If you have to ask, maybe you haven't forgotten. Maybe it just isn't there."

"What?" He looked frustrated. "I mentioned the ranch, gathering another herd to sell, adopting the boys, asking Ward to stay with us. What else is there?"

Isabelle removed Jake's hands from around her waist. "I'm beginning to understand exactly how your mother felt." She opened the door and stood aside. "March yourself back downstairs. I don't think we have anything more to say to each other."

"What! What is it?" Jake said. "I don't want to go back downstairs. The boys will kill me."

"If it's only the boys you're worried about—"

"It's not the boys. I don't want to go anywhere without you. I love you. I want to marry you."

Isabelle froze. "Say that again."

"What?"

"What you just said."

"I want to marry you."

"No, the other part."

"What other part?"

"The important part!"

Jake grabbed her by the shoulders. "You're driving me crazy. I want to marry you. I don't want to go anywhere without you. I love you. I—"

"There! You said it!"

"What did I say?" He looked ready to pull his hair out.

"Don't you remember?"

"Of course I do. I asked you to marry me."

"Not that!"

"Then what the hell is it! Tell me, and I'll say it. Just don't keep torturing me."

"I want you to say you love me."

"Of course I do. You know that."

"But I want you to say it."

"I said it."

"Say it again."

"I love you."

"Again."

"I love you."

"Again."

"I can do better than that."

Jake took her in his arms, kicked the door shut with his foot, and kissed her hard on the mouth.

"There," he said when he came up breathing hard. "I love you. Do you believe me now?"

Isabelle was certain the grin on her face was foolish and besotted, but she didn't care. That was exactly how she felt. "Yes, but it wears off in about fifteen minutes. You'll have to tell me again."

"What are we going to do until then?"

"Think of something."

"What about Ward and the boys?"

"Who's Ward? What boys?"

Epilogue

Isabelle was anxious to get the adoption papers signed and get out of Austin. She would never have believed it, but all the noise and bustle got on her nerves. She didn't think she'd ever grow fond of cows, but some people weren't any better. This judge was one of those people. It had taken nearly an hour to convince him Mercer's report was biased. Buck and Zeke had had to take off their shirts before he'd believe the farmers would have abused the boys.

"You certain you want to adopt all of them?" the judge asked.

"I'd be a great fool to walk in here and ask for them if I didn't," Jake answered irritably.

Isabelle squeezed his hand.

"Well, the man's an idiot," he hissed.

"I agree," Ward hissed from her other side.

"Of course he wants to adopt us," Will piped up. "We catch his cows for him."

"That's not the only reason," Isabelle said.

"Oh yes," Will said, as though adding something he'd forgotten. "We'll be his sons. Then you can't give us to anybody else. Ever."

"I must insist that you wait until sufficient inquiries have been made about Miss Drucilla Townsend's family to pursue adopting her."

"My name's Drew," Drew announced.

"We understand," Isabelle said. "If that's all, I'd appreciate it if you'd sign the papers. We'd like to get back to the ranch. We've got another herd to round up and take to Santa Fe."

"Are you quite sure about this, Miss Davenport?"

"It's Mrs. Maxwell," Isabelle said, "and I'm absolutely positive."

"This is most unusual," the judge said with a frown. "We've never had anybody adopt ten boys."

"It'd put him out of a job if people did," Jake whispered.

Isabelle pinched him.

"Okay," the man said, scrawling his signature on the paper. "They're yours. If you find you don't want them, you have to—"

"We want them," Jake said.

Isabelle watched him head out of the building, the boys streaming behind him. "He's like a Pied Piper," Ward said to her. "They'll follow him anywhere."

"So will I."

"You won't have him to yourself until they're gone. They're going to take every bit of him they can get."

"There's enough to go around," Isabelle said, smiling happily. "More than enough."

Jake

Jake came back into the building. He put his arm around Isabelle's waist.

"Get your own woman," he said to Ward. "This one's wearing my brand."

Isabelle pinched him.

LEIGH GREENWOOD
The Independent Bride

Colorado Territory, 1868: It is about as rough and ready as the West can get, a place and time almost as dangerous as the men who left civilization behind, driven by a desire for land, gold . . . a new life.

Fort Lookout: It is a rugged outpost where soldiers, cattlemen and Indians live on the edge of open warfare, the last place any woman in her right mind would choose to settle.

Abby: She is everything a man should avoid—with a face of beauty and an expression of stubborn determination. Colonel Bryce McGregor knows there is no room for such a woman at his fort or in his heart. Yet as she receives proposal after proposal from his troops, Bryce realizes the only man he can allow her to marry is himself.

LEIGH GREENWOOD

The Reluctant Bride

Colorado Territory, 1872: A rough-and-tumble place and time almost as dangerous as the men who left civilization behind, driven by a desire for a new life. In a false-fronted town where the only way to find a decent woman is to send away for her, Tanzy first catches sight of the man she came west to marry galloping after a gang of bandits. Russ Tibbolt is a far cry from the husband she expected when she agreed to become a mail-order bride. He is much too compelling for any woman's peace of mind. With his cobalt-blue eyes and his body's magic, how can she hope to win the battle of wills between them?

SEVEN BRIDES
LEIGH GREENWOOD

IRIS

Rough and ready as any of the Randolph boys, Monty bristles under his eldest brother's tight rein. All he wants is to light out from Texas for a new beginning. And Iris Richmond has to get her livestock to Wyoming's open ranges before rustlers wipe her out. Monty is heading that way, but the bullheaded wrangler flat out refuses to help her. Never one to take no for an answer, Iris saddles up to coax, rope, and tame the ornery cowboy she's always desired.

___4175-8 $6.99 US/$8.99 CAN

LEIGH GREENWOOD'S
SEVEN BRIDES
Laurel

Although Hen Randolph is the perfect choice for a sheriff in the Arizona Territory, he is no one's idea of a model husband. After the trail-weary cowboy breaks free from his six rough-and-ready brothers, he isn't about to start a family of his own. Then a beauty with a tarnished reputation catches his eye and the thought of taking a wife arouses him as never before.

But Laurel Blackthorne has been hurt too often to trust any man—least of all one she considers a ruthless, coldhearted gunslinger. Not until Hen proves that drawing quickly and shooting true aren't his only assets will she give him her heart and take her place as the newest bride to tame a Randolph's heart.

_3744-0 $6.99 US/$8.99 CAN

SEVEN BRIDES
LEIGH GREENWOOD

Fern

**"I loved *Rose*, but I absolutely loved *Fern*!
She's fabulous! An incredible job!"**
—*Romantic Times*

A man of taste and culture, James Madison Randolph enjoys the refined pleasures of life in Boston. It's been years since the suave lawyer abandoned the Randolphs' ramshackle ranch—and the dark secrets that haunted him there. But he is forced to return to the hated frontier when his brother is falsely accused of murder. What he doesn't expect is a sharp-tongued vixen who wants to gun down his entire family. As tough as any cowhand in Kansas, Fern Sproull will see her cousin's killer hang for his crime, and no smooth-talking city slicker will stop her from seeing justice done. But one look at James awakens a tender longing to taste heaven in his kiss. While the townsfolk of Abilene prepare for the trial of the century, Madison and Fern ready themselves for a knock-down, drag-out battle of the sexes that might just have two winners.

____4409-9 $6.99 US/$8.99 CAN

Dorchester Publishing Co., Inc.
P.O. Box 6640
Wayne, PA 19087-8640

Please add $2.50 for shipping and handling for the first book and $.75 for each book thereafter. NY, NYC, and PA residents, please add appropriate sales tax. No cash, stamps, or C.O.D.s. All orders shipped within 6 weeks via postal service book rate. Canadian orders require $2.00 extra postage and must be paid in U.S. dollars through a U.S. banking facility.

Name_____
Address_____
City_____State_____Zip_____
I have enclosed $_____ in payment for the checked book(s).
Payment <u>must</u> accompany all orders. ❑ Please send a free catalog.
CHECK OUT OUR WEBSITE! www.dorchesterpub.com

SEVEN BRIDES

LEIGH GREENWOOD

LILY

Refusing to bet her future happiness on an arranged marriage, Lily Sterling flees her Virginia home to the streets of San Francisco. In the best saloon in California, she meets handsome proprietor Zac Randolph, and when the scoundrel refuses Lily's kindness, she takes the biggest gamble of her life.

___4441-2 $6.99 US/$8.99 CAN

Dorchester Publishing Co., Inc.
P.O. Box 6640
Wayne, PA 19087-8640

Please add $2.50 for shipping and handling for the first book and $.75 for each book thereafter. NY, NYC, and PA residents, please add appropriate sales tax. No cash, stamps, or C.O.D.s. All orders shipped within 6 weeks via postal service book rate. Canadian orders require $2.00 extra postage and must be paid in U.S. dollars through a U.S. banking facility.

Name_____

Address_____

City_____State_____Zip_____

I have enclosed $_____ in payment for the checked book(s).

Payment <u>must</u> accompany all orders. ☐ Please send a free catalog.

CHECK OUT OUR WEBSITE! www.dorchesterpub.com

SEVEN BRIDES
❦ LEIGH GREENWOOD ❦

VIOLET

Broken and bitter, Jefferson Randolph can never forget all he lost in the War Between the States—or forgive those he has fought. Long after most of his six brothers have found wedded bliss, the former Rebel soldier keeps himself buried in work, until a run-in with Yankee schoolteacher Violet Goodwin teaches him that he has a lot to learn about passion. But Jeff fears that love alone isn't enough to help him put his past behind him—or convince a proper lady that she can find happiness as the newest bride in the rowdy Randolph clan.

___4494-3 $6.99 US/$8.99 CAN

Dorchester Publishing Co., Inc.
P.O. Box 6640
Wayne, PA 19087-8640

Please add $2.50 for shipping and handling for the first book and $.75 for each book thereafter. NY, NYC, and PA residents, please add appropriate sales tax. No cash, stamps, or C.O.D.s. All orders shipped within 6 weeks via postal service book rate. Canadian orders require $2.00 extra postage and must be paid in U.S. dollars through a U.S. banking facility.

Name_____

Address_____

City_____ State_____ Zip_____

I have enclosed $_____ in payment for the checked book(s).

Payment <u>must</u> accompany all orders. ☐ Please send a free catalog.

CHECK OUT OUR WEBSITE! www.dorchesterpub.com

TEXAS TR★UMPH

ELAINE BARBIERI

Buck Star was a handsome cad with a love-'em-and-leave-'em attitude that had broken more than one heart. But when he lost his head over a conniving beauty young enough to be his own daughter, he jeopardized all he valued, even the lives of his own children.

Ever since leaving his father's Texas Star ranch, the daring Pinkerton agent and his lovely partner Vida Malone made it their business to ferret out the truth. But the twisted secrets he begins to uncover after a mysterious message calls him home might be more than anyone could untangle. Saving his father will require all his cunning and courage, as well as the aid of the most exasperating and enticing woman ever to go undercover or drive a man to distraction.
